Also by K.A. Finn

Nomad Series (Space Opera)

Ares

Nemesis

Perses

Chaos

Mania

Cronus

Talos (TBA)

Blackjacks Series (Paranormal Romance)

Breaking Phoenix

Reviving Davyn

Defying Shep (2023)

Unraveling Fallon (TBA)

Broken Chords (Rockstar Romance)

Broken Rock (Tate)

Fractured Rock (Gregg)

Split Rock (Tate – 2023)

Crushed Rock (Luke – TBA)

Shattered Rock (Dillon – TBA)

A bit of a Nomad herself, **K.A. Finn** has wandered around Ireland and the UK for decades before settling back in Ireland with her husband and kids (two and four legged).

Visit K.A. Finn online:

www.kafinn.com
(trailers, excerpts, artwork, playlists etc)

Facebook: kafinnauthor

Instagram: kafinnauthor

Twitter @K_A_Finn

BLACKJACKS BOOK 2

REVIVING DAVYN

K.A. FINN

Copyright © 2022 by Karyn Finnegan.

All rights reserved. This book or any portion thereof may not be reproduced or used in any manner whatsoever without the express written permission of the publisher except for the use of brief quotation in a book review or critical articles

All characters and events in this publication, other than those clearly in the public domain, are fictitious and any resemblance to real persons, living or dead, is purely coincidental

Cover design by Deranged Doctor Design
www.derangeddoctordesign.com

Published by Cooper Publishing
www.cooperbookservices.com

Edited by Desert Mystic Literary Editing
www.desertmysticliteraryediting.com

ISBN: 978-1-914177-38-5

Coming next

BLACKJACKS BOOK 3

DEFYING SHEP

To Davyn

I hope you can forgive me one day

Thea closes her bedroom door and leans against it as she catches her breath. Her black sleeveless tank top is soaked in sweat and clinging to her skin. Every muscle is on fire, every joint aching. The large gash on her arm stings like crazy under the bandage.

She needs a shower but the thought of walking across her room doesn't appeal to her. After a few minutes the sweat on her skin begins to chill so she pushes off the door and shuffles across the vast room to the en-suite. Thea turns on the light and peels off her damp clothes as she waits for the water to heat up.

Seven long weeks have passed since she was kidnapped by the True Order and held in that terrifying underground lab. Since she was rescued she's been on her best behaviour. The True Order are still hot on the Blackjack's heels and the last thing she is going to do is put herself in their sights again.

Fallon had taken the task of training Thea twice a day, six days a week. The compound is safe. There is so much security, she doubts a fly would get through the defences without alerting someone. But it's outside the compound that she's vulnerable. As one of the few humans in the house, she's adamant she won't be the weak link. It doesn't matter how many bruises she gets, how many cuts or knocks. Every single one helps make her less of a hindrance to the team.

Fallon is an incredible teacher and doesn't hold back, and Thea loves every minute of it. She had thrown herself in to her training, eager for any distraction from everything else going on around her.

Things between herself and Court hadn't improved much over the last few weeks. They were still getting used to their new relationship after living a lie for so many years. Accepting that Court is a vampire was hard enough, but finding out that he is actually her father and not her brother, completely turned her world upside down and forever changed their relationship.

In addition to the whole being her father thing, he is still trying to come to grips with his amnesia. Finding traces of his DNA in the Order's lab only added to his confusion. He doesn't remember being there, but the evidence suggests he must have spent quite a lot of time there. That information added another level to the nightmares she's been plagued with since she got back. If she let herself think about him spending time down there, being hurt, having his DNA altered so he could be used as a food source, she would break.

As if all that wasn't hard enough to deal with, the loss of one of the Blackjacks throws things to a whole new level. She steps into the shower, eager to hide her guilty tears under the running water.

Davyn was the Blackjack who killed one of the vampires holding her and brought her to safety in the tunnels. He saved her only to be captured himself. The last image she saw was the feral vampires pulling him to the ground and dragging him along the corridor.

The Blackjacks had searched but, apart from a pool of blood and his gun, they hadn't found him. Davyn had saved her life but paid for her freedom with his own. She'd only needed saving because she had broken the rules and gone out without a Blackjack to watch her and keep her safe. It's all her fault.

She angrily shakes her head, hitting her fist against the wall. She'll never forgive herself. Never. Thinking back on the whole situation, she knows she acted like a spoiled brat. She'd desperately wanted to know what it would feel like to have a vampire feed from her. After a lot of persuading, Davyn had reluctantly agreed.

Her anger turns to something else, something that sends a shiver through her. Having Davyn feed from her was the single most intense experience of her life so far. But then her father found out and the two vampires had fought. She knows why Court was upset, but the whole thing was blown out of proportion and she'd made things so much worse by running away.

She knew there were people looking for Court. She knew the team was doing everything they could to protect her and Court. But that didn't stop her from stealing his car and leaving the safety of the compound.

She needed space, time away to think without all the alpha male vampire stuff clouding everything. But all she did was walk into a trap which resulted in Nix being captured along with her.

Court had gone to rescue Nix while Davyn was sent to save her. She'll never forget the moment he burst into the room she was being held in, and killed the vampire guarding her. He'd taken down anyone in his way as he led her to freedom. The tears flow freely when she pictures him smiling at her as she got to safety. But he wasn't so lucky. She watched helplessly as he'd been dragged away from her and never seen again.

The loss of Davyn had hit every single member of the group. They'd had so much loss, so much pain to deal with over the last few years. First they lose Court, only to have him come back to them three years later, then Davyn disappears. She can see the effect of the trauma on the group. Each had been hit in a different way - Nix especially. Their leader had reluctantly given the order to leave him behind, just like she had all those years ago with Court. She's just grateful that Nix and Court had found each other again and were helping each other through their individual heartache.

She turns off the shower and towel dries her hair before padding across the lush carpet to the wardrobe. Opening the double doors she ignores her clothes and reaches for the last hangar on the left. She pulls the black jacket down and buries her face in the leather. Thea closes her eyes and gets lost Davyn's scent. He had given her his jacket after he saved her from the lab, and she had neglected to hand it over to Nix. She knows it's just a jacket, but she can't bring herself to let it go. It's all she has left of him.

She has to believe he's still alive. There's no other choice for her. Her father came back to Nix after three years. There's nothing to say Davyn isn't alive and well. But if he was, surely he'd come back. From what she can make out, the Blackjacks are all he has. If he could come home, he would. The thoughts had gone round and round her head continuously since he disappeared. As much as she desperately needs to believe he's okay, deep down she fears he isn't. Something is stopping him from coming back to them. Back to her.

She hangs the jacket back in her wardrobe and sits on the end of her bed. The guilt is threatening to swallow her but she can't escape it. Shep has barely spoken to her since they got back. He blames her for what happened. He told her in great detail how he blames her. She knows the others probably feel the same although they are too polite to say it to her face.

Shep is right though. She is responsible for someone she cares about being taken. Maybe if Shep knew how she felt about Davyn he'd back off a little. Maybe it wouldn't make a difference. Davyn had caught her attention the first moment she saw him. His impressive body covered in black leather, and his green eyes glowing when he had burst into Court's apartment. He was spectacular and she was instantly attracted to him. It made no sense. He's a vampire and she's human, but she was drawn to him. Not that he made it easy.

He's standoffish, abrupt, downright rude at times, but she could see something deep inside that she desperately wanted to get close to. They hadn't kissed, barely touched each other, but she'd never felt this level of attraction before.

Thea scrubs a hand over her face and grabs a pair of leggings and a baggy sweatshirt from the wardrobe. After getting dressed, she slips his jacket on, and drops onto the comfortable couch. She takes the TV remote from the cushion beside her and flicks through the channels.

Brooding and over-thinking everything she's done wrong isn't going to help her or Davyn. Hopefully she can lose herself in a random reality show until it's time to fall asleep. Just one night without the nightmares would be great.

~

Davyn spits out a mouthful of blood and wipes his mouth on his sweat-soaked arm. He pushes to his feet and faces his attacker. The male smiles at him, his large fangs tipped with blood - Davyn's blood. The bastard got in a lucky bite, but it won't happen again. His opponent dances on the balls of his feet, hopping around on the dirt ground like it's on fire. He rolls his neck and crooks a finger in Davyn's direction.

'I'm waiting pretty boy.' He waves a knife at Davyn. It's already stained with his blood, but adrenaline is masking the pain from the large slice running down his left arm. He underestimated this asshole. It won't happen again.

Davyn knew this guy was an idiot, but his pathetic taunting solidifies his opinion. He's going to enjoy taking him down. The other vampire lashes out with his fist, but his hot-footed dancing puts him way off the mark. He tries again, and again, tiring with each badly planned swipe.

Davyn bides his time, waiting for the idiot to get close enough, then plants his own fist straight into the cocky vampire's face. He feels the satisfying crack of bones breaking as he smashes the guys nose and hopefully a cheekbone or two.

While the guy nurses his bloody face, Davyn swipes his leg out, knocking him to the ground. Blood is now flowing freely from the hole in his face but Davyn is far from caring. He stomps on his opponent's leg, shattering his knee and putting an end to any chances of this guy getting out of here alive.

Davyn leaves him writhing on the ground, his curses muffled under his hands as he cradles what's left of his face. Davyn stumbles over to the large knife lying a few feet from the idiot. He picks it up and turns the blade in his hand.

He walks back over to the other vampire and without pausing, drops to one knee, driving the blade deep into the idiot's heart. His hands fall from the mess of his face as he dies.

Davyn gets back up and looks at the life he's just taken. It's not the first and unfortunately, it won't be the last. He ignores the crazed cheer from the crowd as he takes a few steps back from the male he just killed. Guards rush into the arena with large electric cattle prods out in front, all pointing at him. He knows the routine well enough by now.

He turns his back to them, holding his hands out to the side. He glances up at the crowd as they fix heavy chains to the shackles welded around his wrists, driving the spikes lining them into his skin. Money is still passing from the bookies to the blood thirsty punters. The well-dressed men and women, both vampire and human, excitedly talk about the match as they sip their chilled champagne and expensive wine.

A few looks are cast in his direction, but all he can see is the greed in their eyes. They don't care that he just killed someone in front of them. All they care about is the thrill of the bet. The sick fucks are actually enjoying themselves.

Once secured, he's dragged from the arena and along the dimly lit corridor back to his cell. Adrenaline keeps him upright and moving along the winding dirt track to his new home. They open the cell and quickly remove the chains before they throw him in. Davyn lands on his injured arm and dark spots dance in the corner of his vision. He rolls over and pulls his arm out from under him. Thick clumps of dirt have stuck to the blood oozing from the wide cut.

He drags his metal bowl of water closer and slowly trickles the contents down his arm, trying to get the worst of the filth out of the cut. The last thing he needs is to lose his arm. He wipes a wet hand over his face, trying to clear some of the blood off it. His fingers brush against the hole at the edge of his eyebrow. It still feels weird without his piercings. He'd taken out the piercing from each eyebrow before his first fight. Didn't want the fuckers he's thrown in with tearing them from him during a fight.

He leaves a little water in the bowl, hungrily drinking the foul tasting, cloudy liquid. It barely quenches his thirst, but it's all he'll get until later. He leans on his side against the wall and closes his eyes. He's tired, hungry, and hurts everywhere.

A guard throws a small plastic bottle of blood through the bars before disappearing back along the corridor. Now that the adrenaline has worn off, Davyn doesn't have the energy to get up and pick up the bottle. He's not sure he even wants it. All they're fed down here is animal blood. He hasn't got a clue what animal it's from, but it's far from fresh. If he doesn't get some proper blood soon, he's not going to last much longer.

He wraps his arms around his naked chest and shivers. The cells are cut from solid rock, the walls damp and cold against his skin. What he wouldn't give for a hot shower and his warm bed. Hell, even a change of clothes would be appreciated. He closes his eyes and tries to drown out the moans and screams around him. Not everyone is taking to this life well. While he's not having any fun himself, he's well used to living in a cage. After his mother died, his father had locked him in one for years. He can survive this. Doesn't mean he wants to though.

He never thought of the Blackjack's compound as anything other than somewhere to sleep and train. After spending who knows how long in this hellhole, he realises he misses it. He misses the Blackjacks and the life he had with them. He'd fought and trained with them - nothing more, but even those two things had become a part of his life.

Then Court came back... with Thea. He knows he has no right to think about her, but tell that to his brain. The second he saw her in the apartment, she was in his head and no amount of effort on his part had pushed her out. Even the fact that she's Court's daughter and a hundred and forty years younger than him hadn't stopped the thoughts. And he'd tried. He really did.

He'd tried to keep away from her, but she wouldn't give him peace. Then he found her at his door when he was releasing his wings. Wings he'd kept hidden from the Blackjacks since he'd joined. He's a Prime. A pure bred male, which means he has the added bonus of having wings. Just his luck to have a fucked up, seriously disfigured wing.

The damn thing ripped his back open every time he had to release it so he'd taken to hiding in his room, blaring music and drinking himself senseless when he had to let it out. Thea had seen the whole sorry show. He'd tried to scare her off. Tried to show why others kept away from him, but she hadn't run away. Instead she'd said she liked his Irish accent!

A few days later, Nix had ordered him to take Thea shopping for some things, as all her belongings had been left when the Order attacked their apartment. He'd enjoyed and hated every minute of the hour-long car trip. And then she mentioned his wings and he fucked everything up by freaking out and saying some shite things to her.

He knows she got out of the tunnels when he rescued her. Court and Nix were close enough to help her get out of the shaft. The rescue may not have gone entirely to plan, but at least he'd gotten her out. That was his main objective. He would have preferred she didn't see him being taken away by the vampires. That wasn't part of the plan. He'll never forget the look on her face as she watched him being dragged to the ground. He may have been hallucinating, but he's pretty damn sure she was crying... for him. It makes little to no sense, but he's nearly positive she was.

He shakes his head and has a stern word with himself. She was probably crying because she was terrified. She had been kept in that place, alone and in the dark. Not surprising she was crying. He may try to convince himself that's the case, but deep down, a little part of him hopes she was crying for him.

No one has ever cried for him. Why would they? He's not someone people care about. There's nothing about him that would appeal to a female – especially someone new to their world. He's disfigured, defective, scarred, unable to feed without feeling ill. Even one of those would be enough to drive her away, let alone all of them.

Someone further down the corridor screams. Davyn buries his head under his arms and focuses on remembering Thea's face, her long dark hair, her scent, the taste of her blood as it hit his tongue. He knows he's just adding to his torture by thinking about her. He knows she could never be with someone like him, but isn't he allowed to dream for a while at least? Get lost in his head instead of his horrific reality.

Knowing she's back with her father and is safe makes being here a little more bearable.

He can't remember much after he was dragged to the ground. There was a hell of a lot of pain caused by boots and hands, then he was shoved down a chute of some sort. The walls had been smooth and the landing hard. While he had been peeling himself off the floor he'd been injected with something and woke up here. The vampires suffering Blood Fever wouldn't have been able to operate a hammer let alone a syringe. Someone in full control of themselves had been waiting down there for him.

He may not remember who took him, but he sure as hell knows who has him. It doesn't take a genius to figure out he's back in Ireland as most of the voices he hears have an accent. Only one vampire in Ireland has the connections, the funds, and the reputation to pull something like this off.

The self-titled Raven King ruled most of the vampires in the country - by force rather than choice. Any one lucky enough not to get in his sights managed to live a normal life, but had to hide the vampire side of themselves like their life depended on it - which it did. Davyn was unlucky enough to have lived under his rule for decades. The man was a bloodthirsty S.O.B. who didn't take no for an answer.

If he is a new toy for the King, this is only the beginning. There will be a hell of a lot more pain heading his way.

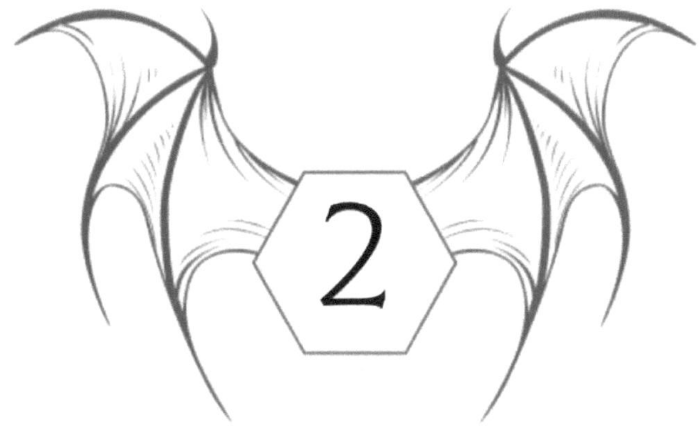

'Hey, you okay?'

Thea jumps when Shep comes up from behind her. Of all the Blackjacks, Shep was the last one she wanted to be alone with. The guy had barely said two words to her since that night in the helicopter when they flew off and left Davyn behind.

He had been beyond furious with her and she couldn't blame him. He'd told her in no uncertain terms - and very loudly - that she was the reason Davyn was gone. Apart from a few grunted words if they happened to bump into each other, she hadn't seen him. Looks like her luck just ran out.

'Not really.'

'Why are you on the garage floor staring at Dav's car?'

Thea doesn't have an answer for that. Over the last few weeks, she found a little comfort down here. She couldn't go to his room - that would be weird. There was nowhere else in the compound where she felt like she could be close to him. She knows how pathetic she looks, but she really doesn't care. It's not like the team could think any less of her. She needed to be here.

If sitting on the floor in the garage and looking at his car helped her to feel a little closer to him, she was going to keep doing it. His jacket was in her wardrobe and would stay there until she could personally give it back. That's all she had. They weren't a couple. They weren't even close. No touching. Nothing except a strange and highly electric moment when he fed from her. That was the full extent of their relationship. He was a highly trained vampire warrior and she was the human who'd ruined his life.

'I don't know,' she replies truthfully.

Shep lowers to the ground beside her and stretches his long legs out in front of him. He pushes his wet hair off his face and crosses his arms as he stares over at the car. 'I was just training with Fallon. She tells me you're kicking ass. That you can hold your own against her.'

Thea nods. 'I wouldn't say I'm holding my own, but I can hold her back for a minute or two. It's nice to have something to do. She's a tough teacher.'

Shep laughs at that. 'Too right she is. She's impressed with your performance though. I've known her years and she's not a fan of throwing compliments around. She only says what she means. Keep it up and you might be ready to go up against me.'

'I think I'll pass for the moment.' Thea isn't in a hurry to go one-on-one with Shep now or ever. He's massive and a deadly fighter.

Shep glances sideways at her then takes a deep breath. 'Listen–'

'You don't have to, Shep.'

'Don't have to what?'

'Apologise for what you said on the helicopter. You were right. It's my fault Davyn is gone.'

'Hold on a second. Apologise?' He snorts loudly. 'I wasn't going to apologise. I haven't got anything to apologise for.'

'Oh. Right.' Okay, so now she's pathetic and mortified. Not to mention she probably just reminded him about their argument and opened that wound again.

'I was going to ask if you'd like to go for a spin?'

She frowns up at him. 'Go for a what?'

He nods over at Davyn's black Range Rover. 'Our boy fucking hates when anyone goes near his car. And I mean glowing eyes and bared teeth kind of hate. My ingenious plan is to piss him off so much he has no choice but to come back just to knock my block off.' He shrugs and smirks at her. 'Worth a shot.'

Thea smiles and looks back at the car. 'I like the sound of that plan.'

Shep gets up and holds out his hand to help her to her feet. He grabs the keys from the safe on the wall and unlocks the doors.

Thea sits back in the cool leather and breathes in the smell. It's Davyn. Shep starts the engine and presses on the accelerator causing the engine to roar loudly. 'That'll really piss him off.'

Grinning, he puts it in gear and drives up the tunnel to the gates. He accelerates down the road, the powerful lights cutting through the absolute darkness outside. After about ten minutes he pulls the car to a stop at the side of the road.

'What's wrong?'

'Swap places.' He gets out and walks around the front of the car. Thea hops out and climbs into the driver's seat, moving it forward quite a bit. She fastens her seatbelt as Shep opens the back door and climbs in.

'What are you doing?'

'Catching forty winks. Don't crash, okay?'

He shuffles down, crosses his arms, and closes his eyes. He may still be angry at her, but he's giving her exactly what she needs right now - time alone with her thoughts of Davyn in something that was... is... his. She smiles and puts the car in gear, then drives.

About an hour later she pulls into the car park at the same spot Davyn had taken her after their shopping trip. She turns around and taps Shep's knee, stopping his snores. He wakes instantly and sits up.

'Hey! It's okay. Sorry, I didn't meant to startle you.'

He slumps back and yawns loudly. 'No problem. Where are we?'

'At the lake. I just wanted to get out for a bit so I thought I better tell you.'

He scrubs his hands through his hair and nods. 'Yep. Good call. Let's go.'

'You can stay here.'

'No chance.'

Shep keeps a fair way behind her as she picks her way along the track to the river. The torch on her phone offers little in the way of a decent light, but she manages to get to the river without tripping or falling. She sits on the same tree trunk she sat on the first time she was here, and glances over her shoulder. Shep sits beside her and looks around him.

'Why here?'

'I made Davyn stop here on the way back from Hereford. He took me shopping after the Order destroyed the apartment I lived in with Court.'

'Right. Never been here before. You want me to fuck off and give you some space?'

'No. Stay where you are. I don't really want to be alone if that's okay. You don't have to talk to me. Just sit.' They sit in a strangely comfortable silence for a few minutes. Thea can't help but like Shep. There's something about the guy that's welcoming. He looks intimidating, but once he cracks a smile, it's hard not to warm to him. Knowing that he blames her for Davyn hurts more than she can say. Probably because she feels the exact same way. It is her fault.

'Can I ask you something?'

He peers over at her and nods. 'Sure.'

'Do you believe that he'll be found?'

Shep doesn't immediately answer, leaving her waiting for a few minutes before he responds. 'Honestly, it's even odds I reckon.'

'Oh.'

'I know that's not what you want to hear, but it's the way things are in our world, Thea. People want us dead. It's a fact. Dav... he's rubbed a lot of the True Order up the wrong way over the years. More than I have, which is something I need to rectify. We all have targets on our heads. That's why we train so fucking hard to be the best we can. And Dav is the best. And no, I will not repeat that ever again. My ego couldn't handle it. And even odds is damn good.'

'It took years to find Court.'

'Yeah. I know. You've got to remember something though. We never stopped looking for him. Not for one minute of one of those days. We just need Dav to hang on until we do find him. That's the key to everything.'

Thea nods but doesn't say anything else. Shep is right. This is up to Davyn. If he is still alive and even remotely in control of his well-being, he needs to keep fighting.

~

Ronan pushes the control to raise the large portcullis, allowing the white panel van entry into the castle. He rubs his tired eyes as he waits for the van to pull in to the courtyard. He was awoken in the early hours of the morning to accept his master's newest fighter.

Ronan abhors this side of his job, but his master is a difficult man to disobey. The fights he runs throughout Ireland and some of Europe are the main source of his income. He doubts anyone would be able to convince him to abolish this horrid sport. His latest fighter had been tried and tested in some of the smaller fighting rings around the country before being brought back to the main base of operations where the prestigious fights were held.

As part of his job, Ronan had to settle the new fighters in, which meant escorting them to their cells and making sure they couldn't escape their chains. He absently massages his left wrist as he waits for the cargo to be unloaded. His master had been unhappy about the fact he'd questioned the treatment of the fighters. To remind him of his place in the castle, his bones had been squeezed to breaking point. The bruise left by his master's hand surrounds his thin wrist turning the flesh an angry red that would no doubt result in an impressive bruise in the days to come.

The back of the van opens and the false wall at the far end is removed, uncovering a large male in a sturdy cage. The cage is wheeled down the ramp and Ronan shakes his head in sorrow. The male has a heavy black bag over his head and his thick arms are chained above him through the bars of the cramped cage. Various cuts and bruises cover his bare back and arms along with a thick layer of dirt. Ronan follows the guards as they wheel the male through the tunnels that snake throughout the foundation of the ancient castle. They arrive at the room where the fighters are processed and Ronan points to the cage. 'Get him inside and secured.'

They do as instructed and drag the male out of the cage bringing him over to the chains hanging from the far wall of the cell. They fasten his arms over his head, leaving his face against the stone and his bare back exposed to the cell. Then Ronan notices the ridges running down the fighters back.

This fighter is a Prime. That explains his size.

Ronan stifles a curse. Having a Prime in the ring will be very lucrative for his master. Ronan had witnessed two previous Prime fighters being readied for the ring and was left with nightmares both times. There's no point having a Prime in the ring unless his wings are out. You can tell the crowd the fighter is a Prime as many times as you like, but without the visual confirmation, it won't work. Unfortunately, the only way to get the wings out of an uncooperative male is to electrocute the base of each one.

Before he can comment further, one of the guards presses a cattle prod against the male's back. The prisoner screams in pain, the hood muffling his cries of agony. Ronan watches in horror as the male is struck again, for longer this time. Ronan grimaces as one large black and red wing slides out through the ridge. The bones lock into position, the skin stretching as it takes its final form. Then the second wing comes out. The fighter screams as the skin tears further down his back to allow the wing out.

The guard quickly pierces the top of each wing and inserts a thick shackle around each of the main bones leaving the male unable to pull them back inside his body. The guard gets to work embedding more shackles down the length of each wing while another locks chains in place, pinning the wings to each other.

Ronan barely pays attention to what they are doing. His entire focus is on the deformed wing being pulled and twisted to secure it to the other one. The fighter struggles as the chains are fitted, locking the deformed wing in place.

Bile rises in Ronan's throat as he swallows deeply to keep everything in check. His feet take on a life of their own and bring him over to the wall. He slowly reaches up to pull the hood off the fighter's head. His stomach falls to the ground as all his worst nightmares come true. Familiar green eyes slowly lift to look at him. The fighter smiles warmly at him even though he's in pain.

'Hey, Ronan.'

'Oh my god! Davyn.'

Ronan's first instinct is to embrace his dear friend, but that would not go down well with his master.

'What are you doing here?' he hisses, trying not to draw attention to himself or to Davyn.

'It's not by choice, believe me.'

Ronan curses his foolish statement. 'Forgive me. I was not expecting you. This is a surprise.'

Davyn winces as one of the guards shoves his face against the wall and begins shaving his head. Ronan wants to shout at him to leave Davyn be, but it would do no good. There is a process each new fighter undergoes and, until finished, they will not stop. When they are done Davyn closes his eyes and rests his head against the wall.

'It's good to see you, Ronan.'

'And you too my friend. However the circumstances are far from favourable.'

Ronan looks up at the guard as he approaches. 'He's ready, Ronan. Should I put his number on him?' The guard looks to Ronan for instruction but he cannot give the one he desperately wants to. Only his master can release a fighter from service. And that only happens when the fighter is killed.

He looks back at Davyn and the young man smiles at him. 'It's okay.'

It's far from okay but Davyn knows the way things work for his master. There is no choice. 'Yes. Then take him to his cell.'

~

'Settled back in again?'

Davyn opens his eyes to glare at the reason he's in this hell. At just under six foot, The Raven King is a lot shorter than Davyn, but there's no mistaking who he is. Just like the last time Davyn saw him, he's still stuck in a time long past in his patched leather trousers made from the hides of animals he caught himself.

Paired with a black tunic style shirt under fur pelts and his long hair in a ponytail half way down his back, you'd swear you had travelled back a few centuries. A serious looking hunting knife hangs from his belt on his left side with the matching sword on the other side. Out on the streets of Dublin he would have been laughed at. In this dark, stone walled setting, he's right at home.

'What took you so long?' Davyn asks, as his visitor silently watches him. 'I've been here for hours.' At least he assumes it's been hours. After his wings were chained together, he had been fitted with new heavy shackles, each one lined with metal spikes that dig in to his flesh, tearing his already damaged wrists. Then one of the goons had given him a new tattoo. This one he has no interest in seeing. His fighter number had been permanently inked on his scalp at either side of his head, marking him as property for the rest of his short life.

Exhaustion had robbed him of the next few hours. He welcomed the safety of unconsciousness. In the peaceful darkness there was no pain, no cold, no gut-twisting hunger. In there were thoughts of his teammates... and of Thea.

'I thought it only fitting I give you time to settle in. Get used to your new surroundings. I wish I was there when Ronan realised who he was processing. I would have liked to see his face. His beloved pet coming home to fight.'

His deep highly accented voice carried the same rasp Davyn remembers from years ago. It helped make his barked orders all the more difficult to ignore. Davyn leans forward trying to take pressure off his aching wings. His deformed wing doesn't fold in the direction it should - never has. The guards had to bend it back on itself to secure it to his other wing. The pain of having it twisted around is bad enough, but the sites where they attached the metal rings are throbbing and the heavy chains are just adding to the pain. 'What do you want?'

'I've been told you've been rejecting my hospitality.' The King nods down at the bottle of stale blood on the floor. 'Drink it. Don't want you keeling over on us. You're my star attraction after all.'

'Drink the damn stuff yourself.' He had planned to drink the contents but the smell alone was enough to convince him otherwise. It's rancid.

The King shakes his head. 'Drink it, Davyn. You don't want me to force you.'

Davyn drags himself to his feet, trying to ignore the way the room tilts as he finally stands. The worst thing he can do is show weakness in front of his captor. He grabs on to the rusted bars, wincing as the spikes on the inside of his shackle digs into his wrist. 'So this is how I get to pay my debt to you. Being used as entertainment in your fighting pit. Bring in funds for your cause?'

'Is it not a fitting hobby for a warrior such as yourself? From what I hear, you gallantly gave yourself in exchange for a human girl. A heroic deed such as that deserves an equally heroic punishment, don't you think?'

Davyn's jaw cracks loudly as he clamps his mouth shut. If he reacted he'd give the King more ammunition. Even hearing the male mention her stokes anger deep inside himself.

'One has to wonder; what was it about this girl - this human, that brought you to make such a reckless decision? Was she your pet? Your donor perhaps?' The King rubs his chin as he examines his prisoner. 'What did you take from her, Davyn, huh? Did you take more than her blood?' He laughs to himself as Davyn snarls. 'I guess old habits die hard, eh Davyn. I'm proud of you.'

Davyn catches himself before he gives away too much by telling the bastard to shut the fuck up. The King pauses then drops his voice, softening his tone. 'I'm sure I don't need to tell you the way things work around here. You betrayed me, Davyn which means you will die when I choose. If you had just stayed with me instead of running off to join the damn Blackjacks, you could be standing by my side where you belong, instead of in there with the rats.'

He faces Davyn. 'I'll give you one shot. All you need to do is kneel before me. Pledge your allegiance to me. Fight for me. It's that simple.'

Davyn looks up and licks his dry lips before responding. 'I'm not going to be one of your assassins.'

'Why not? You were so good at it. Besides, do you really believe being a Blackjack is any different?'

'Don't you dare compare what they do, to what you do.'

The King smiles as he leans against the wall, his broad arms crossed over his chest. 'Interesting. You said 'they' not 'we'. Feeling like a bit of an outsider, Davyn?'

Davyn doesn't bother looking up, not wanting to give any hint that a nerve may have been hit.

'No response?'

'Screw you.'

'No Davyn. Screw you!' he shouts. 'Do you have any idea how much trouble you've caused me? How much I've spent to get you back under my roof? Too much. More than you deserve, I can tell you. No one runs from me, Davyn. No one. You disgraced me and my name by running. You belong to me. You are mine to do with as I please. Always have been.'

The King wipes his face and attempts to steady his breathing. He's always on edge. Always primed and ready to lash out without warning. It's what makes him so dangerous. When he looks back at Davyn he's smiling darkly.

'I'm curious about something. Do the Blackjacks know what sort of monster they allowed under their roof? Have you told them about all the lives you've taken? Have you shared the gory details with them? About how you tore their bodies to pieces and bathed in their blood? Bet that makes for great conversation over dinner.'

Davyn peers up at him but doesn't bother getting into it with him. The King is right. Rumours of what he did in his past life have flown around the compound since the day he arrived. And it's not like he could deny them. He couldn't deny the truth as much as he'd like to. But that didn't mean he corrected any of the details. He was a monster. Probably still is deep down. But the Blackjacks are all he has in his life. He couldn't bear them knowing the full extent of his crimes and have them turn their backs on him.

'They don't know, do they? Still running from the truth, eh Davyn? That's a shame. You were so efficient at enforcing my rule. To this day I have yet to find anyone who can match you in sheer cold brutality.'

Davyn doesn't reply. He has nothing to say to that.

The King crouches down and looks at him through the bars. 'Last chance. Will you join me?'

Davyn shakes his head. 'No.'

The King's eyes darken as his fangs lengthen. 'So be it. Don't say I didn't warn you. Once I leave you're just like all the other prisoners down here. You will fight and then you will die. You will line my pockets and provide entertainment until I'm done with you. It won't mean a damn thing who you used to be to me. You will be nothing more than an attraction that brings me a lot of money.'

Davyn rises to his full height, straightening his wings as much as he can within the confines of the chains. 'I'll gladly spend the rest of my life in chains if it means I don't have to stand by your side for even one second as your son. I'm done fighting. I won't be a part of this.'

The King stares at him for a long time before he straightens and rests his hand on his sword. 'Very well, Davyn. How about I give you a choice. A rare occurrence but I'm in a good mood today. If you don't fight I will personally drag five prisoners out of their cells and slice their throats open right in front of you. One life in the ring or five outside of it. I'll leave you to choose.'

'Fuck you.'

'No fuck you, Son. You don't get to turn your back on me and have a happy life. That's not how it works. I have you back under my control and I promise you, I will make sure you get exactly what you deserve. I'm sure I can come up with a suitable reward fitting for an ungrateful, defective, unwanted, bastard such as yourself.' He spits on Davyn before turning and storming away from him.

'One life in the ring, Davyn, or five out of it. Enjoy choosing.'

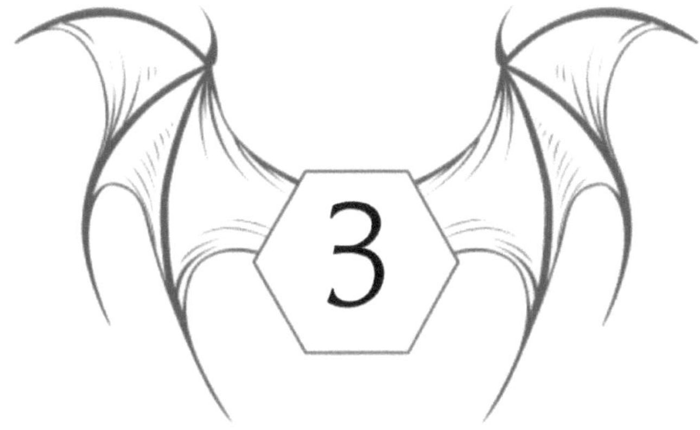

Davyn braces his legs and presses his side against the wall, not that it does much good. His bastard of a father had put the cells in the caves under the castle and extended the foundation walls to keep the prison secure. The added bonus of having them flood twice a day at high tide was an opportunity his father didn't want to miss out on.

When he was a child, fear of drowning while he slept had kept him fighting to stay awake for years. The cells were always cold, either damp, or under a good few feet of water, and miserable as fuck.

The freezing water has made its way to his waist and is still rising. At least the sound of the waves beating against the rocks at the far side of the wall helps to mask the moans and cries of the other prisoners in the cells with him.

He tucks his wings around himself as much as he can, but the chains tethering them to each other doesn't have much give. Another violent shiver passes through his body. The cold is part of him now.

No escaping it. There's no escaping any of this. He spent decades running from his past - from his brute of a father - only to end up in exactly the same situation. If he'd known this would happen he would have just stayed here and let his father kill him decades ago. Save everyone a lot of trouble and him a lot of pain.

Every inch of his body hurts. Not just a dull ache, more like a raging fire. The metal rings secured around the base of each wing pull heavily on his aching limbs. He really needs to pull them back in to his body. Not that that task had ever been a walk in the park thanks to his fucked-up wing, but not being able to retract them left his back in a mess. If he wasn't allowed to pull them in soon, he's going to be stuck with them out for good.

He tucks his hands into his armpits, wincing as the shackles dig in to him, tearing at his wrists. Another shiver works through his starving body. The old bottles of rancid blood he had no choice but to drink might as well have been water for all the good it did him. He swallows again, desperate to keep the last feed where it should be. Blood never settled well in his stomach. This rancid crap is testing him and his willpower. It wouldn't be the first time his father made him drink blood he's later thrown up.

He smiles as someone clears their throat and knocks on the bars of his cell. He looks at the grey-haired, smartly dressed man standing on the raised walkway outside his cell. Davyn rests his head against the cold stone. 'It's a cell, Ronan. You don't need to knock.'

The man smiles affectionately at Davyn as he leans against the bars of the cell. 'No excuse for forgoing manners, sire. I was going to ask how you are, but I fear I know the answer. You look... well, absolutely terrible.'

Davyn pushes upright and stumbles over to his former mentor and closest friend. He falls against the bars and closes his eyes as his head spins. 'I thought I was hallucinating when I heard your voice after I was brought in.'

'As soon as I saw your wing I knew it was you. What happened,

Davyn? How did he get you after all this time?'

'Wrong place at the wrong time. It was going to happen sooner or later.'

'Judging by the wounds on your body, you haven't just arrived in the fighting pits. How long has he had you?'

Davyn shakes his head. 'Don't know. It was just before Christmas when I was captured.' Ronan's gaze drops to the ground. 'What?'

'It's mid-February, sire.'

Davyn hears the words but doesn't want to believe them. He knew he'd been gone for a long time, but nowhere near two months.

'Master?'

'Stop addressing me like that. I was never your master.'

'You may have fought the title, regularly, if my memory serves me correctly, but that doesn't mean it isn't true. I have, and always will serve you, Davyn. Willingly, I might add. In this place that is a rare, if not unheard sentiment.'

Davyn smiles weakly. 'You were more of a father to me than he ever was. I never thought of you as a servant so, for the last time, can we please drop... the formalities.' Unable to hold his weight any longer, his legs fold and he lands hard on his knees, barely keeping his head above the water. 'Sorry. Tired.'

Ronan crouches down in front of him. He reaches through the bars and firmly, but gently, takes Davyn's chin and turns his head towards him. Ronan leans closer and frowns as he examines Davyn's face. 'We both know you are more than tired. He's starving you.'

Davyn pulls his head away. 'The blood he's giving me is weak. Tastes horrible. I'm fine, Ronan.'

'Your eyes are sunken and your skin tone matches the grey rock surrounding you. You need Prime blood. I will try to locate some for you. In the meantime you must feed from me. I can assure you my blood will taste a great deal better than whatever he's giving you.' Ronan rolls up his sleeve and pushes his arm through the bars nearest to Davyn. 'I know you do not want to feed, but you must. Take what you need.' Davyn shakes his head but Ronan thrusts his fist closer to Davyn's face. 'Drink.'

Davyn frowns as the smell of blood hits him. He looks down at the bandage peeking out from under his rolled up sleeve. 'What happened?'

Ronan pulls his sleeve down to cover the bandage. 'I fell.'

Davyn snorts. 'Are we really doing that? What did he do to you, Ronan?'

'I made the foolish mistake of questioning your father. It did not go down well. Now will you please drink?'

'Questioning him about what?'

'Davyn–'

'About what?'

'You of course. While you were being tattooed with your fighters number I confronted him. He pinned my arm to the table with his blade while he made sure I understood it is none of my business. Now, I am going to stay here until you feed so please hurry up. My knees aren't what they used to be.'

Davyn looks back at the frail arm being offered to him. Ronan had been nothing but a loyal servant to his father for as long as he can remember. Of all the people in the castle that deserved to get up close and personal with a blade, Ronan was not one of them.

'I'm fine, Davyn. Please do not insult me by refusing my offer again.'

Davyn gives in. He hates taking blood from the old man, but in his current state, he can't really refuse. He shuffles a little closer and takes Ronan's thin wrist in his hand. His canines fill his mouth and he latches on, hating the wince of pain from Ronan. He takes a lot less than he needs, but enough to give him another day to fight his father.

The only reason he'd survived this long was out of pure stubbornness. He was in a battle of wills with his father and he was damned if the piece of shit he shared some genetics with, was going to win. If living and fighting against him for one more day, gave Davyn one more day to kill the man, he was damn well going to make sure that's what he did.

Ronan wraps a handkerchief around his wrist and pulls his sleeve down. 'Is it true what I heard among the servants? That your father has threatened the life of innocent males if you do not fight?'

Davyn nods. 'If I don't fight or if the fight ends too fast, he'll kill five of the prisoners. Guess he knew I wouldn't be willing to play along with this fucked up circus.' He closes his eyes as Ronan's blood makes its way into his system, helping to take the chill from his limbs 'Believe me, I'd quite happily stand there and go down without a fight, but I'd be sentencing more people to their death. They deserve a chance to fight for their lives. It's a 'damned if I do, damned if I don't' situation.'

'Their deaths are not on you.'

Davyn nods once. 'Nothing either of us can do about it. We're both trapped. I appreciate you coming to see me but you should go.' Ronan's blood isn't settling in his stomach. If he's going to stick a finger up at Ronan's offering, he'd prefer to do it in private. When he doesn't hear the man leaving he opens his eyes again. 'What?'

Ronan shakes his head and curses under his breath, something that surprises Davyn. In all the years he's known him, Ronan had never cursed. 'I can't leave you like this. Not again. I can't watch you go through this again, Davyn. I sat outside this wretched cell for forty-six years with you. Forty-six long, heart-wrenching, miserable years watching you suffer like this. You should not be here again.'

'I'm okay, Ronan. Really.'

'I'd appreciate if you didn't treat me like a fool, sire. You're far from okay.' He takes a deep breath and shakes his head. 'I thought he had given up the search. He hasn't spoken of you for years. I should have known he was planning something. He's been... I guess the best way to describe it is less dark. If I'd known he had you I would have—'

'Would have what? There's nothing you could have done.'

Ronan smiles and nods. 'Perhaps you are right.' He sits on the walkway and chuckles to himself. 'I knew you were still alive. I have for years.'

'How? I've tried to stay off-grid.'

Ronan laughs and Davyn is instantly transported back to his youth and the many hours he spent with his friend. Ronan is the sole reason Davyn survived those decades locked down here. If not for his constant company, Davyn surely would have lost his mind a long time ago.

'You really think someone such as yourself can stay hidden? I have heard rumours. A contact of a contact got himself in a little bother and certain individuals were called into assist. According to him, one of the males was quite intimidating. Apparently when he spoke he had an Irish accent. Can I presume that was you?'

'Why do you assume it was me?'

'There were certain aspects of your fighting style that reminded me of you. I saw you fight your father and brother, Darren, enough times to know your style. Are you honestly going to deny you are a Blackjack?'

Davyn smiles. 'No point. You can see right through me. I don't usually talk too much when I'm in the field. Accent is hard to hide.'

Ronan smiles and laughs. 'That it is. It is quite impressive. I'm proud of you. Have you been a Blackjack for long?'

'Few years. I was living rough, moving round a lot. Got on the wrong side of someone and they were called in. The leader saw something in me and asked me to join.'

'I do not find that hard to believe. I am a little confused though. I have not heard talk of a Prime Blackjack. I would have thought that would be beneficial.'

'They don't know I'm Prime. Or at least they didn't. They do now.'

Ronan nods slowly. 'I see. How have you kept your wings from them for so long? Surely they would have noticed when you released them.'

'Kept it to myself. My back's a mess anyway so the wing ridges didn't stand out.'

'I see,' he says again and Davyn knows he's far from happy.

'What?'

'Can I ask why you did not tell them?'

'You know why. I've got one wing, Ronan. The fucked up one doesn't count. I can't bring any extra help to the team with it. I managed just fine without using them.'

Ronan opens his mouth to say something else but has the sense to not go there. The old man was with Davyn when his wings broke out for the first time. He knows what the process involved for him and why having the wings was more of a burden than an advantage.

'Where were you captured?'

'True Order facility. We were rescuing someone they captured. Got myself caught while getting her out. He have links to the Order?'

Ronan grunts. 'It would not surprise me. He is expanding his business into other areas - lucrative ones.'

'Like what?'

'A drug of some sorts but I am not privy to any details, sire. All I know is that your grandfather would be ashamed of the path his son has taken.' Ronan looks around the cell and shakes his head. 'You come from a long and honourable bloodline. You should not be ashamed of your title, Davyn.'

Davyn laughs harshly. 'Any family pride I had was beaten out of me years ago. Listen, I'm sorry I didn't take you with me. I tried to find you, but I had to get out.'

Ronan reaches through the bars and squeezes Davyn's arm. 'And I was never more thankful that you left when you did. I am well. My only concern was your safety.' He sighs and rubs his forehead. 'It breaks my heart to see you here like this.'

Davyn hopes his smile is convincing, but he doubts it. 'I'm fine. You should go,' he says again.

'I have finished my duties for the day. I can stay with you.'

Davyn shakes his head slowly. 'No. They'll be coming for me soon.

I'm fighting later. I don't want you here. Not for that.'

Ronan looks like he wants to argue, but finally agrees, walking away without a backward glance.

~

Rhain sips his expensive champagne and watches the carnage unravelling below with feigned interest. Fighting pits have been part of life for centuries and would continue to provide entertainment to those with too much money and no taste. The crowd surge to their feet as the stronger of the two males launches on the other, tearing at him with his teeth. The ridiculously expensive champagne tastes bitter in his mouth as he watches the weaker vampire be torn to pieces as the crowd cheers.

He has no interest in the fights. They are vile and barbaric. He peers across at his True Order contact, Barton. The portly vampire is enjoying the show as much as the other spectators. Of course he is. He's a follower. Always has been. If the crowd was silent he'd be following suit.

He slaps Rhain on the shoulder, missing the venomous look thrown at him. 'I made a pretty sum on that fight.'

Rhain nods. 'That's good. Why am I here, Barton?'

'You're not enjoying the fights?'

'Thrilling. I don't appreciate being summoned like this. Why am I here?'

Barton refills his own glass before offering the bottle to Rhain, but he shakes his head. 'The Raven King wants to have a meeting with us after the main fight.'

Rhain rolls his eyes, keeping the reaction hidden from Barton. He had sincerely hoped his one-on-one dealings with the Raven King had come to an end when he delivered the Blackjack to him. Rhain didn't trust the King one bit. He runs his hand through his blond hair and considers his options. He could easily leave here and go home, but that would mean not only irritating the Raven King, but also the True Order.

He winces, doubling over as a cramp twists at his gut.

'What's wrong?'

He shakes his head and forces himself to straighten. 'Nothing. Excuse me a moment.'

'Don't be too long,' Barton calls after him. 'The main fight will begin in ten minutes.'

Rhain manoeuvres through the well-dressed crowd as he desperately makes his way to the restrooms. He locks himself in a cubicle and sits on the toilet lid as another cramp hits, driving the air from his lungs. Once he can breathe again, he fumbles in his suit pocket for the prefilled syringe. He tears off his jacket and rolls up his sleeve, desperate to take the drug before the cramps worsen.

As soon as the medication hits his system, the cramps ease. He holds his hand out in front of him, glaring as it trembles. He's running out of time. He should be working on finding a cure for the Fever instead of humouring sadistic bastards and idiots.

Nothing he can do about that now.

He's here and will have to stay until after the meeting. Rhain slowly gets to his feet, bracing himself against the cubicle walls as his head spins. He unrolls his shirt sleeve and puts his jacket back on. Once he's sure he's alone, he opens the door and comes to a stop when he catches sight of himself in the mirror. His grey eyes are glowing silver with traces of red.

He leans closer to the mirror, hoping he's seeing things. But he's not. There are definitely flashes of red in his eyes.

The final stage of Fever.

Once the eyes fully turned red there's no coming back. Rhain closes his eyes and drops his head down. He hoped he'd have more time. Seems his body has other ideas.

The door to the restrooms bursts open and Barton steps inside. 'There you are. The fight's about to begin.'

'I'll be there in a minute.'

'What's the problem?'

Rhain lets his anger out, hoping it will hide his eye colour. 'Give me a minute!'

Baton nods and backs out. Rhain looks back at his reflection, relieved when all traces of red have vanished in the silver.

He straightens and gets himself together before heading back out into the arena. He takes his place beside Barton but doesn't make an effort to apologise. Barton will die at his hand one day. Rhain is going to make sure of that.

When the main champion is dragged into the ring, he takes a step back from the edge of the viewing area. He's a fool. He should have known the Blackjack, Davyn, would be the star fighter, but he's been so busy with the King and the Order, it never crossed his mind.

The impressive warrior has been through the wars since Rhain delivered him to the King. If not for his sheer size and distinctive tattoos covering his chest and arms he wouldn't have recognised him. The male is bloody, beaten, and filthy.

Barton nudges him in the arm and Rhain barely keeps himself from tearing the limb from his body. 'I've put everything on him. Undefeated.'

Rhain doesn't doubt that. The Blackjacks are a pain in his life but no one could question their training. When the fight begins, Rhain can't help but watch as Davyn speedily kills his opponent. Unlike the previous fights, there are no dramatics, no theatre or showing off to the crowd. He kills the male humanly, if one could use that word for the situation.

Barton cheers and when he slaps Rhain on the shoulder he growls at him. 'Touch me again and I'll throw you in the pit with him.'

Barton nods then clears his throat. 'Relax. We better go. He'll be waiting for us.'

Rhain casts one last look into the pit before he follows after Barton.

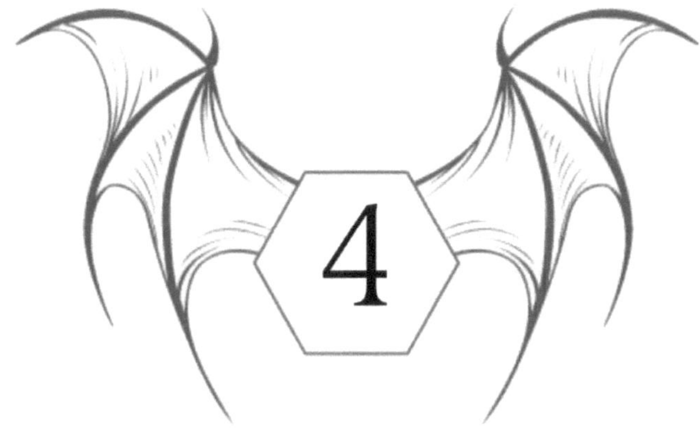

Davyn braces himself as the guards launch him into his cell. The floor is already under a good foot or two of freezing sea water, cushioning his landing a little until he hits the wall and something snaps. Davyn gasps as a sharp pain tears through his good wing. He pushes to his knees, spitting out the mouthful of water he took in when he landed. He glances over his shoulder and curses when he sees what the problem is.

One of the bones is broken, the bloody stump sticking through the flesh part. The little blood he took from Ronan before the fight helped get him through it in one piece, but it's not enough to help him now. Unless he has vampire blood, his body won't be able to regenerate his wing.

He tries to get to his feet but he's running on empty. He'll have to stay where he is for the moment. Or until he has no choice but to get up before he drowns. He hears heavy footsteps echoing through the stone corridor leading to the cells. He licks his cracked lips and steels himself for the fun and games his father will bring. The large male strides up to the cell, keeping to the elevated walkway running alongside the cells.

'So, you live to fight another day, traitor. It was an interesting match.'

Davyn rests his forehead on the cool stone and tries to stay conscious. The male he was thrown into the ring with, didn't have a chance. Even in his weakened state, he was no match for Davyn. He tried to make it as quick and painless as he could, but the end result was the same. Davyn had killed another vampire for the sick entertainment of others.

'Look at me while I'm talking to you!'

Davyn can't be bothered obliging. His father's men push their way inside and force Davyn up on to his knees then lean on the chains linking his wings. He bites out a curse of pain, but he isn't strong enough to throw them off. His father steps in to the cell and roughly grabs Davyn's chin. He forces Davyn's head back as his men keep pressure on his wings, holding him in place.

'This is all I've ever wanted from you. My heir, showing me the respect I deserve. Is that really too much to ask? I gave you life, boy. I gave you everything you ever wanted and look at you. You grew up strong, fierce, intimidating. Stop fighting me, Davyn. Join me by my side. Take your place with me. When my enemies see one of the mighty Blackjacks kneel at my feet–'

'You might as well kill me 'cause there's no fucking way I'll ever willingly kneel in front of you,' Davyn interrupts.

'So, your loyalty is reserved for strangers instead of family, is that it?'

'Loyalty? Why would I have any loyalty to a man who beat the shite out of me day after day for decades? You hated me every day of my life. Never held back showing me how much. You goaded Darren on. Encouraged him to beat me with whatever he could get his hands on.

And you stood by and watched.'

'I was trying to make you strong.'

'You were trying to show me you were the boss. That you could overpower a kid barely out of the change. Bet you gave yourself a pat on the back every day. Big man in charge of everyone in his house. You're a fucking joke. Should have killed you before I left and burned this shit-hole to the ground with everyone in it.' He gets a small kick out of the look of pure hatred on his father's face. He knows he hasn't done himself any favours, but he's beyond caring.

'Why must you continue to fight me, Davyn? I am giving you the chance to be my heir.'

Davyn laughs. 'You only want me as your heir because Darren died and there's no one to take over this circus when someone finally kills you. Just hoping it's me who gets to cut your fucking head off, *Dad*.'

The blow is expected but still hurts like hell. Davyn spits out a glob of blood, pleased when it lands on his father's trousers.

The King grabs the back of Davyn's head and shoves it forward. Davyn manages to take a quick breath before his father pushes his face under the water. He holds Davyn in place and leans close to his ear.

'Your brother died with honour. Darren died defending our name, our legacy. That's something a traitor like you could never understand. He embraced all that I gave him. What did you do? First you disgrace me with those pathetic excuses for wings and then you run like a coward. Your actions disgraced this family. Disgraced my legacy.' He grabs Davyn's shoulder and pulls him upright again. Davyn gasps for breath in between spitting out mouthfuls of sea water.

Davyn looks up at his father. 'Glad to hear I had such an impact.'

His father, or rather the space in between his father's cruel eyes, is all that has his attention. If he really concentrates, he can picture a large hole where a bullet from his gun will enter his father's skull.

'You really want to kill me, don't you.' His father ducks lower so he is eye to eye with him. 'I have to admire that about you. Even after everything I've put you through, that resilience remains. You've got guts, for a traitor. Pity you can't put that anger to better use.'

Davyn continues mentally boring the hole in his father's forehead, seeing the blood ooze out of the wound he's creating in his mind. His father spits on him, then leans his full weight on Davyn's head as he pushes himself to his feet. 'Feed him.'

Davyn is pushed back against the wall by two of his father's men. He shouts out as his wings are crushed behind him, the rough stone cutting into them like a blade. The third man digs his fingers into Davyn's jaw, prising it open even though he fights to keep it closed.

His father picks up the bottle of blood and slowly walks over to Davyn. He takes his time unscrewing the top and theatrically holds it over Davyn's slightly open mouth. Smiling, he tips the contents in, then steps back as Davyn's mouth is held closed.

Foul tasting blood trickles out the corner of his mouth, but with no let up from the men holding him, he has no choice but to swallow. They let him go and he drops to his hands and knees, coughing violently.

'Now, that wasn't so difficult, was it?'

Davyn glares up at the man as his stomach churns. He gags as his father crouches over him. 'I suggest you fight to keep that down. We'll just make you drink it again if it comes out.'

Davyn breathes heavily through his nose and finally manages to convince his stomach to keep the liquid down. However bad it tastes now, he's sure it'll taste worse second time around. The men let him go and step outside the cell.

'What the hell did you just give me?' Davyn asks, barely maintaining the uneasy truce with his stomach.

'It's an interesting bi-product of a new drug friends of mine are working on. When given to mixed-blood filth it is highly addictive. Very useful as you can imagine.'

Davyn glares up at him. It sounds like the drug Shep found where

Thea was being held. He vaguely recalls Shep mentioning something about it being the vampire version of heroin. It was designed for Hybrid vampires, not Primes. 'You're part of the True Order?'

His father laughs. 'No. That lot are too... well, ordered. I prefer to be my own boss. I just use their product. It helps keep my mongrels under control. The thing is, when this blood is given to a Prime it has the same addictive properties, but also has an interesting effect. It brings on Fever. Quite rapidly I might add. A little something to help make your next fight interesting.

'You were good tonight, but it was a tad shorter than I would have liked. A quick stab to the heart is not going to sell seats. A few doses of that and you'll give us a better show. You need to earn your board and keep, both in and out of the ring. My men will give you a few hours peace before they bring you to the castle to get you ready. You'll be the entertainment at the banquet tonight.' His father points to the larger of the guards. 'Keep an eye on him. If he throws up, feed it to him again.'

His father leaves the cell with his guards, locking the door behind him - a futile act. There's no way Davyn would be able to break the chains. He doesn't know what is worse - being addicted to whatever his father gave him, or that he was going to go through Fever. Most vampires battle the urges on a daily basis, a constant fight against the vampire side of their natures. Primes have that fight tenfold.

An invisible hand twists at his stomach. No doubt something to do with the drug. He pulls his legs to this chest when the cramps mix with a shiver, as the cold water continues to rise around him. He gags but keeps the blood in his stomach. One look at his father's man and he knows full well he'd enjoy force feeding him again.

To distract himself, he closes his eyes and tries to think about Thea. He knows Court would have his neck if he even looked at her sideways, but he can't help the attraction. Even if he gets out of here with some of his sanity intact, he'll never act on it. Court is right to be worried about her involvement in this world. She's already been kidnapped and held against her will. The best thing she can do is get as far from the compound as possible. As far from Davyn as possible.

~

Ronan wipes his eyes with a tissue then positions himself in the shadows on the balcony surrounding the great hall. From his hiding spot he can see much of the room below, but it is not a view he is enjoying.

For the last two hours, he has silently witnessed his master play the dutiful host, lavishing food and drink on his guests like they were preparing for the end of the world. It seemed harmless enough until you take in to account Davyn, hanging from his chains at the front of the room. Just like his father wanted, he's on one knee with his head bowed at the foot of his father's throne, but it's far from by his own will.

A collar is fixed around his neck and attached to a steel ring embedded in the concrete platform. The shackles around his wrists are fixed to heavy chains embedded in the walls of the great hall. The chains are pulled taut, yanking the young man's arms back and up at a painful angle. Both ankles are fixed in place with his left leg forward and right leg back, keeping him on one knee in front of his father. As if that wasn't enough, they had unchained his wings and stretched them to their full span, before attaching them to chains embedded in the walls.

Since the first guest arrived, Ronan has had to watch as the young vampire has been subjected to unrelenting beatings and jeering. After the meal, the abuse stepped up a level to include being used as target practice for leftover food and dregs of ale.

Through all the abuse, Davyn has remained motionless, his head down and his wings out, with food, drink and worse, dripping off his head. Ronan didn't want to watch him being humiliated like this, but he can't abandon him. If Davyn is suffering, Ronan will be there with him. Ronan watches in horror as a loud and drunken vampire stops in front of Davyn's down-turned head, pulls down his fly and relieves himself.

He can't possibly allow this to continue. Shame and guilt eat away at him for allowing this to carry on as long as it has. How can his master treat another vampire like this - especially his own son? He always knew the King was evil to his core, but never thought he would do something so vile.

No one in this castle will do a thing to help Davyn - he knows that much. That just leaves him and he hasn't got a clue what to do. He really needs to get word to the Blackjacks, but that's easier said than done. They don't have an advert in the local paper.

He doesn't doubt that they will be searching for him. One of their own is missing. Perhaps they are in the area, searching for Davyn at this moment.

'Hang in there, Davyn. Please hang on a little longer.'

With a heavy heart, he turns away from his friend. His master will be occupied with his guests for another few hours. Perhaps there is a way of locating them and bringing them here to help Davyn?

5

Rhain walks purposefully out the gates of the castle to the waiting helicopter. The urge to run is strong, but he keeps his pace steady. Appearances are everything when it comes to Barton, The Order, and the King. Even now he can feel Barton staring at him as he waits for his own ride to come and collect him.

Rhain ducks as he nears his helicopter and climbs inside. He puts on his headset and tells the pilot to take off immediately. Rhain keeps his attention focused ahead of him as the craft takes off and turns over the castle. Only when he's in the air does he allow himself to look down at the monstrous building.

'How was dinner, sir?' Geraint asks from the seat opposite him.

'Disturbing to say the least. Strangely, watching someone being tortured in front of me ruined my appetite.' If it wouldn't have been to his own detriment, he would have walked away from whatever the fuck the King thought he was doing with that display. The pits were inexcusable. What took place over dinner was... he has no words. Rhain has done many things in his life others would frown upon. But never anything like that.

'I heard he displays his best fighters.'

Rhain nods. 'His guests are openly invited to do whatever they want to the chained fighter.'

'I apologise, sir. I tried to rearrange the meeting but the King was insistent. Why did he want to see you?'

'This blasted drug. He wants more of it. I told him we've lost two labs in recent months, but he has the backing of the Order. I've been told to provide what they need.'

'Or what?'

Rhain raises his eyebrows. 'That was left unanswered. After watching that spectacle over dinner I think I can use my imagination.'

'They had the audacity to threaten you, sir?'

Rhain smiles at his major-domo. 'They attempted to. We need to increase production in the two labs we have left.'

'You are letting them threaten you?'

'How long have you known me? Have I ever let anyone threaten me? No, we play their game for now. I still haven't entirely given up finding a cure.'

'Was the attack severe?'

Rhain smiles at Geraint. He always knew when Rhain had an attack. 'Mild, thankfully. I was able to hide it from Barton. Enough about all of this. I just want to go back to my home and forget about this place.'

'Very well, sir. Perhaps by then your appetite will have returned.'

'Perhaps.' But he seriously doubts that will be the case. What he witnessed tonight will stay with him long after he gets back to the safety of his house.

~

Davyn comes back to consciousness thanks to a boot connecting with his ribs. His father crouches down in front of him and smiles.

'Wake up, Sleeping Beauty. Lost you there for a bit. Were my friends not to your liking?' He laughs to himself as he takes a swig of ale. He licks the froth from his lips then slowly pours the dregs from the glass over Davyn's head. 'You should be grateful – that's the good stuff.' He pushes to his feet and gestures to someone out of view. 'Take him back to his cell and feed him. Then clean the platform, it stinks.'

Davyn watches his father's retreating back then scans the room. All the guests are gone. He must have passed out for a while. Best thing that could have happened to him.

His father's men release his chains, save for the one attached to the metal collar around his neck. Once his wings are secured again one of the guards tugs on his chain.

'Get up.'

He doesn't waste energy looking up at the guard. He barely has enough energy to stay conscious without wasting any of it on his father's men.

'I said get up.' The kick to his legs brings him closer to the ground instead. Davyn braces his hands under him and pushes, managing to get to his knees. 'You walk to your cell or I drag you by your neck, *sire*.' He spits as he says Davyn's title, saliva hitting his cheek.

It takes another two attempts before his legs agree to carry his weight. His wrists are secured behind his back as the second guard takes a knife from his pocket. 'You stink. Probably should wash you first.' He cuts off Davyn's trousers and boxers and lifts a bucket of water from the floor. He throws the freezing water over Davyn and the platform. As painful as it is, Davyn can't help but be a little thankful they've washed some of the filth off his body. He'd give anything for a hot shower. The stench is clinging to his skin, turning his stomach.

Once the platform is clean and he's lost all feeling from the waist down thanks to the ice cold water, one of his father's groupies pulls on the chain attached to his collar. 'C'mon boy, let's take you for a walk.' He pulls on the lead, forcing Davyn forward. Instead of taking him straight to the cell, the guards take Davyn on a tour of the castle. Nothing like parading the disgraced, naked son of their ruler in front of them to reinforce his rule.

Davyn tries not to meet the eyes of the people he passes, tries to look ahead and keep walking, but he's not successful. Every servant, every guard, every damn rat, all look at him with undisguised contempt, pity, or shame in their eyes, and that's something he doesn't want. They eventually take him to his cell and throw him inside. After forcing more foul tasting blood into him, they head back to their mates to get pats on the back and congratulations from everyone.

Davyn shuffles in to the corner, huddles in a ball, and shivers. He thought he could keep going, but now he's having serious second thoughts. Being used as a toilet was a whole new low for him. The sick bastards that seemed to think the sun shines out of his father's ass aren't going to let up. If humiliating Davyn gets them further into the King's graces they won't stop. Beatings he can handle, the other things, not so much.

Too busy congratulating themselves, they had forgotten to unlock his wrists from behind his back. With no way of keeping the cold from seeping into his bones, he buries his head in his knees. After a few breaths, he decides to breathe through his mouth. The stale beer and other things the vampires poured on him, stinks.

He never thought he'd be happy about his cell flooding, but being able to wash himself in the freezing water sounds like heaven. He curls up tighter and closes his eyes. He'll never voluntarily kneel in front of his father. It doesn't matter what he does, his father will never get obedience from him. His only other option is to take himself out of the equation.

'Sire?'

Davyn doesn't bother uncurling from his warm and rancid smelling cocoon. 'Leave.'

'I cannot. Can you come closer?'

'Dammit, Ronan. For once can you do what I say. I don't want you here and I sure as hell don't want any more of your blood. Just go!'

Ronan is quiet for a long time. Davyn isn't under any illusions that he left. He's known Ronan long enough to know his pathetic outburst wouldn't have pushed him away. 'I saw what they did to you. If I could have found a way–'

'You were there?'

'Not as far as your father knows. I was a coward and hid in the shadows. Davyn—'

'Don't Ronan. It's done, okay.'

Ronan's knees crack as he lowers to the walkway in front of the cell. 'It is far from okay, sire. This must end, but I cannot free you alone. Since I questioned his treatment of you, your father will not allow me direct access to your cell. He alone keeps the keys to your bonds. I need help.'

'You're not going to get that from anyone in the castle. And you should be staying away. He'll kill you if he finds out you even fed me.'

'I was not considering asking anyone in the castle for help. I was thinking of further afield. Perhaps you have some friends who could lend a hand? I have searched, but I cannot find a way to contact them.'

Davyn lifts his head to frown at the old man. 'They can't come here.'

'Why not?'

'They won't... I'm just one vampire. They have bigger fish to fry.'

'How can you be so sure they are not looking for you?'

Davyn isn't sure. He knows they tore the country apart looking for Court, so what makes him think they won't do the same for him? He knows he's not at the top of anyone's Christmas card list, but he is one of the team. Maybe they would be searching. A small spark of hope ignites in him, before he quickly extinguishes it. Hope means nothing in this place. He learned that the hard way decades ago. 'Just leave me alone, Ronan.'

Ronan stares at him through the rusting bars of his cell. 'So,' Ronan finally says, breaking his silence, 'he's finally done it.'

Davyn doesn't answer, knowing full well Ronan will continue, whether he responds or not.

'Your father finally broke you. All your fighting over the last few weeks was for nothing. Why the hell did you bother going through all that? Were you just trying to show everyone how tough you are?'

Davyn emerges from his cocoon. 'Give it a rest, Ronan. I can't do it anymore. I can't take another day like today. I can't... I can't do it.'

'So what's your alternative? He's not going to let you die and he's not going to kill you. Tell me how to reach them.'

Davyn shakes his head. He'd give anything to get out of this hell, but not at the expense of the Blackjacks. He'd much prefer to stay put. But then Thea pushes in to his thoughts. He wants to see her again. Hell, he needs to see her again. He doesn't deserve her. He doesn't deserve to get away from here. Not after everything he did before he escaped the first time. His father is right. This is a debt he owes - not to his father, but to all those he's hurt over the years.

'You don't deserve this, Davyn.' He doesn't let Ronan know he hit the nail on the head. It would just give his argument more ammunition. Whatever happens to him, he can deal with it. Knowing that he brought the Blackjacks into this is another story. 'I don't want you here. Get the fuck away from me!' A searing cramp leaves him doubled up on the floor. His fangs ignore all efforts to keep them contained and push out of his gums.

'What's the matter?' Ronan reaches out to him but Davyn shuffles away. 'What has he done to you?'

'Blood Fever.'

Ronan shakes his head. 'You have hardly been fed. That is

impossible.'

Davyn can barely hear his friend. The main sound getting to him is Ronan's blood pulsing through his body. It calls out to the Prime in him, taunting him. 'Altered blood.'

Ronan's frown deepens until he spots the empty plastic bottle floating beside Davyn. 'There's something in the blood?'

Davyn manages a quick nod before another spasm hits him. 'Get out of here. Now!' Before he can stop himself he snarls at the old man. If his hands weren't still chained behind his back he would have grabbed him.

Ronan stumbles back, tripping over a loose rock on the floor. He lands on his back and rolls over to stare at Davyn. He can see the fear on Ronan's face and a piece of him crumbles away. He can never take that back. A part of Ronan will hold on to that fear. 'I'm sorry,' he mumbles, but it's too little, too late.

Ronan gets to his feet. 'It's not your fault.'

Davyn doesn't hear any of the other meaningless sentiments offered by Ronan. The sound of the man's blood overpowers everything else. Davyn stumbles to the back of the cell, and buries his head in his knees, hoping to block everything out.

Davyn blinks, trying to clear his vision as the spotlights turn towards him as soon as he is shoved into the ring. He blocks out the screams coming from the crowd and focuses on his opponent. This one is different to the others. He actually looks like he can handle himself in a fight. Davyn's vision swims again. He needs blood - vampire blood, not the altered, watered down shit he's been getting.

Davyn wipes his hands on the trousers he was given just before the match. They're in worse condition than the pair that were cut off him. They stink and are covered in layers of dried blood, but it's better than going into the ring naked.

The male charges him, his fangs glistening in the spotlights, thick saliva trailing from the tips. Davyn braces his feet, waiting until the last second, then rams his shoulder into his opponents stomach. Then in one fluid motion he pushes upright as his shoulder makes contact. His opponent flies through the air behind him, hitting the electrified mesh stretched across the top of the pit. His body jolts as the current flows through him, filling the air with the stench of burning flesh and hair.

He drops to the ground, wisps of smoke drifting up from his still body. Davyn stalks over to him and grabs the back of his neck, hauling him off the dirt. The vampire comes to, snarling as he lashes out with hands and feet. Davyn's arms are longer than the male's, who quickly runs out of steam and hangs limply in Davyn's grip.

His first instinct is to twist his hand and snap the male's neck. But he doesn't. A more primal urge calls to him, desperately seeking fulfilment. Desperately seeking what his body needs. Blood.

His father wants a show. Fuck it. He'll give him one. He throws the male to the dirt and presses a knee into his back. Preparing for what's going to happen, his gums pulse as his fangs extend. Smelling death in the air, the crowd rise to their feet, cheering loudly, chanting his fighters number over and over until it's all he can hear.

Davyn roars then lunges at the restrained male. He sinks his fangs into his opponent's neck, tearing at the flesh, unable to resist the scent of blood. The blood works through his system, returning feeling and a little warmth to his tired, abused, starved muscles. He doesn't stop - he can't stop. His opponent's fate was sealed as soon as Davyn entered the ring with him. Whether by knife wound, broken neck, or blood loss, he wouldn't be walking out of the ring again. He might as well make himself useful.

The vampire grows weak in his arms but instead of relaxing his hold, Davyn digs his fingers into the vampires neck, his fingernails tearing at the flesh, gouging deep holes which release more blood. He lets the Prime side of himself take the reins. What does it matter at this stage? If his true vampire side can help him survive, he'll use it. A deep growl rumbles in his chest as he senses the life draining from his prey. His fangs throb as he continues to feed, but instead of quenching the searing thirst, it makes it so much worse.

Every mouthful makes him want more. His feeding becomes frantic, more desperate as the need builds. The roar of the crowd is deafening. This is what they paid for. This is the spectacle they wanted.

He stops feeding and gets to his feet. The gate opens but instead of guards with cattle prods, another fighter enters. So, his father wants a bigger show for his paying customers. The crowd goes into a frenzy when they realise they're getting another fight straight away.

The male looks at the corpse, ripped open and bleeding on the dirt floor, before looking at Davyn. Some of the bravado disappears as he realises exactly how much trouble he's in. Davyn watches as one of the onlookers throws a champagne bottle into the ring. With the fight underway, the guards won't be coming in to remove it.

Davyn lunges for the bottle but his opponent gets to it first. The bottle is swung against the side of Davyn's face with such force it breaks, embedding itself in his eye and cheek. He roars as the pain registers through the drug induced confusion. Blood drips from his chin, dropping onto the dirt at his feet. His face is on fire.

While Davyn is distracted, the vampire rushes him with the blood coated bottle again. Davyn sidesteps but either the drug, or his less than peak condition, slows him a little. The bottle slices along his side spilling more blood onto the already soaked floor. Davyn wipes his hand along the wound. His blood mixes with the first victims blood, smearing on his palm.

Davyn snarls at the male and drops to a crouch, sweeping his opponents legs from under him. The male crashes to the dirt, but before he gets a chance to right himself, Davyn helps himself to the broken champagne bottle and drives it into the male's side. It won't kill him but it will hurt like hell. He pulls the male to his feet, and slams his body against the concrete wall. Davyn leans on the bottle and the male screams, cursing him. 'Traitor filth.'

In response, Davyn snarls and buries his teeth into the male's neck.

~

Rhain turns over in his bed and glares at the far wall. Sleep is evading him but no matter what he tries, he can't calm his mind. Guilt has never played a part in his life. Not once, and he has a lot to feel guilty about. He's taken lives with barely a second thought for his victims.

Perhaps his own mortality is affecting him. Perhaps facing his own imminent death has given him a conscience. He looks at his shaking hand, clenching his fist to try to steady himself, but it doesn't work. The Fever is nipping at his heels, gaining ground every day. He shoves his hand under the covers and rolls onto his back.

Whatever it is, since he arrived home from Ireland, he's been unable to get the images of what the King is doing from his mind. Using the bi-product of Rhain's experiments to create a heroin type drug for vampires is something he isn't bothered about. It's not going to affect him either way. It's his own part in what he witnessed that's giving him issues.

He made a mistake.

Even saying the words in his head sounds odd to him, but he can't escape the truth of the statement. He didn't make mistakes. Rhain prided himself on his meticulous planning and thought process. Mistakes didn't happen.

Not until a few months ago. The moment he saw the Blackjack fighting for his life for sport, he knew he'd made his first mistake.

Handing over that Blackjack to the Raven King had been a grave error in judgement. Working with the King had brought nothing new to his search for a cure. Any vampires he collected found their way into his fighting pit, instead of Rhain's search for a cure.

Greed and blood-lust drove the King - nothing more. He was merely using Rhain's extensive fortune to replenish his fighters and that's not something he wishes to be a part of. He didn't spend all these years building his empire to have it associated with something like that. His search for a cure, while unconventional in its methods, was to benefit Primes. The King was benefiting his bloodlust. Nothing more.

It's barbaric. There's no other way to describe it. And he willingly handed over the Blackjack without a second thought. Well, at the time at least.

From the moment he arrived back in the UK, he'd been plagued by the unfamiliar guilt he'd avoided all his life.

'Fuck!'

He throws off the covers and paces his bedroom. There's no escaping it. If he's to get a moment of peace, he has to rectify the situation. Easier said than done. If Davyn had wronged the King in some way, he won't be walking out the front door of the castle without some help. And unfortunately, there's only one group of vampires who will be able to offer that help.

It also wouldn't be an issue if they took care of the King while they were there too. One less irritation to deal with.

He removes a panel from one of the posts on his bed and takes out one of his unlisted mobiles. Geraint knew nothing of these phones. In fact, Rhain has kept quite a bit from the male who runs his house and certain aspects of his business. Self-preservation perhaps. More so the lack of trust. He does have a certain level of trust in him, but if one is truly to survive in this world, you can't afford to fully trust anyone.

He climbs back into bed and waits for a tremor to leave his body before he dials the number from memory.

It rings a few times before a female answers. 'Croft Holdings. How may I direct your call?'

'I'd like to speak to Ethan. It's urgent.'

7

Davyn peels open his eyes and looks at the two bodies laid out in front of him at the foot of the platform.

Like the day before, he had been taken to the great hall after his fight and put on display. All around him, his father's loyal followers eat and drink, completely oblivious to the gruesome scene in front of them.

He doesn't want to believe he did that to the males, but deep down he knows he did. He's done it before after all. That and so much worse.

Dried blood covers the bodies, coating the tears in the visible flesh. Tears he made when he ripped them apart to get their blood. Unable to look away he stares at the flies swarming around the bodies.

The whole fucking scene is like something out of a horror movie.

Like the bodies dumped in front of him, he's badly wounded and covered in blood. With his wings drawn out behind him, hanging from chains attached to the walls, he fits right into this hell.

He groans and closes his eyes. The cramps are getting worse, clawing at his gut, twisting it around itself. Whatever his father is giving him, is doing its job. As much as it disgusts him, he wants more blood. He wants to finish what he did to the two fighters in front of him. He wants to drain any blood left in their bodies.

No. He repeats the one word over and over again, shouting it in his head.

Davyn concentrates on the simple task of breathing as he fights what his body truly craves. He's not going to let his father win. He can't. Not after all this time.

Not after finding Thea.

His gums pulse, his fangs ready to help him get what he needs, but he holds them back. If he lets the Fever win, he'll lose Thea forever.

Someone shoves his head to the side, then warm liquid pours down his neck. From the smell it's only ale, but the night is still young. Plenty of time for more drunken games later. The male shoves his head again, then spits on his cheek before laughing and disappearing out of sight.

Unable to keep awake, he drifts off, only coming to when icy water is thrown over his head.

'How are you doing?'

Davyn opens his eyes and glares at his father, crouched down in front of him.

'That fight must have taken it out of you. You didn't even notice everyone leaving. I'm beginning to think you don't like these meals.'

'Just kill me and be done with it.'

'Kill you? After the performance you gave in the ring earlier? That fight earned me a pretty penny. Also earned quite a bit on ticket sales for your next fight. No, I'll get a few more fights out of you before you turn feral, and I'll have to lock you in your cell and throw away the key. Let you starve to death in the dark.'

There goes any hope of a quick end.

'I must ask. Was that the real you I saw in the pit earlier or the drug?'

'Fuck you.'

The King walks behind Davyn and reappears holding a glass of blood. Davyn's fangs instantly drop and he snarls in spite of his best efforts. His father laughs and places the glass back on the floor behind him. 'That looks like a serious case of the Fever. Got you faster than I thought it would. Never mind. How are the cramps? I hear they can be intense.'

'What cramps?' Cramps isn't the word he'd use to describe them. It feels like someone shoved their hands into his gut and is twisting his insides around like a bowl of spaghetti. The pain is beyond intense.

The King laughs and slaps him on the shoulder. 'Ever the tough guy. Give it to him.' He steps aside and Ronan crouches down beside him. The old man is looking anywhere but at him. Poor guy is between a rock and a sadistic bastard, who will kill him without hesitation.

He removes the top from a syringe and gently tilts Davyn's head to the side. He smiles apologetically at him as he injects the contents into his neck, just above the collar. Davyn gasps as a red hot fire spreads from his neck to every nerve ending in his body. He screams until there's no air left in his lungs.

Unable to think about anything but the searing pain, Davyn slumps to the ground as his chains are released and he's dragged back to his cell. The guards dump him inside and slam the door closed behind them. Davyn scrambles to his feet and braces himself against the back corner. The freezing water is already up to his thighs. He'll be on his feet for a few hours unless he fancies drowning.

He squeezes his hand through the bars against the back wall and hooks a link of the chain connected to his wrist shackle over a broken piece of metal. That broken bar had saved his life countless times when he was a kid. It probably won't work as well for him anymore.

His arms are a lot longer than they were, but it's better than nothing.

Once he's secured, he looks over at Ronan as the old man approaches the bars. His friend seems to have aged a good decade in the last day. 'You okay?'

'I am so sorry, sire.'

'What... what the hell was that stuff he gave me?'

'A concentrated dose of the drug. He doesn't want to feed the Blood Fever - just increase the effects.'

His body spasms as the drug continues its attack. 'People take this? On purpose?'

'It seems so. I have been told the effect on Hybrids is quite different. Forgive me, sire. I had no choice.'

'Nothing to apologise for. This isn't down to you. Fuck it hurts.'

Ronan reaches through the bars and grasps Davyn's hand firmly in his. 'Tell me how to find them.'

Davyn hisses and squeezes his eyes shut. 'No way. Not bringing them here.'

'And I won't sit by and watch you die like this. Tell me or I will do whatever I must to find them myself. Even if it means putting a very public advertisement on that Internet thing. I only hope your father does not see it and punish me.'

Davyn glares over at the old man. 'Really? You're going to try that one on me?'

'For starters. Tell me, Davyn! The Blackjacks were formed to fight for those who cannot fight for themselves. Forgive me, but at this moment that includes you. Unless of course you have something fantastic up your sleeve? Some great plot to escape as you did the last time? If you do perhaps now would be the time to put it into play.'

'Were you always this irritating?'

'Of course,' Ronan replies with a sad smile. 'Davyn, I know you believe you're doing the right thing by sacrificing yourself and allowing that cretin to hurt you. No crime you believe you've committed is deserving of this punishment.'

'I asked him to kill me. When I was…. Fuck…' He can't remember what he was going to say and that scares him.

'He won't kill you, Davyn. Forgive my bluntness but he wants you to suffer. You will die but it will be a slow and painful end.'

'He'll starve me.'

Ronan nods. 'That is a favourite of his. I fear he'll leave you in here and deny you food until you perish.'

Davyn clenches his teeth as another spasm hits. He wants to give Ronan the information, but he's afraid. It hit him when he was on that platform in front of his father earlier. He's terrified they won't come for him. What if Ronan gets in contact with them and they leave him here? He'd prefer not to know. It's easier not knowing.

The agony in both his fangs nearly convinces him to change his mind. If this is what the Fever feels like he gets why so many choose to take their own lives. He's struggling to hang on to his thoughts. The pain is all-consuming.

A firm hand squeezes his, bringing him back from the pain. Ronan is crying, the tears flowing freely down his cheeks. 'I'm not above begging, sire.'

'And I'm not bringing them here. Leave it, Ronan.' Davyn pauses as another hand joins the twelve more in his gut. 'Goddammit! How long does this last?'

'I do not know, sire. Perhaps a few hours.'

He arches his back, gasping as the pain from his broken wing mixes with the pain from the drug working through his system. 'Get out of here. He'll be watching you.'

'Please don't ask me to leave you here like this.'

'Leave me!' Davyn bears his fangs at Ronan leaving him with no doubt that he's serious. 'Leave!'

Ronan bows, then shuffles away, leaving Davyn alone and truly miserable.

~

Rhain steps out of his car and walks over to the pond in the park. At close to three in the morning, there aren't many people around, which is the way he likes it. He closes his eyes, but can't pick up on Geraint. Sneaking out of his own house at his age is ridiculous, but necessary.

Then he senses another vampire. Two vampires. He smiles as Ethan Croft appears at the end of the path and, unsurprisingly, he's not alone. Rhain doesn't mind that he brought protection with him. The man co-founded a group of elite fighters. It stood to reason he would bring at least one of those fighters with him.

As they draw near, some of Rhain's confidence dwindles. The other male is without a doubt a Blackjack. The dark-haired, impressively-built, rather intimidating male is a good head taller than Ethan, who is quite tall himself.

They stop in front of him and Rhain realises what he thought were the sleeves of a top, are actually tattoos on the Blackjack's thick arms. His gloved hands are by his side but Rhain has no doubt he's armed and would kill him in seconds, if commanded.

'Ethan. Thank you for coming.'

Ethan nods. 'I wasn't going to if I'm being honest. But I'm curious.'

'And your friend?'

'He's here to make sure you behave. I strongly suggest you do. He doesn't like you. In fact none of us do. I'm torn between listening to what you have to say and letting him kill you.'

'I understand. Can we sit? Please. You'll want to hear what I have to say.'

Ethan moves to the bench but the Blackjack steps in between them. He looms over Rhain, his brown eyes glowing as he glares at him. 'If you so much as look at him the wrong way I will kill you. I don't care who you are.'

Rhain is momentarily thrown by the Spanish accent, but when the Blackjack bares his fangs at him, he gets himself together. 'Of course. I'm here alone and mean him no harm. I only want to talk.'

The Blackjack doesn't trust him for a moment and Rhain can't blame him. Ethan places his hand on the fighters arm. 'I'll be fine.'

'I'll be watching every single move you make.'

Rhain nods, then the Blackjack begrudgingly steps back, and Ethan sits down. 'Again, thank you for coming.' He glances over at the Spaniard, still giving him pretty impressive death glares from a few feet away. His thick arms are crossed, his nostrils flaring as he takes deep breaths.

'He'll tell us if anyone is approaching. He's astutely aware of his surroundings.'

'His gift?' Rhain asks.

'Is his business.'

Rhain nods. 'I apologise. Strangely, I feel safer with him watching. He's very protective.'

Ethan looks over at his bodyguard and Rhain sees something in his face, something he swears borders on fondness, but he's not going to ask anything. No doubt it would result in his death.

'He is. I'm sure you didn't call me here to discuss him though. What do you want?'

'I know where Davyn is.'

The Spaniard is instantly on him, his hand wrapped around his throat, as he lifts him off the bench.

'Bas, put him down.' Ethan tries to get in between the two of them, but his bodyguard isn't listening.

'I want to help,' Rhain forces the words out, but the iron grip around his neck isn't helping.

Ethan steps right up to the Blackjack and speaks to him in what sounds like Spanish. Rhain knows many languages, but that's not one he has mastered. As Ethan speaks to him, Rhain can feel the pressure around his neck lessening. Finally he is lowered to the ground and the hand leaves his neck. He rubs the bruised skin and takes a few long breaths.

'Thank you.'

Instead of saying anything, he is shoved back on to the bench by Bas or whatever his name is. He steps around the back of Rhain and places one heavy hand on each shoulder, holding him in place.

'I apologise about that. He won't do that again. What do you know about Davyn?'

'I am risking my life by coming here to you like this.'

'And you are risking your life by not talking,' says the deep voice from behind him.

'Powerful vampires are involved in this. Vampires I associate with through necessity. Vampires we could all do with watching out for. Are you familiar with the Raven King?'

Ethan frowns then nods slowly. 'Yes. He's in Ireland, correct?'

'He is. He has Davyn.'

'Why?'

'Personal reasons. I'm not sure why and I'm not in a position to ask. He runs fighting pits throughout the country. Vampires fighting to the death. It's a highly lucrative business for him.'

Rhain winces as the Blackjack's fingers dig into his shoulders.

'I'm trying to help, so please leave my arms attached.'

Ethan calms the situation again with one look. The fingers loosen their grip, but are still firmly in place on his shoulders. Rhain doesn't know what sort of hold Ethan has on this male, but he can't help but be impressed.

'Why are you telling us this?' Ethan asks.

'I'm Prime and approaching my fifth century. You know what that means for me.' He pauses, not sure why he feels the need to explain himself to Ethan. He's known of the male for quite some time. Only a few knew of his connection to the Blackjacks. Both males were using their power, their wealth and influence to make a difference. He's only sorry it puts them on either side of a conflict he wants no part in. He has a lot of respect for Ethan.

'Fever.'

Rhain nods. 'I'm not going to excuse or discuss what I was attempting to do. But I am growing weary of it all. I can slow down the side effects, but I am fooling myself if I think I can stop what has been part of who we are for too long.'

'Trying to right your wrongs?'

'Perhaps. Perhaps it is too late for that. What I do know is Davyn shouldn't have been offered up like he was.'

'And what about Court. And Nix?'

Rhain knew that was coming. 'I can't undo what I've done and I have no regrets about parts of it. Court helped me survive a little longer. I will never regret that.'

And there are the iron fingers again.

'We all want to survive.'

Ethan doesn't stop his bodyguard this time. 'We do, but not at the cost of others. I don't suppose your sudden need to right your wrongs includes telling us what you did to Court?'

Rhain shakes his head and braces for the pain that accompanies that action. He grunts and forces himself to continue. 'There are bigger parties involved. I was not alone in this and I don't have all the information you need. The Order created the drug that removed his memory. I just utilised his blood.'

Ethan nods and the pressure eases a little. 'That's a shame. So what now? Do you expect us just to let you walk away?'

'Yes. Actually I do. You see, I'm still part of that group. I can help you.'

Ethan laughs at that. 'So we let you go and you what? Send us information on the bad guys. I hate to break it to you Rhain, but that includes you.'

'By all means kill me if you want. I can't stop you. But wouldn't it be beneficial to have someone on the inside? Someone who isn't quite agreeable with what the Order are doing?'

Ethan glances up at the Blackjack. 'One moment.' He gets up and takes a few steps away. The Blackjack pulls out a gun that was hidden on his body and points it at Rhain as he speaks to Ethan in hushed tones. He's painfully aware his life is hanging in the balance, but he can't say he really cares at this stage.

He silently watches the two vampires interact, more sure than ever that they are more than just work colleagues. And he can't help but feel a little jealous. He doesn't even have a friendship with someone, let alone anything more. Geraint has been in his life for centuries, but you couldn't call it a friendship. It's a working relationship at most.

After leaving him stewing for a few minutes, the Blackjack turns to face him again and begrudgingly lowers his gun. He glares at Ethan before crossing his arms again and staring over at Rhain. It appears Ethan may have bought him a slight reprieve.

Ethan sits down beside him again and crosses his legs. 'I'm going to have a group of pissed off vampires after this, but I'm willing to see how this plays out. As you say, this is much bigger than you and I. A lot will depend on your intel on Davyn of course.'

Rhain reaches into his pocket but stops as the gun suddenly appears in the Blackjacks hand. 'It's an envelope. You'll need it to get to your team mate.'

The Spaniard nods. 'Slowly, or you'll lose that hand.'

Rhain pulls the envelope from his pocket and holds it out to Ethan. 'Davyn is one of the fighters. The fights are closed to general admittance. Only those with connections - shady connections, can get tickets. I could only get two tickets, so use them wisely. The King will be expecting you to come for Davyn so he'll be prepared. He won't give him up easily.'

'Why is he so invested in Davyn?'

Rhain shakes his head. 'Past dealings. That's all I know. Davyn must have really pissed him off. I've never known the King to be so obsessed with one of his prisoners. That will work against you.'

Ethan looks down at the tickets and smiles. 'I appreciate this. I'll appreciate it more if it's legitimate. Time will tell.' He stands up and holds out his hand. 'Thank you, Rhain.'

Hiding his surprise, Rhain shakes Ethan's hand, ignoring the growl from the over-protective Blackjack.

'You have my number. Use it wisely, Rhain. Next time we meet I hope it's beneficial to us. If not, my friend here will not be so easily restrained.'

'I fully believe that.'

'Walk away.' The Blackjack points his gun at him again. 'I suggest you move slowly.'

Even though it's against his nature, he turns his back on the two vampires and walks over to his car. As soon as he's inside, he locks the doors, even though it's a futile act. He starts the engine then gasps as a cramp twists in his gut. Bad timing as usual. Having an attack in the company of two vampire who want him dead, was not part of his plan.

He closes his eyes and slows his breathing, doing his best to control the pain, to keep a hold on his body. When he opens his eyes again, he finds the Blackjack standing in front of his car, staring at him. His eyes are glowing as he watches Rhain.

Maybe Ethan changed his mind. Perhaps he sent the Spaniard to kill him. But as they face each other, the fighter steps back, moving out of the way of the car. Rhain put his car in gear and pulls away, keeping an eye on the Blackjack in his rear view mirror as he drives away.

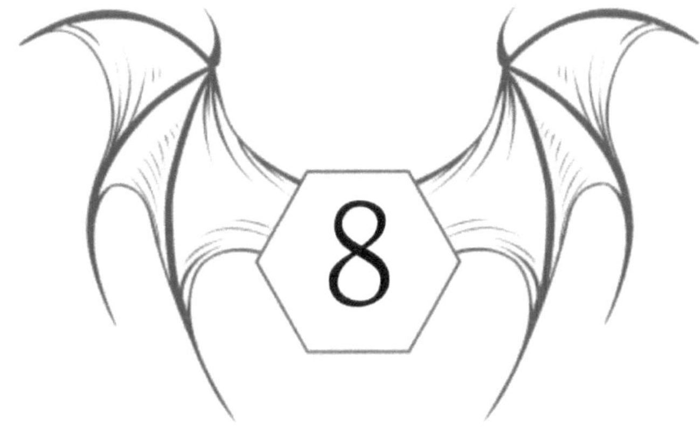

Nix drums her fingers on the table as she waits for the others to take their seat. Sensing her mood, the Blackjacks sit quickly, the room silent as they wait for her to speak.

She turns to face Ethan. 'Please tell me we have something? Anything at all.'

Ethan rarely visits the compound, so the fact he came here by helicopter gives her a little hope he may have a vital lead. He'd asked to take Bastian with him for protection while he had a meeting with a contact. She just hopes it was a positive meeting and they finally have a lead on Dav.

'I wouldn't have called this meeting if I didn't.' He takes a seat beside Shep and passes him a portable drive. Shep plugs it in and turns on the screen at the head of the table. A series of pictures fills the screen, the familiar visage of Davyn at the top. 'I know where Davyn is.'

'Where is he?' Nix jumps in.

Ethan glances over at her. 'Ireland.'

'Are you sure?' Nix asks.

'Well if you'd give me a chance to talk I can explain. I had a meeting a few hours ago with Rhain.'

Nix and the rest of the room fall silent. She looks over at Bas to confirm what Ethan just said. He nods once, clearly as pissed off about the whole thing as she is. 'Rhain! Are you kidding me?'

'I know how it sounds, but he contacted me. He said he had important information and needed to see me.'

'So you just decided to go and see the bastard who took Court? Who has taken dozens of vampires and killed them. Who did who knows what to the vampire fighting for his life along the corridor in our holding cell. I mean are you out of your fucking mind?'

She doesn't usually curse, but this is beyond anything she was expecting.

'I felt the risk was worth it.'

'Really? And what about Bas? Did he have a say in that risk?'

'I knew who he was meeting. It's my job to do what you and Ethan ask. There was no way I would let that male hurt any of our team. Ethan was safe.'

'I'm not doubting your abilities, Bas. I'm doubting Ethan's sanity.'

'Oh thanks, Nix. I appreciate that. Do you not want to hear what he had to say before you lay into me?'

Nix looks over at Court who seems to have shrunk in the last few minutes. 'Go on. And this better be good.'

He gestures to the blurred picture on the screen. 'This is the best picture I can find of a guy called the Raven King.'

Nix looks over at him. 'I've heard of him.'

Fallon nods. 'Me too. Nasty S.O.B. if everything I've heard is true.'

'This guy is at least five centuries old,' Ethan says. 'Prime, and stuck in the old ways. And by old ways, I mean furs and crossbows. His favourite pastimes include a bit of torture, rape, good old fashioned theft, and,' Ethan makes a face then continues, 'there's also a report of cannibalism.'

'Fuck,' Shep mutters from across the table.

'I second that,' Ethan says. 'As Fallon said, nasty S.O.B., plus a bit more nasty on top. This guy and his hired help rule the vampire community across the water.'

Nix tears her eyes away from the picture of Davyn on the screen. 'So why Davyn? Is it because he's a Blackjack?'

'I wish it was.'

'What you mean by that?' Shep asks.

'My team spent the last few hours digging up everything we could possibly find on the King. He works hard to keep himself off any official databases, but we did find something. His real name is Flann Oldranson.

'The House of Oldran is a well know vampire line in Ireland. Flann's father, Oldran, was a highly respected lord and I can't find a bad word written about him. His son Flann took over when he died at the ripe old age of nine hundred and fifty-three. Died in battle by all accounts.'

'Here's to still battling at that age,' Fallon says.

'Agreed. Well, dear Flann wasn't as upstanding as his father as you can tell from his extracurricular activities.'

'Probably overcompensating for being named after a fucking pastry,' Shep mutters.

'Actually it means blood red.'

'Still sounds ridiculous. Not surprised he went for Raven King. So as much as I'm loving this history lesson, what's this got to do with our boy?' Shep asks, his fingers drumming on the table.

'Still working on patience I see. Flann had two sons. The eldest, Darren, died years ago during a tiff with the neighbouring group. His other son is unnamed in the records. He was branded a traitor and a disgrace before being removed from the family records. All save for one detail. Flann was "unfairly cursed with a second son bearing a grotesquely disfigured wing".'

Shep stops drumming his fingers as he whistles. 'Fuck. So Davyn's father is the Raven King?'

Ethan nods. 'It looks that way.'

'That's not so bad then, is it?' Willow asks. 'I mean, if this guy is his father, right?'

Ethan shakes his head. 'From what I've read, it's not going to make a damn difference. This guy is old school. With Darren dead, Davyn would have been his only heir. By turning his back on that honour, Davyn pissed off Daddy Dearest. And I mean pissed off, as in bounty-on-his-head kind of pissed off. He won't be getting a mint under his pillow every day. Flann or The Raven King will be treating our boy to a bit of old fashioned pain and suffering. You need to get him out, before his father kills him.'

Nix leans forward and looks at him. 'I know that face. There's a but coming.'

'Afraid so. Rhain said Davyn is the new star of his father's underground fighting pit. Now, we have no idea where the fights are taking place. It's all arranged in secret and no matter how many doors I knock on, I can't get any information. Luckily, Rhain gave us two tickets to the next match.'

The occupants of the room fall silent as Ethan's words sink in. Nix looks at Court again. He's far from happy, but she sees something in his face she's seen many times. Determination.

'Bastian, I want your view on this. Why did Rhain give us the tickets?'

'Blood Fever has him bad. I watched him have an attack before he drove away. He said he's done with the Order. Wants to end what's happening with them.'

'And you trust him?'

'Not for a second. But Ethan is right. He can help us get to Davyn.

I may not trust Rhain but I do believe he's reaching the end of his life. He had a calmness to him that only comes with that acceptance. I roughed him up a little and he wasn't bothered.' Bastian glances over at Ethan. 'He could be useful to us - if managed correctly.'

Shep laughs at that. 'Manage one of the bad guys? Yeah right. How do we know it's not just a big trap and he's going to be laughing his ass off when we all die horribly?'

Nix has to agree with Shep. 'The only way we'll find that out is when the guns are to the back of our head.'

'I disagree,' Ethan replies. 'I honestly believe he wants rid of the Order as much as we do. The Raven King is working with them. He's another cog in the larger group. If he's removed, it's one less problem for all of us.'

'So you're happy to send two of us in there to test your theory?'

'That's where we may have an issue. The King knows Davyn is a Blackjack. He'll be expecting us to come for him.'

Fallon shakes her head angrily as she slumps back in her seat. 'You can't send one of us. Perfect. So who exactly do you want to send in?'

'I don't know. That's what we have to figure out. We need to send two people who can fit in with the other spectators at the fight. We can then track them to the venue and go from there.'

'I'll go.'

The whole team look over at their resident doctor, Fletch. 'Sorry?'

'I said I'll go, Nix. I'm trained. I'll grant you not as good as you lot, but I can hold my own. I'm also not an active member of the team so I'm not known. Plus I'm not a vampire so I shouldn't set off any vampire alarms. I can just be another rich, bored human who enjoys a bit of blood-sport.'

Fallon jumps in before Nix can comment which doesn't surprise Nix in the slightest. Fallon is protective of her human half-brother. 'Not a fucking chance in hell. You're not going.'

'Oh lay off, Sis. I'll be fine.'

'You'll be dead.'

'Thanks for the vote of confidence. I sincerely appreciate it.'

Nix holds up her hand, silencing Fallon. 'I appreciate the offer, Fletch, but I have to agree with Fallon. I'm not sending you in to an unknown situation set up by one of our enemies.'

'You wouldn't be sending me in. I'm volunteering. What other options do we have? Dav is in that hell hole. We need to get him out. I honestly can't see why you're all being so weird about this.'

'I'll go with him.'

Nix inwardly grimaces when she hears Thea's voice from the doorway.

~

Thea was expecting her father to go completely nuts at her suggestion, but leaping from his seat and dragging her from the room is a bit extreme. 'What the fuck are you playing at, Thea? You shouldn't be down here.'

'That's the part you're angry about?'

His nearly white eyes narrow as he glares down at her. 'Oh I haven't even started yet, believe me.'

'I apologise for eavesdropping, okay? But it makes sense to let me go with Fletch.'

'Oh it makes sense. To who, cause I can guarantee you it doesn't makes sense to me.'

'Or me,' Nix says as she joins Court in the corridor.

Perfect. Now she's going to get it from both sides. 'I've been training every single day. I can take care of myself. And who else are you going to send with Fletch? You can't send one of the team cause no offence, but you lot don't exactly blend into a crowd. And it's like Ethan said, we just have to go to the fight and wait for you to find us. I can handle it. You know I can.'

'So you're telling me you can sit by and watch Dav fighting?' She tries to turn her head away from Court, but he locks his eyes onto her, trapping her until he decides he wants to release her. 'He'll be fighting to the death. Killing another vampire in front of the crowd.'

He pushes into her thoughts, using his special skills to drive his point home. She doesn't know if he's putting the images in her head or if her own imagination is helping her out, but she can see Davyn as clearly as if he was in front of her. Bleeding, suffering, desperately alone and fighting for his life.

'Dad, please...'

Tears trickle down her cheeks, but her father won't let her go.

'Court, I think that's enough,' Nix says and her father finally blinks, releasing her from his hold.

Thea wipes her eyes. 'Wow. Thanks for that.'

'I'm sorry if that was a bit harsh, but I need you to understand what you're volunteering for.' He shakes his head and takes a breath. 'I know you want to help him. I really do, but I'm not convinced this is the way to do it.'

'Court is right.' Nix smiles at her. 'It was a bit of an unconventional way of showing you, but what he said is accurate. What Davyn is doing is brutal, Thea. You shouldn't have to see that.'

'I know. But what other option do you have? I met Rhain. He's a complete dickhead, but I don't think deceit is what he does. He's confident and sure of himself. He doesn't need to resort to trickery to get what he wants. He could easily have captured Bas and Ethan a few hours ago. Instead he offered to help. If he wanted to capture all of you he would have given you six tickets. What good will taking two of you out do?'

'A hell of a lot considering they already have Dav.'

'You know what I mean, Dad. He'd just end up with the rest of you even more pissed off at him than you are right now. Maybe he is on the level with this.'

'Or maybe he's hoping we'll send you in and that'll draw me out again,' Court suggests. 'I'm the cure he's looking for.'

'From what Bas said, it's too late for that anyway.'

'Give us a minute, Thea.'

Her father glares at Nix. 'No way. We don't need a minute.'

Nix smiles at her and nods back along the corridor. 'Please.'

Thea paces her bedroom, wearing a track in the thick carpet. She checks her watch. Thirty minutes. Is that long enough for Nix to convince her father to let her go? She has no idea and she's only assuming Nix is on her side. Maybe the couple have already resumed the meeting, leaving her here to stew. But Thea doesn't think that's the case. Since Court and Nix resumed their relationship, Thea had been spending more time with the Blackjack leader and would like to believe she is getting to know her.

There was something in her face that made Thea think she was more on board with her going than Court was. Convincing her father is an entirely different matter. He may not remember his life with the Blackjacks, but his leadership skills are as sharp as ever.

It's no surprise Nix chose him as her second in command. His methodical approach offered a sense of calm to the group. Unfortunately that means trying to change his mind is like trying to move a tank. She's learning that Nix is one of the few people who has the ability to alter his course.

Whether she can go with the team or not, nothing can quash her elation at hearing Davyn is still alive. He's in hell and her heart is breaking for him, but he's alive, which means the team can rescue him.

She knows they're a long way from bringing him home, but as long as they move quickly, there's a chance they can save him before his father kills him.

Thea angrily shakes her head. She's not going to let her thoughts take her in that direction. She's held onto hope for this long. She's not going to turn her back on it or him. Not yet.

She jumps and places her hand over her heart when she sees Court standing in her doorway. 'Damn it, Dad. Don't sneak up on people like that.'

'Sorry. I knocked a few times. Got a bit worried.' Court leans against the doorframe. 'You okay?'

'Me? Yes. Fine. Why?'

'You're going to make a track in the carpet if you keep up that pacing.'

She forces herself to stop walking and takes up a position in front of him. 'Just a little tense.'

'I kind of got that.' He pauses and crosses his arms. 'Can I come in?'

'Sure.'

Court sits on the couch under the window so Thea joins him and waits for the silence to be broken. She doesn't want to push him into changing his mind. Well, unless he had already decided not to let her go. Best to keep her mouth shut and let him have his say first.

He scrubs a hand over his short hair and then clasps his hands together again. 'First off, I know the way I dealt with Davyn feeding from you was a fucking disaster. I overreacted and I know that. I should have listened to you before I went for him, but in spite of how I handled that, I do understand, Thea.'

'Understand what?'

'How you feel about Davyn.'

She stares up at her father but can't find anything to say. She wasn't expecting that from him. 'Okay.'

'I'm not going to say I'm thrilled about it, but I'm also not going to tell you how you should feel about someone.'

'I don't know how I feel about him. That's the problem.'

'What do you mean?'

'I like him. A lot. But with everything that's going on, maybe it's just a reaction to the situation. Maybe it's guilt playing a part. I don't know.'

Court smiles at her. 'Then don't try to label it. Wouldn't be my first choice for you, but that's my problem.'

'You'd prefer Shep?'

He laughs loudly at that. 'No. I damn well wouldn't. Well played though.' He pauses and rubs his hands together. 'You still blame me for keeping the truth from you.'

'Dad...'

'You really have to learn to listen.'

'Sorry,' she says, recognising the shift in his expression.

'You blame me for forgetting I'm your father. I get that. I wish I knew why I told you I was your brother instead of your father. I wish I could tell you who your mother is. But I can't. There's a good chance my amnesia will keep those answers from both of us. We have no choice but to live with those secrets for the time being.

'What I don't want is for any more secrets or lies getting between us again. You're too important to me. But I can't protect you by keeping you in the dark. All I can do is make sure you can handle what's thrown at you – emotionally and physically. For that I need to let you in.'

'Let me in. You mean the team?'

Court nods slowly, not happy about what he's agreeing to. 'Don't get carried away. It's early days. But as much as I hate the thought of you being anywhere near this world, you're already a part of it. You'll be included in meetings from now on. But you'll listen and I mean really listen. Nix is in charge and I'm the second. In that room you will do exactly as we tell you. I'm not your father in there, and I sure as hell won't hesitate putting you in your place if you step out of line.'

'I understand. Thanks, Dad. I mean that.'

'Don't thank me yet. And I know you want to help save Davyn but don't get ahead of yourself. We're a long way from getting him back.'

'I know.'

'Good. Are you sure you know what you're volunteering for?'

Thea looks up at him for a minute before she answers. Does that mean he's letting her go?

'Are you sure, Thea?'

'Yes.'

He stands up and walks over to the door. 'Come on.'

'Where are we going?'

'To finish the briefing. If you're going to Ireland, you'd better know what's going on.'

Thea hurries after her father as he goes back downstairs to the meeting room. She doesn't dare to speak to him as they walk. The fact he's letting her go with Fletch is astounding. Then again he hadn't actually said he's letting her go in with Fletch. But he also didn't say she couldn't. He's only said she's going to Ireland. He could very well be bringing her with him so he could keep a closer eye on her.

The fact she's invited to the briefing is a good start. She'll find out how much involvement she'll have in the next few minutes. He points to the seat next to Fallon's and she sits, feeling a little out of place among the others.

Nix looks up from the screen she's reading and glances over at her, a small smile on her face. 'I'd like to officially welcome you to the briefing. I'm sure you'll find the seat more comfortable than leaning against the doorframe.'

Thea blushes at the laughs around the table. 'Yeah. Sorry about that.'

'Okay, you and Fletch are going to the fight.' Nix holds up her hand stopping Thea's squeal of excitement before it springs free. 'You will be under Fletch's command. He's in charge. You do exactly what he says. You don't breathe, blink, or even twitch unless he gives you permission.'

'Of course.'

'I guess we're heading to Ireland then,' Fallon says.

Nix nods in agreement. 'I guess so. Ethan, are you sure there's no way of figuring out where they're holding Davyn?'

He shuffles in his seat and straightens his tie before answering. 'No. We've tried to find out but it's a closely guarded secret. I know where his father lives but I doubt the fights will take place there. They wouldn't go to all this trouble to hide the location if it was in the castle.'

Shep does a double take. 'Hold on one minute. A castle. Fucker lives in a castle?'

'He's a lord, Shep,' Ethan says.

'Are you saying Dav is royalty or something?'

'Not royalty, but disgraced or not, he has a title. His official title is Lord Davyn Oldranson. The only difference is his family name. Thanks to his father disowning him, instead of Flannson, he'd be known by his grandfather's name.'

'Fuck me. More than one secret lurking in his closet. Lord Davyn Oldranson. Hey, at least it's better than son of pastry! Lucky escape there.'

'Thank you, Shep,' Nix says. 'I think I have something that'll wipe that smile off your face.'

'You're not grounding me again are you?'

Nix peers down the table at him. 'Have you done something I need to bench you for?'

Thea stifles a snigger as Shep shakes his head briskly. 'Fuck no. Good as gold, me.'

'I seriously doubt that. But no, we'll need you. What I was going to say is that, as we're going to Ireland, we should probably let the other group know we're coming.'

Shep groans loudly. 'Please don't say you mean who I think you mean.'

Ethan grimaces and slumps back in his chair. 'You can make that call, Nix. I'm still recovering from the last time I spoke to them.'

'Spoke to who?' Court asks.

Nix turns to face Court. 'I'm sorry. I completely forgot you won't remember anything about our Irish friends. Okay, so they're a group of... males I guess is the easiest way of describing them. They have eyes and ears everywhere in Ireland. If we're to have any chance of getting Dav out, we'll need their help.'

'Okay, that's great.' Court glances around the table. 'It's not great, is it? Are we not on friendly terms with these vampires?'

'They're not vampires, Court.'

'Then what the hell are they?'

'They're werewolves,' Bastian says while Shep growls to himself. 'A clan of very pissed off, non-vampire friendly werewolves.'

Court stares at Nix, looking for confirmation Bas isn't talking gibberish. 'Werewolves are real?'

'Unfortunately,' Shep grumbles, jumping in before she can. 'Hope you don't have a dog allergy, buddy.'

Nix rubs her forehead then glares over at Shep. 'Please keep comments like that to yourself, Shep. I'm not getting in between you and a wolf.'

'Why would they help us?' Thea asks, hoping she's not overstepping.

'Historically, vampires and werewolves don't get on. It's a long and complicated history that, to this day, still puts up barriers between the groups. One of the oldest families in Ireland is the Whelans. Murtagh and his three brothers are well thought of, but tend to keep to themselves. We've had reason to work with them when we first formed the Blackjacks. They're decent guys.'

'For wolves,' Fallon mutters.

'Okay. Yes. For wolves. If we're to get Dav out we need their help. I'm as thrilled about working with them as you are - believe me. But this is bigger than some ancient feud. This is about Davyn. So play nice. Got it?'

The quiet grumbling isn't entirely encouraging, but no one voices their issues.

'Thank you,' Nix says. 'Now, I'm only going to say this once. We are all going to behave with them. Aren't we Shep?'

'Hey, why am I getting singled out?'

'Because you're a loud mouth dick,' Bastian adds with a grin.

'Oh cheers for the support, buddy. I'm all about getting Dav out. If it means I catch fleas from getting too close to the dogs, I'll deal with it.'

'See, loud mouth dick,' Bastian mutters.

Nix rubs her forehead and looks over at Ethan. 'Let's get over to Ireland ASAP. The sooner we have to end this truce with the Whelans the better. Wouldn't want Shep getting his head bitten off. Literally.'

10

Thea lies against the bulkhead of the helicopter and tries to get some rest. But she can't. How can she possibly sleep when they're so close to getting Davyn back? Whatever excitement she'd felt at the news they knew where he was, had quickly dissipated. Davyn's father sounded truly horrific and knowing that he has Davyn is turning her stomach.

However surreal life had become since finding out Court is a vampire, is nothing compared to what she'd learned in the last few hours. Knowing that vampires exist is hard enough to accept. But werewolves?

How the hell can werewolves be real? Especially in Ireland. It just doesn't make any sense. If they can help get Davyn back though, she'll work with anyone and anything. Having the Whelan brothers willing to meet with them offered a little comfort - but not much. If it was going to take six highly trained vampires and four wolves to even penetrate the pit, she knows getting to Davyn in time is even odds at best.

The Whelans had given them an address for a house in Co. Kerry on the west coast of Ireland that would be a safe place for a group of vampires and werewolves to meet.

Davyn's father owned a castle nearby but, from what she can make out, it's on acres of private land on the coast and is impenetrable from every angle. Having local knowledge from the Whelans will be useful, but Thea can't see how they're going to get inside, let alone get Davyn out.

Court wraps his arm around her and kisses the top of her head. They may still be finding their feet in their new father and daughter relationship, but she can't criticise his support over the last few weeks. Davyn and her father didn't see eye to eye and that's putting it mildly. Her father had used his special mind-powers to hurt Davyn when he had fed from Thea. She understands his reaction, but it had left a bad feeling between Davyn and Court as a result.

That didn't stop Court from being there for her. He may not be happy about her attraction to Davyn but he didn't let it come between them. There's already enough of a rift without adding to it.

'Dad?'

'Yeah?'

'Do you think he's given up?'

Court is quiet for a few minutes then pulls her closer. 'I doubt it. He's stubborn.'

'Did you give up?'

'There's a big difference, Thea. My memory was taken from me. I didn't know if I had anyone who would be looking for me.'

'They could have taken his memory too.'

'Yeah. Maybe. I hung on for three years in that place. He can more than do a few months where he is. You have to believe that, okay.'

She nods and lies against his chest. Her father survived. Even with no memory of his life they found him and brought him back. They'd do the same for Davyn no matter what it takes.

Davyn rests his forehead against the algae covered wall and tries to pull his body higher. He'd hooked his wrist chain around the broken bar but it's not helping to keep him out of the water. The prison is in total darkness and even his vampire eyesight isn't helping to penetrate the gloom. Around him the water swirls as it's driven through the channels at the bottom of the wall.

He wraps his hands around a bar in the ceiling, but he's too weak to haul himself up. The shivers are so intense his muscles ache, adding another level of pain to the cramps and wounds from his last fight.

He doesn't know how he survived this as a child. It probably had a lot to do with Ronan. That man spent nearly as much time here as Davyn did during his early years. Nearly sixty years of his life has been spent in this cell, suffering, in pain, and bitterly cold.

The difference is, back then, there was nothing else in his life. Nothing to miss. Nothing else to think about, except surviving. Back then, this was all he knew. Having those few years with the Blackjacks changed everything for him. For the first time he'd felt like he had a home. Had people who would notice if he wasn't around.

Had Thea.

He laughs to himself as the water swells around him. He doesn't have her. Wanting someone is a far cry from having them. He could never have her. He'd done some horrific things under his father's rule and he'd prefer to die here than ever have Thea know what he's really like.

Davyn gasps and spasms as an intense cramp hits his stomach. He momentarily loses his grip on the bars and his chains slip off the broken piece of metal. Davyn disappears under the water unable to get back to his feet. Every muscle is in spasm. Freezing sea water fills his mouth as another spasm hits, driving the little air from his lungs. This is it. He's going to drown in his cell all alone.

A hand brushes against his shoulder, trying to grab him but they can't get a firm grip. Davyn locks hands with whoever it is and gasps as he is pulled to the surface. Ronan drags him against the bars and wraps his arms around Davyn's messed up wing, pinning him against the door of the cell.

'I've got you. Just breathe through it.'

Davyn focuses on Ronan's calming voice and eventually the cramps ease, giving him a little control over his body again. He tries to stand but his legs aren't ready to support him yet.

Instead he rests his head against the bars and looks up at Ronan. 'Thanks. Cramps caught me off guard.'

Ronan grunts. 'I am just glad I timed my visit so well. I didn't think you would resurface.'

'Neither did I.' He shivers again and Ronan holds his wing a little tighter. 'I would offer you a blanket but I fear it would not do much good.'

Davyn laughs. 'No. Not really. Not that I'm not grateful, but you can't keep coming down here. I don't want him coming after you because of me.'

'Do not worry about me.' He lowers his voice, not that much could be overheard above the waves crashing outside the walls. 'They are coming.'

Davyn looks back at him. 'Who?'

'I have received word from an old friend. Your friends have been in contact. They're coming for you.'

'They are?'

'Why do you sound so surprised? Of course they are. But you must not give up. I know you're in pain and you're tired, but you must keep fighting.'

'Hold on. What friend? The Blackjacks wouldn't just reach out like that.'

'They contacted a four-legged acquaintance. He is trustworthy.'

Davyn stares at Ronan for a few minutes, half thinking he might have misheard. Vampires don't reach out to wolves. It doesn't happen.

'Yes, Davyn. You heard me right. A truce has been made with one clan. Your friends are really coming. My contact has asked me to attend a meeting when they arrive.'

'No Ronan. I don't want you involved.'

'I've been involved since the moment you were born. I will not abandon you, Davyn. If my life ends by helping you get out of here, I will die happy and fulfilled.'

Davyn closes his eyes, resting his head against the bars as he tries to summon the strength to stand. Roman may be willing to sacrifice his life to save Davyn's, but that doesn't mean Davyn wouldn't do exactly the same for the old man. Could make for an interesting rescue if the Blackjacks do come for him.

Thea wraps her coat around her as she steps off the helicopter. The biting wind howls through the trees surrounding the field. If not for the team of vampires surrounding her, she'd be hurrying back to the helicopter as fast as she can. The whole setting is right out of a horror movie.

Court nods towards a small house at the far side of the field. Thick smoke is billowing from the chimney and there are lights on inside.

'That's the rendezvous point. Shep? We good?' Court asks.

Shep closes his eyes and everyone holds their positions as he checks for any surprises. He shudders and grimaces. 'Dogs. Four of them in the house. I can smell their wet fur from here. My allergies are already playing up.'

'Shep—,' Nix warns, but he just grins.

'All clear apart from them, boss. And yes, I will behave. Can we just go - it's fucking freezing.'

Nix leads the way with Shep and Court while Willow, Fallon, and Bas follow, keeping Thea sandwiched between them as they cross the open field. The smoky, earthy aroma of turf smoke hits her as they near the cottage. Clearly the vampires around her sense the presence of the wolves. She can almost feel the tension coming off the group the closer they get to the cottage.

The group comes to a stop as the back door of the cottage suddenly opens and a giant of a man steps into the doorway.

He silently examines them from the doorway, his backlit silhouette hiding all but his sheer size. He's easily as tall as Shep and as well built. That's bound to piss the vampire off.

'Phoenix and the Blackjacks I presume?' His voice is deep and his accent thick. Much broader than Davyn's.

Phoenix nods as she takes a step closer to him. 'You can call me Nix. And you're Murtagh?'

He nods. 'That I am, but while we're being all friendly you might as well call me Murt. I suppose you better come in.'

He steps aside and the vampires file into the cosy living room. A well-used, green couch takes up most of the floor space, facing the wood-burner set back in a wide fireplace. Piles of freshly cut peat turf sit in baskets beside the fire, along with a scattering of various sizes of low stools. A countertop separates the living room from the kitchen area, which is small and dated. A heavy pot is on top of the stove and whatever is inside, smells mouth-watering.

A wooden door sits to the left of the kitchen and another to the right. Presumably the bedroom and bathroom. No pictures cover the white walls, no ornaments on the dresser against the far wall. No TV. No radio that she can see. Whoever lives here clearly likes to be isolated away from the rest of the world. The fire is lit and Thea can feel the warmth working into her, taking the chill out of her bones a little.

The Blackjacks stand and face Murt and the three other men, the tension nearly visible between the two groups. Murt gestures to the seats and everyone lowers slowly as if afraid the other side will attack.

Thea pulls her stool closer to the fire and rubs her hands together as she examines the wolves. The brothers are far from what she expected. Not that she's sure what she was expecting from a clan of werewolves. Until a few hours ago, they didn't exist.

The brothers are tall, but so are the vampires so that's no surprise. Murt may appear relaxed but he's far from it. Thea can see the muscles in his thick arms are tense, his eyes darting from one vampire to the next as he eyes them up.

While the wolves and vampires are sizing each other up, Thea continues her blatant staring at the brothers. It's easy to see the family resemblance between the four men. Each appears to be in their late thirties or early forties with similar thick, dark hair and green eyes.

It's clear Murt is the leader, or whatever wolves call the position. Like Nix, he has an air about him, a quiet confidence difficult to ignore. He pushes to his feet and walks over to the counter. His movements are hypnotically graceful.

Thea can't explain the feeling, but it surrounds the four men. An underlying energy she can't explain. Perhaps it's their wolf side. If they have a side. She can easily drive herself crazy trying to figure all this out.

'Drink?' Murt asks as he takes a bottle from a cabinet against the wall. 'We borrowed this house from a friend. He's fond of the odd glass from time to time. He put some stew on for us too if you're peckish.'

Nix nods and Murt pours each of them a glass. Thea smiles as she takes hers from Murt and his pale green eyes glow as he looks at her. 'So you're the mate.'

She looks around at the vampires, then at the wolves. 'What? Me? No. I'm not.'

'Whatever you say,' Murt replies, but it's loaded with sarcasm. He smiles coyly at her, before taking his seat again.

'Thank you for agreeing to help,' Nix says as she gets things moving in the right direction. 'We appreciate it. This is Court, Shep, Bastian, Willow, Fallon, and Thea.'

'Fionn, Con, and Garret.' The three men barely move and certainly don't give a cheery wave. Then again, neither do the vampires.

Murt leans forward and clasps his hands together as he stares at Thea for a moment, then back at Nix. Thea notices that each brother has a tattoo on the back of their left hand.

'Our clan crest,' Murt explains, and Thea blushes when she realises she was caught staring. He holds up his fist to give Thea a better look. The crest is intertwined with a Celtic wolf which starts at his fingers and disappears under the sleeve of his shirt. 'Marks us as part of the same pack, the same clan or family. It's important to differentiate between clans when you're mixing in our world. Some are trustworthy and honourable. Others not so much.'

'How do you know?'

Murt flashes her a sly smile. 'Oh we know.'

'And which clan are you?'

Murt leans back against the fireplace and examines her as he sips his drink. 'Curious human aren't you.'

Court tenses, his icy glare like a dig in her ribs. She frowns at him and he backs off. 'Like you said, I'm human. I'm still learning about this non-human side of life. How will I understand if I don't ask questions?' She glares at Court again but he doesn't react.

Murt tilts his head slightly in agreement then smiles again. Thea can feel her cheeks redden as his eyes lock with hers. He's a stunning man with an equally stunning smile.

'I can hardly argue with that reasoning, can I? Perhaps if more questions were asked, our worlds would be less distant.' He glances over at Nix who meets his gaze, unfazed. Murt takes another sip of his drink and licks his lips before he looks back at Thea. 'Well, for the record my brothers and I lean towards the trustworthy, honourable side and, as long as I'm clan elder, that will remain the case.'

Murt glares at Shep when he snorts. 'Are your allergies troubling you?'

Thea barely manages to stifle a laugh as Shep's face drops. 'What the fuck?'

'We're dogs, remember,' he says levelling his gaze at Shep. 'Our hearing is exceptional. And you're right. No one seems to like the smell of wet dog, do they.'

'Almost as much as they dislike loud-mouth blood suckers,' Con mutters from behind Murt.

'If I throw one of those sticks by the fire out the door and tell you to fetch, would you race after it?' Shep says before Nix can stop him.

Con snarls loudly, and the hair on Thea's neck stands on end.

'Let's leave them to it, Murt,' Garret says, glaring over at them. 'Let them be torn to pieces. Might just cock my leg and piss on your corpse, Blondie.'

Shep lunges to his feet, but doesn't get far, thanks to Bastian grabbing him by the back of his jacket. 'Sit the fuck down.'

'Only if Fido takes that back.'

Garret gets to his feet and faces Shep. 'Fido? Fuck me, that's original. And coming from the one called Shep! Please tell me you see the irony.'

'Garret, sit down.'

'Yeah, Garret. Be a good boy,' Shep shoots back. 'Sit and I'll give you a doggie treat.'

'Enough!' Nix roars and Shep has the good sense to sit down.

Nix waits until everyone is sitting before she looks over at Murt again. 'I appreciate– we appreciate you agreeing to help us. If anyone on my team has a problem with that I fully expect them to keep their mouths shut. This is bigger than a feud.'

'I agree. I assure you, you won't get any trouble from our clan,' Murt says as he throws a look at each of his brothers over his shoulder. Each brother nods in turn under his cold glare.

'Like I said when we spoke, the Raven King has one of my team,'
Nix says. 'We know a little about him and felt it would help to have
some support from locals.'

Murt clasps his hands together, running his fingers over the tattoo
on his flesh. 'Why did he take him?'

'Does it matter?' Court asks.

'Actually yes,' Murt says as he stretches out in the chair. 'It matters
a great deal. You see, the Raven King takes prisoners to fight in his pit
because he wants to increase his numbers. Or he takes them because
he has a personal grudge. Now, which one is he?'

'From what we can ascertain it's a personal grudge,' Nix says.

Murt nods. 'I'm going to need more than that, Nix.'

'It's his personal business. I don't feel comfortable speaking about
it.'

'What's his name?'

Nix pauses a beat before answering. 'Davyn.'

Murt looks around at his brothers before addressing her again. 'As
in the King's son, Davyn?'

'You know him?'

'Of course. There's not many a wolf or vampire in Ireland who
doesn't know of the King and his sons. Darren was taken out of the
equation a long time ago, then Davyn disappeared a few decades ago,
presumed dead. Are you saying the King's son is a Blackjack?'

'Yes. Why am I sensing a problem here?' Nix asks.

'Because both Darren and Davyn were vile bastards who terrorised
locals for too long. We're not going to risk ourselves to get Davyn out.
Let him rot.'

He gets to his feet and his brothers follow suit.

'What are you doing?' Thea asks before she can stop herself.

'We're leaving. That family needs to be wiped out. Not saved.
You're on your own. Do me a favour and make sure you shut the door
after you leave.'

And just like that, the wolves leave the cottage, taking with them any chance of getting Davyn out. Thea hurries after them. 'Wait! Murtagh, please. Wait! You can't go.'

'Oh I think I can. We're done here.'

'Please!'

Murt stops and turns around. His green eyes are glowing ever so slightly as he peers down at her. His brothers stay back as he closes the distance between them. 'Thea, I'm sorry about your mate. I really am. But there's no way I'm risking my brothers to save a vampire from that bloodline. I'd have a hard enough time justifying helping the Blackjacks to begin with. But releasing Davyn is pushing even my limits. It's a firm no, Thea.'

'But he's different.'

Murt laughs as he turns away from her. 'Of course he is. They always are.'

She grabs his arm, letting go when he growls at her. She shrinks away, seeing a little of the wolf inside him in his glowing eyes. 'I'd warn you not to push your luck, Thea. Or me.'

'I'm sorry. I wasn't trying to push you, I promise. But I need you to listen. Please. Just give me a minute. I'm begging you.'

He draws in a long breath then nods once.

'Thank you. I know you probably won't believe me but Davyn genuinely is a decent person. He's been part of the team for decades and helped to save so many lives. Mine included. I don't know what he did in his past, but I do know he's not that person anymore.'

The words come out in a rush she can't hold back. If Murt and his brothers walk away, Davyn is as good as dead.

'He's loyal, and decent, and will put his life on the line for anyone in trouble. He's not like his father. Nothing like him. I promise you.'

Murt opens his mouth to speak but she doesn't give him a chance to interrupt her. 'He saved my life twice, Murt. Risked himself to get me out.' Not for the first time, guilt claws at her gut, forcing tears out, no matter how hard she tries to hold them at bay, as she remembers the last time she saw him, when the Fever-crazed vampires dragged him to the ground and took him away.

'He was captured while saving me,' she mutters quietly. 'It's my fault.' She brushes the tears away but it's a futile effort. There's no stopping them. 'The only reason he's back with his father is because of me. I was captured and he risked himself to get me out. It's my fault. All of this. And I can't bear the thought of him being hurt because of me. You have to help. Please, I'm begging you.'

'Okay. Okay. Take a breath.'

Thea does just that as she wipes her face again, then looks up at Murt, terrified to see what his reaction will be to her unplanned and slightly hysterical outburst. He's frowning at her, his dark brows tightly drawn together.

'Stay,' he commands, then takes a few steps away, silently followed by his brothers. They talk for a few minutes, then he faces her again. 'If we say yes, you have to stop crying. Con hates when women cry.'

Con holds up his middle finger to Murt, but the older brother ignores him, turning back towards the house instead. 'Get inside, Thea, before you freeze.'

'You're really going to help?'

Murt nods as he walks past her. 'It appears so.'

The Raven King empties his tankard and wipes the froth from his mouth with the back of his hand. His trusted right-hand man, Fergus, refills his tankard and sits in the chair opposite him. 'How much did we take tonight?'

Fergus opens his ledger and moves his finger down the page as if looking for the information which, knowing the vampire, he had committed to memory. 'Between the door, bar, and bets, close to ninety-five thousand.'

Flann is pleasantly surprised by the amount. 'Davyn is a crowd puller. I knew he would be.'

'Yes, but he may be getting to the end of his fighting days. He's getting harder to control. He took down three of our guards yesterday. Killed one of them. He tore the man's body apart.'

Flann scratches his jaw. 'Yes, well, he has lasted a lot longer than the others we gave the enhancer to.'

'Sire, I know he's your son, but–'

'That means nothing, Fergus. I gave him a chance to take his place with me but he refused. He's nothing but a traitor to our kind.'

'So you want him to be punished?'

Flann leans back in his heavy wooden chair and taps his fingers on his desk. What a question. Punishment is irreversible. Flann made it a habit of not giving wrong-doers a second chance. The fact he was willing to move past his son's transgressions was a first for him. No more though. He's done waiting for Davyn to submit.

The boy has too much of his mother in him. That's part of his problem. Flann thought by taking Alana out of the picture it would tame her bastard son, but it made no difference. Davyn was born a disappointment. At least now he had finally found a use for him. It would have been preferable if he could get a bit longer out of him, but if his time has come, so be it.

He gets to his feet and walks down the spiral staircase to the great hall. Davyn is secured to the platform as he had been each night after he fought. His son lifts his head as he approaches and Flann grimaces. 'What happened to his eye?'

'One of the guests dropped a glass bottle into the ring.'

Flann bends down and examines the mess that used to be the right side of Davyn's face. His eye is ruined and there's still glass embedded in his cheek. 'Can you understand me?'

Davyn's blank expression remains unchanged. Perhaps he's too far gone already. Then again, knowing his son he could just be ignoring him.

Flann steps back and sits on the edge of his banquet table as Davyn lowers his head again, letting it hang limply on his shoulders.

'You're right. We may have to cut our losses with him,' he says quietly to Fergus. 'The last thing I need is him breaking out and tearing all of us to pieces. Get everyone together. We'll Bind him tonight while we can still somewhat restrain him.'

'But what about the fights we've scheduled for him in the coming days?'

'He still fights. It will make the match more interesting if one of the fighters is incapacitated as he will be.'

Fergus nods then hurries from the room. Flann turns the tankard on the table as he stares across at Davyn. He's going to enjoy silencing his son once and for all.

~

Davyn's struggles get him nowhere as the four guards pull, push and generally manhandle him along the tunnels. He knows he was secured to the platform again, but can't remember any of his time there. And for that he's thankful. Coherent thought is hit and miss – more miss the last few hours. He has no memory of being taken back to his cell or how long he spent there. He can't even remember what happened to his eye.

He's tried to prise the glass from his skin but gave up in the end. He couldn't see what he was doing and every time his fingers hit against the glass or his torn skin he had to bite back a scream. His world consists of confusion, pain, exhaustion, and gut-wrenching hunger like he's never felt before. It's all he knows.

Through the raging need for blood, a few coherent thoughts make their way out. First, he's being taken to his father. Second, that's not a good thing, and third, it's really not a good thing. He hasn't fought yet today. At least he doesn't think he did. So why is he being brought to the hall?

Rough stone tears at his wings as he is thrown against the wall while one of the guards unlocks a heavy metal gate. They climb up a steep set of stairs and emerge in the courtyard inside the castle's main gate. Home sweet home.

He tries to keep his thoughts in order, but the overpowering urge to feed all but consumes him. His gums throb around his large fangs which refuse to retract no matter how hard he tries. Crippling cramps pull and twist at his stomach, sending spasms of nausea through his body. Every swallow shoves a fresh volley of knives down his throat. He's torn between wanting to tear open each and every throat he sees, and huddling in a dark corner, crying in pain.

He is lead into the great hall in the centre of the castle and he digs his boots into the rough stone cobbles when he sees the hoard that's gathered. His father is sitting in his grotesque throne at the front of the room, his legs crossed, the heavy sword he always carries, resting on his knee. Davyn can't drag his attention away from his father.

Something is wrong. Seriously wrong, and he's about to get the brunt of it. Davyn is dragged through the room, his efforts to dig his feet into the ground doing nothing to slow his progress.

The Fever takes over and he lunges at the nearest vampire, barely missing his target as the guards restrain him. More guards join in, helping to drag him over to the large X frame sitting at the head of the room. He knows full well what it's used for.

Growing up, he had witnessed two Binding rituals and each one scarred him to his core. Fuelled by his growing fear, his Blood Fever charges to the front, but it does no good. His back is slammed against the rough wood and within seconds his wrists, neck, torso, and ankles are chained to the heavy frame.

The guards step back as Flann gets off his chair and slowly walks over to the platform. He knows it won't do him any good but Davyn struggles against his bonds, desperate to break free. The rough wood tears at his bare back as he bucks against it, but it won't budge. The thing was constructed centuries ago, and had survived too many Bindings to count.

'Final chance, son. Take a knee in front of me. Turn your allegiance from the Blackjacks to me and I promise I'll stop this before something happens we'll both regret.'

Davyn laughs harshly. 'You've never regretted a damn thing in your life. Screw you.'

'Should I take that as a no?'

Davyn's only response is to spit in his father's face. He smiles as the glob of blood lands between Flann's eyes. More than once he's imagined putting a bullet in that very spot.

Flann's lip twitches, showing an enormous fang. 'Don't say I didn't give you a chance.' He turns to the crowd and claps his hands, silencing them. When he has everyone's attention, he points at Davyn.

'Most of you will already know, but this traitor is my son, Davyn. Decades ago, he turned his back on me, my name, and my legacy, to join the Blackjacks - a group of mongrels whose sole intent is to destroy old blood. Destroy what we have spent centuries creating.' Flann pauses as the crowd erupts in a chorus of shouting and cursing, all directed at Davyn.

'It's been many years since we've had to Bind one of our own, but our laws are not to be questioned. I stand before you, as your leader, willing to put my own feelings aside for the good of the race. It is with a heavy heart that I must punish my own flesh and blood in such a way, but I would not be doing my job if I forgave such an act of treachery.' He turns to look at Davyn, disappointment plastered on his face. Clearly his father is enjoying playing up to the crowd. Pretending to be the caring father he never was. 'Let's begin.'

Davyn is sure his heart is going to beat right out of his chest. He's been scared before. Living in this castle, fear was a part of life. But seeing the instruments for the Binding laid out on the table in front of his father, has him downright terrified.

He balls his fists and pulls his arms down until his muscles are screaming for relief. Memories of past victims race into his mind, each one trying and failing to get out. As his father drones on about honour and punishment, the dread settles like a rock in the pit of his stomach.

He's not getting out of this.

There's nothing he can do to stop what's about to happen.

Finished playing up to his adoring public, his father walks towards him, a satisfied grin on his cruel face. He's won and he knows it.

Davyn grunts as one of his father's goons approaches him. He wants to beg the male to leave him alone. Hell, to let him go, but his brain isn't on board with that. His attention is on the goblet of blood in his father's other hand. Fucking Fever is taking control again, focusing on the blood instead of the shite situation he's in.

Blunt nails dig into his jaw, prising his mouth open. His father holds the goblet up to the crowd, who cheer loudly.

'This will be the traitors last drink.' The vile grin grows as his father lifts the goblet and holds it over Davyn's mouth.

It's not going to make a damn bit of difference but Davyn attempts to clamp his jaw closed even though his body is craving the blood. The guy in control of his jaw won't ease up, digging those thick fingers in, gouging holes in his flesh.

In spite of his best efforts, the contents are poured down Davyn's throat and his mouth is forced shut. He swallows the blood, but instead of soothing him, it stokes the fire in the battle he's been fighting. The blood hits his empty stomach and sends the cramps into a frenzy. He tries to pull his legs up, to offer some relief to his gut, but he's strapped down firmly.

Flann taps him on the cheek then turns to address the crowd again. 'The purpose of a Binding is to strip the privileges given to all vampires. As a traitor, Davyn has given up his right to feed and to fly.'

'Not that he could anyway!' someone in the crowd shouts.

Flann smiles and nods. 'Very true. Perhaps I should have seen that as a sign of what was to come.'

Davyn clamps his mouth shut as his father picks up a pair of heavy pliers.

No, no, no.

He meets his father's eyes, silently begging him not to do this, but there's nothing there. Never was. His father is dead inside. Cold and cruel.

He thrives on inflicting pain and humiliation. It's how he raised Davyn.

'Open up, son.'

He's not going to stop his father from completing the ritual but he's not going to give in. It's not like it can get any worse for him. His victory lasts a grand total of five seconds. The goon with the steel hands helps him open wide so his father can shove a gag in as far as it will go, stopping him from closing his mouth.

He claws at the chains holding his wrists. He's going to suffocate. A thick vice clamps around his chest, stopping air from getting to his lungs. He's hyperventilating and his father fucking loves it.

The pliers are held up in front of his good eye and slowly turned around so he can see the darkened blood from previous victims. A strangled whimper breaks free but it just spurs on his father.

The pliers snugly grip one of his fangs. Davyn closes his eyes as a wave of dizziness hits.

'Stay with me, son.'

He can't. He doesn't want to see the pleasure his father is getting from doing this to him.

A heavy, sweating palm presses to his forehead as his father braces himself. Then with a powerful swipe of his arm, he tears the fang from Davyn's gums.

White hot pain sears through his skull, radiating out from his jaw to encompass his entire head. Tears pour down his face – from pain or humiliation he doesn't know.

His father's men chant Flann's name over and over again as he repeats the process then holds up the bloodied fangs.

Davyn barely hears the roar of appreciation from the crowd. He's just lost a big part of himself, a part he can never get back. He'll never feed again. If he survives this - which is highly doubtful, he'll be reduced to drinking from a damn cup instead of from the vein.

He squeezes his eyes shut, wishing his father would just end this for him. Kill him and put him out of his misery. He's had enough. If given the option to take a knee in front of his father he'd do it. If he could, he'd beg, plead, swear allegiance. Whatever he has to do in order to end the ritual.

He opens his eyes just in time to see his father launch his fangs into the crowd. The gag is wrenched from his mouth, easing the agony a little but not for long. His father secures a thick leather strap around the top of Davyn's head, pulling it tight under his jaw, tearing into his flesh until it draws blood.

Davyn tries to open his mouth but the strap clamps his mouth firmly closed. The invisible vice tightens around his chest, squeezing his lungs until he's sure he's going to suffocate.

Firm fingers dig into his jaw, tugging at his head until he looks up at his father. 'How are you fairing, son?' His father smiles as he examines him. 'Do you know what I think,' he says quietly so just Davyn can hear. 'I think you would give anything to bow to me. Am I right?'

Davyn wants to scream yes. To drop right now at his father's feet. Instead he can do nothing except concentrate on breathing. In and out, harsh, rapid breaths that barely keep air in his lungs.

His father chuckles to himself. 'I thought so. If only I'd given you a few chances to change your mind.' He jostles Davyn's head, sending a spear of agony through his throbbing gums. 'That's right. I did.'

Davyn whimpers, hating how pitiful he sounds. His torn gums continue to ooze blood into his mouth. He gags as it trickles down his throat, messing with his breathing.

His father disappears from view, reappearing too soon, filling Davyn's field of vision. When he holds up a long suture needle with a length of fine wire threaded through it, Davyn thrashes against the frame, warm blood trickling down his arms and neck from the tight restraints.

'Please don't!'

The words are screamed as loud as he can without moving his jaw. He roars them at his father, again and again, but the sound that comes out is nothing more than a muffled gargle.

'Any last words, son?'

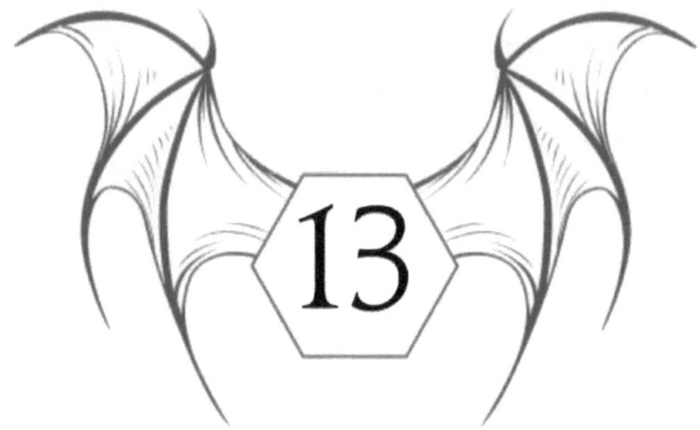

Davyn watches transfixed as drop after drop of blood lands on the platform in front of his face. His blood. He doesn't know which part of his face is bleeding, but it's bad if the steady stream is anything to go by.

Drip, drip, drip.

Each forced breath is taken in time with the drip, like beats in a piece of music. Each one reminding him to breathe in or out.

His rhythm is knocked out of sync as a tankard of ale finds its way over his head and down the back of his neck. He ignores the jeers of the vampire, forcing himself to get back on track with the in and out beat.

He never thought he'd be grateful to the Fever, but after what just happened, it's helping to distract him from the pain. Distract him from the fact that if he fumbles with the next breath, he'll suffocate. Distract himself from the overpowering need to scream until his lungs burn and he collapses.

He'll never forget the feeling of the wire being slowly dragged through his lips, pulling at the sensitive skin, before being pulled taut pressing his lips together. Over and over again, agonisingly slow, until his mouth was firmly sealed shut.

The same wire had been used to stitch his wings in place, before every vampire in the castle had fed from him. They hadn't taken enough to kill him, just to bring him to the edge without any way of saving himself.

He closes his eyes and tries to call unconsciousness to him, but the pain of the wire in his lips, back, and wings is intense and enough to keep him conscious. But that's part of the fun of the Binding. It was created centuries ago by a bunch of power crazed Primes. Left to slowly starve, it was the worst punishment handed out.

His jaw aches from keeping it clamped shut but he's afraid to relax. He doesn't want to feel the pull of the stitches in his lips. The two craters in his gums are still oozing blood which he has no option but to swallow, aggravating his Blood Fever.

Anger burns in him when he hears his father laughing with some males as he enjoys his banquet. The smell of food is enough to drive him crazy, but it's the blood in the air that's causing him the most issues. Every cell in his body is screaming to be fed. He clenches his fists, desperately trying to free himself, but it's a futile effort and only adds his own blood to the vast array of smells in the room.

No one notices, or if they do, they don't mention it. As per the rules, he doesn't exist anymore. He's further down the food chain than the castle rats. His life will continue as it has for however long he has left. He'll fight then be put on display. All he can do is hope his body gives in and surrenders to death soon. He doesn't want to slowly starve to death like this.

He grunts as a boot impacts with his chest, cracking a rib with a surge of stomach churning pain. He grunts, momentarily forgetting about this lips. The sensation of the stitches pulling in his skin turns his already volatile stomach. He breathes heavily through his nose, trying to stop himself from vomiting, concentrating on the drips of blood on the platform.

If he stops focusing on the pain and his Blood Fever, the crippling fear of suffocation will take hold. With his mouth firmly sealed, precious oxygen has to make its way through his blood filled nostrils, past cracked and broken ribs, and into lungs that burn with every pitiful inhale. He tries to slow his breathing down, tries to keep the panic at bay, but he feels his control slipping.

He pulls at his restraints, tearing his wrists and putting more pressure on his lungs. A band of pain clamps around his chest as each breath grates against his broken ribs. He doesn't want his father to see him lose control but he's in no position to do anything to stop it.

The combined effects of Blood Fever, suffocation, and utter despair take hold of him, shattering the last of his control. He screams, forcing the wires to gouge deeper into his lips. His Blood Fever kicks up a gear as the scent of his blood fills the air. He's vaguely aware of his father standing in front of him, smiling at him.

Unable to deal with the assault, his lungs and nostrils choose that moment to stop working together. His ribs squeeze his lungs, stopping air from getting in. Black spots creep in from the edge of his vision as his limbs go numb.

The last thing he sees before he passes out is his father laughing and applauding his breakdown.

~

Nix had looked as surprised as Thea had been when Murt said he would help them. She honestly thought that was it when he walked out of the house. Thea sips her warming drink and tries to focus on the positives. Instead of six going in to get Davyn, there are ten highly trained fighters ready to do whatever they have to do in order to bring him home.

Murt hasn't said anything since he led his brothers back into the house. They'd taken their seats by the fire again after refilling their glasses. He won't break eye contact with Thea and it's beginning to unnerve her. His eyes are glowing ever so slightly but there's no aggression as far as she can tell. It's almost like he's trying to get into her mind.

He rubs his hand over the dark stubble on his jaw then licks his lips, finally releasing her from his eyes.

'Before we take this partnership any further, I need you to assure me you fully understand who you are planning to release. Now Thea here has given me a convincing speech about how good Davyn is, but I need to know you are all aware of who he is. Or was,' he adds, glancing at Thea.

'Davyn's father has no moral boundaries,' he continues. 'And I mean none whatsoever. He will kill, steal, maim, torture, and rape.' Murt pauses and takes a drink before levelling his gaze on Thea again. 'His sons are known for the same. Both of them.'

'We know,' Nix says, surprising Thea.

'You don't believe Davyn is really like that, do you?' Thea asks.

Murt targets her with his green eyes as he smiles coldly. 'You'd do well to believe it, Thea. Whether under duress or not, Davyn has a fair bit of blood on his hands. Anyway, we've promised to help you get him out. Not going to go against that now. I'll leave it to the Blackjacks to control him once we do get him out.'

'Davyn is a Blackjack,' Nix says. 'He is one of us and has done nothing but fight for and protect vampires targeted by the Order. We know who he is now.'

'No, Nix. You know as much as he wants you to know. Each and every one of us is the same. It's part of who we are. Part of what we are. Secrecy goes hand and hand with that.'

He takes another drink and points to the map laid out on the table in front of them. The land owned by Davyn's father is ringed in red, and covers hundreds of acres. 'This is only the land we have knowledge of. I can tell you we haven't found any of his fighting pits. And we've looked. Believe me.

'We've tried in wolf form too, but we can't find trace of anything. But that's what makes the King so dangerous. He's no fool. He's had his fair share of run ins with us in the past. He knows how to cover his tracks.'

'Great fucking help.'

Murt glances at Shep. 'I want to get one thing straight. I get the attitude. I get the tension, and I get the fact that neither side wants to be in the same room as each other. We're risking a lot by even talking to you so I'd appreciate if you drop the fucking attitude. And I'm talking about from both sides.' He glares at his brothers who nod obediently.

The Blackjacks nod and Murt looks back at Nix again. 'We have someone coming to meet with us. He might be able to help. If he can, there's a chance we won't have to send your people in.'

'Who is it?' Nix asks.

'He's agreed to see us in an hour. You'll know more then.' Murt leans back in the chair and stretches his legs out in front of him. 'Right so, I guess all we can do is wait and see what he has to say. How about some food in the meantime? My stomach thinks my throat's been cut.'

Murt lowers onto the couch next to Thea and rests his head on his hand, his thumb brushing over the stubble on his jaw. He doesn't say anything for a minute or two, keeping his pale green eyes on her. Thea fidgets under his intense scrutiny but can't get herself to break the silence. The damn wolf seems to throw her off balance. The four brothers do, but there's something about Murt that's so much more intense.

Maybe being the clan elder made his presence stronger. It makes no sense to her but, it's almost like she can feel the ancient power radiating from him. She has no idea how old he actually is, but something about the way he carries himself hints that he's in the centuries, rather than decades, age group.

Eventually the corner of his mouth lifts into a lopsided grin. 'Who is Court to you?'

'Excuse me?'

The grin widens. 'You heard me, so stop stalling. Every time I called Davyn your mate you looked at Court. So, again, who's Court to you?'

'He's my father.'

Murt laughs and shakes his head. 'Now it all becomes clear. Well isn't that interesting. I take it Daddy isn't keen on your choice of mate?'

Thea looks around the room, but everyone else is either too busy glaring or drinking, to pay Murt and herself any attention. 'He's not my mate, but that doesn't mean I don't want him to be. How did you know?'

Murt shuffles closer, keeping his voice down as he speaks again. 'Wolves have a heightened sense of smell. Much more than your vampire friends do. Please don't take offense, but the overpowering stench of vampire on you is... well, hard to miss.'

Thea blushes and looks down at the napkin she's slowly tearing to shreds. 'I don't suppose showering will help?'

Murt smiles and shakes his head. 'It's ingrained in you. That's what you get when you let one feed from you. Stink hangs around.'

'Stink. Wow, you have a way with words.'

He smiles apologetically. 'I honestly didn't mean to offend. The feud between us has lasted generations. Friendships won't develop overnight. If at all.'

'Can I ask you something?'

'I get the impression you wouldn't be so easily dismissed if I said no. Ask away.'

'Why are you helping? It's not that I'm not grateful. I really am. It's just your brothers seem less than keen. The Blackjacks aren't over the moon about it either. So why would you do this for us. For Davyn?'

Murt takes a long pause before he answers, repeatedly running his fingers over his jaw as he considers her question. 'There's something you need to understand about our species. We're a dying breed. Literally. Wolf shifter numbers are down to a critical level. Centuries of hunting has driven our numbers down. There's a reason wolves don't roam free in Ireland, Thea. We're too scared to.

'When we change we do it on private land that we own, or stay indoors. Neither of which appeals to the animal inside us. The wolf needs space, the freedom to run, to stretch our legs, to hunt,' he adds with a devious twinkle in his eye. Thea wants to know exactly what Murt hunts, but doesn't feel ready to hear the answer. 'But we have little choice. If we're seen, we will be killed.'

'I'm so sorry. That's horrible.'

'It is what it is. If we're to survive we need to form alliances. No matter how much those alliances piss us off. When it comes to your mate though, it's personal too. The King has been on our list for decades, but I've been loath to risk my brothers lives by going in before we're ready. But, with vampire help, now may just be the right time.'

'Why is this personal?'

Murt pauses and his eyes glow fiercely when he looks at her again. 'The Raven King's banquet hall or throne room, whatever the fuck he calls it, is decorated with animal heads from his kills. Wolf heads.'

'Oh my God,' Thea says, as his words hit home.

'Your mate's father has slaughtered, butchered and murdered too many of my clan and put their heads on display in that room. I'll help get your mate out, I swear to that and I am a man of my word. But the only reason I'm risking my brothers' lives... my life, is to kill that man and put my family members to rest.'

~

Shep jumps to his feet and tears the door open, startling Thea. She screeches as Shep hauls an old man into the room and holds him a few feet off the ground. 'Who the fuck are you?'

'Please. I'm a friend.'

Shep holds him up to the group. 'Anyone friends with this guy?' he asks looking around the room.

'Davyn.'

'What did you say?' Nix asks.

The man grips Shep's hand trying to peel his fingers from around his neck, but there's no let up. 'I'm... Davyn's friend.'

Murt storms over to Shep. 'He's my contact. Put him down. He's harmless.'

Shep lowers him to the ground and the man rubs his neck as he coughs. The old man's eyes dart around the room, taking in the wolf and vampire warriors. Then he does the last thing Thea was expecting. He smiles. 'The Blackjacks. You came.'

'Who the fuck are you, old man?' Fallon asks.

'Are you the Blackjacks? Please, I am an old man and no threat to you. I need to know.'

Nix strides to the front of the group and flicks her long black coat behind her. 'I'm Phoenix, leader of the Blackjacks.'

Nix frowns as the old man cries. 'Thank goodness you're here. My name is Ronan. I work for Flann, or The Raven King, as he likes to be called.'

Nix's face hardens. 'Is that so?'

'Yes, but not by choice. Please I need your help. Davyn needs your help. Murtagh asked me to come here tonight to see if I can be of assistance. I've known Davyn since he was a child. He is like a son to me and I've worked for his father for many years. I will help in any way I can to save him and make sure his father dies.'

Nix pauses for a moment as she helps Ronan into the nearest chair. 'Is Davyn okay?'

Ronan smiles sadly and nods. 'He is alive, but okay is not a word I would use to describe his condition. I fear if he is not helped soon he will die.'

15

Ronan settles into an armchair by the fire and takes a sip of water. Nix had introduced each of her team while Murt got the man a drink. Thea barely listened to what they were saying. Her thoughts are focused solely on his last words. They need to get Davyn out now. Making introductions is wasting time. Time he doesn't have.

Court takes her by the shoulders and guides her away from Ronan. 'What?' she hisses as he leads her to the far side of the room.

'You know what, Thea. Calm down.'

She looks at the tattoo peeking out from under his shirt instead of at his eyes. The last thing she needs is her dad to get into her thoughts and see what's really going on in there. 'You need to get him out.'

'I heard. And Nix heard. Neither of us are going to send in a team to get him without knowing what we're up against. You know that, so don't you dare argue with me. Dav wouldn't be on board with sacrificing another team member to get him out. You know that too.'

'So you expect me to just sit here and keep my mouth shut.'

He kisses her on the forehead before she can push him away. 'That's exactly what I want. The alternative is you get back on the helicopter.'

'Fine.'

He shakes his head and goes back to the rest of the group while she hangs back. She'd rather have space away from the others.

Nix sits on the stool opposite Ronan, and Court nods at her before she speaks again. 'We've been doing a little detective work since Davyn was taken. Is his father really the Raven King?'

Ronan smiles at Nix. 'You are very proficient detectives. Flann goes to great lengths to hide his true name.'

'Is he really as bad as we hear?'

Ronan nods. 'A vile, self-important sadist. I would gladly see him with a bullet in his head.'

Shep whistles from the back of the room. 'Now he's talking my kind of language.'

Nix turns back to Ronan. 'So life wasn't pleasant living in an old castle on the Irish coastline?'

Ronan shakes his head. 'Far from it. Flann always wanted two sons; one heir and one back-up. Unfortunately for Davyn he was the back-up. Flann spent most of his time with his oldest son, Darren. His wife, Alana, and Davyn were ignored for the most part.

'Alana was a magnificent woman. Beautiful, smart and completely devoted to her sons. The arranged marriage to Flann was not something she wanted, but back then, there was little choice. He was a lord and you don't refuse a mating at that level. With her permission, I schooled Davyn - in secret of course. Things like reading and writing were considered nothing more than a waste of time.

'When Alana passed away, Davyn's life changed forever. He was taken from his room at the young age of seven and thrown in to a cell in the lower level of the castle. The place is worse than hell. The castle is built over a series of caves which flood at high tide. He extended the foundation of the castle into these caves, creating a most effective prison separate from the castle but also inaccessible from the outside. He cut channels through the foundation walls which allow water to enter and exit the cells, but nothing else.'

'You saying the cells flooded?' Fallon asks.

'Yes. And still do. For the most part, the base of each cell is submerged under water twice a day, perhaps a few feet, maybe more, depending on the tides. Davyn was kept in the cell nearest to the foundation wall.'

'So his cell was under water longer than the others,' Court says quietly.

Ronan nods. 'The poor boy barely slept for years. He was terrified of drowning. The only time he was taken out was to fight against his brother. Flann took great pleasure using Davyn as a training tool. I'm sure each and every bone in his body was broken at least once, if not more. The boy was abused on a daily basis - physically and mentally. His father made sure Davyn knew how unwanted, how useless, how much of an embarrassment he was.

'I am sure they are the ones that caused the damage to his wings. During a particularly brutal battle, Davyn was thrown against the wall of the cave numerous times and was beaten with a stick once he lost consciousness. His brother only ceased the attack when Davyn's back was completely destroyed. His wings emerged a few weeks later.'

Ronan pauses and wrings his hands together. 'I was with him when his wings broke out. I...' He closes his eyes and his voice trails away. 'Forgive me. It was during a particularly bad storm. I went to check on Davyn, as I did as often as I could. He was twenty-six years old at the time, so I knew he would change sooner or later. When I reached the cells I was horrified. His cell was completely submerged. The waves were actually getting through, which made getting to him particularly hazardous. He was hanging on to the roof of his cell, trying to keep his head above the water. As soon as I saw that his eyes were glowing I knew he was going to change. I assured him I would be back and went to find his father.'

Ronan snorts loudly. 'I should not have wasted that time. He barely acknowledged me. Said to leave him where he is. It would 'toughen him up'. I hurried back to Davyn. By that stage he was mid change. I could do nothing to ease his suffering. All I could do was try to hold his head above water while he screamed in agony. I knew there was a problem when the water turned red with blood. He needed to feed to help him but there was no way of holding him above the water and feeding him. I tried but I couldn't do both.'

'So he didn't feed at all during his change?' Nix asks.

Ronan shakes his head. 'He lost consciousness and I supported him until the tide eventually turned. I was so cold I couldn't feel his pulse. I thought he had died. Once I could leave him without risk of drowning, I went back to his father. It took a few hours of begging, but his father eventually gave me the key and sent some men to the cells with me. They brought him to one of the rooms and left me to care for him. His back had been torn open by his damaged wing, but there was nothing I could do to fix it or his wing. He did not regain consciousness for eight days.

'Because his body hadn't had the blood it so desperately needed during the change, he had no interest in feeding. The vital urge to feed, to take blood, hadn't been developed. His body required blood to survive, but the thought of drinking turned his stomach - much as it would a human. Without that basic instinct instilled, it was a daily struggle to give him what he needed. Once Flann saw Davyn's damaged wing, he threw him back in the cell and that's where he remained for the next fifty-three years.'

Ronan takes a drink from the glass of water on the table in front of him before he continues. 'Darren was killed many years later when a rival group attacked the castle. No bad thing if you ask me. The boy was as rotten as his father. Unfortunately for Davyn, Flann couldn't show his face without a suitable heir so, left with no choice, he released him from his prison.

'At this stage, Davyn had never fed naturally. He had been given bottles or cups of blood - which he forced down, but had never taken anything from the vein. Flann was worried if his men saw the 'pathetic excuse for a male', that he'd be a laughing stock.

Davyn was barely alive, let alone a suitable heir. So, in true Flann style, he overcompensated. He filled the great hall with humans and vampires. He took people from the prison below the castle, stole people off the street, found them anywhere they could be found. He threw Davyn in to the room, told him to take his fill and locked the door.'

'I'm not liking where this is heading,' Bastian mutters.

Thea isn't either. She isn't liking any of what Ronan is saying. All she wants to do is hold Davyn. The urgency to get him out is so much more evident. She can't let him suffer like that for a minute longer.

Ronan takes another drink and Thea has to resist the urge to get herself a stiff drink. 'When he finally emerged less than twenty-four hours later, they were all dead. Davyn went from a lonely cell where he was starving, to a banquet. Even though feeding revolted him, he wasn't strong enough to hold back that primal urge when it finally came out. The unfamiliar Prime vampire side took control. He took what he wanted from the people in that room and, when he was done, he killed them all.'

Shep curses as he pushes to his feet. 'Please tell me his damn reputation didn't come from that?'

Ronan nods. 'What they say about him is true. He has killed people he has fed from. But it was not a regular occurrence or because he enjoyed it as the rumours state. That occasion was the one and only time Davyn lost control. I know it does not excuse what happened, but he was not strong enough to restrain that side of himself. It only took a few hours to destroy any chance he may have had at a normal life. That one incident tarnished him for life.'

'No shit,' Shep mutters. 'It was like throwing a starving lion in to a fast food joint. They didn't have a chance - him or them.'

'Anyone else feel about the size of a bug?' Fallon massages the back of her neck. 'I always thought he... damn it.'

'We all believed the stories,' Nix says. 'We can apologise to him when we get him back. How did he get away from Flann?'

'As time passed, Davyn withdrew in to himself. He was plagued with guilt over what he had done. Flann gave him little to no freedom over the next decade or so. He had his heir and he trained him day and night. When he wasn't fighting, he was back in the cell, chained to the wall so he couldn't fly away - not that he could have, poor boy, but Flann refused to give him a moment of freedom.

'Over the years, Flann began to relax his hold slightly. Davyn did precisely what he was told. He fought, he fed, he supported his father and his thirst for pain and blood. I would prefer not to recount the horrors Flann inflicted on his son or, in turn, what his son inflicted on others. Suffice to say, Flann was pleased. He finally had a suitable heir again.'

Ronan smirks. 'That couldn't have been further from the truth. Davyn was just biding his time, playing the dutiful heir until he could break free. Which he did. One morning he had simply disappeared. Flann searched, but Davyn apparently had been planning his escape for years and had covered all his tracks.

'No one heard anything more about him until a few years ago when I heard rumours of a Blackjack with an Irish accent. The description was far from the Davyn I remembered, but I knew it had to be him. He had survived in spite of everything Flann did and was fighting against vampires like Flann and the True Order. I could not have been more proud.'

Thea hugs her arms to her chest, but the chill refused to subside. 'So how did his father find him again?'

Ronan shakes his head. 'I truly wish I knew. I have spoken to Davyn about it and he is unclear. I can only assume he heard similar rumours and put two and two together. Davyn mentioned he was captured in a True Order lab.'

Nix nods. 'Do you think Flann is affiliated with the Order?'

'Perhaps. I would not put anything past the male. As long as it serves his purpose, he has no limits.' Roman glances over at Murt and his brothers. 'Much like you and your new alliance. I presume it serves a purpose.'

Murt nods. 'For now. We've agreed to put our many differences aside and help get Davyn out.

'I am grateful you are willing to assist with this.'

Murt smiles, but it's bordering on something predatory rather than pleasant, and does nothing to ease Thea's chills. 'We want your master's head.'

'I understand, and I sincerely hope you succeed.'

'So you've had contact with Davyn?' Nix asks.

'Many times, yes. He is being kept in the same cell he was in as a child. He has fought in the pits numerous times and won. I'm sure you know what that entails. He has been treated badly by his father. Very badly indeed.'

Ronan nods to himself and pauses. 'Davyn had been fighting honourably until recently. His father didn't appreciate the speed at which he dispatched his competitors. Davyn has been given an enhancer of sorts. I'm afraid I do not fully know what it does, but Davyn is displaying signs of Blood Fever. He has barely been fed, but his eyes are already turning red.'

Thea hears the curses from various members of the team.

'I have no knowledge of where the fights take place. The King's men come and collect Davyn to bring him to the fight. I am not permitted to go with him. You will need to send two people to the fight. I wish that were not the case but there is no other option.'

'We plan to track the two ticket holders,' Nix explains.

Ronan shakes his head. 'That won't work. All spectators are carefully examined and scanned before they enter the fight. Flann has invested too much in these fights. He won't take chances.'

'There is one way we can track them,' Shep says with a grin. 'I can feed from Thea.'

'Oh would you give it a rest,' Court snaps. 'I'm still getting over the fact Davyn fed from her. There isn't a chance in hell you're going near her.'

'Yeah and I totally get that, Court. But I'm a tracker. I'm shit hot at picking up scents anyway, but with her blood in my system, there's no way I can lose her. I'll be able to track them from a distance. Once we get close enough, Bas can do his thing and we'll get the layout.'

Thea holds her breath as Court and Nix have a silent conversation. She doesn't know how the couple do it, but they can have a full conversation, even an argument, just by looking at each other. While the thought of Shep feeding from her isn't too appealing, everything he said makes sense.

Court snarls and glares over at Shep. 'Fuck it. How do you feel about this Thea?'

'I just want to get Davyn out. I'll do whatever I have to.'

'That's the spirit,' Shep mutters. 'You could show a little enthusiasm,' he adds with a grin. 'So are we doing this or what?'

'I do not wish to aggravate a tense situation,' Ronan says. 'But I also agree it is your best option.'

Court points to Fletch. 'Why not feed from Fletch instead?'

'My superpowers work best on a blood bond kind of level. That's strongest with a male and female connection. Don't shoot the messenger,' he adds quickly when Court growls again. 'I can leave the blood bond thing and take my chance on just tracking her, but if you want a sure fire way of being able to find her, Fletch, and Dav, her blood is the key.'

Then Shep's face turns serious. 'I'm not going to fuck around with anyone's life, Court. I'm an exceptional tracker and that's not just me blowing smoke up my ass. I promise I'll find her this way.'

'How long will her blood stay in your system?'

Shep shrugs. 'It's different with everyone. The fight is in three hours. Maybe wait an hour.'

Nix looks over at her. 'Are you sure?'

'Absolutely.'

'Okay, let's get ready to do this. Murt, I presume you and your brothers will be shifting?'

'We're stronger, faster, and can pick up scents better as wolves. We'll probably be able to get closer to the fight without being noticed.'

'Thea, let's get you sorted. Fallon and Bas, do a full weapons check. I want us armed to the teeth.' Nix crouches down in front of Ronan. 'You need to stay here. You're coming back to the UK with us.'

'I appreciate the kind offer, I truly do. But I'm afraid I cannot leave.'

'What the fuck are you talking about,' Shep says. 'You want to stay?'

'I assure you I do not, but if I leave, my master will know something is wrong. Coming here as I have, is already too much of a risk. I need to go back to the castle. If I disappear, there is every chance the King will lock Davyn away. He's waited too long to get him back. He will not risk losing him again.'

'Davyn would want you safe.'

Ronan smiles at her. 'Again, I appreciate your concern. Trust me, I will only put Davyn's life at risk if I leave. I will not allow that.' He pauses and smiles to himself. 'I have loved that boy all his life. He must be saved.'

16

'I'm not so sure about this.'

Thea looks across at her father as she fixes her hair. 'We've been through this dozens of times. I know what I'm doing. Please stop worrying.'

'Are you kidding me? Of course I'm worrying. And he's not helping,' he adds, nodding towards Shep.

'Hey, what did I do?'

'It's what you're about to do that's bothering me.'

'I get it and I fully expect you to kill me if I step out of line. Believe it or not, I can actually feed without jumping on her.'

Court crosses his arms and throws an impressive glare in Shep's direction. 'How is that meant to make me feel better?'

Shep grins and shrugs. 'Fair point. Okay so don't take this the wrong way, but you probably should leave us to it. I don't want to get your fist in my face while I'm doing my thing.'

Court looks over at her again, clearly not happy about what's about to happen. 'Dad, please. Just wait in the living room. I'll be fine.'

With one last threatening glare at Shep, he leaves them alone, closing the door a little harder than necessary.

Thea smiles apologetically at Shep. 'Sorry about him. He's protective.'

'Too right he is. He loves you. So, you really sure you're on board with this? I knows it's a bit weird.'

'If one more person asks me that.'

He holds up his hands and laughs. 'Okay, okay. I get it. Neck or wrist?'

'Neck probably. I'll be wearing a choker necklace later so that will hide the marks.'

'Good plan.' He pats the bed beside him and Thea slowly sits down. She's nervous about doing this with Shep. She absolutely trusts him, but it feels like she's betraying Davyn somehow. And it's weird getting this close to Shep.

'Turn your body so you're facing me.'

She looks into his dark blue eyes.

'You can trust me. I fuck around and act the dick, but you can trust me on this, okay?'

She nods and closes her eyes. There's no way she can look at him, it's too personal. Thea smells his cologne as he leans closer.

'Relax.'

She licks her dry lips and nods. 'Sorry.'

'Ready?'

She nods again then winces as his teeth bury into the side of her neck. It's a very different experience to when Davyn fed from her. Maybe having feelings for him heightened the sensations. Maybe it was just the effect Davyn has on her. Even though it's far from unpleasant, she doesn't get carried away in the moment like she did with Davyn.

Shep may have told her to relax, but she can feel how tense he is. He's as uncomfortable about this as she is. Quicker than she expected, he moves away from her and she comes face to face with his vampire side. Shep's blue eyes dazzle her as he glances in her direction, before standing up and pacing the room. His fangs are very visible and are pretty damn enormous.

'Are you okay?'

He nods. 'Just give me a sec.' She watches him pace for another few minutes not sure if she should call someone in to help him. When he looks at her again, his eyes are back to normal and his fangs have retracted. 'Sorry about that. Your blood has a bit of a kick to it.'

'Are you sure you're okay?'

'I'll be bouncing off the walls for days, but yeah. All's good. Are you okay?'

'Yes. Thanks, Shep.'

'What are you thanking me for?'

'You didn't make that too weird.'

He smiles, and for the first time in months, it's genuine. 'I've got your back tonight, okay?' He grabs a tissue from the bathroom and presses it to the wound. 'Make sure you cover that. I'll leave you to get ready.'

'Thanks, Shep.'

She sits on the edge of the bed and looks over at the dress lying on the chair opposite her. She'll be seeing Davyn in a few hours. Something she's excited about, but also dreading.

After getting dressed, she opens the door to find Court outside her room. She holds her arms out to the side. 'How do I look?'

'Thea–'

She takes his hand and squeezes it. 'I'll be fine. I know the plan.'

'You're surrounded by trained fighters. One of us should be going in your place.'

'Yeah, and you're all vampires. Davyn's father and his men will be expecting the Blackjacks to attempt a rescue. Sending Fletch and I in is the best plan. What happened to the whole 'I'm second in command and not your father' speech you gave me? I'm pretty sure this classifies as one of those times.'

Court smirks at her. 'You don't listen to me the majority of the time and now that's the bit you decide to listen to and throw in my face.'

'I listen all the time. I just may have to work on the 'acting on it' part.'

'I'll go with that. But you're right. I'm shutting up.'

'I'd appreciate that,' she says with a smile. 'Is Shep okay? He went a little weird after he fed.'

'He's hyped up. Nix sent him outside to do a few laps, work off some of the energy.'

Fletch steps out of the other bedroom, wearing a very sharp black tux with a crisp white shirt. His blond hair is secured in a neat ponytail and he's clean shaved. 'You look very smart Mr. Anders.'

'Why thank you Mrs. Anders. You look rather fetching. You got your new ID in your purse?'

Although she has checked numerous times, she opens her clutch and takes out the newly acquired driving licence in the name of Simone Anders. Shep had arranged the new identities for them and had assured them both that the documentation will pass any inspections the security do. She slips the licence back in to her bag along with her lipstick, wallet with fake credit cards, and a phone with fake contacts and diary entries. 'I'm amazed Shep was able to pull all this off so fast.'

Fletch nods as he checks his own wallet. 'He's a genius when it comes to things like this, but for the love of God, please don't tell him I said that. Right, are you all set?'

She nods and smiles even though her stomach is twisting. 'As ready as I'll ever be.'

She follows Fletch and Court downstairs and in to the living room. The rest of the Blackjacks are there with the Whelan brothers, each one looking on edge.

Murt walks over to her and his light green eyes lock on to hers. There's something about looking in the eyes of the wolf that settles her. It has an instant calming effect and she has no idea why. 'We'll be nearby. I'll protect you.'

'Thanks, Murt.'

'We'll meet you outside.' Nix thanks him and takes his place in front of Thea and Fletch. 'Take no chances. If you see Davyn and think you can get him out, don't. I know it'll be horrible but you have to leave him there. We'll be right behind you and we will get him out.'

Both Thea and Fletch nod, even though Thea knows it will be nearly impossible for her to leave him there if they do find him.

~

Thea quietly watches as the Whelan brothers undress. The Land Rover is parked in the old barn waiting for the brothers to transform or shift or whatever they do. It's too risky to have four wolves wandering around the place so Nix will take two of them with Willow and Bas, while Fallon, Shep, Court and the other brothers will take the second car.

'You planning on watching the full show?' Garret asks, startling her.

She blinks, then blushes when she realises she's staring intently at the four men as they take their clothes off and stuff their jeans and tops into rucksacks lying on the floor.

'Sorry.'

Con laughs as he puts his boots in his bag. 'Don't mind him. Getting naked is part of the fun.'

'Does it hurt? When you change.'

'Little Miss Questions aren't you.'

'Garret,' Murt warns. 'Play nice. Our bones realign, our muscles change shape, and our skin stretches then grows fur. Yes Thea, it hurts but it doesn't last long.' He packs away the last of his clothes and they put the bags in the back of the car. With just their boxer shorts on, the brothers face the Blackjacks. 'We're not supposed to shift in front of other species. We're already breaking enough rules. I'd prefer not to add that one to the list. Give us five minutes, then we should be done.'

'How do we communicate once you've shifted?'

Murt grins at her. 'Short answer - you don't. Obviously you can talk to us but to put it bluntly, we'll be wolves. Wolves don't talk.'

Nix smiles at him. 'Of course not. We'll leave you to it.'

Thea follows the others out of the barn and Nix closes the door behind them.

'You really trust these guys not to eat us when they let their dark sides takes over?' The run didn't do much to calm Shep down. He's dancing from foot to foot and looks ready to pounce on anything that looks at him the wrong way.

Nix scowls at Shep. 'We have to trust them. Just like they have to trust us. It's the only way we'll get Dav out.'

Thea jumps as a muffled cry comes from inside the barn. For the next few minutes, the team stand in the cold, weapons in their hands as the bizarre sounds keep coming. Then silence followed by a deep, guttural growl.

Nix looks around at the team. 'Right. I think they're done. Ready?'

The team nods so Nix opens the door and they step back into the barn. Thea and the Blackjacks come to a stop when they see what's waiting inside. The Whelans are gone and in their place are four massive black wolves. She knew they'd be big but each one must reach up to her shoulders at the least. The slightly larger one at the front walks forward and looks at Nix.

'Murt?'

The wolf nods or at least Thea thinks it nods but nothing is making sense right now. Nix is talking to a wolf. It's hardly a daily occurrence.

'Wow,' Shep says from behind her. 'You're fucking big dogs.'

One of the wolves at the back growls and Murt snarls at him, silencing him.

'What? I meant that as a compliment,' Shep says. 'Seriously. I mean I'm impressed. Doesn't happen often.'

The one at the back that growled, snaps at him as he walks past. 'I'm presuming you're Garret.' The wolf cocks his leg and Shep jumps out of the way but the wolf winks at him and walks away.

'Asshole,' Shep shouts after him. 'I was trying to be nice.'

'C'mon,' Nix says. 'We don't want Thea and Fletch to be late.'

The four wolves jump into the back of the cars with the Blackjacks. Court walks over to her and hugs her. 'No chances. Remember your training. Stick to Fletch and keep your head down. Don't attract attention to yourself.'

'I know what I'm doing, Dad. I'll be careful, I promise.'

He nods, then hugs her again before he climbs into one of the cars. Fletch holds out his hand. 'Ready?'

'Yeah. Let's get this over with.' He leads her to the BMW Ethan arranged for them and opens the door for her. As Fletch pulls away from the barn Thea meets Shep's eyes. He winks at her and she smiles back. She just hopes he's as good as he thinks he is.

Thea takes Fletch's hand as they watch the helicopter come down to land. The only coordinates they were given was to an expensive hotel about half an hour away from the cottage where they met the Whelans. The receptionist had smiled sweetly at them before instructing that they wait outside for the helicopter which was on the way.

Davyn's father was going to extreme lengths to keep the location of the fights a secret. She glances over at the other three couples waiting with them on the paved walkway. Like Fletch and herself, they're dressed for a night at a prestigious event, looking relaxed - even excited at what awaits them.

'Can Shep pick us up if we're in the air?'

Fletch wraps his arms around her, pulling her close so he can talk without being overheard. 'That guy is scary good at tracking. He'll find us.'

She looks over at the other couples, catching the eye of a stunning blonde woman. The woman smiles sweetly before turning back to her partner.

'They're looking forward to the evening. What kind of people get dressed up to watch people fight to the death?'

Fletch grunts as he lifts his head to watch the approaching helicopter. 'Sick ones. That's who.'

As soon as the craft lands, they are ushered inside and minutes later, are flying over the hotel. She wants to touch the bite mark on her neck, just to make sure Shep did actually feed from her. Knowing Shep is below them somewhere, tracking her is reassuring, but only if Shep is actually as good at tracking as everyone seems to think he is. Nothing is a sure thing – especially in this world.

They land about fifteen minutes later and are led in to what appears to be a large barn. A short, stocky man enters and smiles widely at the occupants. 'Welcome ladies and gentlemen. If you'll follow me, I have to ask you to undergo a small security check and then we can proceed inside.'

Thea looks around but she can't figure out where they are. She pulls her wrap around her shoulders and shivers as they move to a set of tables at the front of the barn. Four men are waiting for them and spend the next ten minutes removing any electronic devices they find before handing purses and wallets back to the group.

They follow the same man through a set of double doors and into what could be a reception bar in any of the best hotels. Waiters are on hand with trays of champagne and fruit juice. Thea takes a glass of juice, even though she would give anything for a bit of Dutch courage right about now.

The short man claps his hands and waits patiently for silence. 'In a few moments you will be taken to the viewing area where each of our fighters will be on display. Stats, previous wins and the like, will be listed on each of the holding cells. I assure you they are secured and at no time will your safety be in jeopardy. Until then, please help yourself to a beverage.' He bows his head and disappears through the far door.

The murmur of conversation and the clinking of glasses quickly fills the room. Fletch takes Thea to one of the more private booths at the side of the room and sits down beside her. He smiles as he wraps his arm around her shoulder and pulls her close. To anyone looking on, they appear to be a couple cosying up to each other. Fletch leans closer to her ear. 'Shep can track you even in the air.'

'How did you know I was thinking that?'

'Doesn't take a genius to figure out. He does big himself up quite a bit but I've seen him in action. He's scary good at what he does.'

She smiles at him. 'Security doesn't seem to be as heavy in here. I only see two guards.'

Fletch nods. 'Agree. They probably figure they've whittled out any trouble makers by this stage.'

'Wait until a group of pissed off Blackjacks arrives.'

'Indeed.' He nods towards the far door. 'We have to go in there.'

'I know. Oh god, I don't think I can look at the fighters in the face knowing what's going to happen to them.'

'I'm with you there, but we have no choice. We have to act like everyone else here. We've got more money than sense and are super excited about spending an evening watching innocent men killing each other.'

'Fletch—'

'Glen,' he hisses sharply and Thea grimaces to herself. Less than half an hour in and she's already called him by his real name.

'I'm sorry.'

He laughs and clinks her glass, urging her with his eyes to play along. Thea forces what she hopes is a convincing smile on her face. 'Hey. It's okay. You're doing great. I know it's going to be damn near impossible, but you have to go in there and look at the fighters like you would runners before a horse race. The only thing on everyone's mind is picking the winner at the best odds so they can go home a little richer.'

'What happens if he's in there?'

Fletch takes her hand and squeezes it hard. He looks into her eyes, and she knows the gesture is from Fletch to Thea and has nothing to do with their cover. 'Then we hope Shep gets here fast so he doesn't have to fight.'

The door at the end of the room opens, cutting off all conversation. The man gestures for them to follow him inside, so Fletch gets up and takes Thea's hand. She keeps her glass of fruit juice with her. If she didn't have something to squeeze, she's sure they would notice her trembling.

Like the reception room, the light in the adjoining room is dim with plenty of shadows. The floor is made of polished concrete and the echo of expensive shoes fills the void. Two rows of steel cages line the room with a wide walkway down the middle. Each cell houses a vampire, naked from the waist up and chained with their arms over their heads and secured to each side of the cell.

As she finds herself guided by Fletch to the first cell, she notices that each of the fighters has a thick gag in their mouth prising it open, leaving their fangs standing proud. A metal plaque is attached to the front of each cell, with a piece of laminated paper listing the fighter's number, weight, height, and their fighting history.

Just like Fletch said, the other guests are examining the fighters, like they are prize horses before a championship race. Thea tries to keep her eyes averted from the faces of the caged men, discussing their stats with Fletch just like everyone else is doing. After the second man, she knows she has to look at their faces. If he is here, she wants to see him for herself.

She lifts her head and instantly regrets her decision. The man she's facing looks barely older than her. His bruised face is distorted by the gag as he snarls down at her. His blood red eyes target her, glowing brighter when he pulls on his chains, trying to either free himself or kill her - she's not sure which. A crude black symbol she doesn't recognise, has been tattooed to his scalp on either side of his head. The thick lines are clearly visible through his close cropped hair.

'Why are his eyes red?' she whispers to Fletch, even though the sounds from the guests and the fighters will mask anything she says.

'I'm guessing Blood Fever. They must've given the lad that new drug or something similar.'

'What does that mean?' she asks, nodding to his head.

'My vampire is a little rusty but I think it's a number of some sort. Probably his fighter number.' He leads her through the crowd passing cages of fighters. Her feet plant themselves to the concrete when she spots the tips of two wings peeking above the heads of the crowd a little ahead of them. She nudges Fletch and he grips her hand. 'C'mon.'

They weave through the lavishly dressed people and an invisible hand grips her heart, squeezing it firmly in its grasp. As they pass through the onlookers, more of the winged vampire comes in to view. His head is hanging down, but there's no mistaking the Celtic tattoos covering his chest and arms. Like the other fighters, his hair is shaved close to his head so everyone can see the tattoo on his scalp.

'Oh my god.' Fletch squeezes her hand as they come to a stop in front of him. Fletch leans closer to her. 'Don't look love. We need to go. Now.'

She tries to move around Fletch, but he digs his fingers into her arm.

'Thea, I'm asking you not to look at him. Please.'

'Why not?' she hisses, panic threatening to drive her to tears.

'He's been badly hurt, love.'

'Ladies and gentlemen,' their host says from beside Davyn's cage. 'This is our star for this evening's fight. As you can see, he's a Prime, and a highly effective fighter. His owner decided to Bind him due to his unpredictable nature, but that will just make for a more interesting fight.' He bangs on the bars of the cage but after getting no reaction from Davyn, he rams his fist into Davyn's back.

'What does he mean by Bind?' Her question fades away as Davyn rears back, sending the crowd into a clapping frenzy as Davyn growls and pulls at his chains. His struggles die away as he looks at her.

Thea bites the inside of her cheek, trying to keep the tears at bay. He's unrecognisable. His right eye is a bloody mess with what looks like pieces of glass embedded in the skin surrounding it. His broad body is thinner than she remembers, his ribs clearly visible through the blood and dirt ingrained on his skin. Dried blood surrounds both wrists and covers a thick cut on his arm.

But that's not that part that sickens her the most. It's the thick sutures sealing his mouth shut that threatens to force the scream from her throat.

His deep red eye stays on her as she takes in each of his injuries, every single cut and bruise, then back to his mouth and those horrendous stitches.

He recognises her. She's sure of it.

Fletch claps as the man hits Davyn again. 'Play along. We'll get him out.'

She forces her hands to do their best impersonation of a clap. Davyn locks on to her eyes again, and she knows without a doubt he knows exactly who she is. She wants nothing more than to get him out of there, but she can't. Even though they've found him, there's nothing they can do except stand and watch as he fights in the ring.

Davyn tilts his head to the side and his nostrils flare. He growls and pulls at his chains.

'He's getting upset, love. Let's go.'

She allows Fletch to lead her away from the cage and out to the seating area around the arena.

'Why was he calm one minute and then got upset?' Thea asks, as they take their seats.

'I'm only guessing here, but there's a chance he's a tad upset someone else fed from you.'

'What? He'll pick up on that?'

'Oh definitely. Shep's scent will be all over you. But that's what we need right now. Shep should be on his way. Just hold tight.'

~

Davyn waits a few seconds before he lifts his head again. He didn't want to attract any unnecessary attention to the couple. He blinks a few times to clear his vision then stares after the woman. The long red evening dress accents her lean form as she makes her way from the viewing area towards the ring.

The crowd quickly swallows the couple, hiding them from sight. He scans the crowd but they're gone. He could have sworn it was her. The guy beside her looked like Fletch too. But that doesn't explain the scent of another male on her. Someone had fed from her. He recognises the scent, but his brain is too sluggish to identify whose scent it is.

She can't be here. It makes no sense. The Blackjacks wouldn't let her come in to a situation like this. Even if Nix approved it, Court would have a serious fucking problem.

He looks for the woman again, but there's no sign of her. It must have been an hallucination. He's had a few since his father increased the dose of the altered Prime blood. He's also heard a few of the spectators mention how scary his red eyes are.

He knew he was well and truly fucked as soon as he heard that. The Fever has a firm hold on him. At best, he probably has a day or two of useful fighting left in him, before he starves to death. That's assuming his father lets him live even that long.

He catches a glimpse of the woman again. She's standing with 'the Fletch lookalike' at the door to the arena seating area. She is definitely looking at him like she knows him. His heart beats a little faster in his chest, and it has nothing to do with the adrenaline building in preparation for the upcoming fight.

It's definitely her. It's Thea.

He doesn't know how, or why she's here, but she is.

So he did get her out of the lab after all. She's been safe all this time. Knowing that makes everything worth it. He'd live like this forever if it means he got her out. She smiles at him, then disappears through the door with Fletch to take their seats.

She's going to watch the fight. He knows he's scheduled to fight fifth, after the rest of his cell mates have been whittled down to half their original number. He knows his father wants him dead, so he plans on chaining him in the centre of the ring to make it easier for his opponent to take him down. If Thea wasn't here to witness it, he'd happily let that happen.

His thoughts become muddled, so he closes his eyes, desperately trying to hang on to what little sanity he has left. He doesn't want her to see him be torn to pieces. But he doesn't want her to see him kill either. Whatever happens during his fight, it will ruin her image of him forever.

If he could laugh he would. She's seen him like this. No matter if he survives or dies, seeing him caged like an animal with his lips sewn shut will stick in her memories.

His arms tug at the chains but it's not a conscious act. The blood-fuelled side of him wants out. But so does the other side of him. He wants out of the chains, out of the cage, but more than anything he wants the painful stitches gone so he can call out to her. Warn her, tell her to leave this place, tell her to close her eyes and forget this nightmare.

Despair and helplessness threaten to turn the panic that's barely under control, into a full breakdown. He concentrates on Thea, blocking out the taunting of the guard as he shows off the prize fighter for the evening.

Then he feels her. It's faint, but he could nearly cry when the familiar feeling soothes him. Being close to her is somehow reigniting the blood bond. It shouldn't happen after being apart for months, but he's certain what he's feeling is real.

He concentrates on her, using more effort than he should to keep his thoughts from wandering.

But he loses her again. He's barely strong enough to control his own thoughts, let alone connect with her. All he can do is hope Fletch looks after her and doesn't let her see what's about to happen.

Shep stands outside the hotel, surrounded by the stench of wet dog. It doesn't help that the rest of the team are gathered behind him, waiting for him to tell them where to go. Which he's sorely tempted to do. Having a fucking audience isn't helping him sort through the smells around him.

'Okay, you're all doing my head in. Back away all two and four-legged distractions. I can't do this with you lot breathing down my neck.'

He glares over his shoulder as they all give him the space he needs.

'Thank you. Now please keep quiet and let me concentrate.'

He closes his eyes again and concentrates on Thea. Her blood is making him twitchy for some reason. He's fed from a hell of a lot of people - both human and vampire, and they all have a different effect on him. Thea's blood is like nothing he's had before. Which, right now, is fucking brilliant. It doesn't take long to get an image of her in his head.

'They took a helicopter.' He turns to his left and points ahead of him. 'They went that way.'

'Is she okay?'

Shep nods at Court. 'Yeah. Fletch is making her feel safe. She's got this.'

They get back in the cars and Shep is thankful everyone in his car keeps their mouths shut. He doesn't want to fuck this up and risk Dav, Thea, and Fletch. No pressure at all. He closes his eyes again and rests his forehead against the window. He can still feel her, but thanks to them taking to the air, it's not a clear image.

He lets his vampire side out and the scent strengthens.

'You okay?' Fallon asks from beside him. 'You look wired.'

'Just making sure I don't lose her.'

Fallon surprises the hell out of him by squeezing his arm.

Shep blocks out everything else around him and falls into a trance like state as he concentrates on Thea and nothing else. Every now and again he gives directions to Court until he eventually tells him to stop the car. Shep opens his eyes and climbs out. He growls and his eyes glow brightly.

'She's near. Leave the cars here.'

'Are you picking up on any company?'

He slowly nods. 'A few dozen. Male and female, human and vampire. We're too far away for them to get a lock on us.' He shakes himself out of his trance and takes a deep breath. He needs to beat the crap out of something soon. He feels supercharged after Thea's blood.

'Okay, I'll let Ethan know,' Nix says as she takes in their surroundings. 'He can send one of his people to pick us up. Take everything from the cars. We won't be coming back to them.'

Shep makes sure he has his guns and knives then shuts the car door and leads them through the trees to a boring looking barn.

'Huh. That's not in any way exciting.'

'Are you sure it's the right place?' Court asks.

'Yes. She's in there.' He smiles as another scent hits him. 'Dav too. He's hurt though.'

Nix turns to Murt standing to her right. 'I think it's time to go hunting.'

He nods and the four wolves stalk towards the building.

~

Thea stares at the fighting ring surrounded by plush seats, each with a holder for a drink. The large circular pit must be at least two stories deep and is topped with thick wire. Signs are attached to the wire mesh roof at various points, warning of the risk of electrocution.

She follows Fletch around the ring and lowers into a seat in the second row from the front. Two men are raking the rough sawdust floor of the pit, doing a terrible job of hiding the dark patches of fresh blood left from previous fights.

Thea stares ahead of her in a daze. She's trying to play her part, for Davyn's sake, but mentally she's still in the viewing room staring up at him. She'd spent many hours wondering where he is, how he was, and what's being done to him, but actually seeing him in the flesh, she realised nothing could have prepared her for the truth. She knows he's strong and tough, but the Davyn she just saw hanging in the cage was hurting. Behind those terrifying blood red eyes, he's in pain and, right now, there's nothing she can do about it.

The lights go down, plunging the spectators into darkness and highlighting the pit. 'Lie on my shoulder and keep your eyes closed. Put yourself somewhere else.'

She does as she's told, grateful Fletch is being so protective of her. The first few fights go by in a blur of shouting for her. Around her, the crowd feeds off the blood sport in front of them. Fight after fight watched while drinking expensive champagne.

138

She has no idea how much time passes, how many fights she hides from, caught between the need to see Davyn again and not wanting to be anywhere near this place.

Then the crowd surges to their feet, the murmur of excited chatter escalating as the next pair of fighters are led in to the ring. As soon as Fletch's body tenses beside her, she knows it's Davyn's turn.

Before she can stop herself, she opens her eyes and gasps when she sees the occupants of the ring.

A tall, scrawny male is standing to one side, his lips pulled back from his fangs as he faces his opponent. Davyn stands opposite him, held back by three guards as his ankle is chained to the centre of the ring.

'Why are they doing that?'

Fletch shakes his head. 'I don't know love. Can't be for any good reason.'

Once secured, Davyn looks up at the roaring crowd, searching for something. Her stomach clenches when he finds his target - her.

He looks back at the other fighter and stalks around the edge of the ring. The other vampire follows his movements, keeping the same distance between them as he moves position. Once Davyn is facing Thea and Fletch, he closes his eyes. His voice echoes in her head as clearly as if he was standing in front of her.

'Close your eyes, Thea.'

'What?'

'What?' Fletch asks, confused.

'Davyn's talking to me. In my head.'

'He is? What's he saying?'

'Close your eyes.'

'Then I suggest you do as he says. He doesn't want you seeing this.'

Davyn opens his eyes again and she nods at him. With one last look at him, she does as he asked.

As soon as her eyes close, the crowd explodes, chanting a strange word, which she only assumes is the mark on his head.

Fletch pulls her on to his knee facing him as the sounds of flesh hitting flesh fills the air. He presses his lips to her ear as his hands roam over her back. 'Keep your eyes shut, love.'

She tries to keep her eyes shut, but they have other ideas. She looks over the edge and watches in horror as Davyn crouches and faces the other male, ready to continue fighting. Her eyes open wide as she watches the large male circle the smaller one, like a lion cornering a gazelle, the heavy chain dragging along the ground behind him.

The crowd roars as Davyn's kick sends the other vampire crashing in to the wall behind him. Before his opponent can push himself upright, Davyn launches himself across the ring, grabbing the male before he runs out of chain. Fletch turns her face around and looks her in the eye. 'He didn't want you to see this.'

Stamping feet and loud cheers fill the ring. The bell sounds, signalling the end of the fight. Thea turns back to the ring and peers in horror at the victor. Fresh blood covers Davyn's hands and arms. The other vampire's body lies in a crumpled heap on the sawdust ground. The jagged wound on his throat emptying on to the dirt.

Fletch puts himself in her line of vision again. 'Hey. That wasn't him.'

Thea stares at the body at the side of the ring. Davyn ripped his throat out with his bare hands. While she's glad Fletch stopped her from seeing the deed itself, knowing that he had done that - that he was capable of doing that, made her stomach recoil.

Fletch forcefully lifts her chin so Thea is looking at him. 'It wasn't him,' he repeats slowly. 'That was Blood Fever. He couldn't help it. He needs blood Thea. It was an instinct he couldn't fight.'

'Where's Shep?'

Fletch shakes his head then smiles widely as an alarm goes off. 'I'd imagine he's just arrived.'

Shep peers out from behind the wall, then ducks, as a round embeds itself in the stone above his head. 'These Irish fuckers are beginning to get on my nerves, boss. Any ideas how we even the odds a little?'

Nix ducks as a wolf leaps over her head and tears the head off one of their attackers.

'Forget it. I think that'll work,' Shep mutters as he takes another one down. A second wolf joins the first and, with help from the Blackjacks, they clear the entrance to the pit. Court leads the way inside with one of the wolves. Shep has given up trying to figure out who is who. The dogs should be wearing different coloured collars so he can tell the difference.

The team enters the holding area lined with cages, most of them full. No sign of Dav though.

'He must be fighting,' Nix says. 'Where's Thea?'

Shep nods to the door ahead of them and they move forward. Court opens the door, letting Nix through ahead of him. When a pack of wolves and armed vampires appear in the seating area, the punters rush around like a bunch of headless chickens. Shep nearly pisses himself laughing as well dressed males and females scream and desperately try to get out the door at the far side. Let them run. It's the armed fuckers around the edge of the pit that they need to take care of.

He spots Thea and Fletch at the far side of the room. He grabs Bas and they rush around the outside of the pit to them.

'I told you I'm a fucking legend at tracking.' He whistles and one of the wolves turns to look at him. 'Fuck, didn't think that would work. Get these two out?'

'No!' Thea moves away from him and points into the pit. 'Not without him.'

Shep and Bas peer inside and both fall silent. Dav is staring up at them with his fucking lips sewn shut. 'They put him through the Binding,' Shep tells Nix over his comms. 'His lips are sewn shut.'

'Get Thea out of there now! We'll deal with Davyn.' Court throws a vampire over his shoulder and looks over at Thea. He points to the door, leaving no doubt about what he wants her to do.

'I can't leave him.'

Shep turns her face away from Dav. 'You trusted me to find you and I did. Now trust me to get him out of here. Go!'

Thea looks down at Davyn one last time then lets Fletch and one of the wolves take her outside.

Nix hurries over and looks down at Davyn. 'Oh God. Can you get him out of there, Bas?'

He takes off his gloves and places his hand on the electrical box powering the cage roof. It takes less than a second to unlock the box and, after turning off the power to the roof, he focuses on the locks securing the wire in place over the pit. 'Once I deal with these and we open the hatch, he'll be out of there in a flash.

'He needs to get out of here on his own two feet,' Fallon says as she joins them. 'We can't risk darting him while he's like that. It'll take too much to bring him down and that could kill him.'

'Only one option from what I can see,' Shep says. 'You gotta let Dav go.'

'Are you crazy?' his sister shouts over the radio.

'I second Willow,' Bastian says.

'It's not that bad an idea,' Fallon says, and Shep smiles. Trust her to want to go for the risky option.

Nix looks at him. 'You seriously want to release the vampire suffering from Blood Fever?'

'We need something to tip the scales in our favour. He's the best fighter we have. Add Fever to that and we may have a chance. This is his fight anyway. As long as we stay out of his way, he can take them all out for us.'

'He's barely alive, Shep. This could kill him.'

'You know Dav well enough. Do you think he'd want to die in chains or fighting as a Blackjack?'

'Damn it,' Nix mutters and it's all the answer Shep needs.

'I'll see to Dav. You get everyone out of the way.'

She nods and they lift the heavy grid into the pit. Shep vaults over the railing and lands on the floor just in front of Davyn. His team mate crouches, getting ready to pounce at him. Shep isn't an overly emotional guy but when he gets a proper look at his teammate, his breath catches in his throat.

His right eye and the right side of his face is a mass of dried blood. Shards of glass are embedded in his cheek and probably in his eye too. He lifts his head a little and Shep curses loudly when he sees the crude wire puncturing Dav's lips.

'You take it easy, Dav. I'm here to help. I need to cut that chain off you. Then you can go home. You going to let me?'

Davyn looks down at the chain around his ankle then back at Shep.

He slowly rights himself and drops his arms to his side.

'Okay. I'm going to take that as you're not going to eat me… hopefully.'

Shep takes out his gun and points it at the chain. Shep shoots one of the links, freeing Davyn. But it seems Dav isn't in the mood for thanking him. He leaps at Shep, pinning him to the blood soaked dirt. Shep grimaces as Davyn wraps his hands around his throat, growling deep in his chest as Dav squeezes.

'Back… off. It's me.'

Davyn's nostrils flare as he struggles to breathe but that's not going to help Shep. Dav could easily kill him before he collapses himself. Bas appears behind Davyn and tries to separate the two but Davyn is being controlled by instinct.

'He fed from Thea so he could find her,' Bas says as he pulls at Dav's arm. 'He needed to track her. That's it. Let him go, Dav.'

Shep feels like a fucking idiot for not realising why Davyn was so pissed off. No doubt he could smell Shep all over Thea from miles away. Dav frowns and slowly releases Shep, much to his surprise. He thought he was dead for sure. He scrambles out of the way and Bas helps him to his feet. 'You okay?'

He nods. 'Thanks for the save.'

Davyn looks from them to the few guards still standing in the viewing area. He runs at the wall and leaps up, grabbing the edge in his hands and pulling himself over the edge.

'Watch your backs,' Nix shouts over the radio. 'Davyn's loose and he's angry. Keep an eye on him, but steer clear.'

Shep watches for a minute as Davyn moves through the room, slashing, and generally tearing anything in his way to shreds. He's one hell of a killing machine, which isn't exactly a good thing. It's working for them right now, but getting him home could be a problem.

'We've got more company heading our way!' Fallon shouts from the upper level.

Shep and one of the wolves follows after Dav and the others. From the sound of the shots outside, Flann sent reinforcements to stop them from taking his prized possession. Shep takes down two of the henchmen in their way, freezing when Davyn spins to look at him. Shep keeps his gun directed at Dav, waiting to see what he does. He doesn't want to shoot his mate but he will if Davyn decides to get too close.

Davyn frowns as he stares over at him, then turns away. Shep blows out a long breath. That was a little too close for comfort. He's going to need to stay away from Dav until his scent wears off Thea. He slams his fist into another vampire, driving him back against the wall before he shoots the asshole in the head.

'Shep? You okay?' Nix shouts in his earpiece.

'All good, Nix. Just watching his back. You out?'

'Clearing the way as much as we can.'

Shep shoots another vamp that gets too close as Dav coolly and methodically clears any resistance in front of him. 'Pastry dickhead' seems to have an endless supply of idiots willing to die for him. He takes down another and smiles. If they want to die he's more than willing to help them out.

One of the goons grabs Shep by the shoulder, spinning him around. Shep shoves the dickhead off but, instead of fighting back, the vampire laughs at him. He looks down to see what's got the fucker's attention and grimaces. The asshole stuck a syringe in Shep's side.

Shep pulls the syringe out and curses when he realises it's empty. He's about to ask the guy what he gave him, but Fallon takes the vampire out with a shot to the head before he can say anything. Shep quickly hides the syringe in his hand before she can see it. The syringe barely went in to his skin. If he mentions it to her, she'll go all medic on him, and more than likely take him out of the fight. No way that's going to happen.

'You okay?'

He nods, even though his side is burning from whatever he was given. Maybe it did go in a little further than he thought? Whatever. He'll make it back to the UK and deal with it then.

'What are you doing then? Move!'

He rubs his side then stuffs the syringe in his pocket just in case Fletch needs it at some stage, before following after Fallon.

Thea paces the back of the helicopter. She glances at Fletch, but his attention is solely focused on outside. He won't let her go anywhere near the door. As soon as Ethan's man had arrived with the helicopter, she was told, in no uncertain terms, not to set foot off it.

She checks the gun in her hand once more, but it's ready to be fired if needed. Fletch had insisted on giving her a tranq gun in case Davyn tried to get near her. She hopes she doesn't have to use it, but will, if she has to.

'Keep back, Thea. They're coming.'

She ducks into the cockpit as she had promised she'd do, and peers around the corner as, one by one, the Blackjacks burst in to the hold, each one with their weapons raised and directed to the back of the craft. Court looks over his shoulder at her. 'That gun better be ready, Thea.'

'It is.'

He takes a step back, putting himself between Thea and the open door. She peers around Court and her breath catches in her throat. Davyn is standing at the bottom of the ramp. He takes a step forward and then another, coming further into the helicopter. Thea covers her scream when the light hits him.

The first thing she sees is blood. It's on his face, and dripping from numerous cuts on his chest, and from his hands. She didn't think it was possible, but he looks worse than he did when she saw him in the pit. He could be a monster out of a horror movie. Chains hang from his wrists and torn wings, giving him a zombie-like appearance. He growls as he approaches, his movements slow and predatory.

Nix steps closer, her hands in the air.

'Davyn, it's me. Nix. Do you remember me?'

He tilts his head to the side as his red eye turns towards her. His chest rises and falls quickly and his nostrils flair as he hungrily pulls air in to his lungs.

'We want to take you home, Davyn. We want to help you.'

Then he looks over at Thea and his entire expression changes briefly. Almost like for that fleeting moment, he recognises her.

Then everything goes wrong.

The room erupts in shouts as he moves towards her. Thea knows they're just protecting her, but clearly Davyn sees it differently. He sees them as opponents he needs to defeat.

He throws Fallon against the side of the hold then tries to grab a handful of wolf hair as one of them tackles him. Thea doesn't know how he can stand, let alone fight in his condition, but it doesn't matter which of the team he targets, he takes them down.

Thea shouts and jumps back as Davyn kicks Court in the chest, sending him flying backward, narrowly missing her. Thea scrambles back from the warring vampires, dodging her father as he wrestles with Davyn. Court twists around and manages to throw Davyn off him. Davyn crashes into the wall of the craft, smearing blood along the metal. He crouches down, the muscles in his arms pulsing as he holds his position, poised to pounce again.

Everything goes quiet for a few seconds as the Blackjacks and the Whelans wait to see what Davyn does next. Thea freezes as Davyn looks directly at her again. Under the bruises, blood, and gruesome stitches, he's still her Davyn. The realisation of what she just admitted to herself, hits as hard as a punch to her gut.

She cares about him. Deeply. All these months she thought it was infatuation or a crush, but it's so much more. Before Court can stop her, Thea ducks under his arm and approaches Davyn. She lowers the tranq gun, preferring to talk to him instead of drugging him. Thea stops in front of him and crouches down.

'Thea, shoot him. Now,' Court hisses from behind her.

She waves her hand behind her, trying to tell him to back off and let her do this alone. Davyn tilts his head to the side as he stares at her. Wherever she looks, the horrendous wounds dominate. She sniffs as the tears begin to fall.

'Hey, Davyn. Do you remember me?'

He frowns as he silently stares at her. His nostrils flare as he takes quick, shallow breaths. His broad chest rising and falling faster than it should as he struggles to breathe.

'We're going to take you home. But we can't do that unless you calm down. Please, Davyn. Let us help you.'

Davyn is so focused on Thea, he doesn't notice Fallon coming up behind him with a syringe. She manages to empty the contents in the back of his leg before he turns around to attack. The sedative hits him fast. His legs go from under him followed quickly by his arms. He falls face down on the hard deck, but he keeps fighting. His fingernails scrape the metal floor as he tries to pull himself upright.

Ignoring the rest of the Blackjacks, Thea crawls around him. He meets her eyes as he finally settles on the ground, allowing the sedative to do its job.

'It's okay. You're safe now.' His hand slowly moves nearer to hers and she squeezes it, not caring about the blood. 'It's okay. You're safe,' she repeats as his eye closes and his body stills.

~

Thea looks at the person she hurt with her childish actions all those months ago. When she disobeyed Nix and left the compound unaccompanied, she had set in motion a series of events that nearly killed someone she cares about. Davyn came to save her and paid for her freedom with his own. That's something she can never forgive herself for. If Davyn has any sense he'll be thinking the same thing.

If he ever wakes up.

Davyn is strapped to a heavy gurney in the centre of the craft's hold with padded restraints securing him to the gurney as Fletch sees to him. Judging by the look on his face, Davyn isn't doing so good. You didn't need medical experience to know that. Every visible inch of skin is covered in blood. It's even oozing from around the thick shackles secured to his wrists.

Nix is leaning on the head of his bed, deep in conversation with Fletch. She doesn't know what's being said but whatever it is, Fletch keeps shaking his head.

Her eyes move from Davyn to the wolves. Two of the brothers are still in wolf form thanks to injuries they received while helping to get Davyn out. They won't be able to shift back until they're stronger. More pain thanks to her actions. The younger brother, Fionn is cleaning a large cut over Garret's eye while Con helps Fallon deal with Murtagh.

The oldest brother is lying on his side, his thick black hair covered in blood. She knows a lot of it isn't his, except for the blood coating the fur on his side. One of the vampires had stabbed him from what she heard. He's trying to shift back but can't and that's not helping Fallon treat him. She seems to be struggling with all the fur in her way.

'They're all in good hands.'

She nods against Court's chest. 'I know. I'm sorry for not shooting him. I didn't want to do that to him.'

'I know, but that could have backfired – badly. If I can't trust you to do what I say, your future with the team won't be a long one.'

He gently nudges her away from him so he can look at her face. 'Next time I tell you to shoot someone you do it.'

'So there will be a next time?'

'After more training. You'll also need to prove to me you can follow orders. Even from me.'

'Thanks, Dad.'

He smiles and rests his head against the bulkhead then closes his eyes. Just like everyone else on the team he's tired, bleeding, and thinking about what he witnessed in that barn.

Getting Davyn back is only the beginning. She knows that. After seeing a little of what he went through, she fears they may never be able to help him. Never be able to help him get over what he's been through.

Looking at the faces of the Blackjacks in the hold with her, she knows they share her doubts. There's no celebratory slaps on the back. No words of congratulations. Each of them are quietly staring over at Davyn like she is. Even Shep who would usually be full of banter, is lost in his thoughts as he focuses on the floor in between his boots.

It will be some time before any of them will be able to forget what they witnessed today.

21

Thea stifles a yawn behind her hand and adjusts her position on the couch. They've been sitting in the small seating area next to the medical room for over an hour. Her father and Nix are leaning against the far wall, Shep is sitting on the ground with Bastian and Con, leaving the couch for herself, Fionn, and Willow.

Each of the Blackjacks and wolves look bone weary and all need a shower and medical attention. Bastian's forehead is bleeding from a deep cut over his eyebrow. Shep's hand is pressed tightly to his side and his face is smeared with blood, Fionn and Con are scratched and bleeding from too many wounds to count, and a bone is broken in one of Willow's enormous blue wings. Like the others, Willow had refused treatment, leaving everyone to deal with Davyn, Murt, and Garret who are more critical.

The housekeeper, Gwen, opens the door, carrying a tray in her hands. 'No point in you all collapsing while you wait. Fletcher and Fallon have enough to deal with right now.' She places the tray laden with soft drinks, juice, and slices of various flavours of cake on the small table in the centre of the room. 'We're a little low on blood at the moment, so Ethan has arranged for some of his team to come over so you can feed. They should be here in about thirty minutes.'

Nix smiles as she reaches out for a bottle of lemonade. 'Thank you, Gwen.'

'How is Davyn?'

Nix shakes her head. 'Not good.'

'I'll let you know when Ethan's people arrive. You all look like you could do with a good feed.' Gwen smiles at Fionn and Conal. 'Is there anything in particular I can get for you both?'

'We're grand,' Con replies. 'Thanks anyway.'

'If you change your mind please let me know.' Gwen nods then leaves the room, closing the door silently behind her.

Less than a second later, Fletch opens the door and steps inside. 'Well?' Nix asks before Fletch can open his mouth.

Fletch rests his hands on his hips and leans against the door frame. 'Garret is awake and in a foul mood.'

Con smiles at that. 'Sounds about right.'

'He'll be fine. Bit of a headache but with some rest he'll be back on form. He's managed to shift back so that's a good start. Murt is still unconscious after surgery. Fallon repaired the wound but he's lost a lot of blood. He's still in wolf form, but I'm confident he'll recover. They're through the first door on the right, if you want to sit with them. And, I want to have a look at the two of you once I'm done here.'

Fletch moves out of the way to let the brothers past him.

'How's Davyn,' Nix asks once they've left.

'He's in a bad way, guys. Come in.'

He leads them in to the medical bay and walks over to the bed against the far wall. The figure lying on the crisp white sheet is a far cry from the Davyn she went shopping with, all those months ago. His body is still big and broad, but it's peppered with scars and bandages.

She takes a small step closer and bites her bottom lip. Even cleaned of the blood, his beautiful face is unrecognisable. His eyebrow rings are gone, his right eye is buried under yet another thick bandage, and Fallon is leaning over him, gently teasing thick sutures from his cracked lips.

On the table next to him are the shackles that were fastened around Davyn's wrists. Nix picks up one of them and frowns as she turns it over in her hand. Dried blood covers the thick spikes embedded all over the inside. Thea turns away from them and her eyes are instantly drawn to his wrists. Thankfully, Fletch has already bandaged his wounds so she can't see the deep holes left by the shackles.

Fletch runs a hand over his hair, brushing it back from his face. 'Physically, he's got broken ribs and more than his fair share of cuts and bruises. His right eye is badly damaged. Pulled a fair bit of glass out of it and his face. Depending on how he gets on over the next few days, it may regenerate to a certain degree, but I'd be surprised if his sight isn't permanently affected. Fallon is trying to get the sutures out of his lips, but it's no easy task. He's so dehydrated she's having trouble getting the damn things out without causing more damage. They used the same wire to stitch his wings in place.'

Thea wraps her arms around herself, horrified by what she is hearing.

'Are his fangs gone?' Nix asks

Fletch nods. 'Until Fallon manages to get the wire out of his lips I can't examine his mouth properly, but it looks like his fangs are gone. His father put him through the full Binding ritual. He left nothing out.' Fletch gestures to Davyn's neck. 'They even fed from him. His neck is a mess and so are his arms. Pretty much ripped him apart. There's also the issue of his wings. I haven't removed the shackles from them yet, but as you can see, the good one is badly broken. It'll take a few hours to assess the damage fully, but to put it bluntly -

they're fucked. I may need to call in some help before I tackle them.'

'What are his chances?' Nix asks.

Fletch shakes his head as he looks down at the bed, and his shoulders drop slightly. 'In normal vampire circumstances, I'd give him fairly good odds. Usually a good feed would deal with most of the injuries. The problem is, thanks to the Fever, drinking blood will do him more harm than good. He needs to drink to heal and for his body to regenerate, but if he gets too much it'll increase the side effects. I don't know how to handle this to help him.'

'Any of his injuries life threatening if he can't take blood?'

'To be honest, I'm not overly concerned about any of those injuries. Don't get me wrong - they're nasty and I wouldn't wish them on my worst enemy, but it's mostly superficial. It's the drug he was given that's giving me headaches.'

'How so?' Nix asks.

'Well, I just got his bloodwork back and his system has a truck load of the same stuff Shep found in the underground facility in it.'

'Will it work out of his system?'

'Aye, it should, but that's not the only issue. He's in full Blood Fever, guys. I mean end stage. His body is acting like he's been drinking Prime blood for years, which we all know he hasn't.'

'That doesn't make sense,' Shep says. 'You can count his fucking ribs. How can he be that far gone when he's starving to death?'

'It's the drug. It's brought on Fever without him having to overdose on actual blood. His intake has to be carefully monitored and limited to the bare minimum.'

'Why do I hear a but coming?' Bastian asks.

'That would work if his father hadn't stitched his mouth closed and refused him blood, for who knows how long. Judging by the muscle loss, his diet has been shit since he was taken. His body is shutting down. You never get Blood Fever this bad along with starvation. I'll be making this one up as I go, I'm afraid.'

Nix lowers onto the desk and crosses her arms. 'So he's starving, but we can't risk giving him what he needs, cause it will make him worse?'

Fletch smiles grimly. 'That's the problem.'

Thea struggles to get her head around everything she's hearing. Blood Fever and blood starvation are terms she never thought she'd hear in normal conversation. She watches in silence as Court sits down beside Nix. 'Can we keep him restrained until the drug is out of his system? At least that way he can get the blood he needs, without being a risk to himself or us.'

Fletch nods. 'We can either force him to go cold-turkey - on blood and the drug, or we feed him little and often, to get his body back in condition, then wean him off. Whichever option, it's not going to be an easy ride.

There's also a chance he won't be able to shake the addiction. He's a Prime. Blood Fever can be fatal. Even if he does come through it, there's no saying what kind of damage it'll have done to him. We may never get our Davyn back. I need you guys to prepare for that. I'll get one of the holding cells ready. It'll be his home for the foreseeable future.'

He pulls his hand through his hair and blows out a long breath.

'What the hell did he do to deserve this? What sort of sick bastard even considers sewing his son's mouth closed?'

'He didn't choose his parents,' Shep mutters from the back of the room. 'No one has that choice, Doc. Why don't you keep your opinions to yourself and just get him back on his feet.'

Shep pulls his arm out of Willow's hand and storms out of the room.

Fletch frowns after him. 'I'm sorry. I didn't mean to offend him.'

Willow smiles and shakes her head. 'Ignore him. He's just worried about Davyn.'

Fletch smiles kindly. 'Hey, we're all worked up, tired, and

emotional. Leave Dav with me for a bit. You all go back to the waiting room. Fallon will be with you as soon as she gets these obnoxious sutures out of his mouth.'

Thea shuffles after the rest of the team and settles in for a long wait. Willow suddenly gets up and points to the door. 'I'll just check on Shep. Be back in a bit.'

Thea lies down against Court. Shep came through for them all today and she couldn't be more grateful. Hopefully his reaction is just down to tiredness like Fletch said, but his comment seemed to come from a personal level. She closes her eyes and puts it to the back of her mind.

'What the hell is your problem?'

Shep ignores Willow and continues ploughing through his pull up's. Maybe if he blanks her she'll leave him alone. But in true Willow style, she isn't put off by his attempts. She moves around in front of him and crosses her arms. 'You know full well I'm not going anywhere until you talk. So talk.'

Shep groans and drops down from the bar. He wipes damp hair from his forehead, ruffling the spikes under his palm. 'What you fancy talking about, Sis?'

Her eyes narrow and her hands move to her hips. What this girl lacked in years and experience, she made up for in attitude - well, when it comes to him anyway. He doubts she throws attitude around with Nix and the others. Lucky him. He rolls his shoulders but the band of pressure across his chest increases. He feels fucking rotten and a fight with Willow is the last thing he needs right now.

'About Dad obviously. You bit poor Fletch's head off when he mentioned Davyn's father. It doesn't take a genius to figure out your issue with Dad brought on that little outburst.'

Shep laughs harshly and looks out the one-way windows overlooking the garden. Yeah, he did a great job hiding his daddy issues. Willow knows they don't get on but he'll die before he tells her why. 'Listen, Wills. It's been a long day, okay? I need to work off some of this adrenaline before I crash for a few hours. And you should get Fletch to fix your wing.'

'Fine. You don't want to talk about it. Big shock! And I'm perfectly capable of looking after myself, Shepherd. How about you think about getting patched up and feeding? You're smearing blood all over the place and judging by that pathetic attempt at a work-out, you're about to collapse.'

He sneers at her as he reaches down to grab his towel from the chair. 'Give me a fucking break, Wills. And don't call me Shepherd. You know I hate that.'

'Which is exactly why I do it.'

'Real mature, Sis.' He storms past her but she grabs his arm. Shep growls and bares his teeth at her before he reins himself in. 'I'm not in the mood for a lecture. Dav's the one you should be worried about.'

She reaches for his hand but he pulls it away. Willow grabs it again, refusing to let him go. 'I'm worried about you, Shep. I know seeing him like that was...' She takes a deep breath and shakes her head. 'You can talk to me, you know that, right?'

He squeezes her hand before slipping it out of his. 'I know. I'm just wound up, okay.'

She nods, then her eyes lock on the scars peeking out from under the arm of his sleeveless t-shirt. They're barely visible unless you look closely, but that doesn't change the fact they're there. He always tried to keep them covered around her, knowing it would trigger a shitload of questions - none of which he ever answered, or ever intended to answer.

His kid sister will never know how he got the seven hundred and fifty-three neat tally marks running up both legs and along each side, stopping just under his armpits. Even having her eyes locked on them makes his skin crawl. 'I'll feed, okay? Just back the fuck off and leave me alone.'

He hurries away, disappearing into the male changing room, hoping she'll get the message. It works, but it won't hold her off for long. She's right, which only makes things so much worse. He should get patched up and feed – ideally before he falls on his ass.

He pulls up the bottom of his t-shirt and examines the puncture mark barely visible on his side. He absolutely should tell Fletch about it, but he's got enough to deal with looking after Dav and the fleabags.

And it's not like the needle went in deep. His jacket is fairly thick. At most the tip would have pierced his skin. Shep curses himself. He's not a fucking idiot. You only need the tip to go in.

He'll feed, grab a shower then see how he feels. Maybe whatever it was will work out of his system.

~

Nix looks up from her screen when Fletch knocks on her office door. 'Hey.'

'Sorry, am I disturbing you?'

Nix shakes her head. 'To be honest, I've been staring at the screen for the last hour. My mind isn't on it. How is he?'

Fletch shakes his head as he sits down. 'It's his wings that are giving me the headache at the moment. They're a mess, Nix. And by mess, I mean a real fucking mess. I can set bones but this is so far beyond that. He needs someone specialised in this area to help him.'

'You know of a vampire wing specialist?'

'Not quite,' he admits with a small smile. 'But, I do know one of the best orthopaedic surgeons in the area. I could give her a call.'

Nix leans back in her chair and takes a long breath. 'I'm taking it she won't be familiar with vampires.'

'Nope. Well, as far as I know. I haven't seen her since I came on board with the Blackjacks. That's why I need you to okay this before I reach out to her.'

'What are his odds if we don't use your friend?'

'That's a tricky question, Nix. His wings, his overall physical condition, and his addiction are three separate issues. Now, not having wings myself, I can't say how not having wings will affect him, but I reckon it won't go down well. He clearly has issues with his wings, but in their current condition, there's every chance he won't even be able to pull them in to his body, let alone do anything with them. They're critical, Nix. I'm only talking hours before I can't do anything more for them. My friend can... well, hopefully do something for them.'

Nix sighs, and brushes her hair back from her face. Highlighting the fact that vampires exist to yet another human, wasn't at the top of her to-do-list today. She trusts Fletch. No question of that at all, but bringing someone new into the fold is always a risk.

But forcing Dav to live for even a day, with wings that do nothing except hang lifelessly down his back... that's no life for him, especially after everything he's endured over the last few months.

'Do what you have to. Give me a shout if she agrees to come here. I'll get things ready for you.'

'Thanks, Nix. Keep everything crossed she doesn't run when I mention the whole vampire thing.'

Fletch smiles, then leaves the room, closing the door behind him. Nix stares at the closed door and crosses her fingers under her desk.

Doctor Annie Simmons closes the last of the files on her desk and shuts down her computer. She stretches and pulls out her hair tie, running her fingers through her tight black curls. Slumping back in her chair she closes her eyes. She's exhausted. This shift seems to have gone on forever. It's time for a long bath, a glass of wine, then bed, and she can't wait.

A soft knock on the door startles her. Suppressing a groan, she forces herself to smile. 'Yes.'

She glances up and breaks into a genuine smile when she sees who has just walked into her office. 'Fletcher Marsh? Is that really you?'

Fletch smiles and hugs her back when she gets up to embrace him. 'Hey, Annie. You look great.'

She waves away his compliment. 'After a shift that feels like it went on for three days, I doubt it. Sit, please.'

He drops into the chair at the far side of her desk and grins at her. It may have been years since she last saw him, but time had stopped for him. Apart from the addition of a beard and longer hair, he's still as striking as ever. 'Got a minute to talk?'

'A minute? It's been years, Fletch. I think I can spare you a little time.'

'Yeah, sorry about that. I should have stayed in touch. It's been a crazy few years.'

'I thought you'd been abducted by aliens or something. Where the hell have you been?'

'I've been around. My new job is keeping me busy.'

She leans back and narrows her eyes. 'And what is this mysterious new job, if you don't mind me asking? I mean we were close all through medical school, then you just vanished. I have colleagues in most of the hospitals in the country. No sign of you though.'

'Checking up on me?'

'Absolutely. So, are you going to tell me what you're up to? Are you still practising?'

'It's in my blood, Annie. No way I'm walking away from medicine.' He pauses and scratches the back of his neck. 'Just working with a different breed of patient.'

'Breed? What are you talking about?'

Instead of answering, Fletch takes her coat off the rack next to her door and passes it to her. 'It's a bit difficult to put into words. How about I show you - if you're game of course?'

Without hesitation, Annie passes her white coat to Fletch and slips on her long, black woollen coat. 'Oh, I'm game. Where are we going?'

His mischievous grin comes back. 'Wales. I've got some friends I'd like you to meet.'

'Wales? But that's hours away.'

'I have a way of getting us there a little faster. It's on the roof.'

Annie stops buttoning her coat and looks at him. 'Excuse me? You have a helicopter?'

'You don't?' he asks with a wink.

'Oh ha ha. But seriously, you have a helicopter?'

He holds out his arm and she links her arm with him. 'How about I show you?'

They take the elevator to the roof and Annie can't believe what she sees when the doors open. 'You really have a helicopter?'

'Well, it's not actually mine, but I can borrow it when I need to.'

'And you can fly it?'

'I don't think it's a good idea to take one out unless you can actually fly it.'

She slaps him on the chest. 'I forgot how much of a smart arse you are.'

He opens the door of the impressive black craft and helps her step inside before walking around the front and getting in.

Fletch turns to face her and takes a deep breath. 'Right, so I'll take us away from the city for a bit, then land, and I'll tell you more about my friends.'

'Why not tell me on the way?'

'I'd prefer not to be keeping us in the air while I tell you. Not so sure what your reaction will be.'

He passes her a headset and winks before starting the engine. Annie doesn't bother asking him to explain. She knows Fletch well enough to know he's stubborn and won't talk until he's ready. Clearly he has this planned out, so why not let it play out the way he wants.

~

Fletch finishes speaking and watches Annie's face go through a range of emotions. Everything from humour, to confusion, to shock, and back to a desperate look of humour. The ten minute flight to the rooftop of one of Ethan's buildings has passed in silence. No doubt she was trying to figure out what he could be involved in. After seeing the various expressions she's just shown in the last few minutes, being the resident doctor for a team of vampires wasn't one of the options she'd considered.

'You okay, Annie?'

She frowns at him then smiles. 'Okay. You got me. What's the punchline?' she asks, finishing with a nervous laugh.

Fletch shakes his head. 'No punchline, Annie.'

She turns in her seat and faces him. 'You don't honestly expect me to believe you work as a doctor for a group of vampires.'

'Some with wings.'

Annie holds up a hand. 'Sincere apologies. I forgot that small detail. What the hell is going on with you, Fletch?'

'I know it's a lot to take in, but I haven't lost my mind.'

'Fletch, I've known you since medical school, and I care a lot about you, which is why I have to tell you that you're stark raving mad. You know that, right? You're taking about flying vampires, Fletch.'

'Do you trust me?'

'This has nothing to do with—'

'Do you trust me, Annie?'

'Well, yes. Of course I trust you. I got into a flipping helicopter with you, didn't I? But this is different. You're talking about flying vampires, Fletch.'

'I know. And believe me, I know how crazy it sounds. All I'm asking is that you trust me enough to come with me. I'm asking for a few hours of your time. If I haven't convinced you by then, I'll bring you home and never mention any of this again.'

Fletch silently watches as she decides what to do. He has no doubts he'd be acting the same if he didn't have a vampire as a half-sister. She finally nods once and he releases the breath he was holding.

'Thank you.'

'Yeah well, don't thank me just yet. I don't believe a word you're saying to me. The only reason I'm humouring you, is because you're a friend. That's it.'

Fletch starts the engine and leaves the rooftop.

She doesn't say anything else until they get to the compound so Fletch leaves her to it. He lands the craft beside the bus and shuts down the engine.

'Is this it?'

'Yep. Well, the garage.' He nods towards Nix, standing to the side of the garage space. 'She's my boss.'

'And she's a vampire.'

'Yep.'

'She doesn't look like one. Then again I don't know what I was expecting.'

'Maybe a cape or something like that?'

She smiles briefly. 'Yeah. Maybe.'

'Ready to meet her?'

Annie shrugs. 'Absolutely not, but I said I'd do this, so let's go.' She follows him over to Nix and Fletch makes the introductions. 'So, Nix, are you one of these flying vampires?' she asks, the smile on her face saying she doesn't believe any of what Fletch told her.

Nix removes her thick woollen cardigan and passes it to Annie. Underneath she's wearing the leather waistcoat she dons for fighting, which has two slits at the back for her wings to fit through. She takes a step back and Annie stumbles backwards in to Fletch as Nix releases her wings. She stares in confused shock at the large bat-like limbs catching the light as Nix gently moves them.

Nix take a step forward and Fletch is surprised that Annie doesn't move away. 'Annie, I know what Fletch told you seems like something out a Bram Stoker novel, but as you can see, we do exist.'

'But... how?'

Nix shakes her head. 'Like humans, we've been around for quite some time. And just like humans, there are good vampires and not so good ones. Myself and the others living here, are good. Whatever is going through your head right now, please believe that you are safe. I promise you.'

Curiosity gets the better of Annie and she moves away from Fletch to slowly approach Nix. She reaches out to touch one of her wings but pulls her hand back before she makes contact.

'It's okay,' Nix says.

Annie runs her hand along the webbed skin and smiles slightly. 'I'm touching a vampire's wing. Didn't think I'd be doing that today. I have to admit that's kind of cool. So Fletch, why am I here?'

'I think it's best we show you.'

Annie didn't think anything could shock her as much as learning that vampires do exist - and that they have wings, but she was wrong. Fletch and Nix stand at either side of a large gurney holding a horrifically injured male vampire. She approaches the prone figure and wipes a hand over her face as she looks down at him.

'What happened to him?'

Nix gestures to Fletch, silently asking him to explain. 'This is Davyn. He was kidnapped nearly two months ago. Nix and her team finally found him and brought him home a few hours ago. He was forced to fight for sport, then beaten and drugged as the cherry on the cake.'

She sees something on his lips that turns her stomach. 'Are those suture scars?'

'It's an ancient ritual called a Binding,' Nix explains. 'They used a pair of pliers to remove his fangs, then his mouth was sewn shut, and his wings were sewn in place.'

'My god. Who did this to him?'

'His father,' Fletch says.

'His father?'

She swears she hears Nix growl. 'Don't worry about him. His cards are marked, but for now, we need to get Davyn sorted.'

'What can I do to help?'

'Are you sure about this, Annie?' Fletch asks.

'What can I do, Fletch?'

Fletch walks around the table to the gurney helping to support Davyn's broken wings. 'His wings are a mess, Annie. One was broken inside his body decades ago. It was never dealt with and healed arse-ways, while still inside him. He needs someone with a hell of a lot of experience to fix them. We were kind of hoping you might be willing to step in.'

She looks over at Davyn and the enormous torn and broken wings on the table behind him. 'Have you any x-rays of the damage?'

Fletch turns on the screen on the wall and Annie walks over to examine the information. 'Wow, this is bad. How long have they been like this?'

Nix shrugs. 'The deformed wing was broken about a century and a half ago - maybe longer, and the other a few weeks ago.'

'Did you say a century and a half?'

'As far as I know he's one hundred and seventy years old.'

Annie raises her eyebrows. 'Remind me to ask what night cream he uses.' She looks back at his wings and carefully runs her fingers along the smooth skin. 'It won't be an easy or quick operation but I'm sure I can help him. I'll need some time to carefully study both him and his x-rays. I can't promise he'll ever be able to... well, fly.'

'We're not even thinking about flying,' Fletch says. 'He just needs to be able to pull them in without tearing his body apart. The poor lad has been through enough.'

'How do the wings go back inside his body in the first place?'

Nix turns around and lifts up her top. 'The ridges that run down our back is desensitised skin. The wings come out through these ridges without causing us any pain.'

'But Davyn's damaged wing comes out through regular skin,' Fletch explains. 'Imagine what it would be like pushing that beast through your skin. No thank you.'

Annie raises her eyebrows as she examines the x-rays again. 'No thank you indeed. Okay. I'm on for this. I'll need to steal your room for a bit. It's time Davyn and I have some time alone. Is he anaesthetised or unconscious?'

'I've given him a sedative, but he's so poorly I don't think he'll wake up any time soon.'

'That suits me just fine.' She takes off her coat and hands it to Fletch. 'Right. Let's get you sorted, Davyn.'

~

Rhain looks up from the screen when Geraint enters his home office. 'I'm sorry to disturb you, but I have the Raven King on hold for you.'

'Oh that's not good. What the fuck does that deviant want?'

'There has been an incident.'

Rhain nods, takes the phone from Geraint and watches as the man leaves the room. He has a fair idea what the incident is. In fact, he is positive he played a part in that incident. The Blackjacks retrieved their stolen comrade. Perhaps now Ethan will be more open to working with him, instead of trying to kill him.

Rhain takes a sip of water to moisten his throat, but it's not water his body is craving. He's trying to lengthen the time between feeds but his body is not agreeable. He picks up the receiver and pushes the button. 'This is Rhain.'

'The bastards took him.'

Four words and his theory has been confirmed. 'Which bastards are you referring to?'

'The Blackjacks of course. They broke into one of my pits and took him. They had stinking wolves with them.'

That surprises Rhain. 'Wolves? Are you sure?'

'I think I know what a fucking wolf looks like,' the King scoffs. 'There were four of them. Fucking monstrous ones at that, so it must've been one of the older clans. I have associates looking for them, but with the feud, I am not having much luck.'

'I see. Can I ask why you are telling me this?'

'I need your help.'

'I'm not getting involved with wolves.'

'We have a deal. You will help me find them.'

Rhain clenches his jaw. Fucking bastard is pulling his strings and he doesn't appreciate it. 'I'll see what I can do.'

'I know you will. I want my property back. I also want the heads of the four dogs for my wall. Find them.'

'I will certainly do what I can to capture him again, but unless he shows himself, that will be difficult.' Impossible more like it, but no point mentioning that. The King won't care in the slightest.

'There is one more problem.'

'What?'

'From what I can gather, one of my associates injected a Blackjack with the enhancer. The raw product. It went into the male's side but, as the Blackjack killed my man, I have no idea how much of the drug was administered.'

Rhain stares at a knot in the wood of his antique desk for a long few minutes. There goes his truce with Ethan. Save one of the team, only to have another put in danger. 'Is that so? Was it a male or female Blackjack?'

'A male. As I said, the Blackjack dealt with my man, but that doesn't erase the issue.'

'I understand. Thank you.'

Rhain ends the call and continues to stare at his desk. He's still staring at a knot in the wood when Geraint enters his office again.

'Is there a problem, sir?'

'Not a problem as such. I'd describe it as a monumental fucking disaster. The King let the Blackjacks and four wolves free Davyn. Now he's ordered me to find Davyn and the four wolves so he can exact revenge.'

Geraint's eyes open wide at the mention of wolves. 'What in the world were wolves doing working with vampires?'

'Who knows. If it is true, it won't have done them any favours either. I doubt the other wolf clans will be thrilled about them siding with vampires, no matter the reason.'

'And you've agreed to find them?'

Rhain leans back in his chair and rests his hands on his knees under the desk. He's sure the trembling is due to Fever, but it could also be anger. Being told what to do by that cretin didn't help. 'I have no intention of involving myself with anything wolf related. They'll have their own issues with the clans. Besides, we may have a bigger problem. A thug hired by the Raven King injected a male Blackjack with a pure dose of the enhancer.'

Geraint nods solemnly. 'That is a monumental disaster. I presume it was one of the Hybrid males?'

'Yes. There is only one Prime Blackjack and the Raven King just let him escape. This mistake could open a whole Pandora's box of potential issues.'

'I have not heard of any Blackjack death.'

'No, neither have I. It's still early days however. The raw form of the drug could very easily kill him within a few days. If it doesn't, there's a chance he will develop the Fever.' The list of all the horrible ways the male could die is too long to count and Rhain has seen far too many of them.

The one side effect that concerns him however, only came to light recently. In a small number of cases, Hybrid males given the enhancer developed certain Prime traits. Traits he has no doubt this Blackjack male would not appreciate.

He grabs the edge of the desk as a particularly intense cramp works through his gut.

'Sir?'

'I'm fine, Geraint. Leave me.'

He drops his composure when he hears the doors closing. Geraint is invaluable to him, but sometimes he just needed to suffer alone. Having the male witness his slow decline is humiliating.

Not that the process could be referred to as slow any longer. It's speeding up, bringing him closer to a stage where he would have to end things, before he lost too much of himself.

At least, with Davyn's freedom, he's managed to clear a little of his conscience.

If Geraint, The Order, or The Raven King ever finds out he sent the Blackjacks tickets to the fight, he would have a target on his back within minutes. But he didn't intend on them ever finding out. It's just a shame the King is still breathing, but if he knows Nix and her team, that will be rectified shortly.

Something he can tick off his list before he dies. Not that he wants to die. Far from it, but time is against him. He's out of options.

He has a few weeks of the drug left and that's being optimistic. He's already cut his dose back to the bare minimum. It just might be time to begin getting his affairs in order.

Nix looks up from her desk as Fletch knocks on the door. 'Got a minute, Boss?'

She closes her laptop and gestures to the chair in front of her. 'Sure. Is Davyn okay?'

Fletch sighs as he drops into the chair. 'I'd love to say yes, but we got a bigger problem than I first thought.'

Nix's throat instantly dries. 'Another problem? What sort of problem?'

'He's deteriorating - fast. I thought he'd be strong enough to get over this, but the last few months have clearly taken their toll on him. His organs are shutting down. He's starving to death in front of me, Nix. Unless we can do something drastic right now, he's not going to make it through the next few hours, never mind serious surgery to fix his wings.'

'Okay, I don't suppose you have an ingenious idea up your sleeve?'

'I wouldn't call it ingenious. More reckless and risky.'

'You want to feed him? I thought that wasn't a good idea?'

Fletch grimaces. 'We have to deal with both issues separately. We did plan to give him little and often. Try to manage the addiction, while physically building him up again over time. We don't have that time anymore.

Thanks to the Binding and his shite condition, he needs a massive transfusion of blood pretty damn fast or he's not going to make it. And that's before we even get to his wings. Damn things are disintegrating. I'm afraid to touch them. The skin is flaking off if you even look at them sideways.'

'What about fixing them? Is that still a possibility?'

'Fingers crossed. Annie is going over his x-rays, planning the procedure. He needs his wings repaired - no question. There's no way we can leave him in agony every time he has to take them in or out. I'm thinking that we can give him a good feed before surgery. I don't want to give him enough to start regenerating his wings, but he does need a hefty amount to get him through the surgery.

'Once Annie is done, I'll give him everything we have - vampire and human blood. His wings will need all the help they can get to regenerate. If all goes to plan, his wings should be healed and over the surgery in a few days. We won't know if the surgery worked until he's with us enough to pull them back in to his body. Until then, I'll wrap them to prevent any further damage.'

'Why not just leave the surgery until he's stronger?'

'We discussed it, but I seriously don't think his wings will last that long. We need to set the broken bone in his good wing anyway. Might as well do the lot while we're at it. Save him the pain further down the road.'

'Is the cell ready for him?'

Fletch nods. 'I've got a gurney down there. Fallon is securing it to the floor as we speak. It'll be fitted with steel restraints - padded of course. I'm loathe to put him back in that situation but it's either that or he could kill the lot of us.'

Nix leans back in her seat. The last thing she wants to do is bring more difficultly to Davyn's world by feeding his Fever, but Fletch is right. There's no point dealing with that if his wings have shrivelled up and fallen off. He's lost enough already without that. 'Damn it.'

'I'll take that as a yes.' He gets to his feet and opens the door. 'We don't have a choice.'

She nods as he leaves, but his final words don't give her any relief.

~

Thea adjusts her position on the couch and rests her head on Court's lap. He continues scrolling through the iPad resting on the arm of the couch as he rubs her hair. Davyn went into surgery five hours ago and there's been no sign of Annie, Fletch, or Fallon since. It may not be a life threatening surgery, but his quality of life is going to depend on what Annie can do for him and his wings. If she can do anything for him, full stop.

She glances up at Court, but he's focusing on the screen. He hasn't left her side since Davyn was taken in and she can't put into words how much that means to her. He's taking the time to continue reading through years of reports he either missed out on, or can't remember. At least he has something to occupy his mind. Staring at the far wall and thinking about what they're doing to Davyn is driving her crazy.

She jumps when the door opens, but it's just Shep. He smiles and sits on the armchair next to them. Instead of filling the silence as she expected him to, Shep stretches his legs out and crosses his arms, then closes his eyes.

Thea hasn't seen a lot of Shep since they got Davyn back. As she's looking over at him she can't help but worry. He doesn't look well. She's not even sure vampires get sick like humans do, but if they do, Shep looks the part. He's pale and she could swear he's quivering. The last thing she's going to do is put herself in his firing line by saying anything about it. He's probably exhausted, and worried about Davyn like everyone else is.

Thea nods off for the next hour or so, waking when Annie and Fletch join then, taking two of the free seats.

'Well?'

'Well,' Fletch says. 'This woman to my right is a certified genius.'

'You fixed his wings?' Court asks.

Annie nods. 'I have to admit I'm rather chuffed at myself, but yes, I did. Now, he's got a long way to go before we'd even consider the remote possibility of getting him off the ground. But I was able to reconstruct his damaged wing. He's under heavy sedation and will stay that way for the next two days. His wings are being held together by pins and a lot of bandages. We can't risk him damaging them at this stage. They need time to heal.'

'Hopefully the feed we gave him beforehand will help with the regeneration.' Fletch wipes a hand over his face. He's another one to add to the list of exhausted people in the house. 'All we can do is keep things crossed.'

'You told Nix?' Shep asks.

'Yeah. She's telling the others. Listen, I can't let you in to see him at the moment. Maybe a little later.'

Thea nods and smiles even though she desperately wants to see him.

Fletch and Annie get to their feet and leave the room to go back to Davyn again. 'I better get back to it. You okay?' Court asks her as he stretches and shuts down the screen he was reading.

'I'm fine, Dad. Thanks.'

'You fancy training with me?' Court asks Shep, who grins widely.

'Absolutely.'

Shep glances at her before he follows Court out the door. She could have imagined it, but she swears he winked at her before he left. Maybe now things are looking up for Davyn, he'll be able to forgive her for getting him captured in the first place.

Doesn't mean she'll ever be able to forgive herself.

Thea knocks on the door and waits until she hears a gruff, 'Yeah,' then enters. She smiles when she sees Murtagh in the bed, back in human form and sitting up.

'Nix said you're going back home in a few hours. I just wanted to see how you are before you leave.'

He pushes up the bed, grimacing as he adjusts his position. 'How's your mate?'

He grins as he says the word mate, fully aware of how it would make her feel. 'He's doing okay considering everything he's been put through. They've spoken of Blood Fever and addiction and I'm lost, Murtagh. This isn't my world. I don't understand half of what's going on.'

'Not many do.' He turns on his side and his soothing green eyes meet hers. 'There's one thing you need to know about vampires and wolves. As much as we don't get on, we do have one common trait. We're tough. And I don't just mean physically strong.' He places his tattooed hand on his chest. 'I mean in here. We've been hunted, killed, brought to the brink of extinction time and time again. You don't survive that without being resilient. I know a little about your mate. Not many of our kind haven't heard about the Raven King and his sons. Davyn survived what would easily destroy most people. He will survive this too.'

'I wish I was as sure as you are.'

'Just be there for him. That's all you can do.'

Thea nods. 'Always. So, how are you feeling?'

Murt smiles as he shuffles up the bed. 'I'll be grand. Just another scar to add to all the others. I'll be on my feet in a few hours. We heal fast, but your vamp friends get the added bonus of being able to drink to speed up the process. We just have to wait it out.'

'So what are you going to do now?'

Murt shrugs and smiles. 'Head home and try to stay alive and hidden for a while longer. Keep Garret and Con from starting fights with anyone who looks at them the wrong way. I'll need to be at full strength to deal with the second one.'

'Good luck with that. It's like that here with Shep sometimes.'

'I can well believe that.'

'Do you think working with the Blackjacks will put aside some of the tension between your races?'

She barely knows Murt, but you'd have to be an idiot not to see that the smile he gives her is put on. 'Who knows. It's been going on a lot longer than I've been around. And I'm heading towards five hundred years old. Can't see this arrangement putting an end to the bad blood so easily.'

He frowns and adjusts himself in the bed again. 'We'll just have to keep going as we are and see what happens. The way I see it, whatever the Order is doing with vampire blood is far more of an issue than some ancient feud, but I don't get a say.'

Thea gets up and hugs Murt. He pauses for a moment before hugging her in return. 'Thanks for everything, Murt. I mean that. I don't think the Blackjacks could have got Davyn out without you and your brothers.'

'My pleasure, Thea.'

She releases him and brushes a tear away. 'Sorry. I'm an emotional mess at the moment. I'm going to miss you guys.'

'My brothers will probably never admit it, but the feeling is mutual. It's certainly been interesting. You never know when you'll need our help again. We're only a few hours away. You got my number, right?'

'Yeah, thanks.'

'Now go and be with him. He'll need you to help him through this.'

Thea straightens her shoulders and smiles at Murt. Easier said than done, but she's absolutely going to try to help Davyn. 'Safe trip home, Murt.'

He nods and Thea leaves his room so he can rest before he goes back to his life. She genuinely hopes she'll see Murt and his brothers again. She laughs to herself as she walks through the compound back to the main residence. Her circle of friends contains more vampires and werewolves, than humans at the moment.

~

Without opening her eyes, Nix feels in the dark for her phone. The glass of water and jewellery box land on the floor before she finally feels it under her hand. 'Yeah.'

'Hey, boss. It's Fletch. You good to talk?'

'Go ahead.' She lies back on the bed and tries to convince her brain to wake up.

'Davyn just came to. He's... well agitated is probably the best way to describe him.'

'His restraints holding him?'

'We wouldn't be having this conversation if they weren't. And after what I just witnessed, I'll be leaving the restraints firmly in place for the time being. Besides, I'd prefer he didn't move around too much until his wings have a chance to begin regenerating. I'm hoping he'll calm down once he's had some time to get used to his new home.'

'Okay. I don't want him alone. You okay to sit with him until I get there?'

'Of course. I'll send the rota out to the others. Our boy won't be by himself until he's out of this.'

'Thanks, Fletch. I'll come down to see him in a few minutes.' She turns off the phone and sighs loudly as she turns to face Court. His blue eyes are full of concern as he drapes a large arm around her shoulders. 'You okay?'

She shakes her head. 'This is going to sound terrible, but I was hoping he'd stay asleep a little longer. A few weeks would have been great. Give his body a chance to recover.'

Court smiles and kisses her on the forehead. 'Dav probably wishes the same. We all do. We'll help him get through this. You know that, right?'

Nix wants to believe him, but she's seen vampires suffering from Fever before. And the effects are so much stronger in Primes, and so much more deadly. 'I know, but that's not going to help him - medically I mean.' She buries her face in his chest and closes her eyes.

Court holds her close as he runs his hand through her hair. The tears come before she realises she's crying. It doesn't take long to soak his bare skin as they keep coming, refusing to stop.

He leaves her to her misery until the tears turn to a mix of sobs and a lot of face wiping. Perfect leadership display again.

He takes her face in his hands and moves away so he can look at her. 'Talk to me, Nix.'

She tries to shake her head, but his glowing eyes lock on to hers. 'That wasn't a request. Talk.' He softens his command with a small smirk.

She sniffs and smiles at him. 'Now I know how irritating that is when I say it to you.'

'Talking is the best cure for amnesia and for crying. C'mon.'

Nix moves away from him and lies flat on her back. Court rests his head on his hand as he examines her. 'This stays in this room, right?'

'Nix.' His tone tells her he would never consider breaking her confidence.

'Sorry. Shit. I guess I'm questioning my leadership of the Blackjacks.'

'I thought we talked about this?'

'We did. But I keep letting you down. My decision has left you with no memory and now Davyn is... I knew by leading the group against the Order we would have injuries and losses. But what happened to you and Dav... it's nothing you can prepare for. How can we possibly mount a defence against a group who does things like this?

'We still don't know what they did to you, which gives me nightmares to think about. That was bad enough, but now Davyn's father performed the Binding on him, after beating and starving him for months. How can I train you all for something like that? It's impossible, Court.'

'He survived. So did I. You trained us for that. That's all you can do. It's all any of us can do. Survive. Besides, I'm not doing too badly out of my amnesia. I've found a family, a daughter, you. If I had to lose my memory to get all that, I can deal. Dav will too. He's strong.'

'I know. I just wish I could...'

'Locking us in the compound won't work, so get that thought out of your head. We'll continue to fight and to deal with the results. Nothing's changed, so tell that nut of yours to knock it off,' he ends, tapping his finger against her forehead. 'Even without knowing you, I trusted you when you took me from the warehouse, and brought me back to this weird, and slightly messed up house. We all trust you. Sounds like it's time you trusted yourself.'

He gathers her in his arms again as the words sink in. She knows her fighters have faith in her. They wouldn't do what they do, unless they trusted her and her orders. That doesn't mean trusting her is the right thing to do. Yes, Court is alive and well, but he's lost all but two years of his life. There's no recovering from that.

Seeing the little she has of Davyn since they got him back, perhaps losing his memory would be a bonus. Healing his body is one thing. Fletch is one of the best doctors she's ever met. But what if the damage to Davyn runs deeper than physical scars and broken bones?

Davyn clenches his fists and pulls against his restraints. His muscles scream in protest, but he can't get free. And he's tried. He needs blood. It's all he can think about. His gums are throbbing in time to the raging headache he can't escape from. He can't escape any of this. He needs to work out the cramps in his stomach, arms, and legs, but the chains are too tight. The pain from the cramps is at war with whatever is going on with his wings and eye. He can't see anything out of his right eye. It feels like there's something stuck to his face and it's itching like crazy.

He's fucking miserable.

Someone approaches him and a dark haired female peers down at him. He snarls at her, but instead of cowering away from him, she looks sad.

Something in the back of his mind is screaming at him. Something, or some part of him recognises her, but the overpowering need to feed is too strong to give her much thought.

She's saying something to him, but her words don't get through the fog in his brain. A male comes into view and he smells blood in the air. He growls again and tastes blood in his mouth. But it's his own blood. He's bitten his tongue or the inside of his mouth. He can't tell. His tongue runs along the holes where his fangs had been torn from his gums. He can't feed.

Despair builds on the rage that has control of him. He needs to feed. But he can't. He's going to be stuck in this hell forever. Trapped in a body that craves something it can't have. Always craving something that will kill him.

He pulls at the restraints again and shouts in frustration when he can't break them. The male and female speak to him again, but the words don't register. The male injects something into a bag hanging to the side of the bed and the urge for blood diminishes a little.

In the few seconds before the sedative takes him away, Davyn's mind clears. He looks up at the two people by his bed and instantly recognises Nix and Fletch. He's back at the compound. They saved him.

He opens his mouth, tries to thank them or say anything to prove he's still here. Prove he's worth saving. That they have to fight for him. Beg them to fight for him. To save him from the pain. But whatever Fletch gave him wins and he drifts away from them.

~

Thea frowns when she finds Fallon at her door. The vampire has never come to her room before and she immediately fears the worst. 'Fallon. Hi. Is everything okay?'

'Can I come in?'

'Sure.'

She steps aside and Fallon strolls in, her arms wrapped around her torso. She looks around the bedroom for a minute then settles her gaze on Thea again. 'Thought you should know, Davyn's awake.'

Thea smiles widely as she lowers onto the couch. After everything she's heard about his condition over the last few days, she'd tried to stay hopeful, but she was struggling. The fact that not one of the Blackjacks themselves seemed to be taking the positive angle, didn't help. 'Sorry. I'm just a little surprised. That's great. How is he?'

Fallon shakes her head. 'Not good. He's agitated. Confused. Exhausted. In pain. The best thing all round would be if he'd stayed unconscious longer. He's going to be suffering and there's nothing Fletch or I can do about it.'

Thea swallows as her throat suddenly tightens. 'Oh, I see. That's terrible. Does Fletch think he'll be okay? Are you any closer to finding blood for him?'

Fallon's face gives her all the answer she needs. 'No. Not yet.'

'So what's the plan? I mean long term. If you don't find something suitable what will that mean for him?'

'Well, if we don't find something soon, we may have to keep him in the holding cell and give him diluted Prime blood. It's either that, or we risk losing him. He can't keep going like this indefinitely.'

'He's getting weaker, isn't he?'

Fallon nods. 'Human blood is keeping him alive but it's not giving him all the nutrients he needs. As a Prime, he should be stronger and faster than the other Blackjacks, but he's nowhere near that. Hey, Fletch hasn't stopped looking, okay. And Ethan's team are on the case. We just need to find the right combination that will keep him fit and strong, but not feed the addiction.'

'That easy, huh?' she replies sarcastically.

Fallon leans against the wall and shrugs. 'He's got a long way to go before that becomes a problem. Blood Fever doesn't just go away, Thea. I've seen strong vampires fall to it. As a Prime it's part of him. His father just unlocked it. He's addicted to blood, and I guarantee he will do anything he has to, in order to feed. But we can't let him because it'll just make him worse.

'It's like denying a drug addict their drug of choice, then forcing them to go cold turkey, while everyone around them is flaunting that very drug in their face. Each and every one of us has what he wants. And that makes him a danger to us. And, if that's not enough, he's also got to deal with everything he went through in the fighting pit. He's not on solid ground yet. Far from it. There's still a hell of a fight ahead of him and there's a chance it's a fight he won't win.'

'Oh... Right.' Thea bites the inside of her cheek to keep the tears in place. Fallon isn't the sort of woman you cry in front of.

The vampire sits down beside her and looks over at her. 'I'm sorry.'

'Sorry about what?'

Then Fallon smiles for probably the first time since she met her. 'I understand you care about him, but you have to prepare yourself for the possibility that the Davyn you like, may not come back. I need you to prepare yourself for the worst case scenario. If you're prepared for that, maybe it won't hurt as much if it happens.'

'What do you mean by the worst?'

'If we can't get him back, can't get him to where he's safe to be around, we'll have to make a decision about his future.'

'You mean like with the team?'

'No, Thea. I mean like with his life. He wouldn't want to survive in chains and we're not going to lock him up in a cell, and watch him die in agony.'

Thea takes a little too long to figure out what Fallon's saying. 'No. You wouldn't...'

'If it spares him from suffering, yeah, we would. You'd prefer to visit him every day in his cell and watch as he gets weaker and weaker? There won't be any of our Davyn left. Just a 'being' with a raw need for blood. Nothing more.'

Thea wraps her arms around her chest, desperate to get some warmth back into her body. But it's not going to work. How can it, after hearing something like that. As much as she doesn't want to believe what Fallon just said, she knows every word of it to be true. Fallon doesn't come across as someone who would lie.

Fletch and Fallon can deal with his body, but she needs to try to reach him. Try to somehow make sure he can find his way back. The alternative doesn't bear thinking about.

'Thanks for being honest with me. I had no idea what was at stake.'

'That's why I wanted to speak to you, Thea. I know everyone is trying to remain positive, but I've seen Fever first hand. I've seen how it destroys vampires. Dav is one of the strongest males I know, but...' She shrugs. 'I lost someone I cared about. Not to Fever thankfully. I just thought you should be prepared. Not that you can ever really prepare for something like that. At least you have all the facts now.'

Thea nods. 'I appreciate that. And I understand, really. Do you mind me asking who you lost?'

Fallon licks her lips as she stares down at her clasped hands. 'My mate. I'd prefer not to talk about it.'

'Of course. I'm sorry for asking. It was insensitive of me.'

'It was the obvious question. It still hurts to talk about. He still hurts to talk about.'

Both women fall silent, but it's far from awkward. The small insight into Fallon had helped Thea to see the stand-offish woman differently. Losing someone you were in love with... Thea stops herself before she lets that thought pull her away with it. Davyn is still alive. There's still time to save him.

'Do you think I'd be allowed to see him?'

Fallon nods and looks over at her again. 'I'd like to see someone stop me from letting you in. Wouldn't end well for them.'

Thea laughs as Fallon pulls her to her feet. She had no doubts about that whatsoever.

28

Thea stops beside Fallon outside the high security holding cells and tries to calm her racing heart.

She is nervous about going in there with him. Seeing him unconscious in Fletch's room is one thing. Awake and agitated is another. Fallon steps aside and gestures for her to go inside. She walks into the room outside the holding cell and can feel the tears building.

Davyn is sitting on the ground pressed into the corner of the cell. His enormous wings are wrapped in heavy gauze and beat against the metal wall in time with the violent shudders working through his body.

'What should I do?'

'I'm sure you've seen enough TV shows. Talk to him. Just be here with him. I don't have the right or wrong answer. I don't even know if anything he's hearing is getting through his need for blood.'

Fallon pulls up a chair and places it a few feet from the cell. 'Do not move from this spot. His chains can't reach anywhere near the bars, but I don't want to get it in the neck from Nix or Court if you get hurt.'

Thea obediently sits down, suddenly feeling like she's overstepping her mark here. This is way out of her comfort zone or expertise.

'I'll leave you to it for a bit.' Fallon points to a panel on the wall beside her. 'Hit that if there are any problems. One of us will get here fast. You're also on camera so we'll see if something is up with him. I promise you're safe though. He won't be getting through the chains and the bars. But if he gets upset, step outside. Don't try to talk him down. Easier for you if you leave him to it.'

'Does... does he know I'm here?'

Fallon squeezes her arm. 'Who knows. He recognised you on the helicopter so I hope so. I'll be back in a few.'

Thea jumps when Fallon closes the heavy door behind her and waits a few seconds before she convinces herself to look over at Davyn.

His head is resting on his knees as he slowly rocks back and forth. The white t-shirt and black joggers are soaked with sweat and cling to his thin body. Thea wipes her sweaty palms on her jeans. She was desperate to see him, but now that she's here, she doesn't know what to do. She doesn't even know if he'll be able to understand her.

His rocking suddenly becomes more pronounced and he lurches to his feet. The heavy chain holds his arms behind him as he scrambles across the small cell. He jolts to a stop as the bonds hold him back after a few steps.

Davyn screams in anger and pulls hard against the chains, but there's no give. The padded shackles are a far cry from the spiked metal ones his father used, but Thea still hates the sight of them. Hates the sounds they make as he fights against them.

He lifts his head and she finally gets a proper look at his face. The bruises and cuts have healed leaving his skin pale but unmarked. His shaved hair is beginning to grow out, covering the ugly fighting pit tattoo his father gave him. She's also relieved to see the holes left by the wire sutures have closed, but unfortunately the same can't be said for his eye. It had been too badly damaged for his body to regenerate. The thick gauze covers half his face, hiding the wound until it heals properly.

Thea wipes away a tear, desperate not to let him see her cry. He had been through so much by his father's hand. The added disgrace of having his fangs taken and his wing broken, on top of losing an eye, and all this Blood Fever nightmare - she can't see how he can come through it all.

He growls, his bloodshot red eye boring into her.

'Hi Davyn. Do you remember me?'

He pulls against his chains, his bare feet sliding on the ground as he tries to break free. Frustration building, Davyn's lips peel back from his teeth. A deep, feral growl rumbles in his chest as he looks at her like she's lunch. Instead of launching himself at her, he paces back and forth, shaking his head as he mutters incoherently to himself.

He suddenly stops pacing, focusing on his restraints and the sudden need to tear them off his arms, leaving red marks in his flesh. As he scratches, he drops back onto his mattress and tries to pull the bandage off his face, but thanks to the chain around his waist, his arms won't reach that far. Frustrated at not being able to reach, he screams and hits his head against the wall again and again.

Thea jumps when Fallon touches her shoulder. 'Time to go.'

She shrugs out of Fallon's grip. 'I can't leave him like this. Just give me a sec.' Thea moves closer to the bars and crouches down to get on the same level as him. 'Davyn. It's Thea. Do you remember when you took me to Hereford? It was nearly Christmas.'

It takes a minute but his movements slow and he leans forward to look at her. Fallon nudges her. 'Keep going.' She steps back to the far side of the room, giving Thea space.

'You bought me chestnuts.'

He peers over at her, his red eye looking straight at her.

'I'll never forget the look on that shop assistant's face when you smiled at her in the changing room.'

He may not say anything to her, but he's calm so that's all that matters to her.

'I'll be outside,' Fallon says before leaving the room.

Thea takes out her mobile and picks the first book she finds. 'Can I read to you?'

There's no response from him, but she still has his attention so she begins reading.

~

Davyn watches his 'hallucination' read to him from the other side of the bars. She's more beautiful than he remembers. Her hair is a little longer too, but he really likes it. Whatever his father is giving him is good. His dreams are so realistic.

She pauses and smiles at him and he'd give anything to smile back. But he can't. He can't do anything. He's stuck in a body that isn't on board with listening to him. All it wants is blood. Her blood. He can smell it, hear her heart pumping it around her body. The cramps that are always twisting his gut, intensify.

The cravings are trying to take him over again. He won't let them. He needs to stay with Thea. Just another few minutes. That's all he wants. He ignores the pain and concentrates on her voice. She's talking to him, but he can't make out what she's saying over the sound of her heartbeat.

'Stay with me.'

He doesn't know how those three words pull him back, but it works. The uncontrollable urge to feed fades again.

'That's it. Just stay here with me, Davyn.' She smiles at him and reads again. He doesn't know what she's reading. It doesn't matter.

It's the sound of her voice that's keeping him grounded. After a while he closes his eyes. He's so tired but doesn't want to sleep. If he sleeps he'll wake up back in his cell.

'You can sleep. You're safe. I'll stay with you. I promise.'

As much as he tries to stay awake or stay in this hallucination, he can't. Instead he drifts away to the sound of her voice.

~

Thea looks up as Shep opens the door to Davyn's cell. 'You okay?'

She glances over at Davyn, asleep on the mattress on the floor before getting up and walking outside to Shep. 'He just dropped off. I don't want to wake him.'

'I'm to give you a break if you want it.'

'I'm okay to stay for another while, thanks.'

Shep nods slowly. 'Spending a lot of time here, aren't you?'

'I just want to pull my weight. You all have training to do. I have extra time.'

'You ditching your training?'

'Of course not.' Thea hates that she feels nervous around Shep. Ever since he fed from her she's been on edge around him, avoiding him entirely whenever possible. He hasn't made things weird, it's all her.

Shep leans against the wall and crosses his arms. Thea tries to look relaxed but Shep always intimates her. He's a great guy, but his sheer size makes it nearly impossible not to be a little wary. 'You doing it every day?'

'At least an hour every day with Fallon or Willow.'

He nods again but she can't tell if he's happy with the answer or not.

'What's the book?

Thea holds up the phone to show him the book. 'It's a thriller.'

He raises an eyebrow as he looks down at her phone. 'Looks

interesting.'

'I don't think he's really listening, but it's better than sitting in silence.'

Shep tilts his head to the side slightly then blows out a breath. 'Listen, I'm not trying to be an ass - really. And I have Davyn's back. I just don't want... damn it.' He scratches the side of his head and pushes away from the door. He paces the concrete floor outside the cell, his Converse making no sound as he walks back and forth.

'His dad really fucked him up, okay? As much as I want him back to his rude, highly volatile self, it's going to take time - if ever.' He looks at her, his deep blue eyes as serious as she's seen them so far. 'You get that, right?'

'I know that, Shep. I realise I've messed up a lot over the last few months, and I fully understand how miserable Davyn is because of that. I was there when Fletch was explaining everything that... everything that his father did to him. I saw the wounds, the horrendous stitches...'

A shudder runs through her body as the image of his prone, broken body slams in to her mind. 'Believe me - I get it. I get that he went through months of hell without any hope of getting out. I get that he's in a world of pain right now. I get that he's scared, confused, angry, and going through things I will never understand with all the Fever stuff.

'I also get that he's in there because of me. If I hadn't gone off on my own, I wouldn't have been captured and you guys wouldn't have had to come to get me out. Every cut, every bruise, every damn stitch is down to me. I can't change that, no matter how much I want to. I can't stop him hurting. I just know that if I was hurting, I wouldn't want to be alone. I know that - to me - being alone would make things so much worse. I don't want him to feel like he's alone. I know he's not,' she adds quickly when he frowns at her.

'I know you guys are sitting with him. I just want to be a part of that.' She looks down at the phone in her hand and shrugs. 'I don't know him, so I can't talk to him like you all can. All I can do for him right now, is read to him. That's it. That's all I have to offer him. A stupid book. It's pathetic.'

He stops pacing and faces her, his hands loose by his side as he examines her. 'Fuck. I honestly wasn't trying to be an ass. Epic fail.'

'You weren't being an ass. You're looking out for him. I get it.'

He crosses his arms again and looks down at the ground. 'In spite of what some fucking idiot may have said to you - this isn't your fault.'

He looks up and smirks at her. 'In case you didn't guess, I'm the fucking idiot. This isn't on you, Thea. I was angry and I shouldn't have taken it out on you. The odds of one of us getting nabbed by the bad guys is high, every time we go out. You may, or may not, have figured out by now, but I occasionally let my mouth run away with me, before my brain catches up.'

'No, you were right, Shep.'

'No. This might be one of those times when I fucked up. Believe it or not, I actually was looking for you, to maybe apologise in some way for what I said that night we lost him.'

'You were?'

'I say I may have been. I don't do apologies. Never wrong, so no need.' He smirks at her, but that's as far as he gets with his attempt at an apology. Thea doesn't mind. She'll take it.

He holds out his hand. 'Move on?'

She shakes it, squealing in surprise when he pulls her into a tight hug. 'Can't. Breathe.'

He releases her and grins. 'You need to toughen up.'

'I'll keep that in mind.'

Shep nods towards the cell door. 'So, Fallon reckons you're helping him. Got to agree with her. He's a lot calmer than he was a few days ago. Better get in there and keep the grumpy Irish git company.' He smirks to soften his words, then frowns and reaches out to brace himself against the wall.

'Are you all right?'

He blinks a few times and wipes his face. 'Yeah. All good.'

'Are you sure? You're really pale.'

'Vampires don't usually get that good of a suntan.' He winks at her but Thea isn't convinced by his performance. If anything she'd say he was about to throw up.

'I'll leave you to it.' His smile is thin and a little forced as he pushes off the wall.

'Shep—'

'Get in there. Dav needs you.'

Thea frowns down the corridor after him as he slowly makes his way around the corner. She's not quite sure what just happened, but she gets the feeling there's something wrong with him. Do vampires even get sick? She has no idea. Court never did, but that doesn't mean it never happens.

Thea goes back into the cell and sits in the chair opposite Davyn. She places her phone on her lap and looks over at him. He's facing her on the low cot, but his sleep doesn't look peaceful. Tremors work through his body, rattling the chains against the floor as he stirs.

Even though he's asleep, she continues reading to him. It's either that or stare at his gaunt, thin form. After a few chapters, she glances up to see him staring at her. His lone eye is solely focused on her, looking intently at her as she reads. She stops and lowers her phone.

'Hey. I didn't know you were awake. How are you feeling?' She's not expecting an answer, but talking to him makes this a little more normal.

'I'll start this section again. I'm not sure how much you missed...'

Thea's voice trails away as Davyn pulls himself across the floor as far as his chains will allow, then sits and stares at her. Thea gets off her chair and moves closer to the bars, gasping when she gets a better look at him. For the first time since he woke up, his eye is green. The same, familiar, sparkling green that grasped her attention from the very start.

'Davyn?'

His head tilts to the side as he stares at her. His green eye locks on to hers as he slowly places a shaking hand on his chest. Davyn swallows a few times then frowns when he tries to speak. He furrows his brows in concentration and tries again. 'Yours.'

His voice is rough and barely more than a whisper, but the word rings out loudly in the empty space. It takes her a few seconds for the meaning behind his first spoken word to break through her confusion. He presses his hand firmly to his chest and nods towards her. Is he saying what she thinks he's saying?

'What do you mean?'

'Yours.'

His level gaze leaves her with no doubts. She smiles as she places her hand over her heart and holds it there, mirroring his actions. 'It's yours too,' she says, knowing in that instant, that although it makes less than no sense whatsoever, she means it.

Davyn lies in his cell listening to Thea reading to him. He's struggling to keep hold of consciousness, but he'll fight with every ounce of strength he has left, if it means he gets to hear her voice.

He has no idea how much time has passed since they rescued him. Hell, he's not even sure they have rescued him. This is all probably just another drug and Fever induced hallucination. He'll wake up in a few minutes up to his neck in freezing water. Or worse. His lips will be sewn shut and he'll be on that terrifying platform in front of his father.

No. He's in no rush to go back to that. He'll force himself to stay awake.

She tucks her long hair behind her ear as she reads and he wants to reach out and touch it. Everything about what he's seeing feels real, but he's terrified to let himself believe he's free. If he does and he finds out it's all in his mind, it would destroy him.

He slides his hand across the floor towards her but his chain won't reach.

'It's okay, Davyn. I'm here.'

She's crouched on the ground at the bars of his cell, smiling at him. 'Can you hear me?'

He can, but his voice is done cooperating for the moment. Damn head won't move either. Controlling his body is hit and miss, and right now it's a definite miss. Every limb, every muscle, feels like it's made of lead.

The only thing he manages to move is his finger, but you'd swear he'd grabbed her hand by the smile she gives him.

'I'll take that as a yes.' She stretches out on the floor opposite him and reaches her hand towards his. It still isn't close enough to touch but the fact she did it, gives him a little comfort. 'You have to fight this, Davyn. I'm begging you. Each and every one of us is here for you. We'll help you however we can, but you need to come back to us. I need you to come back to me.'

He desperately tries to give her some acknowledgement. Some hint that he'll do whatever she wants him to do, but his vision begins to swim. He's going to wake up now. Going to be plunged back in freezing water.

Davyn looks at her face as he's dragged away from her again back into the darkness.

~

Willow walks by Shep's door then stops and turns to glare back at it. She's due to sit with Davyn for an hour so Fallon can check on the other male they rescued from the lab. The poor guy isn't faring much better than Davyn. There could be family out there somewhere desperately looking for him. Maybe a sibling waiting for him to come home. As much as Shep irritates her, she couldn't be without him.

They hadn't grown up together but Shep had been a big part of her life for the last twenty years. He took being a protective big brother to a whole new level, but she didn't mind... most of the time. Having him near, made his irritating need to control her life bearable.

She loves her big brother more than he'll ever know, but sometimes - actually, most of the time, he's infuriating, stubborn, big-headed, arrogant - the list could go on and on. No matter what he's like, she hates fighting with him. He's always been there for her. No matter what she needed, she knew all she had to do was ask, and he'd make it happen. Fighting with him just doesn't sit well with her. Especially after everything that's happened lately with Court and Davyn.

Fallon won't mind hanging on another few minutes. Willow knocks on the door, but gets no reply so she tries again. Still nothing. Willow turns the handle and slowly opens the door. Shep would be less than thrilled about her invading his privacy, but he's barged into her room enough times in the past, so let him complain.

She peers into the dark room but there's no sign of him. She places her hand on his unmade bed. It's warm. 'Shep?'

Something crashes in the bathroom and Willow hurries over to the door and knocks. 'Shep? Are you okay?'

When he doesn't reply, she opens the door and gasps. He's on the floor writhing in pain. Blood stains the floor and his lips. He coughs, and more blood pours out of his mouth. Willow drops down beside him as she pulls out her mobile and dials Fletch. 'You need to come to Shep's room. Quick.' She lets the phone fall to the floor and rubs the side of her brother's face. 'Fletch is on the way.'

Shep tries to talk, but it ends in an unhealthy cough, followed by more blood. 'It's okay. Don't try to talk.'

Willow holds his hand and strokes the side of his face as he struggles with the pain of whatever is going on with him. She can feel the tears on her face but doesn't take her hands away from him. 'Please be okay. Please.'

Shep smiles at her, then loses consciousness.

Davyn opens his eyes and takes in his surroundings. He's in a cell, but it's not the one in his father's castle. The air is clean and cool. No hint of mildew or stale sweat. He closes his eyes again and digs his fingernails into the palms of his hands. He needs to wake up. He can't be here again. Can't keep torturing himself by dreaming about being back at the compound. Back with Thea.

Not that he was, or could ever be with her. He's a monster. Seen and done horrific things she has no business knowing about, or being a part of. The best he can hope for is being able to watch her from afar.

He laughs to himself. What's left of his mind is leaving him. His life is going to end drowning in a cell, or bleeding out on the floor of the fighting pit.

Time to wake up.

He digs his fingers in to his flesh but nothing happens. Davyn opens his eyes again and looks down at his hands. There's blood oozing from the cuts on each palm. He turns his hands over. His skin is clean, his cuts bandaged with a fresh dressing. He frowns at the heavy chain around his waist that's attached to a padded cuff. There's a matching one on his other wrist, securing him to the fixed anchor point embedded in the steel wall.

Could this be real...

Ignoring the chains which have been part of his life for weeks, he gingerly touches his right eye, feeling thick padding secured by strips of tape. Judging by the pain, whatever is going on under the bandage isn't good. His trembling fingers explore his hair, the soft strands feeling unfamiliar to him. He's never been vain, but he is relieved his hair is growing out. He never saw the vile fighting tattoo on his scalp, and he plans on keeping it that way.

The searing pain from the sutures in his lips and wings is gone, but a part of him is afraid to check, just in case they're still there. He holds his breath and bends right over so he can reach his mouth. He brushes the tips of his fingers against his mouth, closing his eye in relief when he finds them gone. He can feel indents left by the wire but he doesn't care about that. He drops his hand and takes a few deep, relieved breaths.

The Blackjacks got him out.

He doesn't know why or how, but they saved him. Fragments of memories come to him, but none that makes any sense right now. It's all jumbled, like trying to differentiate between a dream and reality.

He tries to push himself on to his back, groaning as every muscle and bone in his body screams in protest, but something stops him from rolling over. He looks back at his wings and frowns in confusion. The two bandaged wings are resting on the wide bunk behind him. He cranes his neck to get a better look.

The deformed wing has somehow been repaired. It's still smaller than it should be, but even through the padding, he can clearly see it's the correct shape. He can't help the large smile that erupts on his face. He never thought his wing could be repaired. It came out of his body bent the wrong way, and he assumed it would always be like that.

'What do you think?' a strange female voice asks from outside the cell. He looks up and instinctively goes into defensive mode. He snarls at the woman but instead of backing away, the dark haired woman holds up her hands as she walks closer to the bars. 'It's okay, Davyn. I'm a friend. My name is Annie. Fletch brought me in to fix your wing.'

Davyn growls, silently eyeing the stranger. The door to the holding cell opens and Nix joins the woman. The stranger turns to Nix. 'He's back with us. I don't think he's warming to me. Certainly a lot calmer though.'

Nix nods and faces him again. 'Davyn? Do you know where you are?'

He swallows a few times but instead of soothing his dry throat it just irritates it more. 'Compound.'

She smiles, clearly happy with his answer. 'Annie is a friend. You can step down.'

He does as he's told, but not by choice. The exertion has sapped any energy he had. He flops down on the mattress, not caring if he lands on his wings or not. Nix opens the cell and slowly approaches, her hands out in front of her, like he's some sort of wild animal. Probably fitting after how he's spent the last few months. 'You good?'

He nods, unable to find the energy to do anything else. She smiles and crouches down in front of him. 'Welcome back, Davyn. This amazingly talented surgeon is Doctor Annie Simmons. Fletch used to work with her. She's got a knack for fixing badly healed bones.'

He blinks a few times as his fuzzy brain struggles to take in the information. 'She fixed my wing?' He doesn't recognise his own voice. He swallows but his throat is raw from disuse.

Nix smiles and nods. 'It'll take a lot of physical therapy, but Annie is convinced you'll be able to pull them in without causing you any pain.'

Davyn frowns. 'Can...' He winces and swallows again. 'Can I fly?'

Annie appears beside Nix and holds out a plastic cup of water which Davyn accepts. 'I'm hopeful, Davyn. For now the important thing is to arrange physical therapy for your wing. With a lot of work, who knows. I'll leave you and Nix to talk. I'll come check on you later.' She smiles kindly at him, then turns to leave them alone.

He sips from the straw, spilling half the contents over his hand thanks to a badly timed fit of the shakes. Nix takes the cup from him, placing it on the ground beside the mattress.

'How long was I gone?' He's not sure he wants to know how much of his life his father has taken from him yet again.

'Just shy of three months. We got you out a week ago.'

He instantly writes off the three months. Damn all he can do about the lost time now. It's the week back in the compound that disturbs him. He has little to no memory of that time. 'What was wrong with me?'

Nix sits on the edge of the mattress beside his knees and crosses her legs. 'Your injuries and blood starvation nearly killed you. It was touch and go for a bit. In order to give you a fighting chance, Fletch and I made the decision to give you a pretty hefty feed. It was either that or risk losing you. Unfortunately, that caused serious problems with Blood Fever. Your body and wings recovered, but you've been delirious, confused, lost, since we got you back. It took its toll on you... on all of us I guess.'

'I've been going through withdrawal?'

'According to the blood results, you were given the drug we found in the facility. It's seriously addictive,' Nix says. 'Do you remember any of the time you were gone?'

'Everything up to just after the Binding.' He frowns and shakes his head. 'I remember my father kicking me in the ribs and I ...' He closes his eyes as the memories hit him like they just happened yesterday. The sensation of the wire digging in to his lips as he struggled to breathe will stay with him forever. He jumps when someone touches his arm. He opens his eye and stares at Nix. Her eyebrows are drawn in concern.

'Am I clean now?'

'We hope so. The aggression you've been exhibiting is all but gone, but we want to leave the restraints on for another day or so, if that's okay?'

He nods and closes his eye. Sleep is calling to him and he's struggling to fight it. 'What about my eye?'

'I'm sorry, Davyn. We hoped it would regenerate, but it hasn't.'

'So I'm blind in that eye?'

'Yes. Fletch has it covered for the moment. The skin around it was badly damaged by the glass. Fletch is working with Ethan to find something we can give you to keep you fighting fit without aggravating the Blood Fever. I do have some good news however.

While you were unconscious Fletch took a few moulds of your mouth. He's got prosthetic fangs made for you.

Now I know they're nowhere near the same thing,' she continues quickly before he can comment, 'but I've seen them. Once they're fitted, you'd be hard pushed to tell the difference. He didn't want to fit them until you were conscious enough to have it done. You'll be able to feed from the vein again.'

He closes his eye as the relief washes over him. While he was never a fan of feeding from anyone, somehow having the option taken from him hit more than the rest of the Binding.

He feels the mattress move under him as Nix comes closer. 'I know it's probably the last thing you want, but I'm here for you if you need to talk about anything. We all are.'

He nods and attempts a smile. 'I'm good.' But it's a lie. He's never suffered from Fever before and he never wants to again. He's finding it difficult to concentrate, his heart is about to burst out of his chest, the damn ringing in his ears is starting to get on his wick and there's a red hot poker running through his gums.

'How did you find me?'

'We had help from an unlikely source, but I'll tell you more about that later. Your friend Ronan helped too. He's a genuinely decent man.'

Davyn nods. 'He is. Did you try to convince him to come with you?'

'Of course. After hearing a fraction of what your father is like, there was no way I wasn't going to offer.'

'Said no though, didn't he.'

'I'm sorry. He was worried if he disappeared, your father would suspect something was up. He insisted on staying.'

'Figured as much.'

He groans as a gut churning cramp pulls at his stomach. He buries his face in the pillow to hide the cry of pain as the cramp twists his insides.

He doesn't want to do this in front of Nix. He's one of her fighters.

She needs him fit and in control of his emotions. Not this snivelling, broken mess.

Why didn't Ronan leave? He should be here, safe in the compound with Davyn. Stubborn, infuriating man, always put Davyn first, no matter the risk to his own well-being.

Hot tears spill out of his eye as the humiliation of his punishment, mixes with the crippling guilt of leaving Ronan behind again. He screams into the pillow, not giving a damn that Nix is still sitting beside him witnessing his brilliant display of falling apart.

The cramp tightens its grip on his stomach, twisting it into a knot that has him crawling up the bed on all fours, until his head hits against the wall. His fingers dig into his flesh, trying to tear the demon out of his body. It adds its own cry of despair to his screams.

He feels something sharp on his upper arm, before the screams die down, leaving him locked in the dark with his pain again.

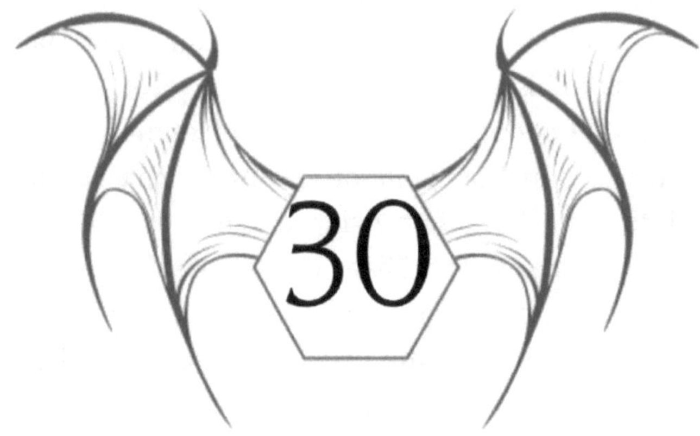

Fallon opens the outer door of the containment cell and walks up to the bars. The machines keeping the patient alive, hum and beep softly in the background. He's been unconscious since they found him in the lab where Nix was being held, months ago. Fletch had given him a few days at most, but the patient had refused to give in. How the weak specimen had survived this long is a credit to him.

She unlocks the cell and steps inside, checking the readings before allowing herself to look at him.

Fallon always prided herself on being able to remain unemotional while out in the field. Over the years, this had leaked in to her personal life, helping to keep most males at arm's length. It was something she regretted at times, but had come to accept. She thought having Fletch and her team mates in her life was enough.

Sitting beside this man, something stirred inside her that had been long forgotten... or ignored. Something she swore she would never feel again. Never let herself feel again.

She was attracted to him.

Fallon could nearly laugh out loud at the absurdity of that thought. Trust her to choose an unconscious, broken, human, who would more than likely be a basket case, if he ever wakes up. Fletch had no idea what had been done to him while he was imprisoned.

Fletch said that Court had been well looked after while he was a prisoner. This man had not been as lucky. His many wounds had been treated. His bones set. But until he wakes up, they won't know how his treatment had affected him mentally. If Court was anything to go by, there's a strong chance he won't have a memory even if he does wake up. And that's before they begin to deal with his blood.

He's human, but his blood is giving Fletch headaches. There's so much mixed in with it, he's struggling to tell what exactly is pumping around his body. He's been hooked to an IV since they got him back to the compound, in the hopes that it will help to flush his system eventually.

She checks all the readings on the various monitors then looks down at his still body. He's thin and wouldn't stand up to a fight with a child right now, but his face is frustratingly appealing. Fletch had shaved his matted hair and thick beard leaving his sunken cheeks visible. In the few weeks he's been here, his black hair has grown and she has to stop herself from touching it.

His malnourished body is broad and tall, even for a human. With a bit of meat on his bones he'd be quite impressive. Her fingers trace over the extensive tattoo of a horned steer skull on the left side of his chest. The artwork is spectacular and had given rise to his temporary name. Until he woke and could tell them his real name, he was being called Austin. Shep had wanted to call him Tex but he'd been overruled - much to his annoyance.

Being renamed would be the least of his problems. He's showing symptoms of Blood Fever which makes no sense. The illness is reserved for vampires. Why would they want to give a human Blood

Fever? How would they give it to a human? The disease was driven by the uncontrollable need for blood. Austin wouldn't have that need. Well, not unless they somehow altered him. But to what end?

Fallon sits down beside him and watches the captivating man sleep. Being attracted to a human is beyond ridiculous. She's over a century old and, unless she is killed in battle, should live for another few centuries. Austin must be in his early-to-mid forties. He's already lived nearly half his life.

That's the reason humans and vampires have no business being together. It brought nothing but heartache when the human died too soon. Dav would have that with Thea. He'll have to live centuries without her, knowing what he'd lost. Why do that to yourself? Better to be alone. Protect yourself from the inevitable loss. Better all-around to avoid that pain.

She doesn't think her heart could take it again.

~

Thea prises her arms from around her body and forces them into the back pockets of her jeans. She shouldn't be here. She knows that, but when Fletch tore past her on the way to the cells, she knew there was something wrong with Davyn.

Fletch slumps back on the floor and blows out a long breath. 'You okay, Nix?'

She nods. 'I'm fine. What the hell was that? I thought you said he was through the Fever? Why did he just fall apart like that?'

Fletch packs the syringe away in the case. 'That wasn't Blood Fever.'

'He was screaming.'

'He just woke up after being through hell and back. The poor lad is traumatised. His father tortured him for months and forced him to kill for sport. He's confused, in pain, and downright bloody miserable. What you just heard was Davyn - not Blood Fever.'

Thea slowly approaches the bed, ignoring the look cast in her direction by Nix and Fletch. Thankfully neither of them stops her and for that she's grateful. 'I thought once he was through the drug addiction, he'd be all right.'

Fletch smiles at her. 'That would have been the best case scenario, Thea. There was no possible way of knowing what else he would be dealing with until he came back to us.' He taps the side of his head. 'Up here I mean. Nix, can you help me roll him onto his side.'

Davyn has collapsed on his front on the mattress, but between the two of them they manoeuvre him over and Fletch adjusts Davyn's wings on the floor behind him. 'That should give him a few hours peace. Unfortunately, the cramps will be with him a while longer. He's still addicted to what he was given. He may be through the aggression, but he's a long way from the finish line. I'm not even sure what his finish line is.'

Nix nods. 'I know. Any word from Ethan about a safe donor for him?'

'Nothing yet. They're checking donors on file, but it's a tricky one. As a Prime, he needs Prime blood to fully function. Thanks to the drug, even a sniff of Prime blood will bring him back to the way he was when you found him. Big no-no. Trying to track down a Hybrid vampire with strong enough blood, is like finding a needle in a vampire haystack.'

'And if he doesn't find someone?' Thea asks, not sure she wants to hear the answer.

Fletch looks over at Davyn and frowns. 'Let's just keep everything crossed we do.'

Nix paces the room, keeping her eyes on Davyn. 'How long until he's critical?'

'It actually did him a favour giving him the large feed before surgery. His body is faring better than I thought it would. In his current condition, he can survive on mixed blood for a few weeks, but after that he's going to go downhill fast.' He squeezes Thea's arm and smiles. 'Hey, we're not done yet, love. He didn't go through all that for us to lose him at this stage. Might as well leave him to rest. He'll be asleep for a while.'

'I'll sit with him for a bit if that's okay? I'll stay away from him, I promise.'

Nix stops pacing and opens her mouth to argue but sighs instead. 'Fine. His chains can't reach too far but make sure you keep your distance just in case. I need to check on Shep then I'll come back for you. Don't argue with me on this, Thea. I've got two of my team down at the moment. I don't need to add you to that list.'

Thea nods and waits for them to leave her alone with Davyn before she lowers onto the ground and hugs her knees to her chest.

If she leaves the cell, she'll go to back to her room and think. At least if she's here she can concentrate on just looking at him. Not that seeing him like this is sitting well with her. She glances behind her to make sure she's alone, then crawls closer to him. His skin is pale and covered in a fine sheen of sweat. No doubt that's thanks to the Fever.

She wishes more than anything that she can go back in time and do things differently. So many things. Knowing she is the one and only reason Davyn is here like this, is something she'll never be able to get over. Not only had her actions hurt him so badly, she's also ruled out any chance there might have been at maybe taking things further with him. And that's probably the hardest part to swallow.

Thea examines his face and the guilt intensifies. There are still faint marks on his lips from the wire. He's probably going to be blind in one eye. He's lost his fangs. Each of those things will be a daily reminder of her stupidity.

~

Shep opens his eyes and blinks to clear his vision.
'You're awake.'

He looks at Willow and frowns. 'Seems so. What happened?'

Fletch and Nix appear beside Willow and the three of them face him, each one clearly pissed off, no doubt with him. Fletch tucks some hair behind his ear, then crosses his arms. 'What happened is, you've been holding out on me, Shep. On all of us. Big time.'

'What are you talking about?' Fletch jabs him in the side in the exact same spot he was injected. 'Ouch. Oh, that.'

Willow thumps him in the shoulder. 'Are you freaking kidding me? Oh that? Yes, Shepherd. That small detail. I mean were you ever going to tell us about it?'

'Would you please stop calling me Shepherd. And of course I was going to tell you.'

Nix curses under her breath. 'Like hell you were. You were going to do your usual laugh it all off, and deal with it yourself, routine.'

She's got him there. 'Okay, so maybe I was. But you all had your hands full with Dav and the dogs,' Shep says, not liking the three against one thing going on. Fletch he can handle. It's Nix and Willow that are giving him the evils. And he knows better than to get on their wrong side.

'So you keep quiet about being injected with who knows what?' Fletch says. 'You should have told me. It doesn't matter what's on my plate, I'm not going to turn any of you stubborn fuckers away. You should know that.'

Shep grimaces at the hurt on Fletch's face. 'I didn't mean that as a dig at you. At any of you. I just thought... I don't know.' Fletcher sits beside him and leans forward, clasping his hands together. 'Okay. I know that look. That's not a good look.'

'You've been out of it for just shy of twelve hours. Willow found you writhing in agony and vomiting blood. You remember that?'

'Kind of. What's wrong with me?' No one is in a rush to tell him which sets off alarm bells. Willow isn't even looking at him. 'Hey? What's wrong with me?'

Fletch licks his lips and turns to face him. 'I got your blood work back just before you woke up. I'm sorry Shep, but it looks like you were given a high dose of the enhancer.'

'The same stuff they gave to Dav?'

'It's similar...'

'Why do I get the feeling there's a 'but' coming?'

'But,' Fletch continues, 'from what Ethan's people can tell, it's a purer form of what Davyn was given.'

'So I'm going through the Fever?'

'Partly.'

'For fuck's sake, Fletch. Just tell me and stop beating around the fucking bush.'

Fletch turns his computer screen around and points to the x-ray on the screen. 'That's you. Well, your back to be precise.'

Shep doesn't immediately see what the problem is, but when he does, he has to hold on to the sides of the bed to keep himself from falling off. He looks over at Willow and knows she can see the same thing he can see. 'That's not right. I mean it can't be. Nix, this is a joke, right?'

She shakes her head. 'No, Shep. It's not a joke. Fletch took the x-rays three times.'

Shep looks back at the x-ray, still not believing what he's seeing. 'But I'm a Hybrid.'

Fletch pauses, and Shep barely stops himself from shouting at him again. 'Not entirely. Well, not anymore. Shep, the drug they gave you is altering your DNA to give it Prime traits. And those,' he says pointing to the mass at either side of his spine. 'Those are wings. Big fucking wings.'

Davyn taps Bastian's shoulder and the male comes to a stop, supporting Davyn's weight as he catches his breath. Fletch had released him from the cell, on the condition he stays in bed. Problem is, he needed help to get back to his room. His damn wings are not cooperating as usual and make walking near on impossible. 'Need a break for a sec.'

Bas lowers him onto the seat next to them and Davyn doubles over, his arm tight to his stomach. The cramps aren't letting up yet, turning his insides to a volatile ball of pain. Bas crouches down in front of him. 'You good?'

'Yeah. How's Shep doing? Heard he collapsed.'

'Fletch is still going through the rest of the results.' Bastian attempts a smile which falls short. 'You're both giving Fletch grey hairs.'

'Need to keep him busy.'

Bas smiles at him. 'He can't complain life is boring here.'

Dav nods tiredly. He's lived in the same house as Shep for years. He knows full well if something took him down, it's not good. Whatever is wrong with him, Dav doesn't have the energy to worry about it right now. His priority is getting back to his room and collapsing on his bed.

Every part of his body is either aching or downright painful. Fletch had fitted his new prosthetic fangs a few hours ago, but now his gums are throbbing, adding to the overall misery he's feeling. The addition of the black leather eye patch covering his damaged eye, is pissing him off too. He's not being ungrateful. Far from it. He's just tired of being in pain.

'Okay. Let's go.' He stands up and leans heavily on Bastian as they continue along the corridor.

He can feel Bas looking at him as he shuffles along the corridor. 'You sure you're good to be alone in your room? You don't look so great.'

'I don't feel so great. But I want to be back in my room. I want to deal with this without a fucking audience.'

Bastian takes more of his weight, as his legs decide they're not on board with keeping him upright. 'You're part of a team, Dav. You're not dealing with this alone.'

Davyn nods, but doesn't reply. He's not sure he wants them watching him battling this. The drug is out of his system, but the after-effects of Blood Fever are the real killer.

Bas opens his door and slowly lowers him onto the bed. Dav rolls onto his side and tries to ignore the fact that Bastian has to help him move up the bed. His fucking wings are a real pain in the butt, but they're a pain he's going to have to get used to for the next few days. Until they're healed, he's stuck with them out.

Bastian stands back and grimaces. 'You don't look particularly comfortable.'

'I'm not, but it's fine. No way to get comfortable with the wings out.'

He disappears into the walk-in wardrobe and comes out with another four pillows. He slips them under Dav's wings and pulls the duvet up. 'Any better?'

'Yeah. Thanks.'

'You need anything else?'

'No. I just want to sleep.'

Bas nods and turns off the light, shutting the door behind him. Davyn lies in the dark and closes his eye, opening it quickly when his fucked up brain puts him back in his cell. He reaches out and turns on the bedside light. Not much of a warrior if he's scared of the dark.

He gasps as cramps twist his insides. This is his future. This is all that's left for him. That human doctor fixed his wings, but he's not thinking about his wings right now. It's the addiction. It's his fucked up eye. It's the fact he can't feed without driving himself towards full blown Blood Fever. It's the feeling of the wire in his lips. He can't escape any of it. Can't see any way of getting through this.

He squeezes his eye shut and wraps his arms around his stomach. Maybe they should have left him where he was, cause right now, letting his father kill him is a hell of a lot better than this.

~

Rhain drops the barbell to the mat and takes the towel from Geraint. 'What the fuck do you want, Barton.' He's not usually a fan of cursing, but this irritating male is pushing all his buttons lately.

Barton frowns at the weights on the mat, then up at Rhain. 'Am I disturbing you?'

'Yes.'

'Can we talk somewhere more...'

'No. Speak her, or leave me to my business.'

Barton nods and sits on the edge of the weight bench, wrinkling his nose at the wet towel on the floor beside it. 'The Order would like to know how you are getting on.'

'I'm well, thank you.' Rhain knows he's acting like a child, but Barton and the relationship with the Order is testing his patience. He's also aware that Ethan will be expecting something useful from him soon. Having the Spaniard sent to speak to him is not something he's eager for. Rhain had researched some of the markings on the male's arms. The list of crimes the marks represent was troubling, even for someone in Rhain's line of business.

'I meant with the drug. I would like to see one of the labs.'

Rhain stalks over to him and towers over him. 'No.'

Barton attempts to get to his feet but Rhain is too close so he lowers onto the bench again. 'Excuse me?'

'I said no. I work with the True Order. Not for them. I do not answer to you, or to them. Lines are being blurred and I do not appreciate that.'

'The Order—'

'The Order does not own, or control me. I am providing the product as promised. How I do that, or where I do that, is not your concern.'

'You are forgetting your place, Rhain.'

The anger he keeps a tight hold on, breaks free. His wings burst out of his back, the silver limbs encircling Barton and the bench. His thick black talons bury into the ground, trapping the weedy male.

'No, Barton. You and your bosses forget your place. You came to my business unannounced. Now my home. I will not tolerate your constant intrusion into my life. If you keep pushing me, I promise you, I will push back. I didn't get to where I am by not knowing how to cover my tracks. Am I making myself clear, or do you need me to spell it out for you?'

Barton shakes his head briskly and Rhain watches as a bead of sweat works its way down his forehead. 'You don't need to spell it out.'

Rhain leans down and smiles at Barton. 'Good. Now I'd appreciate if you would kindly fuck off and let me get back to my workout.'

He lifts one wing a few inches off the ground, leaving Barton with no choice but to crawl out from under it to escape. Geraint gestures to the door and Barton hurries from the room.

Rhain waits until he hears the door at the far end of the external corridor close, before he shouts and drives his wings into one of the floor to ceiling mirrors lining the gym.

'Sir?'

He hadn't heard Geraint coming back into the room. 'Is he gone?'

'Escorted from the property. He will need a new suit. I believe he may have soiled himself. You realise what you've just done.'

'I answer to no one, Geraint.'

'I am aware of that, sir. But the Order may see it differently. Your actions will be reported back to them. First you kill Vincent, then you threaten Barton.'

'They have no proof I killed Vincent. If I have to take the same action with Barton, I will leave no proof behind.' He turns to look at Geraint. 'Why are you so concerned? You've been cautious about my involvement with the Order from the beginning.'

'As I still am. But involved you are. I would not be doing my job if I did not warn you about your actions.'

Rhain scrubs a hand through his hair. He's struggling to calm down. Maybe he should have decapitated Barton. It probably would have satisfied his anger. 'Check on the latest shipment.'

'I should see to the mirror first.'

'The shipment, Geraint. Let's not give the fucking Order anything to complain about.'

Geraint bows stiffly and leaves him alone. He can't tolerate much more of this. The link with the Order must be broken. But not yet. He has nothing of use for Ethan. Offering to bring them down from the inside is all well and good. Unless he finds something concrete the Blackjacks can use to dismantle the group, Rhain's future will consist of being a pet for the Order for the rest of his life, or dying at the hands of Ethan's Spanish protector. Neither option is particularly appealing.

~

Davyn pushes himself up the bed when someone knocks on his door. He doesn't really want any company, but he's not doing himself any favours being here alone. He can't stop the constant replay that's going on in his head. Sleep ends in nightmares which come to him while he's awake too. A distraction might not do him any harm.

That all sounded fair enough, until he sees who steps into his room. Court stays by the door and smiles at him. 'Can I come in?'

Dav tries to get himself further up the bed, but his wings aren't cooperating. 'What do you want?'

'Not to beat on you again, I promise. I just need a few minutes. Please.'

Davyn nods, so Court walks around the bed, leaving the door open a crack, and Davyn is grateful for that. At least he's not trapped in a room with the pissed off father of the human he fed from. Not that he'd be able to make a run for it.

Court sits on the chair beside his bed and rests his arms on his legs as the silence settles. The Court sitting beside him is a different Court to the one Davyn went on his last mission with. He's been taking advantage of the training room. Davyn looks down at his own frail body and realises if Court decides to deck him, he'll probably break.

'How are you?'

Davyn will play along for the moment. 'Fine.'

'You look a hell of a lot better than you did when I last saw you. That's good.'

Davyn nods, not sure what the hell is going on. Court hates him. When he drank from Thea, Court had quite rightly been furious and used his 'mind fuck powers' to well and truly mess with him. In those few minutes Court was in his mind, Dav could feel the contempt the second in command had for him.

220

Court straightens in the chair and rubs the back of his neck. 'Okay, so I'm going to get right down to it. I should have come to see you a long time ago. I need to talk to you about Thea.'

Davyn's tongue sticks to the roof of his mouth as he waits for the punch.

Court leans forward again and Dav can't help but think he's as uncomfortable about this encounter as he is. 'Listen, I don't quite know how to say this to you, but thank you. You saved her life, Davyn and I owe you.'

Davyn hopes his breath of relief is hidden from Court. He was expecting a punch not a thank you.

'It's grand.'

Court shakes his head. 'No, Davyn. It's absolutely not grand. I don't even know how to begin to thank you. And I owe you an apology for what I did to you. I had no right pushing into your head like I did. I'm ashamed and disgusted at myself. I understand if you can't forgive me. I honestly couldn't blame you.'

Davyn knows Court saw a little of his memories when he got into his head. Dav had been powerless to stop sharing snippets from his brutal childhood. And he can't meet Court's eyes because of that. Not that he'd risk eye contact in case Court decided to go for round two and pull out more shite from his past.

'It's grand, really.'

'You can look at me. I've got a good hold on my powers.'

Davyn looks at Court, but only so he can finish this conversation and get back to wallowing alone. In hindsight, being alone was a hell of a lot easier than whatever this is.

Court's unnerving pale blue eyes meet his and he smiles. 'If you ever need anything, Davyn, just ask. I mean that. If you hadn't gotten to Thea when you did, I... well, I don't even want to go there.'

'It's grand.' Davyn hears the flippant reply coming out for a third time but it's all he can come up with.

Court shakes his head. 'Don't let me off the hook so easily. I acted like an over protective father when I attacked you. I don't appreciate you feeding from my daughter, but I know it was what she wanted. I should have let you explain, instead of forcing myself into your mind. I launched in and made everything ten times worse.'

'We both fucked up,' Davyn says, finally getting his brain to form an actual sentence. 'You were right. I shouldn't have touched her. But I swear I didn't hurt her, Court. She's your daughter. I wouldn't—'

'I know, Davyn. I know. I'd really like if we could start over.'

Court holds out his hand and Davyn stares at it for a few seconds before grasping it.

'Thank you, Davyn. I appreciate the second chance.'

He stops himself from replying with it's grand, leaving it at a nod instead.

Court gets up and gestures to the door. 'I'll leave you to get some rest.' He gets as far as the door before he stops and turns back to him. 'What I saw when I was in your head. It hasn't gone any further. It never will. You have my word.' He closes the door, leaving Davyn alone again.

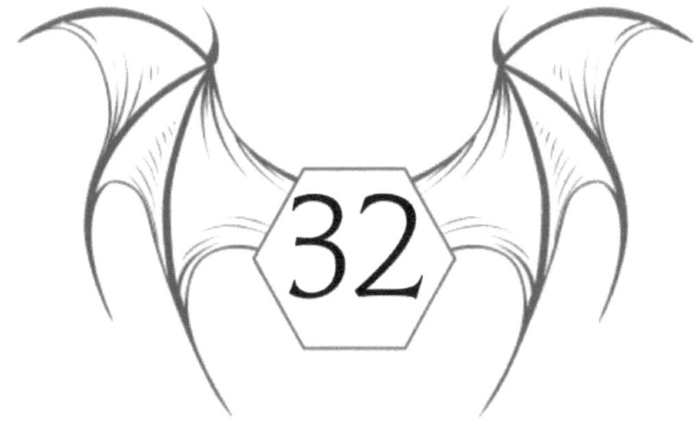

Thea walks up to Davyn's door, lifts her hand to knock, then lowers it again. She's been completing the same ritual for going on seven minutes, and she's starting to piss herself off. She went to see him in the cell, only to find that she was too late. Annie and Fletch had let him come back to his own room to recover.

She silently kicked herself every step of the walk from there to here. Seeing him in the cell would have been so much easier than his private room. The last time she was here was when he fed from her. That hadn't gone too well for her, and she wasn't keen on repeating the experience. Especially after what had happened between them.

She pushes her shoulders back and straightens her t-shirt. She had thrown on the first one in her drawer and is now adding that choice to her list of regrets. The faded, and slightly too big t-shirt had a picture of a unicorn on the front. It had been relegated to her pyjama pile a long time ago and was most definitely not something she wanted someone she's attracted to, seeing her in.

She glances down at the faded multicoloured unicorn and grimaces. As if a t-shirt is going to make one bit of difference. This is Davyn she's talking about. She doubts he keeps an eye on the latest fashion trends. His entire wardrobe seemed to consist of his fighting clothes, faded blue jeans, scuffed biker boots, and a few black t-shirts.

She pushes her hair off her shoulder, somewhat grateful that she at least took the time to wash and style it after her training session earlier. 'Right unicorn, let's do this.'

Before she chickens out... again, she knocks three times and holds her breath, a small part of her hoping he doesn't answer.

A gruff, 'Yeah,' from inside the room stops any chance of her making a run for it. She licks her lips, smooths out the unicorn again, and opens the door. A soon as she sees him, her feet plant themselves to the floor.

He's lying on his side, propped up on half a dozen pillows. It looks like his first priority after escaping the cell was to spend some time on himself. His thick hair has been shaved at the sides and back again, but not enough to show the crude tattoo on his head. The top is much shorter than usual and standing up in soft spikes. His scraggly beard has been trimmed and hugs his strong jaw. He'd also put back in his eyebrow rings, helping to make him look more like his old self.

His enormous wings lie behind him, taking up their fair share of the bed. Each one is wrapped in heavy gauze, securely protecting his wings in a moisture rich cocoon. While in his father's custody, he had lost a lot of muscle making his t-shirt seem a little too big for him. In spite of the enormous wings, he seems a lot smaller than she remembers, and that upsets her.

'You okay?'

His question brings her out of her thoughts. She looks away from him, focusing on the damn unicorn again. The creature's mocking smile does nothing to help her embarrassment. 'Yeah. I... I just wanted to see how you were. Or are. How are you?' She clamps her mouth shut and hopes he loses consciousness in the next few seconds so she can make a run for it.

He pulls himself up the bed and she swears he smiles. 'I'm good. Are you okay?'

'Me? I'm fine. Why?'

'They took me to the ground before I saw Court and Nix get you out of the lab. I hoped you were okay but I didn't know for sure.'

'You guys got me out in time. I owe my life to you, Davyn. I can never thank you for what you did. When the others came back and said they couldn't find you... it's my fault this happened to you.'

'No it isn't.'

'If I hadn't–'

'My father did this to me - not you. He was going to get me sooner or later.' He looks away and shrugs. 'Anyway, we're even. Nix said you talked me down on the helicopter. You saved them and me from having more blood spilt.'

'I did that partially out of selfish reasons. I just wanted it all to end. For everyone to be safe and back here. It was dumb luck. I honestly didn't think you'd listen to me.'

Davyn closes his eye and sucks in a breath. In spite of her best efforts, she takes a step closer to him.

'Are you all right?'

'Yeah. Just taking a little longer than usual to regenerate.'

'Is that because of the drug you were given?'

He nods. 'Among other things.'

His brief smile doesn't help to ease Thea. Everything that happened to her father and to Davyn is like something out of a nightmare she could never imagine. A nightmare she's finding it difficult to escape from. Most nights she finds herself back in that place. 'I could hear the donor vampires screaming...' Her words trail away as the sounds come back to her. Did her father scream like that, alone, in the dark, terrified about his future? Did Davyn?

'Hey, you're safe.'

She blinks and looks up at him, coming back to the present. He tries to sit up, but doesn't manage to complete the manoeuvre, flopping back on the pillows. 'I know.' She forces a smile trying to reassure herself as much as Davyn. 'I just wish the Blackjacks had managed to find the guy responsible for that place. Make sure he couldn't continue whatever he's doing.'

He runs a hand over his hair and looks away from her. 'They will.'

She immediately notices he hasn't included himself in that statement. Deciding it best not to mention she noticed, Thea stuffs her hands in the back pockets of her jeans as she searches for anything else remotely intelligent to say to him. True to form, Davyn doesn't offer any conversational help as he stares at her. 'Right, well I better let you get some rest. I just wanted to thank you.' She turns to leave, but he stops her as she gets to the door.

'I don't remember a lot of what happened after I was rescued, but I do remember you reading to me. Well, I'm hoping I'm remembering right and it wasn't some drug-induced dream.'

She looks at him again and smiles. 'You remember?'

'Just bits. I'm having a hard time separating what really happened, from whatever my fucked up brain invented. I'm just glad I got something right.'

Thea's face remains the same but a little bit of her sinks at the news. Whatever small hope she had that he'd remember what he said to her in the cell, disappears. He was so out of it, he could have been saying anything to anyone and he wouldn't remember. 'I just thought reading would be a better option than making idle chit-chat.'

'I appreciate you taking the time to do that.' He swallows deeply a few times then pushes the covers back and slides his legs out of the bed. 'Bathroom. Back in a minute.' She has to stop herself from rushing over to help as he tries, unsuccessfully, to get up. 'Fuck,' he mutters under his breath. His head drops to his chest and Thea wants to cry for him. The most feared member of the Blackjacks has been reduced to needing help to get off his bed.

Without a word, she moves over to the bed and offers him her hand. He lifts his head to look at her outstretched limb. His shoulders sink slightly and he curses to himself again. Davyn takes her hand and she supports him as he finally gets to his feet. She helps him shuffle over to the en-suite and, trying to give him a little privacy, sits on the end of his bed as he closes the door behind him.

Five minutes later the door slowly opens and a very pale Davyn shuffles out. 'Sorry about that. Stomach still isn't right.'

'Don't be silly. It's fine.'

He tries to make his own way back to the bed, but he stumbles, catching himself on the door jamb before he hits the ground. 'Damn wings.'

She slips her arm under his and brings him back over to the bed. 'Other side,' he says when she heads to the near side. 'I can't turn in the bed with these things out.'

Thea slowly walks with him around to the other side of the bed and stands out of his way as he slides back onto the mattress and manoeuvres himself on to his side again. 'You have to do that every time you want to get in and out of bed?'

He nods tiredly. 'Just while my wings are out. They weren't designed with beds in mind.'

'How long do you have to have them out for?'

'Few more days. Fletch wants to make sure they don't fall apart when I try to pull them back in. If I'm not strong enough or they're not strong enough, it'll damage them and me.' Davyn looks away from her and rubs the back of his neck. 'Speaking of wings, I owe you an apology for the way I was with you, when you arrived. I was a dick. I had no right speaking to you like that.'

'You've got nothing to apologise for. I was snooping in your business. After seeing what I have since I've arrived here, I know you had a point. I was sticking my nose into matters I know nothing about.' She laughs. 'I guess I thought that vampires only existed since

I found out about Court. We were both learning about what he was at the same time. I'm still struggling to get my head around the fact you've existed for... well, a long time, and I still have a lot to learn. I deserved to be put in my place.'

'Like hell you did.' He tucks his arm under his pillow hiding his eye patch. 'My issue with my wings had nothing to do with you. But you were right. I should have told the others I'm a Prime.'

'Well, it's all out in the open now, and that's a good thing. So, Lord Davyn Oldranson... I'm not sure of the protocol for being in the presence of a vampire lord.'

He smiles slightly as she bows. 'Fuck the protocol. Never played a part in my life. It's a title - nothing more. And no bowing or calling me sire.' His face drops and he looks away from her. 'I don't want any part of that. Ronan is the only one who insisted on using my title.'

His voice trails away and Thea instantly regrets her joking. He had to leave someone important behind in that place. Someone close to him. Someone who, no doubt, called him sire and treated him like the lord he is. 'I'm sorry about your friend.'

He nods and picks at the sheet covering his chest. Thea's eyes drift to the spot where he had so forcefully put his hand less than a week ago. She can still hear his gravelly voice as he uttered that one word - yours.

She knows it's not the same, but she begins to understand how Nix must have felt when her father forgot what had happened between them. More than anything, she wants to touch him, wants to feel that powerful chest under her hand, and, as selfish as it sounds, wants to continue to be the one to help him through this, but he doesn't need her anymore - not that he needed her in the first place. It was more that she needed to spend time with him. She doesn't want to accept that their time alone has come to an end.

He reaches for the glass of water by his bed and drinks from the straw. She tries not to stare but she can't help looking at the eye patch covering his damaged eye. He catches her looking and she turns away quickly. 'Are you going to be okay? I mean, will you be able to go back to the Blackjacks... you know, like properly?'

He shrugs and looks up at her again. 'I hope so. Fletch thinks my eye is as good as it's going to get, which is pretty much fucked. Lost my sight in it completely.' He looks away and shrugs. 'As long as I can still fight and not drag the team down Nix will put me on rotation again.'

'That's good,' she says again. She pulls her eyes away from his face and gets up. 'Well, I better leave you to get some rest.'

She walks towards the door, desperate to stay but unable to think of a valid reason. 'Thea?'

'Yes?'

He opens his mouth, then closes it again. The silence hangs for an awkward few seconds. 'Thanks again.' She smiles and closes the door behind her, wondering what he really wanted to say before he talked himself out of it.

Davyn stops outside the gym and takes a few deep breaths. Fletch is waiting inside so he can monitor Davyn while he attempts to pull his wings back in to his body. Every single time he's released or retracted his wings in the past, the pain was intense. While he wants them in his body, he's not looking forward to actually doing the deed. He'd tried to convince Fletch to let him do it in private, but Fletch wasn't having any of it.

Drinking himself senseless while he did it, sounded like the perfect solution. Damn doctor probably knew what he'd planned to do. Nix had backed Fletch up, which just made the whole thing that much more irritating. He's been releasing and pulling his wings back the same way for nearly two centuries. The last thing he wants to do is change that now - especially when it's always gone hand in hand with a shed load of pain.

He takes another deep breath and forces his feet to carry his pathetic ass inside the room.

'I was about to send out a search party.'

Davyn ignores the cheery doctor and stops in front of the heavy metal frame embedded in the floor. A favourite of his during training, the ladder would give him the support he needed so he wouldn't land on his ass, and embarrass himself any more than he already has.

Needing help and monitoring while he pulls his sorry excuses for wings back into body, is pathetic. The sooner he can get this over with and find a bottle of anything that will help numb the humiliation, the better.

'Right, as chatty as ever,' Fletch mumbles from behind him. Davyn looks over his shoulder as the door opens. His stomach drops when Fallon and Annie step into the room and stop beside Fletch.

'Why are you here?'

'I've asked Fallon to help with your wings,' Fletch says, handing his sister a pair of scissors. 'There's a lot a wrapping keeping those rather monstrous limbs safe and secure. It'll be quicker to free them with help.'

'And I wouldn't miss this for the world,' Annie says. 'I put a lot of my expertise and exceptional skill into those two bad boys. I want to see if I've done you justice.'

Davyn looks back at the ladder. Monstrous is right. He closes his eye and curses himself. He's just adding more topping to his pathetic cake, but he can't seem to stop. He may have escaped his father and the Binding, but he's doing nothing but carrying on his father's work. His father always called him useless and weak, and he's doing a damn fine job proving the bastard right.

He jumps as someone touches his wings. 'Hey,' Fallon says in a soft voice, which only adds to his uneasiness. Fallon doesn't do soft with anyone. 'We're just cutting the bandages off. It'll be okay. Just keep still.'

He nods but doesn't say anything. He looks up and meets his reflection in the floor to ceiling mirror on the far wall. He barely recognises himself. Thin, weak, broken, only one eye - he's far from the warrior he used to be. Cool air hits his wings and he directs his gaze in the mirror to what Fletch and Fallon are doing.

He doesn't ever remember seeing his wings like this. Brought up to detest them, he barely looked at the limbs when they were out, and in his father's castle, they had been chained behind his back. Until now, he never realised how large they actually are.

Fletch, Annie, and Fallon step back. 'Okay, Davyn. Can you open them?' Annie asks. 'Take it at your own pace. I just need to see if everything has healed.'

Davyn focuses on the wings in his reflection and wills them to do as he's asking. The right one does as it's told and he manages to stretch it to nearly its full span. The female doctor had done an impressive job. As soon as he saw the jagged spear of bone tearing through his wing, he thought that both his wings would be useless, but it looks as good as new. It takes him a few seconds to notice that the deformed wing is also moving outwards.

Thanks to the direction of the original break, the wing only ever stretched behind him - never to the side as it should. He laughs as it moves in and out with the other one. The movements are weak and the reach pretty shite, but it's the shape it should be.

Davyn ignores everyone else in the room as he takes a few minutes to familiarise himself with his new and improved wings. The heavy red skin is still fragile, but a few days inside him would fix that.

'I'm guessing that's a happy face?' Annie says from his left.

'Yeah. Thank you.'

Annie's squeezes his shoulder. 'You're more than welcome.'

Fletch and Annie carefully examine the wings for a few minutes as he hangs on to the ladder. He's exhausted already and he hasn't even pulled them in yet.

Fletch smiles as he walks around to face him. 'They're looking good, Dav. I think it's time to tuck them back inside you. Are you okay to give it a shot?'

'Better get it over with.'

Fletch slaps him on the shoulder. 'That's the spirit. Annie, you happy?'

She nods at Fletch. 'More than happy. Even with your slightly slower than usual regeneration, they've healed remarkably well. The fact you can move your left wing is impressive.'

'Okay, this is where it gets serious. As your wings have been out for so long, it may take your body some time to adjust to having them back inside you. You may feel a little...'

'It'll hurt. I know.' Davyn's wings had been held out of his body by his father as a punishment when he was younger. He had passed out from the pain when he was eventually allowed to retract them again.

'Whenever you're ready then.'

Davyn closes his eyes. He doesn't want to look at the others while he does this. It's bad enough having them here, without looking at them while he makes a fool of himself. He blocks out all the sounds around him and concentrates on his wings. It takes a few seconds but his body has the good sense to do as it's told. The skin to either side of his spine splits, as the repaired wings seek the refuge of his body. He leans heavily on the ladder as the pressure of the limbs retracting, threatens to topple him off his feet.

Davyn holds his breath, waiting for the searing pain that goes hand in hand with this act... but it doesn't come. The sensation is far from comfortable, his body feels like it's being stretched to beyond its capacity, but it's not painful. Usually his flesh tears as the deformed wing forces it's way inside, but not now. Unless nothing is actually happening and the wings are stuck half in and half out. He could be hanging on to the ladder for the next ten minutes waiting for the damn things to fully retract. It's a fucking joke.

'Well done, mate.' Fletch slaps him on the back. 'How do you feel?'

Davyn opens his eyes and stares at his reflection. His wings are in. 'What the fuck?'

'What's wrong?' Annie asks, her voice full of concern.

'They're in.'

'Isn't that the point?'

'It didn't hurt.'

Annie smiles at him. 'That's very good to hear. How are you feeling?'

Exhaustion suddenly hits him. 'Tired.'

'I'm not surprised. Let's get you in to one of the rooms beside the surgery. I'd like to keep an eye on you for a little longer.'

Davyn nods, then looks back at the mirror. He's still finding it hard to believe they went in without any pain. Maybe he'll be able to release them without pain too. He follows Fletch to the medical centre and climbs on the bed offered to him.

'Try to get some rest. Your wings have been out for a hell of a long time. It'll take your body time to get used to them again. Are you in any pain?'

Davyn shakes his head. 'Uncomfortable, but not painful.'

'How about I give you something to help you sleep? You look exhausted.'

Davyn's initial reaction is to say no, but he stops himself. He hasn't been able to sleep without waking up with nightmares. Maybe if he's knocked out he can get a few hours peace. 'Yeah. Thanks.'

Fletch prepares the injection and Davyn lies back as he injects him in the arm. 'I'll check on you in a bit.'

Davyn nods but is already feeling the welcome pull of unconsciousness.

Davyn opens his eyes and blinks to clear his vision. Everything hurts, but in a good way. It feels like he's done a few hours in the gym. More importantly, he can feel his wings inside - back where they belong. He may hate the damn things, but he'd prefer to have them in, than stuck out and getting in the way. He rolls on to his side and freezes.

Thea is curled up on the chair beside his bed. Of all the people he'd expected to see when he woke up, it wasn't her - not that he was expecting anyone to be sitting with him. He knows it's probably all kinds of creepy, but he can't help but watch her as she sleeps. Her dark hair has fallen over her face and she's hugging her legs to her chest. He'd give anything to be able to gather her in his arms and hold her while she sleeps.

He thought her blood had worn out of his system long ago, but when she's close to him, he can still feel her. It's like her presence reignites the effect her blood has on him.

He licks his lips. Hell, he can still taste her on his tongue. He had heard rumours of certain humans whose blood could drive a vampire to distraction. A few of his father's men had fallen foul of the curse, but he never put much stock in the claim. Now he's not so sure. There's something about it that's slowly driving him crazy, but he can think of worse ways to go.

Unless he's not as over his drug addiction as he thought. The idea doesn't sit well with him either. He shakes his head. What he feels when he's near her, is completely different to what he experienced thanks to his father's drugs. The feeling itself isn't unpleasant. Distracting, yes, but not painful. The gut twisting agony he went through during the initial withdrawal, is no comparison.

Thea mutters in her sleep and he frowns. He could have sworn she said his name. He briskly shakes his head. Now he's hallucinating. Maybe there is something wrong with him.

He grabs the eye patch from the table next to his bed and slips it on. Vanity has no part in hiding the milky coloured eye. It's shame. He should have been able to block the attack in the pit. His father took a lot from him over the weeks in captivity, but losing his sight in his right eye, that's down to him.

Thea stretches and yawns loudly as she opens her eyes. She wipes her mouth with her sleeve, before she realises he's awake and looking at her. She pushes up in the chair and fumbles with her hair. 'Hey! I mean hi. Sorry. Was I asleep? I didn't mean to fall asleep.'

'You been here long?'

She tries to get to her feet, but curses and sits down again. 'Ouch. Leg is still asleep. No, not long. Well, I'm not sure.' She checks her watch and grimaces. 'Shoot, maybe longer than I thought. Em... how are you feeling?'

'Good.'

'Really? I mean they're pretty big. Does it not hurt having them back inside you?'

'Our bodies are designed to take them.' He shrugs. 'You'd have to ask Fletch about how it works.'

She smiles and looks down at her watch again. 'I probably should let you get some rest.'

'I've just woken up.' His gaze travels up her body, stopping at her lips as she licks them. 'Rest is the last thing I want right now.'

He curses himself as soon as the words have escaped. Whatever fleeting hope he has that she might not have heard him, disappears as she freezes and looks at him, colour touching her cheeks. He clamps his mouth shut in case any more stupid statements make a run for it. Thea tucks her hair behind her ear then looks him straight in the eye. 'Do you need anything? Are you hungry. Do you want me to get you some food... or some... something to drink?'

Not unless it's your blood. Luckily that comment has the sense to stay locked in his head, but the fact it materialised at all freaks him out. He's having a hard enough time distinguishing reality from nightmares. If he can't tell the difference between what he's saying in his head or out loud, he's in for a fun time. 'No, I'm good.' Before he can say anything else Thea nods and jumps to her feet. She opens the door, and closes it quietly behind her without another word.

Davyn throws himself back against the bed sending pain through the newly healed wounds left by his wings. 'Fuck, that hurt.' He covers his face with his hands, both angry with himself for forgetting about his back and frustrated about what he said to Thea. He needs to get his shit together before he embarrasses himself.

The door bursts open and Thea steps inside again, closing the door behind her. She leans against the door, both hands behind her grasping the handle.

'In the cell you said something, and I need to know if you really don't remember saying it, or if you do and seriously regret it.'

He pushes himself upright and sits at the edge of the bed staring at her, hoping she's not going to say what he thinks she's going to say. He knows exactly what she's talking about and really doesn't want to go there.

'What?'

'You put your hand on your heart and said something.'

Davyn feels like he's going to be sick. He never expected to be having this conversation with her. The only things he clearly remembers, are seeing Thea at the castle, and letting his guard down in the cell, all but admitting his feelings for her. He clenches his jaw and focuses on the clock on the wall, instead of her face.

Thea slowly shakes her head as she watches him. 'Oh my God. You remember. Why didn't you say anything?'

'I thought you didn't want to talk about it. I just wanted to forget the whole damn thing.'

'So you do regret it? That's all you have to say. I'm a big girl, Davyn. I can take the truth.'

He looks back at her and knows this is it. He has to tell her the truth no matter how painful. 'Of course I regret it.'

~

Thea feels sick when she hears his words. It was bad enough thinking he didn't remember saying what he did, but knowing that he regretted it... that's too much for her. She nods and smiles weakly before leaving his room. She waits until she's rounded the corner before racing back to her room and locking the door behind her. She sits on the edge of her bed and stares at the wall opposite her.

So, that's that. Whatever small hope she's been clinging to has been squashed. It was a ridiculous notion in the first place. She's not even thirty yet and he's a few decades off two hundred years old.

She laughs harshly to herself. That's one hell of an age gap. As if that makes the slightest difference to anything. He's a vampire. Age should come a distant second to that. He's a vampire lord and warrior from an ancient bloodline. He should settle down with someone like him.

A knock at the door brings her out of her thoughts. She holds her breath, hoping whoever is there gets the message and leaves.

'I know you're in there, Thea. Open the door.' Davyn knocks again, harder this time. 'I'm not leaving, so just open the damn door.'

She pulls the door open. 'I'm embarrassed enough as it is. I don't need everyone else to hear about this. Will you keep it down.'

'Everything okay?'

Davyn turns to growl at Bastian. 'Mind your own damn business. Go.'

'You okay, Thea?' Bastian asks, clearly not thrilled with what's going on.

Thea smiles and nods at Bastian. 'I'm fine, really. We've just had a slight disagreement.'

Bastian takes a few steps closer to Davyn. 'Fletch is looking for you. He wants to know why his recovery room looks like a hurricane flew through it.'

'I'll talk to him when I'm done. Back the hell off and let me talk to her in private.'

With one last look at Thea, Bastian slowly backs down the corridor, stopping at the bench under the large bay window. He sits down and crosses his arms, clearly with no intention of leaving Thea alone. Davyn ignores his team mate and follows Thea in to her room, closing the door behind them.

Thea sits on the end of her bed. 'What do you want, Davyn?'

He drops heavily in to the chair and takes a few breaths. His face is pale and his eyebrows are drawn as if he's in pain. 'Why did you run off like that?'

'The conversation was done. I thought you could do with some rest.'

'I wasn't done and I told you I didn't want any more damn rest. I was trying to tell you...' He sighs and shakes his head. 'I don't know what I was trying to say, but I know I wasn't finished.'

'Do we really have to have this conversation? You regret telling me what you did. I get it. You were confused and under the influence of whatever your father gave you. We really don't have to talk about it anymore. I'll get over it.'

He rubs his forehead then drops his hand down on the arm of the chair with a thud. 'That's my point, Thea.'

'I'm glad we agree.'

'Will you stop talking for one minute so I can talk?'

His gruff command has the desired effect. She gestures for him to continue, wishing he'd get it over with and get out of her room, so she can wallow in self-pity by herself. Having him here, rehashing the regret he feels, isn't helping.

He leans forward, resting his arms on his legs and looks up at her, locking on to her with his glowing green eye. 'I don't regret what I said. When I said it in the cell, I was as clear headed as I am now. What I regret is that, by saying it when I did, I've left you wondering if I meant it or not.'

He laughs to himself as he drops his gaze. 'To be honest, I thought you wanted to forget it ever happened. You didn't bring it up, so I left well enough alone.' When he looks at her again, he smiles slightly and places his hand on his heart. 'It's still yours, Thea. Has been since the first moment I saw you,' he adds quietly .

Thea is at a loss for words. She had imagined him saying those words to her, but had accepted that he never would. She looks across the room at him, searching for any hint that he may be having a laugh with her, but there's nothing. If anything, she would have said he looks a little nervous. 'Do you remember how I replied?'

'Everything is muddled. I was going from the castle to the compound in my head, and couldn't tell what was real or not.' He glances up at her and taps the side of his head. 'Up here you played along.'

Thea can barely believe this is happening. She'd seen and heard him say the words that day in his cell, but like he said, his mind wasn't clear while he was recovering. That doubt had tarnished what he had said. But here he is. This stunning vampire is sitting a few feet from her, saying that he has feelings for her. After everything she did to him, he still cares. And that stuns her.

'Why are you crying?'

Thea wipes her face, surprised to find tears on her cheeks. 'Sorry, not sure where they came from.'

'I should go. I've upset you.'

She shakes her head. 'No. Absolutely not. I'm not upset. I'm relieved.'

'You're crying because you're relieved?'

'I'm relieved, because I told you my heart belongs to you too and I meant it,' she responds with a smile.

His face breaks in to an enormous smile that stuns her. 'Really?'

'Of course, really.'

He tries to stand up, but gasps in pain and slumps back in the chair. He holds his stomach as he sucks in a deep breath, screwing his eye shut. Thea hurries over to him, dropping to her knees in front of him. 'What's wrong?'

'Got up too fast.' He opens his eye and smiles weakly at her. 'I'm fine.'

He's not fine, but she lets it go... for now. 'Will you let me help you back to Fletch? You probably should be resting.'

'You really said it. It wasn't in my head?'

'I really said it, Davyn.'

He tips his head forward, resting his forehead against hers. Thea closes her eyes as his rough hand touches the side of her face and the other slides around the back of her neck, holding her close to him. His thumb slowly rubs against her jaw and she takes a minute to enjoy the contact with him. Or does, until she can feel the tremors working through his body.

She wants to kiss him, but it doesn't feel like the right moment, even after everything they've said to each other. He's still a little guarded, but she's not sure if that's down to his health or her. Whatever the reason, she gets the impression she has to take things slow with him. At least while he's recovering.

But she doesn't mind. There's something going on between them and, for now, that's all that matters. There are bigger bridges to cross with him. Making sure he's well is the important thing right now.

'You look a little pale. Will you let me take you back to Fletch?'

He nods and she takes his arm, helping him to his feet. 'I'm sorry.'

Thea pushes back from him. 'Sorry about what?'

'You shouldn't have to do this for me.'

'Hey, never apologise for that. Your body has been through a lot lately. Don't try to push yourself too hard.'

He nods again and Thea walks beside him through the house and back to Fletch. They finally get back to Fletch's room and she helps him back onto the bed.

She's still trying to process the fact he meant what he said in the cell. But what happens now? Usually there would be a kiss or something like that, but he barely looks like he can stand, let alone consider doing anything romantic.

'Where the fuck did you go?' Fletch asks as he comes back into the room. 'You know you could have asked me to unhook you from the monitors, instead of tearing the leads from the machine.'

'I was in a rush.'

Fletch points to the bed. 'Lie down. Is everything okay? I mean the reason for you rushing off like that.'

Davyn looks over at her and the faintest of smiles makes a brief appearance. 'Yeah. It's great.'

Fletch looks from her to Davyn then shakes his head and walks over to a set of drawers. 'I'm pretty sure I don't want to know. Okay, so I'll give you a once over, then you can probably head back to your room. You feeling okay? Any residual pain. Oh and I'm expecting the truth and not just a brush off.'

'Back is aching, stomach feels off, and I'm still really fucking tired.'

Fletch stares at him over his shoulder. 'Wow. That actually sounded like the truth. How's the hunger?'

Davyn glances at her before answering. 'Manageable.'

'Got it. We're on the case. I know you'll probably be itching to get back to training, but you're going to have to take it easy for now. Your regeneration will be slower because you're not feeding. Can't have you putting yourself in the middle of a scrap, until you're back in tip top form.'

'Has Ethan had any luck yet?' Thea asks, even though she knows the answer.

'Not yet,' Fletch says. 'There are still a lot of donors to access. We'll find one suitable.'

Not caring that Fletch is in the room with them, Thea takes Davyn's hand and squeezes it. He looks over at her and she could nearly cry at the look of utter despair in his face. He's accepted they won't find someone.

She holds his hand tighter. She hasn't given up hope and there's no way she's going to let him give up either. Not at this stage. Not when they've finally found each other.

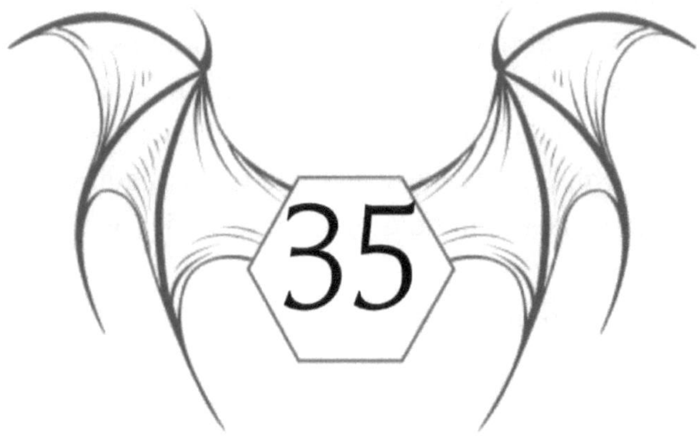

Davyn straightens his shoulders as he walks towards Fallon. He'd prefer to be anywhere other than here, but there's no point having wings if he doesn't know how to use them. Of all the females on the team, Fallon was the one that he picked to help him.

Willow and Nix are great, but he knows he's going to get pissed off with whoever helps him. He's already on edge and he hasn't done a damn thing yet. If he's going to get confrontational with any of them, he'd prefer it was Fallon.

The last thing he wants to do is get on the wrong side of Nix. And if he did anything to Willow, he'd have Shep to deal with. In his current condition, Shep would destroy him without even trying.

Fallon turns to face him and crosses her arms. The red-haired Blackjack is one hell of a fighter and without a doubt, top of the list of team members he'd happily go into a fire fight with. He grimaces at the thought. He doubts Fallon would have him at the top of her list right now.

'You're late.'

'I know,' he replies. There's no reason. Unless dragging his feet is a reason.

'Take off your top.'

Davyn pull off his t-shirt and throws it on the ground beside him. He can feel Fallon's eyes on him as she walks around him and stops at his back. It's a mess of scars from centuries of damage, thanks to the broken wing. He's a good few inches taller than Fallon, but for some reason, he feels small and weak under her scrutiny. He'd lost so much muscle mass while his father had him, he must look pathetic next to her.

'Can I touch your wing ridges? I just want to check they're working correctly.'

He nods, but he'd prefer she didn't go anywhere near them. He braces for the pain as her fingers probe his skin. But there's nothing. He can feel the pressure of her touch but that's it.

'Any pain?'

'No.'

'That's good. I was just pinching you. Now that Annie has realigned your wing it will travel out through the ridge. You shouldn't feel a thing. Release your wings.'

His body tenses at her words. It's a reaction he can't keep under control. It doesn't hurt to release them anymore, but the memory of the pain is going to be difficult to get over.

'Your body has healed well,' Fallon says from behind him. 'Trust the process. It won't hurt you.'

Davyn concentrates on his wings, feeling them moving inside his back. Little by little, they emerge from the ridges. The bones push out of his back and stretch, locking into place to form two intact, well-healed wings.

'Did it hurt?'

Davyn smiles as he shakes his head. 'No. Not at all.'

Fallon is showing one of her rare smiles when she walks around to face him again. 'Told you. Now, are you ready to see if you can do anything with those monsters?'

Half an hour later, Davyn kicks the living shite out of a pile of tyres. He's worn out, sore, and totally fed up. Fallon hands him a bottle of water and looks down at the tyres. 'Better now?'

'I'm fucked off.'

She smiles and takes a drink before answering. 'Really? Never would have guessed. You're improving, Dav.'

'I can flap my wings. Flap them. That's it.'

'Yeah and before you were taken, you couldn't even release them without screaming in pain. Being able to move it is a big deal. Between you and me, I didn't think Annie would be able to do anything with that wing.'

She's probably right, but he's not in the right place for giving himself a pat on the back for something so simple.

'Hey? Dav. Look at me.'

'What?'

'Why are you being so hard on yourself?'

'The only thing I'm good at is fighting. It's all I've ever been good at. Like this, I'm useless.'

Fallon sighs and sits on what's left of the pile of tyres. 'How long have you worked with me?'

He shrugs. 'Two decades?'

'Do I ever sugar coat anything?'

'Never.'

'So when I tell you I'd go into battle with you as you are right now, you'd believe me, right?'

Davyn looks down at the ground as her words register with him. Fallon never spoke anything but the truth. That was part of the reason he respects her as much as he does.

'You have a team of highly trained vampires backing you. As much as I don't particularily like them, the Whelans have your back too.

And more importantly, you have Thea. That human is crazy about you, Dav.' She gets to her feet and walks over to him. 'The warrior I have fought with for decades, would never doubt his abilities in the field. You have wings. That means you haven't lost anything. And I'm going to do my hardest to show you how much of an asset they actually are.'

Davyn tries his best to look enthusiastic even though he feels anything but. Fallon can fly. Her wings don't hinder her in any way. There's a strong chance his wings will never be strong enough to hold his weight in flight. How exactly can they be an asset while he drags them behind him during a fight?

'How is it going in here?'

Davyn turns to face Nix as she joins them in the training room. He isn't in the mood to talk to anyone else. All he wants to do is go back to his room and feel sorry for himself.

'He's doing really well,' Fallon answers before he can say anything.

'That's great. I have to say you certainly look the part Davyn. Your wings really suit you.'

He nods not sure how to respond to that. He's still getting used to them knowing he has wings in the first place, let alone liking the damn things. He's just grateful they don't hurt anymore.

'Fallon, could you give us a minute?' Nix asks, immediately making Dav feel on edge.

'Of course,' Fallon pats him on the shoulder then leaves him alone with Nix.

'Take a seat.'

He sits on the bonnet of the car behind him and Nix joins him. She looks down at her hands as she takes a long breath. 'I know following hierarchy rules isn't exactly what we do here, but I feel I need to in this instance. I need to show you the respect you deserve as a Prime Lord.'

'What are you talking about?'

'You'd be within your rights to take control of the group.'

Davyn raises an eyebrow as he turns to look at her. 'What?'

She shrugs. 'No one would question it.'

'Except me. Just because I have a title, doesn't mean I'm the right one to lead.'

'The right is yours, Davyn. I'd be doing you a dishonour if I didn't step down.'

Davyn stares at Nix for a few minutes, but she's being serious. 'Nix, there's no fucking way I'm going to take over. You lead the Blackjacks. End of story.'

'Are you sure?'

He snorts. 'Nix, I know I've had my own set of issues since I joined, but that doesn't mean I was going around with blinkers on. You're a damn good leader. Always have been.' He straightens and gestures to the well-equipped training room. 'All this exists because of you. The Blackjacks only work because of you.'

'Ethan has his part to play.'

'I have no problem with Ethan, but he'd be cowering in the corner in a puddle of piss, if you left him to deal with all of us alone. You make this work. I haven't got a fucking clue how, but you manage to keep all of us working as a unit... well, most of the time.'

'I'm lucky to command a fine group of warriors.'

Davyn shakes his head. 'We're all more than a little fucked up. Me with my daddy issues. Court and his memory thing. Bas and whatever those fucked up tattoos of his mean. Shep's...'

He blows out a breath and shakes his head again. 'Who knows what's waiting to jump out of Fallon and Willow's past. And there's the guy we rescued from the lab, fighting for his sanity in the cells. We're a sorry group of broken, beaten, and seriously screwed up fighters.' He lifts his head and smiles at her. 'But you make us better.' He scratches his head and clears his throat. 'Yeah, well. You know what I mean.'

Nix returns his smile. 'Thank you Davyn. You know, in all my years leading the Blackjacks, I've never had one of my fighters praise my leadership. Hearing I'm not making a complete mess of it, is an unexpected, but welcome thing. Especially hearing it from you.'

'It's the truth.'

'Well, I for one, am grateful Lord Davyn Oldranson chose to be part of our team.'

Davyn suppresses the chill that courses through his body at hearing his full name. It has nothing but bad memories. 'Lord Oldranson was my grandfather. I'm just Davyn. No interest in taking over the family business.'

'No offence, but after seeing the family business I can't blame you.' She stands up and takes off her shirt, revealing her fighting waistcoat underneath. 'Fancy showing me what you can do? I promise I won't drop you on your ass.'

Thea looks around her as she approaches the door to the training area. She's only ever been in there with Fallon and Willow, and isn't sure whether she'd be allowed go in without supervision. Before she pulls open the heavy door, she checks the light beside it is green. The last thing she needs to do is walk in, in the middle of a training firefight.

She may have been here about half a dozen times before, but the sheer size and scale of their main training area still leaves her speechless. Outside, it looks like an old factory. Inside, there are houses, streets, various sized buildings and plenty of room for the winged vampires to train and hone their skills, both in the air and on the ground.

Fallon had put her through her paces in here and, even though she had gone easy on her, Thea had been bruised and aching after each session.

She walks around the corner of the first building and stops in the shadows. Davyn is sitting on the roof of the house opposite her. He's topless with his stunning wings out behind him. Thea goes into the house and follows the stairs to the attic. Davyn doesn't react when she manoeuvres around his wings and sits beside him.

The awkward silence drags on. Clearly Davyn isn't in one of his rare chatty moods. Thea glances over at him and frowns at the blood on the side of his face and smeared on his arm. 'What happened to you?'

'Training. It's nothing.'

'Are you okay?'

He takes a deep breath, but that's as much of an answer as she gets.

'Why are you sitting up here. There's not much of a view.'

'I think I'm done, Thea.'

The sudden comment surprises her. 'Done with what?'

He lifts his arm off his leg and gestures to the training area. 'All this. The Blackjacks.'

'Why? Has something happened?

When he turns to look at her, his green eye is glowing. 'My father happened. I'm out of breath climbing the fucking stairs up here. I've got one eye. My reaction time is shite. And I can't fire a fucking gun while I'm like this.' He holds up his hand and Thea can't help but notice the tremors. 'I can't fight while I'm like this. I'm useless while I'm like this.'

Thea takes his hand, still feeling the tremors working through him. 'Who have you been training with?'

'Fallon mainly. And she's kicking my ass. Nix just spent thirty minutes with me. Handed me my ass on a plate.'

She turns his head to face her. 'You've just been cleared for training again. Don't be too hard on yourself. It'll take time to get back to where you were.'

'And what if I can't get there? What if they can't find a donor for me?'

She forces herself to smile, even though the thought of what he's facing terrifies her. 'We have to stay positive, okay? There's still time.'

Davyn rests his head against her hand and smiles at her. 'How do you do that?'

'Do what?'

'Make me feel better.'

The comment takes her completely by surprise. Whatever is going on between them is confusing her so much. She can't figure out their relationship - if there is one. But when he says something like that, all the doubt disappears. 'I'm glad I can do that for you. I wish I could do more.'

He shrugs and looks out over the buildings. 'Yeah, well, that's on me. Don't think anyone can bring me the last part. I've got to pack it all in, or keep pushing and hope I can bring something to the team.'

'Just keep fighting, Davyn. You've come so far. You deserve this. You deserve to get your life back.' He smiles at her then looks at the tiles under his legs. He's right. No one else can do this part for him. He needs to see for himself, needs to prove to himself that he can fight and be a valuable member of the team. None of the training has left him. His confidence has.

She bites the inside of her cheek to keep the tears that are always threatening to spill out, at bay. If they don't find someone he can feed from, none of that will matter.

Just another thing she can't help with. 'I'm hungry. Do you want to get some lunch?'

'I'm not really hungry.'

'So you just want to sit up here all day and stare at the roof tiles?'

He glances at her and, when he smirks briefly, she can't help but smile. He may be doubting everything in his life right now, but he's smiling at her more and more. And she loves it. 'Fine. I'll join you.'

He stands up and pulls her to her feet. Thea yelps in surprise when he gathers her in his arms and drops off the edge of the roof, landing gently on the ground. 'A bit of warning next time thank you very much.'

He places her back on the ground and shrugs. 'Quicker than the stairs.'

'Well us mere mortals are used to the stairs.'

'Us vampires tend to take quicker routes when we can.' He takes a step back and closes his eyes. Thea is about to ask what he's doing, but understands when his wings begin realigning so they can retract inside his body. Davyn opens his eyes and rolls his shoulders, then grabs his t-shirt from the ground where he left it.

'I don't think I'll ever get used to seeing you guys do that.'

'Helps that it doesn't hurt anymore. I don't dread having to do it.'

'I suppose it's one good thing to come out of all this. I'm sorry. I didn't mean that.' She curses herself for even suggesting anything that happened to him because of her is a good thing. Thea turns towards the door, hoping he doesn't comment and just follows her from the room. But he grabs her arm and stops her escape.

His amazing green eye locks on to her and glows. 'It is a good thing, Thea. The pain I felt every time I had to release or pull my wings in... it's indescribable. My flesh was being ripped open, over and over again by one of my limbs. What I went through in Ireland... getting my wings fixed makes it worthwhile. I mean that. It's spared me from a few hundred years of being torn apart.'

'That's good then.'

'Yes. Are you all right?'

She tries to convince him with a pathetic smile, which just makes him frown even more. There's no way she's going to go into the whole blame thing with him. If she apologises for what happened, it'll just open a Pandora's Box of regret, shame, and pain. He's getting over what was done to him. She has no right to go back there, just so she can get forgiveness from him. It's selfish and something she doesn't deserve.

'I'm fine. Really. Just tired and hungry.'

He keeps his glowing green eye on her for another few seconds, then gestures towards the door. Thea takes the lead with Davyn beside and a little behind her. Instead of looking forward to having a meal with him, she's lost her appetite and, sitting opposite him while the results of her stupidity face her, isn't appealing.

~

Shep pulls on a pair of jeans, and grabs a long sleeved black t-shirt from the chair at the end of his bed. Fletch will go fucking nuts at him, but he needs to get out of the compound for a while. He's done with being examined and stared at like he's a freak. Yeah, so he's growing wings inside him. That's no big deal.

He laughs loudly at his own statement. Okay, so maybe it's a big deal. But it doesn't mean they'll keep growing, or that the damn things will tear out of him.

Watching what Dav had to go through, that one time he witnessed him freeing his wings, has well and truly turned him off following in his footsteps. If he's not meant to have wings, how the hell would they come out of him? He hasn't got wing ridges like the girls and Dav. That just leaves a lot of pain and blood for him, if they do decide to pop out and say hi.

Fletch had rejected his suggestion of amputating the fuckers before they get a chance to come out. Saying they don't know exactly what they're dealing with, is a cop out. Just cut open his back and remove the things. It's simple. Well, in his head it's simple. Apparently the medical heads in his life don't agree.

He slips on the t-shirt, wincing as his shoulders object to the movement. His body isn't on board with doing anything like moving and that's just pissing him off even more. His go-to, blowing off steam hobbies, were kicking the shit out of something or someone in the training room, and sex.

Unless he plans on just lying there and having someone else do all the work, option two is out. He prefers to be in charge. Prefers to be the one in control. Not being able to move his fucking arms over his head without wincing, kind of puts a stop to that.

So not only is he unbelievably horny, he's also pissed off, wound tight like a spring, and maybe a little bit scared.

He laces his boots as that last feeling hits home again. He's tried to dismiss it, tried to ignore it. But it's fighting back. He thought when he joined the Blackjacks, he'd be able to control the fear that was part of his life for so long. And, up until recently, he's had a handle on it. He swore years ago no one, or nothing, would make him feel like that again.

Shep runs his hand over the scars on his side and swallows. He's not going to throw up. He's not going to let it own him again. He can't.

He's strong. He's a warrior. He's fought for vampires for years. Helped countless vampires stay free from The Order. Not many he knows would be able to do that. If he lets the fear take him again, he's worthless - to Willow and the team.

Thoughts of his sister help settle his mind. He'd die for her without thinking about it. His sister is the most important person in his life, and he will protect her, no matter what - even if it means protecting her from him. He's lied to Willow her entire life. Every single day he's protected her by being deceitful. If she knew...

'Fuck!' He stands up and scrubs a hand over his face. 'Enough, Shep. Get it together.'

After taking a few deep breaths he grabs his jacket, helmet, and phone from the bed and leaves his room, disobeying Fletch and Nix.

He gets as far as the garage before he's rumbled. Seems Nix can either read his mind or was keeping an eye on him. She's leaning against his Harley, her hands resting on the saddle to either side of her.

'Hey Nix.'

'Hey yourself. Care to tell me where you're going?'

'Going? What makes you think I'm going anywhere?'

Nix crosses her arms and raises an eyebrow. 'I don't know. Maybe the fact you've got your helmet in your hand. It's just a guess though.'

Shep glances down at the helmet and smiles. 'That would give it away, wouldn't it? C'mon boss. I feel fine. I'm going stir crazy being locked up in here.'

'I'm glad you feel okay, Shep. But that doesn't take away from the fact you were given a drug we know nothing about. A drug that is changing your body so much, you're growing a set of wings inside you. Please tell me you see that as a big deal.'

'I get that, Nix. I'm not an idiot. But they're not full wings. Fletch said they're not fully developed, and there's nothing to say they will. Fuck's sake, Nix. I need to get out.'

'Where are you going?'

He resists the sudden urge to bare his teeth at her. 'You going to be on my back from now on? Do I need to get a permission slip before I leave? Is that how this is going to go?' He knows she's just looking out for him, but right now he doesn't want that. All he wants to do is leave the compound and get some fresh air.

'I've got one of my fighters wondering if he has a future on the team after being tortured for months, another has amnesia, and you're growing wings, Shep. Of course I'm going to be keeping an eye on you. On all of you. I worry sick about all of you the second you leave this place, let alone dealing with some mysterious drug too.

'You honestly can't blame me for that. We've just got Court back. Dav is going through hell. And now this is happening to you. To be honest, if I could lock the lot of you up and never let you out again, I would. You lot are more than just a team I manage. You're friends and I'm seriously worried about you all.'

He reigns in his anger and nods. He can hardly have a go at her for looking out for her team. 'Fair point. Please Nix. I just need to get out of here for a few hours. That's all. I won't do anything stupid or go looking for trouble.'

She sighs and shakes her head but he can see the signs. She's weakening.

'I promise I'll leave the locator on my bike turned on. And I won't take this off,' he says, holding up his wrist, to show her the leather band with the tracker in it.

Nix quietly examines him, then nods once. 'I want you back here before sun up. No excuses.'

'Loud and clear boss.'

'And if you get even the slightest twinge of anything off, you call one of us immediately. We'll come and get you. Please don't take any chances, Shep.'

'You got it.'

Before she can change her mind, Shep swings his leg over the seat of his Harley and puts on his helmet.

Thea climbs into the bus and finds Davyn sitting at one of the tables surrounded by maps, glaring at a laptop.

'What are you doing in here?'

Davyn glances up at her and smiles before looking back at the map. 'Good place to get peace.'

'Sorry, I'll leave you alone.'

'No. I meant peace from everyone else. I just needed some time alone with these, to try and figure it out.'

She peers down at the map but doesn't recognise the area. 'What are you doing?'

He scrubs a hand through his dark hair then gestures over the map. 'I was held at another smaller fighting pit, before my father moved me back to his castle. I'm trying to figure out where it was. It's probably a lost cause, but might as well give it a go.'

Thea sits and watches him work. She doesn't know why she isn't leaving him to it. The whole point of tracking down Davyn was to have a chat with him, but what he's doing is more important than her feelings.

'Do you want anything?'

She blinks and looks over at him. 'Sorry?'

Davyn gets up and grabs a bottle of water from the fridge. 'Do you want anything?'

'Oh. Sorry. No, thanks. I'm fine.'

She watches Davyn as he sits down and turns his attention back to the map. She hasn't known him long, but she knows without a doubt, he's not looking at the map. He's back in the castle which is marked with a red circle at the far side of the map. He's back in his cell or in the fighting pit. He grunts quietly and discretely moves his hand to his stomach. But not discretely enough. He's still getting cramps but is doing his best to keep it to himself.

'Davyn?'

He looks up at her and the frown disappears. He may even attempt a weak smile, but there's a strong possibility she imagined that.

'What's going on with us, Davyn?'

'What do you mean?'

She had the whole speech planned out, but sitting in front of him and actually having to say the words, is throwing her off track.

After a few minutes of slightly awkward silence, Davyn sits back and raises an eyebrow as he waits for her to speak.

'Okay, so a few days ago you told me your heart belongs to me and I said the same. But we haven't progressed past that. And I know that's down to me too but...' She trails off as his frown deepens, then fades to show nothing on his face. And that's what scares her the most.

Davyn licks his lips, and scratches his jaw as he looks at the map again. She needs him to say something, anything to help break the awkwardness surrounding them. Instead, he stares at the map for a ridiculous amount of time. So long, Thea fears he's trying to tell her that he wants her to leave him alone. That he likes her, but there's no way there can ever be anything between them.

'Thea...'

Here it comes. The rejection she was dreading. She straightens in the seat, subconsciously bracing herself.

'I'm one hundred and seventy years old. You don't get to my age without doing things you regret. In my case I've done more things I regret than I'm proud of. What I said to you in the cell, and again in your room - I still mean that. I wouldn't have said it unless I did. Believe that. But my life, what I've done...' He scrubs a hand over his hair as he focuses on the map again. 'It stops me from being with you.'

'Stops you? How?'

'In my head. I would give anything to be with you, Thea. I mean that. I've never felt like this for anyone else before. But as much as I want you, I don't think I can be with you.'

She gets to her feet and stands beside him. 'Even if I want this as much as you do?'

'You're an incredible woman, Thea. And you've got a career in your future. You can make something of yourself outside of this world. Live away from the fighting. Away from wondering if I'll come back every night I go out on patrol. Away from having a vampire like me attached to you for the rest of your life.'

Thea takes his hand and squeezes it, but he doesn't return the gesture. 'Davyn—'

'I've thought about this over and over again,' he says, interrupting her. 'It's the only thing I've thought about, but I can't find a way around the things I've done.'

'What about me? What about my feelings?'

'I'm trying to protect you and your feelings.'

'By running away?'

'That's not what I'm doing.'

'Really? It sounds like you are. It sounds like there are too many obstacles, so you've decided it's best to not bother trying.'

He gets to his feet, backing her against the wall of the bus as he towers over her. 'Obstacles? You're human and I'm not. That's a pretty fucking big obstacle, Thea. And as much as both of us would like otherwise, it does make a difference.'

He pauses and his eye glows softly as he looks at her. Thea's heart races in her chest. Being this close to him always has this effect on her, but it's not just his proximity that's making her dizzy.

He's going to end whatever chance they had. Deep down she knows her time with Davyn, however short, is about to come to an end. She'll never know what it's like to fall asleep on his chest. To wake up with him. To have a future with him in it.

She wants to tell him not to say anything. To let her leave with a little of her dignity intact. But she doesn't want to leave him. This stunning man is everything she wants, everything she needs.

He licks his lips and moves his body closer to hers, until he's all she can feel. All she can smell.

'Thea, you'll never know how much I wish it could be different. You'll never know how much I wish I could pick you up, carry you back to my room, and claim you as mine and mine alone. But there isn't a force on Earth that will convince me to risk you like that. I care about you too much to be in your life. I won't do that to you.'

Thea feels her eyes welling up at his words. Davyn reaches up and gently wipes tears from her cheek.

'It's for the best.'

'Best for who?'

'You, Thea. You'll own my heart until the day I die. I've no doubts about that. But I'm going to protect your life by keeping out of it.'

He rests his hand on the side of her face and gently kisses her forehead before moving away from her. Thea watches in stunned silence as Davyn climbs down from the bus and walks away from her without a backward glance.

~

Davyn keeps it together until he gets into the gym. The rest of the team are on rotation or asleep, so he's got the place to himself. He pulls off his t-shirt and faces the punching bag. Not bothering with gloves, Davyn strikes the bag, watching as it rattles on its chains. Then he hits it again. And again. He only stops when his blood smears the smooth surface of the bag.

'Fuck!'

Davyn strikes the bag one more time, before leaning back against the wall, worn out, and fed up. He slowly slides to the ground and sits on the floor staring at the far wall.

The conversation he'd just had with Thea, had been brewing in the background since he'd told her how he felt. He'd been an idiot. A selfish one at that, which is even worse. He had no right to tell her how he felt. Whatever feelings she thought she had for him, were only enhanced when he told her he... what? Likes her? Loves her?

Whatever he's feeling, admitting it to her had only hurt her. And that's the last thing he ever wanted to do.

That doesn't mean he's going to change his mind. He can't. Thea should be with a human her own age. She deserves so much more than someone as fucked up as him.

He rubs his forehead, as his past crimes come back to haunt him. Not that they ever fully leave him. He's been waiting for over a century for a fucking break from them and is still waiting.

Davyn holds up his fists and grimaces at the blood covering his knuckles. Fletch is going to have his neck for adding another injury to his already knackered body. His injuries won't heal rapidly if he's not feeding.

Another big reason for keeping Thea at arm's length. If he's not feeding, he's terminally fucked. No way he's going to let her watch him either wither away and die from starvation, be lost to the Fever, or have to be killed if he loses his mind again. And right now those are the only options facing him.

'Hey. You okay?'

Davyn is so lost in his personal misery he doesn't notice Shep come in and sit beside him on the ground.

'How long have you been there?'

'Long enough to know you're in your head somewhere. You okay?'

Davyn considers coming clean and opening up to someone for the first time in his long and miserable life, but changes his mind. 'Yeah. Just trying to get my head straight.' He looks over at Shep and takes a second to examine him. 'You look how I feel.'

Shep laughs and rests his head against the wall. 'Yeah, and you look how I feel. Guess we're both fucked, huh? Both of us have issues with what we are. Both of us are trying to escape life in general.'

Davyn is surprised to hear Shep speak like that. Out of everyone in the compound, Shep could usually be depended on to see the positive in any situation, even if there wasn't any. 'Any more changes?'

Shep shakes his head. 'Nope. Just the beginnings of a set of wings I don't want. Guess I just have to keep my fingers and toes crossed they've developed as much as they're going to. Might still escape this fuck up by the skin of my teeth.' He grins at Davyn, but even he can tell it's half-hearted. 'So, what's got you more miserable than usual?' He winks to soften his words but apologises anyway. 'Harsh. Sorry. I guess my humour radar is knocked out of whack.'

'Finding wings in your back would probably do that.'

Shep laughs again. 'Wow. Was that your attempt at taking the piss?'

'Attempt. I'll leave it to you.'

'Probably best. I'm going to stick my impressive neck out there and say that this has something to do with Thea, right?'

Davyn looks over at him but doesn't answer. Shep's grin tells him he doesn't have to.

'She's fallen for your Irish charm?'

'Seems so.'

'So what's the problem?'

'She's human.'

Shep nods thoughtfully. 'Yeah but there are ways around that. If you really want to be with her long term.'

Davyn snorts. 'No fucking way. I'm not linking her life to mine. I'm not doing that to her.'

'Fair enough. I see where you're coming from and I guess it's still early days. But maybe in a few months or a year it could be an option.'

'I don't know.'

'I'm just saying that it's a two way thing, Dav. If she likes you and you like her, keeping apart doesn't seem like the best option. We're here for a hell of a long time, Dav. Finding someone to spend that time with is rare. Especially in our world and with what we do.'

'I don't want to risk her.'

'But isn't that her choice to make? All I'm saying is you shouldn't push her away cause you think it's the best thing for her.'

'It's more than just that though. I've got a fucked up past, Shep. How do I even go there with her?'

Shep absently scratches his side along the line of scars. 'She loves you, Dav – past and all. I mean Ronan didn't hold back when he spoke to us. Thea knows you've killed, but she's still here. She still loves you.'

'That easy? How do you talk about that sort of shite?'

Shep shrugs. 'Beats me. Thankfully I haven't had to go there with anyone. Don't plan on going there either.'

Dav turns his head to look at Shep. 'So you plan on being single for the rest of your life? What about being here for a hell of a long time?'

'I was talking about you, not me. I'm more of a solo warrior. The mysterious loner who doesn't have any ties.' He shrugs again and grins. 'Really gets the ladies going. Anyway, back to you. Talk to Thea. If she's anything like her father, she's strong willed and sensible. Give her the facts. Let her make up her own mind.'

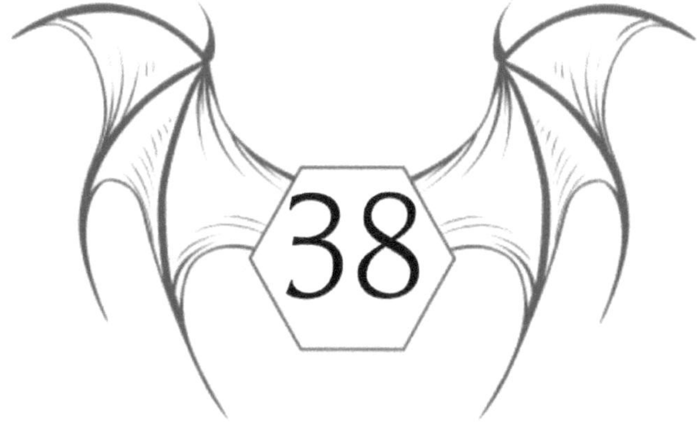

Davyn slumps into the chair opposite Nix and Fletch and watches as Ethan hurries down the corridor towards the meeting room. It's either good news or bad news. Ethan rarely just pops in and he's usually more reserved than he appears right now.

Without greeting anyone in the room he sits at the head of the table and smiles at them like he's won the fucking lottery. In a complete break from the norm, his usually perfect hair is tousled, his tie is undone and crooked, and it looks like he's been wearing his shirt for a few days.

'Ethan? You okay?' Nix asks, clearly noticing the same dishevelled appearance.

'Thea.'

Nix shakes her head. 'Thea what?'

He pulls his chair closer to the table and scratches his head. 'Sorry. We've been at this for a few days. Bit short on sleep. Anyway, she's the key to this. I can't believe it's taken us so long to find this, but by the time we went through the samples from the team and the staff at the compound I had pretty much scrapped the idea. But I was wrong. We all were. We just hadn't found the answer yet. It's really pretty exciting - if it works, but we're all confident it will. I mean why wouldn't it?'

'Ethan! Shut up for a second,' Nix shouts, startling him into silence. 'You're babbling and I haven't got a clue what you're talking about. Take a deep breath and give it to us again - in one sentence if possible.'

He takes a deep breath and attempts to straighten his tie but ends up pulling it over to the other side instead. 'Sorry. Like I said, extreme lack of sleep. It's Thea's blood.'

Everyone around the table stays quiet, waiting for the rest of the sentence, but Ethan is clearly finished. He sits back, a large grin on his face as he waits for them to sing his praises.

'What about it?' Davyn asks, getting pissed off and irritated by the mention of Thea's name. He doesn't like where he thinks this is heading.

'Oh right. You can drink her blood. Davyn I mean, not you Nix. I think I was looking at you when I said that. Anyway, her blood is unique. It has all the properties of a Prime - probably thanks to her mother. Well, it would be thanks to her. Anyway, her blood is safe, but it also has everything he needs to survive. Everything you need, Davyn.'

Nix and Fletch smile widely at the news, leaving Davyn sitting at the table with three extremely happy people.

'I wasn't expecting to hear that,' Fletch says. 'That's great news, Ethan.'

'I know. I'll send everything over to you, Fletch, so you can look at it, but from what we can make out, she should have transitioned. Because she didn't, for whatever reason, her blood isn't as addictive as it would have been if she had changed. In fact, it shouldn't be addictive at all. It's technically normal vampire blood with a Prime kick to it.'

Davyn stares at Fletch, then across at Nix and back to Fletch again. 'This is a joke, right?'

Ethan shakes his head, his grin still in full force. 'Not a joke at all.'

'This is good news, Davyn,' Fletch says. 'I'd just like to take a sample of her blood so we can test Ethan's theory. Why do you look like I've just kicked a kitten?'

'I can't drink... not hers.'

'It'll just be a sample at first,' Fletch says. 'You won't be drinking directly from her. I'd also like to restrain you if you're okay with that? I'm confident this will work, but better safe than decapitated, right.'

Nix rolls her eyes and Fletch shrugs.

'What? I'm trying to lighten the dire situation that Davyn is clearly in - although I haven't got a fucking clue why. This could save your life. You did hear Ethan right? They've found you a blood donor, Dav. And she's right here living under the same roof. I mean the odds aren't worth mentioning, mate. This is... I don't know... absolutely the best scenario any of us could have imagined. Why the frown?'

'I appreciate everything you and your team are doing, Ethan.'

Ethan sits back and shakes his head. 'Don't you even consider saying what I think you're going to say.'

'I can smell her.'

'Excuse me?' Fletch says.

'When I fed from her before, her blood tasted different. It had a different effect on me. The bond was strong even at that stage. As soon as I got close enough to her, it came to life again. I'm struggling every time I'm near her. The craving hits and I'm terrified I'll act on it.

'If I drink her blood and the addiction kicks in again, I'll target her. I'll hunt her down and kill her without thinking about it. Doing this puts her at risk and that's not going to happen. I'm not going to lose...' He shakes his head, shutting off the words.

Davyn slumps back in the chair and rubs a hand over his face.

'I won't have her keeping me alive, just so I can turn on her one day and kill her when the addiction sets in again. I've seen vampires in my father's court becoming obsessed with their donor. I've seen what they can do to them, when the Prime side takes over. I'd prefer to die than have that happen.' He stands up and walks to the door. 'Final answer.'

~

Thea's smile at seeing Fletch at her door quickly disappears when she gets a proper look at him. 'That doesn't look like a happy face.'

'Can I come in?'

She steps aside and Fletch takes a seat on the couch under the window.

'Is Davyn okay?'

'Yes and no. Stubborn git. Sorry, Thea. Okay, so Ethan found a donor for him. Someone with strong enough Prime traits in their blood to sustain him without tipping him too close to the edge.'

'That's amazing. Where is the donor?'

'Well, that's where we hit the jackpot. It's you, Thea. Court is the first Hybrid in a long line of Primes. We're also assuming your mother, whoever she was, was Prime herself. Technically you should have transitioned. Even though you didn't, your blood is exactly what Davyn needs. I couldn't have planned it better myself if I tried.'

Thea can't express her relief at hearing that. Even though Davyn had shot down the idea of anything between them, she still loves him and if her blood can save him, he can have every drop.

'Okay, so what do you need me to do?'

Fletch grimaces and blows out his cheeks. 'Well, that's where we've hit a bit of a snag. He's refused to take your blood. As in categorically, flat out, totally and utterly never going to happen, refused.'

Thea isn't in the least bit surprised to hear that. In fact, she was expecting it. It doesn't help ease the hurt at hearing the words however. Knowing that Davyn would rather starve to death than drink her blood, is pretty much as final a rejection as you can get. 'Right.'

'Don't go taking it personally, love. He's worried he'll become addicted to your blood. And I get what he's saying. Usually the team mix up their donors. It helps dilute the blood, so there's no chance of them getting too drawn to one particular donor. With you being the only card left, it'll put you in a wee bit of a precarious position. You will be keeping him alive. You and you alone. That's one hell of a weight to put on your shoulders. And an impressive target on your back.'

'Do you really think he'd hurt me?'

Fletch shrugs. 'I'm not putting money on it either way. But it's not just Dav I'm talking about. It's anyone who may have a score to settle with him. By taking you out, they'll eventually be taking him out. After the team sorts out his father, he'll be heir to a powerful seat. That'll irritate some vampires.'

Thea swallows as she wipes her hand on her jeans. She hadn't thought about any of that.

Fletch rubs her arm and smiles at her. 'Hey, he's got a little more time before he deteriorates. I'll keep looking, okay. It's a big ask for the both of you. Take some time to really think about what you want.'

'I think I need to talk to him.'

'Yeah, well good luck with that one. He's not in a particularly chatty mood today.'

Thea thanks Fletch and he leaves to look for another solution that doesn't exist. If there was an alternative they would have found it already. Davyn is only going to survive if he drinks her blood. But for some reason, hearing him say it like that brought the reality home, like a slap across the face.

She'd be the only thing keeping him alive. How does she begin to process that? And what about Davyn? She hadn't even thought about it from his side.

She comes to a stop outside Davyn's room and stares at the wood. Okay, so she understands his hesitation. Understands that he needs to think about it. But a firm refusal? Is he worried about putting her in danger because he cares about her, or just because he doesn't want anyone hurt keeping him alive?

Whatever is going on with him, she's not going to let him throw his life away because he's being stubborn. Surely they can find some way of feeding him without making him think he was risking someone's life.

Thea pounds on Davyn's door, not letting up until he yanks it open. 'What?'

She pushes past him and rests her hands on her hips as she glares over at him.

'What exactly are you doing?'

Davyn looks around him then shrugs at her. 'Nothing.'

'You won't take my blood.'

He nods and sits on the side of his bed. 'Right.'

'Is that it?'

'It's my choice, Thea.'

'So you're telling me you would rather starve to death than drink my blood? Are you seriously telling me that?'

'It's my choice.'

She wipes her hands over her face and groans in frustration. 'You can't just keep saying that. This can save your life, Davyn. You need to take this seriously.'

'I am, Thea.'

'Then why won't you drink my blood?'

'Vampires can hurt their donors when they feed. I've hurt my donors. I've killed them when I couldn't control myself.'

Thea loses her train of thought for a moment upon hearing that. 'Okay, so you don't drink from me directly. You can be restrained. Or Shep and Bastian can be on standby if something happens. There are loads of options besides starvation. You're giving up and I can't let you do that.'

'This isn't about giving up. That's not what I'm doing.'

'Is that so? What else would you call this? Risking starvation above all the other options available, sounds like giving up. Why aren't you fighting, Davyn? After everything you've been through, do you really want to just give up at this stage?'

'I'm not giving up. Fletch is looking for another option.'

'Do you really think he's going to find a better option than someone under the same roof as you? Take my blood, Davyn. Buy yourself some time. Please.'

'No.'

She growls and fists her hair in frustration. 'You are the most infuriating person I've ever known.'

He storms over to her, forcing her back against the wall. He places a hand to either side of her head, caging her in with his broad body. She lifts her head to keep eye contact with him. 'I've killed too many people in my life. I will not add you to that list.

'Every time I'm near you, I can hear your blood pumping through your gorgeous body. Its intoxicating scent consumes me. I can hear your heart beating from outside the fucking door. I'm a vampire who's addicted to blood. That doesn't just mean I want to drink loads of it. It means that I could very easily tear you apart, and feed from you until you're dead. You need to understand that, and keep the hell away from me. Tell me you understand.'

'You wouldn't do that to me.'

He leans down, his green eye glowing menacingly, and his fangs showing as he parts his lips. 'How exactly are you going to stop me?'

'Davyn—'

'I'm stronger than you. Faster than you. There's nowhere you can hide that I won't find you. So, tell me how you're going to stop a highly trained vampire who is addicted to your very scent?'

Her throat tightens as his words hit home. 'I couldn't.'

'Exactly.' He pauses and leans closer to the side of her neck, breathing her in. 'I want you so badly, Thea. At this moment, my feelings for you are stronger than the call of your blood. That's the only thing keeping you alive. But that could change without warning. I will not be responsible for hurting you. Do you understand?'

She nods, feeling numb after his outburst. 'I understand.'

'Then you know you have to turn around and walk away. Please. I'm begging you to walk away from me.'

With the fight taken out of her, Thea turns and quietly closes his door behind her.

39

Davyn pulls his car into the car park and shuts off the engine. He grabs the paper bag off the passenger seat and climbs out, slamming the door behind him. Coming back to this car park had been completely unplanned. The last time he was here was when he brought Thea to Hereford, so she could do some shopping.

He sits on the wall that surrounds the car park and looks over the lake. He pulls the bottle of whiskey from the bag and places it beside him. He doesn't particularly want to drink, but he can't think of a reason not to. He's tired, hungry, sore, on edge, and generally pissed off at everyone and everything.

Thea.

Of all the people on the Blackjack database, why did it have to be her?

Fate must really be fucked off with him right now. He doesn't trust himself to feed from anyone. Apart from Ronan, he's killed most people he's fed from. He's fed from Thea before, but that wasn't a proper feed. He'd gone through the motions with her, but barely took anything from her. And even those few mouthfuls had been too much. Even now he can still taste her, can still smell her.

He reaches out for the bottle, but his hand trembles so much he nearly knocks it off the wall. He growls and his fangs drop. It's getting worse. The pull to blood - any blood, is getting stronger. He's starving, and it's only a matter of time before he succumbs to it. As long as he falls before he hurts anyone, he honestly doesn't care.

He clenches his fist, begging his body to obey and steady his hand. He wins this battle, but it's becoming increasingly difficult to fight back. He glances over his shoulder as a truck pulls into the carpark and stops in the entrance. The door opens and Davyn lowers the bottle before taking a drink.

'I thought I could smell traitor in the air.'

Davyn bares his fangs and growls when he recognises him as one of the vampires from his father's hoard. 'Eoin? How did you find me?'

Eoin smiles as he climbs out of the truck. 'I drank from you, remember. I fed from you, while you hung from your chains, with your lips sewn shut. I've been wandering around this backwards shithole for days, unable to pick up on your exact location. Never expected to just stumble on you like this. To be honest, I'm surprised I'm the first one to find you. Well, part of the first group.'

Davyn swallows as another car pulls in behind Eoin's and four more males join him. 'He sent you to get me?'

'Let's just say you've upset him. A few teams were dispatched to ask you to return home. He's keen to have a father and son reunion. He misses you.'

'He's just pissed I survived the Binding.'

Eoin shrugs. 'Perhaps. He may also be upset at the destruction your friends left when they broke you out. Best you come back with us.'

'No.'

He smiles at Davyn. 'Oh, I was so hoping you'd say that.'

The group closes the circle around him, so Davyn pulls out his gun and takes out the nearest body to him before they realise what's happening. While the others get their shit together, Davyn races over to his car and starts the ignition.

The thick tyres spin on the gravel as he reverses out of the spot and turns towards the exit. Without stopping, he rams his car into the other vehicle, catching it at the back and shoving it out of the way. With a screech of metal he scrapes through the gap and slams his foot on the accelerator, putting as much distance between him and Eoin.

Before he's even reached the main road, two sets of headlights pierce the darkness behind him, gaining ground fast.

He knows these roads like the back of his hand, but they have a serious advantage on him. His blood is in their systems. It doesn't matter where he hides, they'll find him unless he can get enough distance between them. The last thing he wants to do is lead them back to the compound.

He drops a gear, forcing the powerful car around the corner at breakneck speed. As soon as he clears the bend, he accelerates again, trying to get some breathing space, but they're relentless. No doubt his father will have a bounty of some sort on his head. There's no way these fuckers will walk away from that.

Davyn curses and ducks as something hits the side of his car. He glances in the rear view mirror. 'Fuck.' They're firing on his car which not only pisses him off, but also means he's in more trouble than he thought.

His father made sure all his men were excellent shots.

He throws the car around the corner, and takes off along the narrow road, but a few seconds later the headlights are back in his rear view mirror. Davyn grunts as his car is rammed from the rear.

'You're really pissing me off now. Stop fucking with my car!'

They hit him again, pushing him to the side nearer the ditch. He drops gears again and pushes his car around the corner, then brakes hard and leans out the window. He fires at the driver the second they round the corner, killing him. The out of control truck scrapes along the side of the Range Rover, as it slides off the road into the trees.

One down.

But Eoin clearly isn't giving up so easily. With a thrust of power, he barrels into the back of Davyn's car and this time he can't control it. Davyn curses as his car leaves the road, the wheels spinning in the air as it flies down the side of the valley.

It lands with a bone jarring jolt, then continues its journey down the side of the valley, until it hits a boulder and flips.

Davyn can do nothing except brace himself as much as possible, as his car tumbles into the ditch and heads down the hill. It seems like a ridiculous length of time being thrown around like a rag doll, but his car eventually comes to a stop and everything goes quiet.

He groans and peers out the shattered windscreen. The moonlight illuminates the ruins of Llanthony Abbey in front of him. Before he can recover, the windscreen explodes and he's dragged through the glass and thrown away from his car. He lands hard and rolls before he comes to a stop against the stone wall of the abbey. He licks the blood from his lips and tries to push himself off the ground, but as soon as he moves his arm, he curses in pain. It's broken. A few ribs too.

He's kicked on to his back and Eoin grabs him around the throat, pulling him to his feet. 'I thought you were meant to be some sort of warrior. A Blackjack, right?' He laughs in Davyn's face then throws him over the remains of the ancient wall into the abbey. Davyn crash lands against the far wall, grunting when he hits the ground, jarring his broken ribs.

Eoin approaches him, taking his time as he saunters through the doorway and over to Davyn. 'I have to say I'm a little disappointed, my lord. Here I was all ready for combat with a mighty Blackjack, with a formidable warrior, and instead I get this. Can you not even give me a little slap at least? How about a kick? Give me something so I at least feel like you're trying to make this hard for me.'

Davyn clenches his teeth and pushes himself to his knees. He's fucked. Not feeding properly for months has left his body in shite condition. He's no stronger than a human and bleeding out just as fast. 'What's... the bounty?' He couldn't care less but needs a few seconds to catch his breath before he's thrown across the ruins again.

'Oh that's the best part. Whoever brings you back to the King will be given the honour of killing you. Then he will transfer your title to them. That means when I kill you I will take your place as your father's heir. I'll be a lord. Think I'll like that.'

Davyn isn't surprised to hear that. His father still needs an heir. Either that or everything he's worked for will fall to the other families when he dies. It's a lifelong sentence of servitude. Eoin is welcome to it.

'Get up, my lord.'

Davyn peers up at him.

'I said get up.'

Davyn doesn't know how he does it, but he manages to get upright, using the rough stone wall to haul his bleeding body off the ground.

Eoin releases his wings, stretching the enormous yellow limbs out behind him. Davyn grunts as Eoin strikes at him, driving a talon into his side. He laughs as Davyn wobbles and drops to his knees. Blood pours from the circular wound in his side.

'Your father wants your heart beating or, failing that, your body still warm. I won't take any chances like he did. Think I'll bring you back dead.'

He drives his wing towards Davyn again, piercing the other side.

Davyn falls forward, catching himself before he lands on his face. As Eoin laughs at him, Davyn decides to even the odds a little. Or at least tip them slightly in his favour. Eoin stumbles backwards when Davyn's wings make an appearance.

Eoin laughs and claps his hands. 'Oh that's better, sire. Glad to see a bit of fight left in you.'

Using his wings to lever himself to his feet again, Davyn faces Eoin and leans against the wall of the abbey while he catches his breath. 'I'll be damned if I'm letting you take me anywhere.'

Eoin smiles, showing his fangs. 'Is that so? Considering you're using the wall to hold you up, those are fighting words.'

Davyn grits his teeth and stands tall. When he pulls his wings off the ground he wobbles slightly but remains standing. 'You're not taking me back.'

Eoin snarls and lunges at Davyn again. Gravity helps Davyn duck the yellow wing that swipes through the air where he was standing a second ago. He rolls to the side and attacks Eoin with his good wing. It hits home, but Eoin is too strong and too fast for it to do much damage.

Davyn shouts in pain as a talon slices across the back of his leg, severing tendons and crippling him. He falls onto his back, cracking his head against a rock embedded in the ground. Eoin stands on Davyn's good wing, pinning it to the ground.

'Valiant effort, my lord. Now I think it's time I put you out of your misery.'

Davyn looks up at the stars, instead of at Eoin. He doesn't want to die ,but if that's what fate has planned for him, he wants the sky to be the last thing he sees, not Eoin's smug face.

But then he thinks about Thea, and the urge to live takes over. He can't go back to his father. Dead or alive, he won't fall at his father's feet. Won't surrender to him ever again. If he is to die here, it will be while fighting.

In a last ditch attempt to get up, he thrashes his wings, hoping to knock Eoin off balance.

Nothing happens. Eoin stays where he is, but doesn't make a move to kill him. Davyn looks away from the sky to Eoin. The male is staring down at him with a confused look on his face. It takes Davyn a few seconds to see what the problem is. Eoin is impaled by a thick black talon which disappears into his stomach.

Davyn follows the talon to the red wing it's attached to. His dud wing. The damn thing moved. It's never moved and certainly not that much.

He pulls it back, dropping Eoin to the ground. Davyn pushes himself onto his side and watches as Eoin collapses on the grass and dies. No loss. The male was a fucking dickhead.

Davyn lies back and looks up at the sky. His car is a good few feet away from him. It could be at the other side of the damn planet, for all the good it will do him. Problem is, his phone and the emergency beacon are in it. Unless Eoin can help him out.

Cradling his broken arm to his chest, he digs his talons into the ground and pulls his dead weight across the grass to Eoin. There's so much blood smeared over the grass, he's surprised he's not dead yet.

Dark patches form at the corners of his vision, as the blood continues to leave his body. He'll be dead in a few minutes. No way even Fletch can fix him at this stage. He's fine with that. The only thing he doesn't want is any more of his father's men showing up and claiming his body.

Davyn feels in Eoin's pockets and finds his mobile. It takes a few attempts to key in Ethan's number and hit dial. There's no point ringing any of the team from an unknown number. They won't answer.

Davyn rests his head on Eoin's leg as he waits. Exhaustion is chasing after him so he gives in and closes his eyes.

'Hello?'

Davyn clears his throat, grimacing when his broken ribs grate together. 'Ethan...'

'Yes. Who is this?'

Davyn takes a few breaths and forces himself to speak again. All he wants to do is sleep. 'Dav. Got jumped. I'm... hurt...'

'Where are you?'

Davyn pauses to cough up a mouthful of blood. 'Track... my car...'

That's it. He's done for. He drops the phone and lies against the fucker his father sent to kill him. Looks like he got his wish.

Thea stares out the window of Court's Defender, scanning the surrounding landscape speeding by the window. Within minutes of getting the call from Ethan, the team had dispatched to go and get Davyn. Ethan hadn't said much about the call with Davyn. Just that he had been attacked and was hurt. Badly.

Thea looks down at the phone, the small red dot on the screen signalling Davyn's car. They were coming at the location from different angles. Davyn hadn't said if there are more enemies in the area. They have no idea if they're heading into an ambush.

She can feel Court glancing over at her before he focuses on the road again. 'Under your seat.'

She looks over at him. 'Sorry?'

'Take out the gun from under your seat. Check it. Make sure it's ready to fire.'

Thea stares over at her father, not quite believing what she just heard.

'Yeah. I'm telling you to take out the gun and I'm telling you to use it if you have to. I checked your training records. According to Fallon you're pretty damn good. I know full well you won't be staying in the car as soon as we find him. I want to make sure you're armed just in case.'

Thea reaches under the seat and pulls the gun from its holder. She checks the weapon carefully, all too aware Court is watching her every move as he drives.

She places it in the pocket of her jacket and smiles at him. 'Thanks for trusting me with this.'

Court nods as he focuses on the road ahead of them. 'I want you to be able to protect yourself.'

He slams on the brakes all of a sudden and Thea lurches to the side as he turns off the road onto a dirt track. 'Sorry. His signal goes this way.' Court contacts the rest of the team on his radio. 'We're approaching his signal. Anyone else close?'

'Not yet,' Shep replies first. 'About two minutes behind you. Looks like he's near the abbey, so it could be an ambush. Plenty of hiding places there.'

'I can't see any other cars around the area,' Fallon says from somewhere above them.

'You picking up on anything, Shep?'

'Nope. Just us.'

Thea's heart races when she sees wide wheel tracks ahead of them. Branches hang over the path, torn from the trees as if something large crashed through it. Court pushes his Defender forward, following the path Davyn's car took.

When they clear the trees Court curses loudly. A black Range Rover is on its side with the bonnet embedded in a tree. She knows it's his car, but a small thread of hope refuses to let go. There's probably dozens of black Range Rovers in the area. Even as the thought goes through her mind, the thread breaks. It's his registration on the back.

'Dad. It's his.'

He brings the car to a stop and points at her, silently telling her to stay put. 'We've found his car just up from the abbey. I'll keep you posted.' He ends the transmission on his radio and keeps his finger pointed in her direction. His nearly white eyes meet hers and she can't turn away. 'No fucking with me, Thea. You stick to me and don't move from my side. Come on.'

He gets out of the car and walks around the front to meet her. Court hands her a torch, then leads the way through the trees to the overturned car, gun raised in front of him. He crouches down at the windscreen and peers inside.

'Is he...' Thea can't bring herself to finish the sentence.

'He's not inside.' Court's eyes glow as he looks around the clearing, trying to find Davyn in the dark. Thea slowly plays the torch over the grass, hoping but also dreading what she might find.

'Let's try the ruins. He's not out here.'

Thea obeys her father, staying by his side as they walk over to the hulking form of the abbey, its skeletal structure appearing all the more ominous in the moonlight.

Court suddenly comes to a stop and lifts his head. 'Blood.'

'Where?'

He scans the darkness and nods towards the back of the abbey. 'That way.' They go around the back of the structure, through an opening that once would have held an impressive door. When her torchlight lands on the ground to her left, her feet stop moving. Davyn is sprawled across another vampire and they're both covered in blood. It's everywhere.

Court keeps his gun trained on the other vampire while he crouches down and checks them. 'Davyn has a faint pulse. Other guy won't be giving us problems. Fletch, you hear me?'

'Got you, buddy.'

'We need you A.S.A.P. Davyn is in a bad way. He's still with us but

I can barely feel his pulse. He's lost a hell of a lot of blood.'

'On the way. Fallon, stabilise him until I get there.'

Thea shouts in surprise as Fallon appears out of the sky and lands beside them. She shakes out her wings then pulls them into her body. 'Will do.'

She crouches down beside Davyn and checks his wounds. 'Can you manoeuvre his wings while I turn him over?'

Thea steps aside as Court and Fallon flip him onto his back. It's so much worse than Thea feared. It looks like he's been torn open.

She watches in a daze as Fallon and Court empty their field kits and try to stop the bleeding. Then Fletch, Shep, and Nix arrive, their voices blurring into white noise.

She blinks when Court pulls her away from the scene. 'Hey? Did you hear Fletch?'

'Fletch? What?'

'Dav is dying. He needs blood. I'm not happy about it but you need to feed him or he's gone.'

'But he didn't want me to feed him.'

'He can have that fight with me after we save him,' Fletch says as he unpacks supplies from his kit. 'Right now, unless you give him blood, he won't last the next few minutes. We've got no choice.'

Thea nods and kneels down beside Davyn, trying not to look at the gaping wounds in his sides and leg. Fallon takes her arm and attaches the transfusion kit, inserting the other end into Davyn's arm.

'Will this work?'

Fallon shakes her head. 'Touch and go right now. Just sit tight and let your blood help him. It's all we can do for him until we get back to the compound.'

Thea watches her blood disappear into Davyn's arm as Fletch and Fallon try to stabilise him and deal with his wounds. She focuses on Davyn's face, and tries to block out the sounds of his wounds being seen to.

Fletch curses as he throws a wad of blood soaked gauze on the ground. 'This isn't working. He's losing too much blood. He needs to drink. Thea, can you try to feed him?'

'Feed him? How? He's unconscious.'

Fallon leans in and holds her hand out. 'Give me your arm.' She takes Thea's arm and brings it to her mouth. Thea hisses in pain as Fallon bites her wrist. She moves Thea's arm towards Davyn's mouth holding her wrist up to Davyn's lips. 'Come on, Davyn. Drink.'

Panic builds in Thea as he remains motionless. She can feel his teeth against her wrist, but his canines are withdrawn. His breath comes in shallow gasps against her skin. She runs her hand through his hair, keeping away from the wound on the side of his head. She closes her eyes, pretending they're alone and far away from his wrecked car.

'Davyn. You need to drink. Please, Davyn.' She turns her wrist, rubbing the bite marks against his bottom lip then back to his fangs. 'Damn it, Davyn. Don't do this. Drink!' She pushes her wrist against the tip of one of his canines and gasps as his fangs extend and he closes his mouth around her wrist.

She continues to stroke his hair as he feeds. Court is keeping a close eye on what's going on but she doesn't mind. He's just keeping her safe.

'Is he going to be okay?'

Fletch shakes his head. 'Don't know, love. You're helping him more than I am right now.' He fixes a bandage over the wound in Davyn's side and sits back. 'Get him loaded now. Fallon, can you fly ahead and get the trauma bay ready? We're far from done with him tonight.'

She nods and takes to the air as Court and Bastian carry Davyn over to the bus. Thea stays where she is as Fletch removes the transfusion line and bandages her wrist, then helps her to her feet.

'Come on. You can go in the bus with him.'

Thea climbs on board and sits opposite Davyn, keeping away from him as Fletch attaches various monitors to him. Perhaps it's just her imagination, but she could swear there's more colour in his checks.

Fletch squeezes her shoulder as he passes on his way to the front of the bus. 'You saved him, love. He's stabilising already. I don't care what issue this stubborn idiot has with your blood. I've seen the effect it has on him. He needs it whether he wants it or not.'

Thea smiles at him as he disappears to the front of the bus. Fletch is right. She's not going to take no for an answer on this. Not when Davyn's life is at risk.

Davyn groans as consciousness comes back to him. He takes a deep breath, gasping as a heavy weight presses against his chest.

'Take it easy. Your wounds have just sealed. You don't want to be opening them up again.'

He opens his eyes and looks at Fletch before closing his eyes again. 'What the hell happened?' Davyn yelps as someone thumps him in the shoulder. 'What the hell?' He frowns as he opens his eyes to see Nix glaring down at him.

'That was for disappearing, and nearly getting yourself killed. I thought Fletch told you to keep out of danger until you fed? What the hell were you thinking? I'm pretty sure we had a conversation when you first came to, about being part of a team. You remember that?'

He shuffles up the bed, wincing as every bone and muscle in his body screams in protest. 'I know that, but–'

'There is no but, Davyn. Do you have any idea what you put everyone through? We've just got you back, and you pull something like that on us. It's not on.'

'I know. I'm sorry, Nix. I just needed to get away.' He jumps as the door opens and the rest of the Blackjacks come in. Court shuts the door behind him and crosses his arms. Davyn pushes up the bed, suddenly feeling like he's trapped. 'What's this?'

'This is your friends, your team mates - your family, showing you that we're here for you, idiot,' Shep says.

Bastian rolls his eyes. 'Was the idiot bit really needed?'

'Too damn right it was. He's acting like an idiot. I should know, I do it enough myself.'

Willow glares at her brother, then steps in front of him. 'What he's trying to say in his usual dumb-ass way, is that you shouldn't have to face any of this alone.'

'We're a team, Dav,' Fallon says. 'You got a problem. We all have a problem. That's the way it works.'

Davyn is struck dumb. He's heard all the 'team talk' before, but he never thought about what it really meant. It went over his head. Until now. With the group of vampires standing in front of him, the meaning behind the words hits him like a bullet to the chest.

'I'm sorry. I fucked up.'

'Too right you did,' Shep mutters. 'But I guess we can forgive you.'

Dav smiles at the team. 'Thanks. So, how bad is my car?'

Shep slowly approaches him and holds out his phone. 'I'm sorry, but it didn't make it. Not worth salvaging.' Davyn looks down at the photo of the wreckage and growls as he takes in all the damage.

Shep pulls the phone away before Davyn can throw it at the wall. He loved that car. 'I'm going to kill them for this.'

Nix steps in front of the others. 'Okay, back up a little. Kill who exactly? What do you remember?'

'Some of my father's men jumped me at the lake. We fought and I managed to get back in my car. I took off... ' He shakes his head, willing the memories to come back to him, but the rest is a blur. Had his father's men forced him off the road?

'How'd they find you?' Bastian asks. 'They wouldn't have followed you from Ireland - would they?'

'They tracked me. After the Binding everyone in his court fed from me. They picked me up from that. Guess they got lucky and were close enough to sense me.'

Court curses as he lowers onto the corner of the counter. 'Great. So they've tracked you from Ireland to Wales. That's a problem. How many came for you?'

'Four, I think.'

'And how many fed from you?'

'Forty, fifty maybe. I wasn't exactly keeping count.'

'Will they all be able to pick him up?' Court asks.

Nix blows out a long breath. 'Possibly. It all depends on how much each of them took. The more blood consumed, the stronger the link to the donor. I would've thought the effect would have worn off by now though.'

'Unless it has something to do with the enhanced blood Davyn was given,' Fletch suggests. 'Maybe that in turn enhanced the effect drinking his blood had on the others.'

'Whatever the reason, it means we could have a big fucking problem heading our way,' Shep says.

'So we bring it to them instead.'

Everyone turns to look at Davyn. 'You what?' Shep asks.

'I'm done running from my father. I shouldn't have left Ireland without killing him.'

Fletch snorts. 'You were hardly in any physical state to do anything about it.'

'That's no excuse. As long as he's alive he's going to keep coming after me. Image means everything to him. By escaping for a second time, I'll have disgraced him - really disgraced him. He'll have lost face with his men, and his reputation will have taken a hit.'

'Then why are his men willing to come over here and face you and all of us?' Bastian asks.

'He has an inner circle of men who have been with him for as long as I can remember. My father has them so brainwashed they won't know how to do anything else. They've been following him for centuries. They're not going to stop now. They'll want to get into his good books by bringing back my head. With me dead, his reputation as someone you don't mess with, will be restored with the other elder families. It'll be a win for him. I have to kill him. It's the only way to end this.'

'Are you sure?' Nix asks, looking anything but convinced about what he just said.

'I'm sure. Without my father, his men won't know their arses from their elbows. They're only fighting because it's what he wants. They couldn't give a fuck about me, or any misplaced loyalty I should've had for my bastard of a father. They only want his approval. They're not going to risk their lives for no reward.'

'So you want to go back to Ireland and fight?'

Davyn nods. 'Yeah. I don't want to, but he won't leave the castle. Especially now he knows the wolves are after him too.'

'Oh great,' Shep mutters. 'We got to get them involved again?'

'I know all the secret entrances to the castle, so I can get us in. But I think we could do with their help if they're up for it.'

'There is one condition,' Nix says silencing the group. 'You feed, or you stay put. End of story.'

'What?'

'You're only talking to us right now, because Thea fed you at the crash site.'

'Hold on. Thea fed me?'

'Now don't get all agitated about it,' Fletch says. 'You were dying and that girl's blood saved your life.'

'You had no right to let her to that. I told you I didn't want her anywhere near me! What the hell is wrong with you?' He glances over at Court but his face is unreadable.

Fletch jabs a finger in Davyn's chest, ignoring the growl he gives in return. 'Now you listen to me and quit growling. You were dying. Again. A lot of people put in a hell of a lot of work to save you the last time. Do you honestly think I'd just sit back on the grass and watch as you bled out?'

'It was still my choice.'

'You were unconscious, you stubborn man. I could hardly ask you. Thea was on board with it.'

Davyn finds himself glancing over at Court again. 'She was,' he says, but her father doesn't look happy about it. 'She was safe the entire time. I promise you that.'

Davyn looks at his wrists. 'Where are my restraints?'

'Firstly, you do not have your own set of restraints,' Fletch says. 'Stop being dramatic. Secondly, you had no adverse reaction to her feeding you, Nothing. Not a hint of red in your eye. No craziness or trying to kill people. You fed, stopped, and your body started regenerating. Pretty damn fast too, I might add. She's fine, and you're doing better than you have since we got you back. I mean you actually look bigger if that's even possible.'

Davyn pauses before launching into a verbal attack. His first instinct is to tell Fletch and Nix exactly what he thinks about letting Thea anywhere near his teeth.

Nix moves closer to his bed and stands beside him, blocking out everyone else. 'Fletch is telling the truth. You had no adverse response at all. We're out of options, Dav. It's Thea or no one. There is no one else. Ethan has checked and double checked. I understand your reservations, I really do.'

She pauses and looks away for a moment. 'You're the best fighter I have,' she says, holding up a hand to stop Shep from arguing. 'But do you seriously expect me to let you go into battle with your father while you're like this? I need my fighters to be in top condition. As it is, technically we're down to five. I'm still on the fence about letting you join in, Shep.'

'Ah Nix. C'mon. I'm fine.'

'And like I said to Dav, it's my decision. You both do exactly what Fletch tells you to do for the next three days. Three days,' she says again when they both try to jump in. 'If he clears you, then and only then, can you leave the compound.'

'Fine,' Shep mutters, clearly as thrilled about the condition as Davyn is.

'Good. And Dav?'

'Clear.'

'Fantastic. Now I'll have a chat with Ethan and then try to get a hold of Murt again to see if they're open for round two. Wish me luck.'

The team file out of the room leaving him staring down at his hands. The cuts have already healed to faint pink lines. They'll be gone in another hour or so. Davyn pulls the sheet aside and lifts the bandage from his side. The holes from Eoin's talons are visible, but further along in the healing process than he expected.

Davyn slides out of the bed and makes his way into the bathroom. The reflection he sees in the mirror over the sink isn't what he was expecting either. He looks healthy. Not feeding properly over the decades had left him thinner and paler than he should be. And Fletch is right. He does appear larger.

Davyn smiles as he looks at himself. As a Prime he should be taller, stronger, bigger than the rest of the team, but he always fell short compared to Court, Bas, and Shep. Not anymore. With Thea's blood in his body, he's finally the Prime he should be.

He's still furious they took that risk with her life, but maybe it was the right decision. It must be hours since he fed from her and, instead of fuelling the cravings, the pain has dulled. Davyn lifts the eyepatch from his eye, half expecting to see a red pupil, but it's milky white. No sign of red in either eye.

He slides the patch back in place and allows himself to enjoy the moment. He's stronger than he's been for a long time. Thea is safe.

He hasn't tried to kill her.

He meets his reflection again and smiles. Maybe this will work with Thea.

Then his mind takes him back to the castle, his father, and his past. If he even wants to consider something with Thea, he's going to have to talk to her about his past. About what he did. It's only fair she has all the facts before she agrees to anything. And that's not a conversation he wants to have.

Davyn stuffs his hands in the front pockets of his jeans as he glowers at the handle of Thea's door. He checks along the corridor in either direction, but there's no one else around. Court and Nix are having a meeting with Ethan, Shep is being examined by Fletch and Fallon again, and Willow is training with Bas. There shouldn't be anyone eavesdropping on this conversation. He doesn't want to have this talk with Thea in the first place, let alone with other people around.

He licks his lips and knocks on the door. After a short delay she opens it, clearly surprised to see him there. 'Hi.'

'Can I come in?'

'Of course you can.' She steps aside and gestures for him to come in. He slowly walks in, feeling like he's doing something he really shouldn't. She closes the door behind him.

'Wow. You look really good. A lot healthier if that makes sense. How are you feeling?'

'I'm a bit sore, but alive. Thank you for saving my life. You didn't have to do that for me.'

'Why wouldn't I? I care about you, Davyn. Of course I was going to do anything I possibly could to help you.' She sits on the end of her bed and pats the covers beside her. Davyn sits, feeling increasingly uncomfortable being in her room. Maybe he should have done this somewhere a little more public after all.

'Have you changed your mind about me being your donor? Will you take my blood now?'

He licks his dry lips, hating the nerves that always seem to appear when he talks to her. Fighting a room full of True Order vampires would have him less on edge. 'No. I haven't changed my mind.'

Thea nods slowly. 'Right. Wow.'

'You're angry.'

He frowns when he catches her wiping her face. Fuck. Now he's made her cry. 'Of course I am.'

'At me?'

She nods again and glares at him. 'Who else? My blood saved your life yesterday. I saw it. I saw the wounds closing up right in front of my eyes. All because of my blood.'

'I know—'

'I genuinely care about you Davyn. Do you have any idea what it was like to find you covered in blood, with gaping holes in your sides. I thought you were dead, Davyn.'

'I didn't mean to put you through that.'

'I know you didn't, but it's part of your life. As much as I want to keep you and my father safe, this is what you do. You go out and sometimes you come back hurt. It's not so bad for the others, but you're putting your life in serious danger, because you don't have any way of regenerating anymore. The tremors have eased today, haven't they?'

Davyn frowns as he holds up his hand. He hadn't even noticed that, but she's right. His hand is steady for the first time in months.

'See. And have you looked at yourself in the mirror? You're healthier and stronger looking than you've been in a long time. But you still won't take my blood.'

She sniffs and wipes her face again. 'So yeah. I'm a little angry at you. Angry that you're willing to die, instead of taking what will save your life. All because it's my blood. Do you have any idea how ridiculous that sounds?' He looks down at his knee, surprised to see her small pale hand resting on him. 'Talk to me. Please, Davyn. Make me understand. What's going on in your head?'

'I want to be able to take your blood, Thea. I really do. And maybe it won't cause the issues I thought it would. I didn't react badly to it. But I still don't know for sure what it would mean for you long term. That's what's worrying me.'

'Then we take it day by day. Feed by feed. There's not a lot else we can do.'

She makes it sound so simple. Like it's not a big deal. But that's just because she doesn't understand. Time to change that.

'Were you there when Ronan told you about my past? About what I've done?'

She nods slowly. 'Yes.'

'When Darren was killed and my father locked me in the great hall with all those people, I lost control of myself. I'd been starving for decades and all of a sudden I had more blood than I could ever want. I didn't want to hurt anyone in that room. I said it over and over and over in my head as I stared at their terrified faces. I didn't want to hurt them.'

He can remember every single detail as if it happened an hour ago. Talking about it with someone he cares for so deeply is painful, but she needs to know. 'Everything that happened after that is a bit of a blur. The smell of their blood in their veins, their hearts beating in their chests, it all hit me at once. My fangs ached and my wings broke out, but I didn't feel the pain. The urge to feed overpowered everything else. It was so much stronger than my promise not to hurt them. I tried to stop - I really did, but it was stronger than I was. I killed every single one of them, Thea. I tore their bodies apart after I was done taking what I wanted from them.'

The urge to throw up is strong, but he keeps a hold of it. What he did to those people is unforgivable. They were prisoners of his father, just as he was, and he slaughtered them.

Thea squeezes his hand, offering comfort he doesn't deserve. 'I did that to them without having Fever. If I lose myself to that side of my nature again while I have Fever, I don't want to think about what I could do. But it's part of me now. I'll always be on the edge between control and my true nature. That makes the risk to whoever I feed from so much higher. I want to live, Thea. I want to be with you, but I'm not going to save my ass by risking your life. I love you too much.'

~

Thea turns to look at him, but he's focusing on the floor. 'What did you say?'

He shakes his head and takes a deep breath. 'I'd prefer to die than risk you for even a second. If I continue to drink your blood there's a chance I'll become addicted to it. It's happened before and I can't... not with you.'

Clearly he's not keen on making eye contact, so she kneels in front of him and rubs his legs. 'You love me?'

'Yeah. Sorry.' Thea laughs and he lifts his head. 'Why are you laughing?'

'Why are you apologising for loving me?'

'I was apologising for the way I told you. I wanted to tell you, but not like that. I'm not good at this stuff.'

'I think you're pretty amazing at it. Davyn?'

'What?'

'I love you too.'

His frown deepens then the most amazing thing happens. He smiles. A proper full face, beaming smile. 'You do?'

'Yes. And that's why I'm willing to take the risk with you. Please Davyn. I can't lose you again. You have to try this. We can take whatever precautions you want. But you have to try. And in case you've forgotten, you did feed from me before and you didn't kill me. In fact you single-handedly tore through an underground vampire stronghold to save me.'

'I'm dealing with Blood Fever now. That'll increase the effect your blood has on me. And I didn't take a lot of your blood last time.'

Thea nods. 'Yeah I heard you getting sick before I left your room. Was that because you don't like feeding or was it my blood?'

'Actually, it was the first time I've ever taken blood and it didn't make me feel sick. I was scared I'd get hooked because it was so different. I made myself get sick so I wouldn't risk you.' Davyn leans over and rests his forehead against hers. 'Your blood isn't the issue. It's the fact I don't hate it that's the problem. I liked it too much. If I hurt you...'

'You won't. I can ask Dad to knock you out if anything happens. I'm sure he'd be on for that,' she adds with a smile.

Davyn snorts. 'You got that right.' He tilts her head back and looks her in the eyes. 'You really love me? Even after hearing about my past. You still want me?'

She rises up and kisses him. The act surprises him for a moment but it doesn't take him long to let go a little. His hand brushes against the side of her face, his long fingers combing through her hair as he pulls her closer. Thea's heart hammers in her chest when Davyn growls deep in his chest, the rumble vibrating through his body as he kisses her. Thea wants to touch him, to take things further but she holds herself back.

She'll go slow with him. Take it one kiss at a time if that's what's needed. Thea rests her hand on his chest and he growls again as his canines drop.

He pulls back from her, but doesn't appear to be freaked out or regretting what just happened. If anything, she'd bet money he wants to take this exactly where she does.

His glowing green eye is burning as he looks at her in a way that leaves goosebumps on her flesh. His lips are parted slightly, showing the tips of his fangs. His broad chest is rising and falling, and she could swear she can hear him purring.

'Fine.'

Thea licks her lips as she tries to get her body to calm down. 'Sorry?'

'I'll drink your blood in a secure room and we'll go from there.'

'Really?'

His lips brush against her again. 'I don't know why I'm fighting you over this. It's too late for me anyway.'

'What do you mean?'

'I mean I'm already addicted to you, Thea. I'm addicted to your smell. To your taste.' He kisses her again, his fangs scraping against her tongue making her moan. 'Your sounds.'

'You are?'

'Yes.'

She closes her eyes when he kisses her again. Being kissed had never had this effect on her before. But she's never been kissed by Davyn. 'I absolutely second everything you just said.'

Davyn pulls her to her feet and she sits beside him again. 'I'm still not happy about this but I'll try. For you.'

She squeezes his hand in hers. 'That's all I'm asking. So, are we a couple now?'

Davyn smiles at her. 'I don't know. I've never been in a relationship with anyone. I don't know the process. I'll have to tell Nix though. Which means Court will find out.'

Thea's smile dies a little. Court did say he understood how she felt about Davyn, but that doesn't mean she's eager to test him. But being on the same team is very different to dealing with them as a couple. Or whatever the vampire equivalent of that is. 'I'll deal with my father. The priority at the moment is getting you ready to fight.'

~

Thea peers in through the window in the door of the gym and blows out a long breath. Her father is alone. That should make the next part a little easier to deal with. She pushes the door open and makes her way across the room to the bench, taking care not to startle him.

When they lived in that shitty apartment he had often gone to the gym around the corner to work off the surplus energy the vampires always seem to carry with them. She's noticed the change in him since coming here. Living with others like him, had helped him deal with this nervous energy. Having constant access to a state of the art gym and training room didn't do any harm either.

The changes hadn't just been in his overall manner. His body had appreciated the extra attention. In the last few months, he'd grown into a well-trained fighter, just like Bastian and Shep. In fact, he's outdone the two of them, not that she'd ever say that in front of Shep. Heaven forbid she does anything to hurt his monstrous ego.

Court drops the barbell back on the rack and smiles at her when he sits up. 'Hey. I didn't hear you come in.'

'I didn't want to interrupt.'

'I'm done.' He wipes his face with a towel and frowns at her. 'What's wrong?'

'Nothing. I just need... can we talk?'

'Always.' He pats the bench beside him, then changes his mind and nods towards the one next to it. 'Better sit there. This one is covered in sweat. So, what's up?'

'Did Fletch tell you they're going to give Davyn more of my blood?'

He nods. 'You okay with that?'

'Of course. It helped him after he was injured.'

Court takes a drink from the water bottle by his feet, then wipes his mouth with the back of his hand. 'It did.'

He looks away, a sure sign he's not happy about the conversation. 'I'm okay with this. I really am.'

He glances back at her, absently running his hand over the black wings tattooed across his chest. 'I'm not. The thought of you being a donor for one of us is seriously pissing me off. And that's putting it mildly.'

'And you feeding from Nix is different?'

'Yes it is.'

'How, Dad?'

'Because she's a trained fighter and you're my daughter. That makes it different.' His face softens as he leans forward, resting his arms on his legs. 'I don't want to keep going around in circles with you. You're doing this and I will, in time, get my head around it.'

'He only needs a small amount of my blood every few weeks to survive. It's not like he'll be draining me every night.'

'How exactly did any of that help?'

She grimaces, realising she should have just stopped talking. 'Sorry. But you know what I mean.'

'Yeah. I know. So, I'm guessing by the way you can't look me in the eye, that you're making things official with him.'

Thea's mouth opens and closes, making Court laugh out loud.

'Wow. If that's you playing dumb, you're doing a lousy job.'

'But how—'

'Because it's clear you're in love with him.'

'It is?'

He moves to sit beside her. 'Thea, I'm madly in love with Nix. I know what it feels like. I know what it looks like. I may be heading towards a century and a half but that doesn't mean I don't get it.

Believe me.'

'So you're okay with this?'

'Fuck no,' he answers with a smile. 'It's not my business though. I already told you that. I appreciate you coming to talk to me. I really do. If I'm being honest I didn't think you would.'

'Why wouldn't I?'

'I know things are still... strained between us. It genuinely means the world to me that you wanted to tell me like this.'

Thea reaches over and wraps her arms around his neck.

'I'm sweaty.'

'I don't care,' she mumbles against his neck as she pulls him into a hug.

Davyn stretches his legs out in front of him. He's been locked in the cell for close to an hour and, so far, he hasn't had any negative reaction. Fletch had given him more of Thea's blood, but she had to promise to keep away from him until Davyn's convinced he's not a danger to her.

Davyn has forced down blood his entire life, hating the taste of the stuff every single time. Until he tasted hers. He liked it. Really liked it. It didn't make him sick. For the first time he wasn't revolted by what he is, or what he has to do to survive.

It's too soon to let his guard down, but maybe, just maybe, with his wings fixed and being able to feed, the shame at what he is, would lessen. Maybe.

Fletch checks his watch from outside the bars and stretches. 'You still good?'

'I feel stronger, but nothing I'm worried about.'

'That sounds encouraging. You on for the next test?'

Bringing Thea into the room could change everything, but they need to know. Deep down he's assuming the worst. His track record is as bad as it can get, but there is a chance things will be different with her. There's a chance he'll be able to feed from the woman he loves without hurting her. A small chance, but even a small chance is worth hanging on to.

'Davyn?'

He nods and Fletch opens the door calling Thea in from outside. She smiles when she sees him, and sits on the chair Fletch was in a minute ago.

'Hi. You okay?'

Davyn looks at Thea expecting to be overtaken with the need to take more blood. But that's not the need he's feeling right now. He wants her, but hurting her doesn't come in to it. Far from it. Her blood is making him stronger, linking them to each other, which is bringing out a protectiveness he's never experienced before.

She's his. And he is without a doubt, hers. And that's all he can think about.

Fletch clears his throat and Davyn realises he's been talking to him. 'What?'

'Back with us then?'

'What?'

'You went a little... well... three's a crowd sort of thing. I'm going to give you two a minute. Thea, best keep him in there. Do not open that door, okay?'

Fletch leaves them alone and Davyn gets up. Thea meets him at the bars but keeps a little back from him. He knows she trusts him but he told her the rules and she's sticking to them. 'Are you okay?'

He nods. 'Yeah. I think I'm okay.'

'What was with the growl a minute ago?'

'I growled?'

'Oh yeah. I'm getting the impression it wasn't a growl I should be worried about though. Fletch muttered something about god-damn vampire hormones or something like that.'

'Sorry. I'm just getting my strength back.' His body may want her but he's far from ready to even go there with her. That's a whole other hurdle for further down the path. He'll just have to ignore her scent which is suddenly all he can smell.

She's turned on. He can sense it. She's turned on by him and what his growl meant and she's not alone. He wants his mate. Wants all of her. Wants to taste her, wants to mark her as his.

She licks her lips and the growl comes out before he realises what he's doing. 'I'm sorry. It's your blood. I guess my vampire side is being recharged.'

Thea smiles and takes a step closer, still out of his reach. 'Don't apologise for that. I like it. A lot. It sounds sexy as hell.'

He rolls his shoulder as the pressure builds across his back. Now his damn wings are joining in, begging to be released.

'Are you okay?'

'Yeah. Wings are uncomfortable.'

'Why don't you release them? You're in there anyway. You can't do anything.'

He pulls off his t-shirt and throws it through the bars to her. The relief at letting his wings out is quickly diminished when the need to be with Thea increases tenfold. He grabs the bars of the cell and peers down at her. Thea reaches through the bars and pulls off his eye patch. 'Wow.'

'What?'

She smiles up at him. 'Both your eyes are glowing. I didn't know the damaged one could still do that. It's glowing white. It's beautiful.'

Ruined, destroyed, messed up, blind. Those are words he'd use for the eye. Hearing her call it beautiful helps lift some of that shame.

'Why are you smiling like that?'

Thea takes a long breath as her eyes wander down his body then up to his face again. 'I'm smiling because you are unbelievably sexy right now. You're all big, and broody, and yeah... I like seeing you let go like this.'

'This is the side of me you should fear.'

Thea places her hand over his. 'I'll never fear you, Davyn.'

He rests his forehead against the bars. 'I don't deserve you.'

'Stop talking like that. Just concentrate on getting stronger. So, are you happy so far? About your reaction to my blood I mean.'

Apart from being more turned on than he's before, he's happy. 'Yeah. So far so good.'

'Fletch said I can give you more if you want.'

He shakes his head. 'Not yet. I want to take this slow.'

'Of course. You're in charge of this. By the way, I spoke to Court. You know, about you and me.'

Davyn's fire is rapidly extinguished at hearing those words. 'Did I just have my least meal?'

She laughs and pushes him in the chest. 'Don't overreact. Actually he was great about the whole thing.'

'He was?'

Thea nods eagerly. 'Well he's not entirely thrilled about it, but he says it's not his business.'

'So he's not going to kill me?'

'Stop being dramatic. No he's not. We can both just relax and concentrate on getting you back on your feet properly.' She sits down and takes out her phone. 'I still have that book I was reading to you when you were sick. Do you want me to continue with it? I need a distraction.'

'From what?'

She gestures at him while she scrolls through her phone. 'From you looking like that.'

Davyn sits down beside the door and smiles. He's never had someone say things like that to him before. 'Yeah. I'd like that.'

~

'I don't think this is a good idea,' Davyn says.

'I can't keep going to Fletch to donate my blood for you to drink. Isn't it much easier all round if you drink directly from me?' Thea knows Davyn wouldn't want to try feeding directly from her but, it's the obvious next step.

It may sound simple but the look he gives her says the exact opposite. While she absolutely has no problem keeping the fridge stocked with her blood, she'd prefer he took it from her. When he fed from her it was the most incredible experience. But she understands why he's not keen. Even now, his hand is trembling slightly. He's not in complete control of the addiction and that's what's giving him a reason to hesitate.

And the fact he's being chained to the wall of a cell probably isn't helping the situation. It's just the latest in a long line of bizarre things that have happened since she came to the compound. Davyn had asked Court to make sure he was secure and she gets why. Of everyone in the compound, her father would be the one to make painfully sure she was safe.

He's living up to expectations too. Davyn is pinned to the bars of the cell with a ridiculous amount of chains. Her father was either playing it extra safe or just wanted to make a point. His ankles, knees, waist, upper chest, elbows, and wrists are secured. Perhaps a little too tightly by the look of the red skin on his exposed flesh.

Davyn peers down at her but is far from happy. If anything, he looks like he's about to throw up. 'You okay? Are the chains too tight?'

'No. I don't want to hurt you.'

'You won't. I trust you.'

He shakes his head then rests it back against the bars. 'I hope that's justified.'

'How do you want to do this?'

'Your wrist. I'm not feeding from anywhere else. Not yet.'

Thea pushes the wooden step over to him and climbs up, bringing her face level with his. 'Hi.'

He smiles at her. 'Are you absolutely sure you want to do this, Thea?'

'I'm sure, Davyn. So, what do you want me to do?'

'Leave the room and forget all about this, but I know you won't.'

'Glad you know me so well already.' She rests her hand on his chest. 'You've done this before with me. Just trust yourself.'

He peers over her shoulder at Court and Nix, both holding tranq guns.

'Forget them. Pretend it's just you and me.'

'And your father.'

He has a point but there is no way she'll be able to convince Court to leave the room. Being with Davyn like this, with him here, isn't ideal for her either, but they don't have a choice. Hopefully, if he sees that Dav can be trusted, he'll back off. 'Look at me.'

His eye locks on her and he nods. 'Yeah. Okay. Let's get it over with.'

Thea doesn't comment on his terse reply. He's stressed and worried about the entire situation. She holds her wrist up to his mouth, pressing it against his lips. Thea's heart races in her chest as his breath tickles her skin.

Having Court watching his every move isn't helping. As ridiculous as it sounds, Davyn just needs to try his best to ignore him. Thea waits for what seems like a good few minutes before his mouth opens and his fangs scrape against her wrist. As soon as he latches on and begins feeding, Thea couldn't care who else is or isn't in the room.

She pushes herself against his chest and wishes his arms were around her like the last time.

Then he stops and places a kiss on her wrist over the wound. 'Are you all right?'

She nods, still waiting to come down after whatever feeding Davyn does to her.

'Back away from him, Thea,' Court says from behind her. 'If he's going to react, it'll be when you're taken away from him.'

Thea smiles at him as she runs her hands along his arm. He's so tense his muscles are trembling under her touch. 'You'll be fine. Trust yourself. I do.' She kisses him on the cheek, loving the way his head tilts ever so slightly towards her, pressing his skin to her lips.

She climbs off the step and walks over to her father. He hands her a tissue for her wrist but keeps his eyes firmly on Davyn as she presses it over the wound. 'You okay?'

'I'm fine, Dad. Really.'

Nix moves closer to Davyn and examines him. 'How about you, Dav? How do you feel?'

He pauses for a moment then frowns and nods. 'Yeah. Fine, I think. But I've never fed from someone like Thea.'

'You mean someone you care about.'

'Yeah.' His eye darts to Court before focusing on Nix again.

'Well in my experience, the feelings are so much more intense when it's someone you care about. We'll unchain you but might leave you in the cell for an hour or so. Just see how it progresses.'

'Fine by me. I want you all to trust me.'

'We trust you, Dav. Maybe you should try having a little trust in yourself. Thea, you can stay with him, but outside the cell.'

'Of course.'

'Great. Court, unlock him and make sure he can't get out of the cell. I'll have a chat with Fletch. Let him know how it went.'

Thea follows Nix from the cell as Court unchains Dav then joins them, firmly locking the cell behind him. Court points to the chair at the far side of the room. 'Stay back just in case. I'll check on you in a bit, okay?'

'Thanks,'

Thea waits until they're alone before she drags the chair closer to the bars. Davyn rubs his chest where the chain had cut into his flesh. 'Are you sure I didn't hurt you?'

'I'm absolutely positive. Come here.'

He slowly approaches the bars and lowers to the ground. Thea holds out her hand and, after looking at it for a few seconds, Davyn takes it.

'I am fine. Great even. You have to stop worrying.'

He targets her with his green eye, but he doesn't look happy. Not that he ever really looks happy. 'I've killed a lot of people I've fed from, Thea. You can tell me to stop worrying as much as you want. I'm still going to worry.'

'That was a different time and place, Davyn.'

'A century is nothing for a vampire. It feels like it happened yesterday.'

'What if with me it will be different? Hear me out. Maybe your feelings for me will make things different. You keep saying I should fear the other side of you, but it's all you. You're a vampire and I get that. The glowing eyes, your teeth, those stunning wings. It's all part of you. And so is the need for blood. You really need to stop trying to separate the two sides of yourself. It's like me trying to take my arm off. It's a part of me.'

'So you're saying I should relax and see what happens.'

'No, not exactly. I'm more saying that you shouldn't automatically assume you're going to hurt me. You've never hurt me. And from what I can gather you've never hurt any of the Blackjacks. I'm just saying trust yourself a little more. You might be surprised.'

Davyn walks back to his room with Thea beside him. Having her blood keeping him alive is such an incredible feeling. He's stronger than he ever remembers being before. Fletch and Ethan were right. Her blood is just what he needs, what he's needed his entire life.

'What are you smiling about?'

'I feel strong again. It's been a long time.' She squeezes his hand and that's another feeling he could get used to. He's shied away from physical contact for so long it's taking time to accept someone touching him again.

Now he just needs to convince himself to make the next move with her. He hates that she's taking the lead more than he is, but everything about this is so new he honestly doesn't know how to act. And that's pissing him off.

'I told you it would be okay.'

'Yeah but you were just saying that. You didn't know.'

She brushes his comment away with a flick of her wrist. 'Stop raining on my parade. You fed from me. I'm still very much alive and you're looking healthier than I've ever seen you look before. I'd class that as a success.' She reaches up and kisses him on the cheek. 'Maybe next time you won't be so quick to dismiss other people's ideas so fast.'

He opens his bedroom door and steps aside to let her in. After locking the door behind him Davyn sits on the end of his unmade bed, suddenly unsure about what to do now. Thankfully, Thea is on the case.

She slides onto his lap and wraps her arms around his neck. He likes the feel of her on top of him like this. Likes it a lot. It takes a second to convince himself to lift his arms and place his hands on her hips. She smiles at him and Davyn instantly feels himself go hard under her. He wants her. Badly.

Before he can second guess himself again, he leans down to kiss her on the cheek. But Thea takes things up a level by turning her head so he gets her lips instead.

Her hands dig into his hair, pulling him closer to her and he doesn't resist. His hands squeeze her hips, then he slides under the hem of her t-shirt and touches her skin. It's smooth, and soft, and he wants his hands all over it.

Thea moans against his mouth and he has a hard time not growling in response. He wants her so badly it hurts. His cock is aching like never before. But when his gums throb he stops kissing her and slides his hands out from under her shirt. 'I'm sorry.'

'Sorry for stopping I hope.'

His fangs drop so he leans back on his bed, putting more distance between them. 'I get too worked up around you.'

She smiles at him and it does nothing to calm his body down. 'That's exactly what's supposed to happen, Davyn. If it helps, I'm worked up too. I didn't want you to stop.'

'But I have to.'

Thea sits back on his legs and straightens her top. 'Right. Well this is going to be a bit of stumbling block in our relationship isn't it. I'm going to be blunt with you, Davyn. I would like to have sex with you. And I mean I really, really, really want to have sex with you.

'You have no idea how much I want to see you naked. I want to feel you inside me. I'm so turned on right now and I'm not helping myself by talking like this, but it's the truth. Do you not want that with me?'

'Of course I do.' He wishes his past actions didn't keep getting in between them but he's beyond terrified of hurting her and it's crippling him. 'I don't want to keep letting this get in the way, but my head puts up this block and I…'

He sighs and rubs his hand over his face. 'I want you, Thea. That day when I first fed from you… it was so difficult for me. Your smell, the feel of your skin, it all drove me crazy. And then I had your blood and I knew I wanted you and only you.'

She pushes him back on the bed and straddles him.

'Thea—'

'Shut up for a second. What you just said, did you mean it?'

He looks up at her and knows he meant every word. 'I love you, Thea. I want to give you everything you need and deserve.'

'Thank goodness for that. To be honest, I was kind of wondering if you were having second thoughts. You're impossible to read sometimes.'

He runs his hands up her legs loving the sight of her on top of him, even fully dressed. 'I'm not used to all of this.'

She leans down and kisses him tortuously slow. Her tongue slides into his mouth and runs over his fangs. When she stops and smiles at him, Davyn knows he'll do anything to be with her properly.

'I have a plan. Do you trust me?'

He nods and swallows, trying to moisten his throat. 'Yeah.'

'Okay, so go and train or hit something for a few hours then come back here.'

'Why?'

She kisses him quickly and pushes off his chest. 'Just go and don't come back for a few hours.'

Davyn doesn't argue. He has no idea what she's going to do but he does know training will help. He's got so much energy since feeding from her, he could do with blowing some of it off before he takes things too far with Thea.

~

After one of the best workouts he's had... well, ever, he showers in the gym then heads back to his room.

He opens his door and comes to a stop when he sees his new room. He barely recognises his personal space. He steps back and checks he's at the right door just to be sure.

'Well, what do you think?'

Davyn steps into his room and turns around. The bed is made, probably for the first time ever, the new set of pale grey linen matching the thick rug on the floor. Colourful artwork hangs from the walls instantly brightening his space. She's even packed away his clothes, uncovering the couch which also has bright cushions on it. He can't remember the last time his room looked so welcoming and clean.

'It's amazing. It looks like a different room.'

'Well it kind of is. Gwen had all this downstairs in the store room. I'll have to have a search through her stash for my room. Anyway, it's just a little more homely feeling in here now. I didn't touch any of your stuff. I just put your clothes away - that's it. You deserve a nice space to relax.'

'Thank you, Thea. It looks incredible, but I'm confused. This was your plan?'

She shakes her head and stuffs her hands in the back pockets of her jeans, suddenly appearing nervous. 'No. That wasn't exactly my plan. I was just on edge waiting for you to get back so I organised the rest. My plan is a little more... extreme I suppose you could say.'

'Extreme? Now I'm on edge.'

'Please don't be. I've just never done anything quite like this before. I'm not sure how it's going to go down.'

'This conversation isn't exactly doing a good job of putting me at ease. What do you want to do?'

'I think it's best I show you.' She reaches down beside his bed and drags a heavy sports bag across the floor. 'That's the plan. Well, inside the bag.'

More confused than ever, he frowns at her, then crouches down and opens the bag. What's inside fills him with dread, before it quickly ebbs away to excitement as he realises what this could mean for Thea and himself.

Davyn picks up one of the heavy restraints and lifts it from the bag, smiling slightly as he peers over at her. 'Does Fletch know you took these?'

She blushes and shrugs. 'I think it's best we don't think too much about who knows what about what. I have them and that's all that matters. I have a drill and some anchor points for the wall. I thought we could secure the restraints to the wall so you can't move.' Thea pauses and shrugs again. 'Good idea or not?'

He drops the chains back in the bag and straightens. 'Good idea. I would have suggested it but I didn't know how.'

'So you're on for this?'

'Yes.' He'll stay in chains if he means he can be with her. 'Are you sure you want this? I mean with me like this.'

'I love you. I'll try anything to prove to you we can be together.'

He pulls the drill from the bag and hauls his bed away from the wall. 'Pass me one of the anchor points. Better make sure I can't get out of these.'

'You okay?'

Thea nods and smiles as he sits beside her on the couch and looks over at the bed. It didn't take long to fix the anchors to the wall and floor. With the chains and cuffs fitted, the freshly tidied room looks more like a dungeon. 'Not exactly romantic is it?'

'I wouldn't know,' he answers with a small smile. 'I'm learning as I go. You don't have to do this. I get it's weird and far from ideal.'

'I'm more worried about you.'

'Me? Why?'

'It's the chains I guess.'

Davyn nods slowly. 'You thinking about my father?'

'That sounds so wrong, but yes.' She takes hold of his hand and can't help but look at the scars around his wrist. 'Every suggestion I come up with seems to end up with you in chains. That's not fair. Not after what your father—'

'Don't go there, Thea. There's no comparison. The restraints on the end of those chains are padded, not lined with rusted spikes. I'm in my room with you, not in a cold cell or a fighting pit. I won't be comparing this with anything that happened in my past. I'll just be thinking about you.'

'So what now?'

Davyn scrubs a hand over his face as he takes a long breath. 'Well, that's up to you. You need some time or–'

She straddles his legs, wrapping her arms around his neck. 'I've waited long enough, Davyn.'

His smile drops and Thea knows he's worried. Time to show him they can be a couple and do things like this, without him losing control.

Thea kisses him again, taking her time, distracting him as much as she can from the worry, fear, and the dread he seems to carry with him all the time. She leaves his mouth, kissing along his strong jaw and down to his neck. He jerks and growls softly, startling her. 'Are you okay?'

'Yeah.' When he smiles at her, it pushes all the doubts about her plan aside. He wants this as much as she does. 'Better lock me up then. If you're sure.'

'Oh I'm sure.' To prove her point, Thea takes the bottom of his t-shirt in her hands and slowly uncovers his chest. Davyn lifts his arms over his head so she can take it off. She runs her hand down his broad chest, tracing the heavy lines of his tattoo down to his stomach.

She gets to her feet and holds out her hand. After a brief pause, where she fears he might change his mind about the whole thing, Davyn takes it and stands up. She slowly opens his belt and unzips his jeans. Davyn swallows thickly as he watches what she's doing.

Thea pushes his jeans down his legs and takes a minute to appreciate the view in front of her. Even hidden under the black material of his boxers, she can't stop staring at his body – specifically his groin.

He either notices she's staring and has stopped undressing him, or maybe he's just eager to get things moving, but he kicks off his boots and finishes taking off his jeans.

Then his control slips. In the blink of an eye, he goes from reserved to dominant.

He crushes her against his chest, pushing his arousal against her as he kisses her. She gasps as his hands grip her ass, squeezing hard while his tongue invades her mouth. He picks her up and moves back towards the bed. Then he growls, a deep rumble in his chest that sends goosebumps over her skin.

'Is that a growl I should be worried about?'

Davyn nuzzles against the side of her neck and she swears his fangs brush against her skin. 'No, but you should chain me now, just in case.'

'Lie down.'

Davyn takes off his boxers before he lowers onto the bed and stretches out for her.

She'd thought about Davyn's body a lot since she saw him with his wings out a few months ago, but seeing him naked in front of her, is better than anything she could have imagined in any of her fantasies.

His body is pure muscle. Every single inch toned to distracting perfection. It takes her a minute to focus her attention on what was clearly visible under his boxers. Like the rest of him, his cock is stunning and intimidating. She's never been with someone his size before. The thought of that thick cock inside her excites her and also makes her a little nervous.

His lips part slightly, showing the tips of his fangs as he watches her intently. Thea climbs onto his bed, taking one of the wrist restraints in her hand. She runs her hand up his arm, gently massaging the solid muscles under her fingertips until she reaches his wrist and wraps her fingers around it, pinning it to the bed. Thea leans down and kisses along his arm as she holds his wrist down.

'Thea...'

Hearing her name growled in that deep, low voice has her smiling against his skin as she places kisses along the underside of his arm.

'Shush.'

He growls again but doesn't interrupt her. Thea releases his arm and slowly licks the underside of his wrist. Davyn holds his breath then groans.

'You like that?'

He nods, his glowing green eye firmly locked on her. 'Yeah.'

She draws her tongue along his wrist again, then locks the first restraint in place. Once she's sure it's secure, she straddles his broad body and smiles down at him. 'Okay?'

He nods again and licks his lips. 'I could get used to being chained up like this.'

Thea kisses him, dragging her tongue over the tip of his fang, earning herself another deep growl. 'I like it when you make that sound.'

'Good. I can't help it. You bring it out of me.'

Thea kisses him again as she holds his other wrist to the bed. She traces her finger along the sensitive area on his wrist. The contact is barely there but he hisses and his body vibrates under her. 'You do like being touched there.'

'Only by you.'

His words mean so much to her. For most of his life touch had meant pain. The fact he's willing to let her touch him, and is actually enjoying it, is empowering. She doesn't want to stop showing him how thrilling being touched can be.

Thea locks the second restraint in place then turns to deal with his ankles. She doesn't want to touch his dick yet, not until he's fully restrained. More for his benefit than hers. If something does go wrong it could set him back and potentially put a stop to anything like this happening again.

She gives each leg the same attention as his arms, but unless she missed it, his legs aren't as sensitive. Maybe the feeding sites have heightened sensations. Definitely something to focus on.

Thea locks the final restraint in place and climbs off him. 'Can you get out?'

Davyn pulls against the chains, the muscles in his body tensing as he strains. 'No.'

'That's good.' She takes a minute to just marvel at the vampire laid out in front of her. Having him restrained to the bed as he is, isn't as bad as she thought it would be. If anything, knowing she's in control of what's going on is such a turn on.

She looks at his face and his glowing green eye. 'Do you have any idea how sexy you look right now?'

Then he smiles and flashes her the tip of one of his fangs which nearly has her moaning in delight.

'I'm going to touch you now, okay?'

'I want you to do whatever you want to do.'

~

Davyn can barely believe what's happening to him right now. When Thea had produced the chains he'd accepted it was the only way he could safely be with her. It wasn't ideal, but keeping her safe was the only thing he cared about.

But being chained up by Thea was nothing like he expected. Or could ever have imagined. She had somehow turned the task into something pleasurable. And he couldn't love her more for it.

'Are you comfortable?'

He smiles at her, loving the slight blush on her cheeks. Her body is responding to what's happening. He can smell it.

'Yes.' He's not, but he couldn't care less. All he wants is Thea on top of him.

She slowly pulls off her t-shirt, dropping it to the ground beside her. Then she unfastens her bra, sliding the straps down her arms, until that too lands on the ground. Davyn's dick twitches against his stomach at the sight of her breasts. He licks his lips at he watches her nipples tighten when the cool air hits them. The urge to touch them, to touch her, increases and he strains against his bonds.

The scent of her arousal intensifies when he does this. Does she like that he obviously wants to touch her, but can't?

His thoughts turn back to her body when she kicks off her shoes and opens her jeans, moving her hips from side to side as she pushes them down her legs, far too slowly for his liking.

When she slides her thumbs under the waistband of her panties, he growls deeply, startling himself. The air is heavy with the scent of her arousal. She likes him growling. It's not something he feels he has any control over at the moment, but if she likes it, he won't try to stop.

The growl deepens when she steps out of her underwear and stands naked in front of him. He wishes he could put into words how beautiful she is, but he can't get his brain to form an intelligent sentence.

Training has transformed her body in the last few months, toning her legs and arms. A few small scars mark her stomach and legs, no doubt from training with Fallon, but they do nothing to take away from her appearance. She's fighting to be a part of his world and that makes him so damn proud.

'You're looking at me strangely.'

'I was just thinking you look like a fighter.'

Thea blushes and glances down at her body. 'Really?'

'You're incredible.'

Thea climbs on to the bed and traces her fingers along the tattoo running up his chest. 'Is there anything you want me to do? Or not do?'

'I don't know. This is all new to me.'

'You'll have to tell me if you like what I'm doing, okay?'

He nods and lifts his head, desperate to kiss her. Thea smiles seductively then touches her lips to his. Her tongue teases his lips apart, sliding into his mouth as her hand massages his chest.

A fire burns deep in his gut, building as she invades his mouth, brushing her tongue along the tips of his fangs while her fingers trace up his side and over his nipple.

He bites back a curse and holds his breath as she does it again, his nipples hardening under her touch. 'Fuck, Thea.'

'That good?' she asks as she moves from his mouth to his ear, kissing his earlobe before sucking it.

'Fuck, yes.'

'What part,' she asks before licking along his ear again.

'All.' He can't do the whole talking think while keeping himself together. She hasn't even gone near his dick and he's struggling to hold back.

When Thea presses her lips against the side of his neck he bucks on the bed, pulling against the chains.

'Wow. I think I found another sensitive spot.'

He swallows thickly and nods. 'Yeah. I like that.'

She traces her finger down his neck and he growls. 'Is that a sensitive spot for all vampires or just you?'

'I don't know. Never been touched there before.'

She goes back to what she was doing, clearly enjoying figuring him out. His body spasms again when she gently nips his neck, and he lifts his hips, desperate for some friction, something to rub the damn thing against.

He meets Thea's eyes as she moves from his neck to his chest, kissing, licking, and sucking. Her breasts rub against his skin, her hard nipples brushing against his own as she moves lower. Her hot skin against his, the smooth flesh sliding along his, has him dizzy and breathless. He wraps his hands around the chains to ground himself. But it doesn't work.

'Just keep breathing, Davyn.'

He didn't realise he was holding his breath. Exhaling on a long breath he closes his eyes, focusing on her touch, on her fingers, mouth, and tongue as they work in perfect harmony.

He rears up, his arms straining, as her warm, wet tongue swipes against the head of his dick.

She smiles wickedly and does it again as he watches in stunned silence. 'Breathe.'

Fuck, he has to stop doing that. In and out. In and out. His breath leaves his body in pathetic short gasps as her tongue flicks against him. He's breathing in time to her licks and he's about to hyperventilate.

'Relax, Davyn.'

Easier said than done. He's never been touched there. He dealt with himself every now and again when the need became too difficult to ignore. But this... he flops back on the pillow and gasps as she sucks him into her mouth. Yeah, he's going to completely disgrace himself by coming too fast, or fainting because he's not breathing again.

As he takes another breath she pulls back, releasing him while still sucking. The pressure is blowing his mind. He won't last long. Not that he really knows what the right length of time is.

Thea wraps her hands around the base of his dick, standing him upright. Her eyes meet his again as she slowly slides him into her mouth. This time she doesn't stop, taking him deep into her throat. Thea swallows, her throat constricting against his dick.

The growl that rumbles deep in his chest sends her into a frenzy. With one hand still wrapped around his base, she puts the other on his stomach and moves her head back, then takes him deep into her mouth again. The heavy chains rattle as he fights to get free. But this has nothing to do with harming her. He wants so much more, wants it so much harder. Needs to feel all of her.

His guttural growl spurs her on. She peers up at him as she sucks his dick and when she moans against him, he responds the same way. He knows his fangs are on full display and his eye is glowing. But she likes that. He knows that now, so he doesn't try to hide it. Thea moans again and runs her tongue along him as she sucks him, swirling it around his crown as she rises, then flattening it against him as she takes him deep into her throat again.

A heavy pressure builds in his balls as she tightens her grip around his base. 'Thea... I'm close.'

He expects her to stop. To take him out of her mouth and let him finish himself. But she clearly has no intention of stopping. He lifts his head off the pillow, squeezing the chains in his hands as she sucks him harder.

She continues to push him harder, his body trembling uncontrollably, his legs and arms pulled taut as every muscle contracts. He's going to come in her mouth.

Shit.

The thought is more than he can handle. His hips move of their own accord, rising and falling in time with Thea's motions. She moans again and her fingernails dig into his stomach as he pushes himself into her mouth over and over again.

His growl builds to a loud roar as he releases into her mouth, his hips pumping as the orgasm rips out of him. And still Thea works him, keeping him going, using her wicked tongue to draw out his pleasure as long as possible.

For how long he has no idea. His dick just won't stop. It wants so much more of what she has to offer.

When he's finally spent, his hips still. In and out. He needs to breathe, but he's seriously struggling. He gasps as Thea slowly releases him and crawls up his chest to look at him. Her beautiful face is flushed, her lips swollen and wet. Ignoring the fact he can't breathe, Davyn lifts his head up and kisses her. He groans against her mouth as he tastes her.

'You taste incredible.'

She smiles against his lips. 'I taste of you.'

For some reason that spurs his dick into life again. His stomach clenches and his hips move against her, pressing his dick against the back of her thigh.

'You like that, huh?' Thea peers down at him, wiping sweat soaked hair from her forehead.

'I liked all of that. I've never experienced that before.'

'I love how your body responds to me,' she says as she sits back on his lower stomach, resting her pussy against his skin. 'You are unbelievably sexy all worked up like this.'

'I'm only worked up because of you.'

She momentarily holds her breath as his dick twitches against her ass. Thea glances over her shoulder and smiles. 'You're ready again?'

He nods not sure what to do. All he knows is that he wants more.

'Do you want to be inside me, Davyn?'

He growls and she smiles again. 'Yes. Please, Thea.'

'You never have to beg me, Davyn. I'll always want to do this with you.'

His damn hips rotate at hearing that. They have a life of their own.

'Oh God, Davyn. That's so hot.'

'Can't stop them.'

She laughs and kisses him deeply before reaching down to wrap her hand around his, squeezing gently. 'Time for more?'

He nods without hesitation. 'Yes.'

46

Thea can honestly say she's never been so turned on before. Davyn's hard, defined, stunning body takes her breath away and that's before she even touches it. The way he responds to her, the sounds, the groans and growls - is captivating. Everything about this vampire is addictive. Driving him over the edge was sexy and she had to remind herself to breathe as often as she had to remind him.

She runs her fingers down his shaft, loving the way his stomach muscles contract as he hisses. 'I'll just put a condom on you, okay?'

He licks his lips then shakes his head. 'There's no need. We don't carry or pass on human infections and I can't get you pregnant.'

Thea freezes at his blunt reply. The fact vampires don't transmit any nasties makes sense. But the pregnancy thing gets to her more than she thought it would. Does he mean he can't ever get her pregnant? 'You can't get me pregnant?'

He shakes his head. 'You're not ready.' He flashes her a brief smile. 'You're a few days off that.'

Thea feels her cheeks redden. 'You can pick up on that?'

He nods. 'Yes.'

Thea raises her eyebrows and files that away with everything else she's learning about his species. She doesn't want to think about who else in this house can pick up on her body clock.

His glowing green eye meets her. He's frowning slightly. He's overthinking again. Thea rests her chest against his and adjusts her position, placing her pussy over his dick. Davyn's hips rotate and she groans. 'I want to do something first.'

He frowns again. 'What?'

'Can I take off your eyepatch?'

Davyn licks his lips and his gaze drops from hers. 'Why?'

'I want to see your eyes while we do this. Both of them.'

'It's... it looks disgusting.'

Thea places a kiss on the leather patch. 'Don't ever call any part of you disgusting. Everything about you is beautiful. I mean that.'

A lot of awkward silence fills the next minute or so but he eventually nods once. He lifts his head, giving Thea room to pull the eye patch away. He lies back but keeps his eyes closed. Thea takes a minute to look at the spiderweb of scars spiralling out from his eyelid to his cheek and forehead. She kisses the damaged skin. 'Look at me.'

He does as he's told and Thea smiles even though her heart is breaking for him. The milky eye still has a green iris, but it's so pale it's nearly white. 'So handsome.'

He frowns briefly then smiles. She just made his day by telling him that. And it's the truth. She wishes he didn't have to endure what he did, but his eyes are beautiful. She doesn't care what colour they are or how many scars he has.

Thea tilts his head down and kisses him as she rubs herself against his dick. Davyn takes a few seconds to relax again, but when his tongue pries her lips apart and slides into her mouth, she knows he's back with her again.

She wants him to be able to be himself when he's with her. No eyepatch, no holding back, and no chains. Not that she's overly unhappy about the chains after what just happened. Watching his powerful arms straining and pulling against the restraints had her on the edge of coming, too many times to count. Telling him to breathe, gave her a few seconds to get herself together.

His hips buck against her when she traces her fingers along his neck. God, she loves how that area is so sensitive. Not for the first time her mind drifts to thoughts of him biting her, while he's inside her. Pinning her at two points to his hard body as he takes what he needs from her, his spectacular wings out, cocooning them. Before she knows what she's doing, Thea nips at his neck.

'Fuck!' His deep, curse is full of raw need. She pushes back from him and her clit pulses when she sees him. His lips are pulled back, two deadly fangs on show which is hot as hell. Then she meets his eyes and instinctively rubs her aching pussy against his shaft. Both eyes are glowing brightly; one green and one white. All she needs now is his wings and the fantasy will be fulfilled.

In time, hopefully.

His nostrils flare as he breathes heavily while levelling his wanton gaze on her.

'You okay?'

Instead of answering, he rotates his hips again, with more force this time. And she's more than ready for him. She reaches down and takes his dick in her hand, slick with her juices and hard as stone. Without thinking about whether she can take all of him or not, she holds him upright and positions him at her entrance.

They both groan at the same time and it's sexy as hell. 'Don't move, okay. Let me do this part. You're big.'

He doesn't respond, but his hips still as he watches her. Thea slowly moves, gradually working his thick dick deeper. 'Just breathe,' she says, instructing herself as much as Davyn. He takes a breath and she hears the deep growl. God, if that sound isn't the most erotic thing she's ever heard.

She lowers slowly, until she's stretched wide to accommodate him. She runs her fingers along his chest to his groin. There's still a good few inches left to take. Moving slowly, she lifts up, then slides back down a little further. It takes another few minutes, but she eventually takes all of him.

She rests on his hips, loving the feel of his balls against her as she sits back. He's filling her more than she thought possible. Stretching her more than she's ever been before. He's consuming her, sending tingles of pleasure through her entire body by just being inside her.

'Am I hurting you?'

She shakes her head. 'Just give me a minute.'

'You look like you're in pain.'

His concern for her is sweet, but this is a pain she can handle. 'You're rather big, Davyn.'

'Is that good?'

She smiles and nods at him. 'Oh yeah. It's very good.' Thea proves her point by moving her hips, rubbing their bodies together as his dick fills her. Davyn's eyes roll back and he groans. 'See. Very good.'

Finally used to him, Thea rests her hands on his chest and lifts her hips up and down again, beginning slowly and building speed as her body not only accepts, but craves him.

He lifts his head again. The pleasure, mixed with what she can only describe as awe, sends goosebumps over her skin. He's magnificent. This one hundred and seventy year old vampire lord is at her mercy, and loving every second of it. And he's far from alone in that. Every muscle in his broad chest is taut, his arms pulling against his restraints, but not because he's trying to get out. He's holding himself back.

'Let go, Davyn.'

His glowing eyes meet her. 'No.'

Thea rises and drives him deep inside, gasping as he fills her to her limit.

'Please Davyn. Let go. You won't hurt me.'

'I can't, Thea.'

She pumps her hips faster, her hands splayed on his sweat slick chest. 'Please…'

She wants to kiss him, to bite his neck again, but doesn't want to get too close to his fangs. She trusts him, but this is about building his confidence more than anything. There's no way she wants to do anything that'll put that confidence at risk.

Then his hips rotate under her, his movements increasing, driving his dick deeper with each thrust of his hips. He's taking over and Thea has no reason to argue. She falls forward, pressing her breasts against his chest, her hands to either side of his body, digging into the sheets to ground herself.

His breath is coming in hard pants, his chest rising and falling rapidly as he gets lost in the sensations. Thea's pussy clenches against his cock as a deep purr builds in his chest. She can't get enough of that sound. When it turns to a rumble of a growl Thea matches his movements, slapping their sweat slicked bodies together.

He's close. The trembling in his limbs is increasing, his pants hard and his thrusts faster. 'Oh God Davyn.'

He growls loudly which hits her straight in the clit, sending a spasm through it, that has her crying out. She pushes off his chest and looks at him. Teeth bared, eyes glowing, he's pure raw male energy. 'Make me come, Davyn. Please.'

'Never have to beg,' he responds in a deep rumble in the same words she used earlier, and damn if it didn't hit the spot. Thea usually has to play with her clit to come, but that's not going to be necessary this time. Her left hand leaves the bed, resting on the side of his neck. As her climax creeps closer, she digs her nails into his skin.

Davyn growls loudly and rocks against the bed at a mind-blowing pace. The air is filled with the heady scent of sex, the sound of his body slapping against hers as he fucks her. The pressure starts to build in her core and causes her stomach to clench tightly as he drives her towards what's promising to be an unforgettable orgasm.

When it hits, Thea's whole body spasms violently. 'Oh fuck, Davyn!' She's aware of him snarling, but that's it for the next few minutes. She's lost in waves of pleasure, riding them out as Davyn continues to keep her there, refusing to let her come down. Every glide of his dick against her clit sends spasms of pure pleasure through her body. Her pussy squeezes him impossibly hard, intensifying the sensations overtaking her.

Her own wave of euphoria is interrupted when Davyn gives a strong thrust and shouts out. She moans as his dick releases inside her, the hot stream filling her as he continues to pump his hips. Thea hangs on to him, draped over his chest as he rides out his orgasm.

She loses all concept of time as he pulses inside her, the deep purring in his chest the only thing she can hear. When he finally stills she can't move, not that she wants to. She'd be content to lie on his chest for the next few hours, listening to the steady beat of his heart.

A heart that belongs to her, and for that, she cannot be more grateful.

~

Davyn stares at the ceiling above his bed as he makes a valiant effort to catch his breath. He can hear and feel Thea's heart racing in her chest as she lies on top of him. He's still buried deep inside her and is in no rush to extract himself. Not that he could move being pinned under her as he is. She affectionately runs her fingers through his hair as she lies on top of him.

He didn't hurt her. The fact he could give her what she wanted, without putting her at risk, is better than he ever could have imagined.

Maybe next time he could be with her without the chains. Maybe he could feed from her while they are together.

Thea lifts her head and smiles lazily at him. 'Hey.'

'You okay?'

She nods. 'Oh yes. I'm very okay. How about you? Any side effects?'

'No. I feel... great. Really great actually.'

'That's a relief. Do you think I can unlock you now?'

'Yeah. Arms are going dead.'

Thea climbs off him and picks up the key from the top of the chest of drawers at the far side of the room. She unlocks his ankles then his arms, dropping the chains on the floor with a thud. Davyn rubs his arms to get the circulation going again, before shuffling over a little. Taking that as an invitation, Thea climbs back on the bed beside him and lies against his chest.

Davyn takes a few minutes just to enjoy holding Thea like this. He's never held anyone. His mother held him when he was a child but, when she died, the only physical contact he had, was when his father or brother beat him. Nothing even close to right now. Thea runs her hand across his chest and the movement is so soothing. If she just did that to him for the rest of his life, he'd die happy. Something he never thought would happen.

She groans softly and hugs him closer. She seems to have enjoyed what they just did. Not that he had a lot of input chained up the way he was. The one and only time he'd been with a female, was when his father released him from his cell over a century ago. The female had seen to him, but that was as far as it went.

For all intents and purposes, he's a one hundred and seventy year old virgin. He had been terrified about hurting her, but also about not being good enough for her. In a way, being restrained had helped his confidence. There wasn't a lot he could do, so it was down to her to be with him, how she wanted.

Now he knows what she likes, how she moves, and how she feels. Maybe next time, if she trusts him enough to leave the chains off, he'll have a better chance of not letting her down.

'What are you thinking?' she asks.

'Just glad we could do this,' he says, keeping it simple. He's not about to open up to her about his real thoughts.

'Was it what you expected?'

He shakes his head. 'Nothing is what I expect with you.'

She lifts her head and smiles at him. 'Is that a good or a bad thing?'

'Good. Always good. Thank you, Thea. I have no words to describe that.'

'How about absolutely fucking incredible.'

He laughs and pulls her closer, not ready to let her go. 'Yeah. It was.'

'Would you be happy to maybe do this again, without the chains next time?'

'Yeah. I think so.' He knows he was desperate to touch her. Knows he wants his hands all over her, but that wasn't because he wanted to do her harm. Nothing he experienced while they were together, gave him reason to think he would hurt her.

She props her head up on her hand and looks up at him. 'You're still worrying, aren't you?'

'Always. I don't want to hurt you.' Her face drops and her hand stops caressing his arm. 'What?'

'Nothing.'

'Thea...'

'I owe you an apology.'

He pushes back from her. 'For what?'

'I know you said it's not my fault, but it is.' She traces her finger over the scars surrounding his eye and he gets what she's apologising for. He grips her wrist in his hand and moves it away from his face.

'Now you listen to me. I don't bullshit, Thea. If I say it's not your fault, I mean it.'

'But I ran off. I left the compound when I wasn't meant to. I was the one who was captured by Maddox. Because of that Nix was captured and so were you. What happened to you is my fault, Davyn.'

When she came to see him after he came to, she had mentioned something along those lines, but he'd dismissed her apology as not needed. Never for one second did he blame her for what happened. She was captured. It was his job to save her. What happened with his father was completely separate.

'Have you been blaming yourself since I was taken?'

She sniffs, and he realises with horror that she's crying.

Davyn moves to the far side of the bed so he can properly look at her. 'You have.'

'How can I not? You wouldn't have been there if not for me.'

He tilts her chin up. 'Look at me. Thea, look at me now.'

She meets his eyes and he puts as much conviction as he can into his voice.

'Now you listen to me. It wasn't your fault. My father has had a bounty on my head since I left. It was only a matter of time before he got me. Nothing you did could change that. Besides, you saved me, Thea. I'm only here because of you.'

She frowns and wipes her eyes. 'What?'

He absolutely doesn't want to do this with her, but she deserves to be able to move on from this. They deserve it. 'I can't describe the Fever. Unless you've gone through it, it's difficult to comprehend. I was trapped in here,' he says, tapping his finger against his head.

'I was aware of what was going on around me some of the time, but I didn't know what was real, or what was a hallucination. I remember you reading to me, remember you talking to me, and I focused on that as much as I could. I'd concentrate on trying to hang on to consciousness, or sanity, or reality, - whatever it was. I just focused on you, Thea. You were the one to truly revive me. You got through. Got through all the madness and the noise.'

'I did?'

He smiles and cups the side of her face. 'Yes. If you hadn't reached me like you did, I'd be lost forever in my head. Your blood is keeping me alive, but you've done so much more for me the last few weeks. Besides, thanks to you, I have two functioning wings.'

'You really don't blame me?'

'I really don't blame you. Not one bit. I don't want to hear you mentioning this again, okay?'

She nods and smiles. 'Okay. Can I ask you something?'

'Of course.'

'Are you sure you want to go to Ireland again?'

Davyn pulls her close and looks into her eyes. 'I have to end this thing with my father. He's never going to stop unless I end him first.'

'I know. I'm just worried about afterwards.'

'What do you mean?'

'I did some research on your father.' Davyn's throat dries at her words, but he doesn't interrupt. He'd prefer she kept as far as possible from anything to do with his father. 'You have to claim his throne.'

'Yes. I can kill him but, unless I take his place, someone else will, and this will continue. To end it, I have to take my place as head of the house.'

She nods but won't meet his eyes.

'That doesn't mean physically. I'm a Blackjack. My place is here. I love Ireland but this is my home now. With you.' Her smile is one of relief. 'You thought I'd stay there?'

'I didn't know for sure.'

'I'll rule the Oldran house, but just in name. I have no intention of continuing what my father did. But if I'm the ruler of the house, I control what is done in its name. I can protect what my ancestors created.'

'By destroying what your father did?'

'Yes. Growing up under his roof I never hoped for a future. Being part of the Blackjacks gave me a sense of belonging.' He traces his fingers down her face. 'You brought me back to life in a away I never thought possible. I owe you my life, Thea. I only hope my love is enough of a repayment.'

She crushes her lips to his, her kiss sure and confident. 'How about no more talk about guilt, or owing, or anything like that. I say it's time we both put the past behind us and enjoy what's in front of us.'

'I'd like that.'

He wraps his arms around her, wishing more than ever he could share in her optimism.

Davyn takes his seat at the end of the table and tries to stop himself from shuffling around. He's on edge. Has been since his father's men ambushed him. He doesn't want his old life and his new life mixing with each other. He's ashamed and embarrassed by everything to do with his life under his father's rule. When he joined the Blackjacks he finally felt like he had a purpose. Like he could make a difference.

It's his own fault though. All of this is. If he had just killed his father before he ran the first time, none of this would be happening. Who knows how many lives he could have saved. How many vampires he could have spared from being tortured and forced to fight.

'Davyn?'

He jumps when Nix's voice breaks through his thoughts. Not only is Nix staring at him, but so are the rest of the team. 'Sorry.'

'Are you okay?'

He nods and sits up straight. 'Yeah, Nix. I'm good.'

Nix examines him for a good minute, so he keeps his face

emotionless, trying to convince her that's how he feels. Thankfully Ethan arrives, distracting Nix from her examination. Ethan sits heavily in his seat, looking flustered and exhausted. Dav has worked with the guy for years. He never saw him with even a hair out of place.

'What the fuck happened to you?' Shep asks in his usual 'no holding back' way.

'I'm a little concerned about sending you lot back there, with little to no intel.'

Davyn can feel Thea looking at him, but he can't turn around. He doesn't want her to see how unsure he is about the whole fucking thing. 'I know my way around the castle.'

'It's more than the layout of the castle. I'm just not convinced about this course of action if I'm being honest.'

Nix holds up her hand to silence Shep, before he can argue with Ethan. 'What are you saying?' she asks Ethan.

'I'm wondering if it might be best to delay this, until you have time to formulate a solid, well informed plan.'

'We've acted with less information,' Bastian says, his voice strangely hostile.

Ethan takes a few seconds to lift his head and look at Bastian. 'This is different. I'll decide if you have enough intel or not.'

Bastian curses under his breath in Spanish, which is a sure sign he's pissed, but he doesn't say anything else. He follows the rules. Always did. If Ethan and Nix say no, he'll accept it.

'I have to agree with Bas,' Nix says. 'We've got Davyn. He can provide a lot of intel.'

'He was a prisoner, not part of his father's inner circle. Decades ago, he might have been able to give us an idea of what sort of manpower and support his father has. I'm sorry, but that isn't the case any longer. I'm not going to risk all of you by giving the green light too early. Give me a few days to go over everything.'

Nix nods, but keeps frowning at Ethan, who completely ignores her. 'Very well. Until then, keep up with your training. I want us prepared when we do go.'

Davyn notices she said 'when' instead of 'if'.

He'd prefer to get the whole thing over and done with, but if Ethan has bought him a few days to get this head straight, he's going to take it. Facing up to his father is going to test him to his limits. Given the option, he'd take on a few dozen True Order fighters any day.

~

Ethan walks across the hangar towards his car, desperate to get out of here before he's cornered. He's exhausted and pissed off. Refusing to give the green light to the assault in Ireland, had gone down as expected.

Badly.

He hates disagreeing with Nix. It always puts him in a bad mood. Deep down, he knows she understands his reasoning, but that doesn't mean she's the slightest bit happy about it. And that goes for rest of the team too. Which is why he's making a hurried tactical retreat.

Understandably, they want to end this nightmare for Davyn. He does too. More than anything. He just can't bring himself to risk...

He curses himself as he walks around the helicopter to the line of vehicles at the far end of the garage. He's being selfish by refusing to let them attack. He knows he is, but it's something he has no control over. That's the part that's irritating him. He's putting his own feelings ahead of Davyn's. And he hates himself for it.

He clicks the remote on his key and the lights on his BMW flash. All he wants to do is go home and have a stiff drink. Give himself time to figure out how he's going to explain his actions. He steps around to the driver's side and comes to a stop.

So much for having time to come up with an explanation.

He has no idea how Bastian beat him down here. He thought he had a head start, but clearly luck is not on his side. The impressive fighter is leaning against the saddle of his black Ducati glaring over at Ethan. That's what he gets for parking his car next to Bastian's bike.

'Hi Bastian.' His voice betrays his nervousness. 'I wasn't expecting you.' Which is a lie. He knew Bas would want answers, just not as fast as this, and ideally, not face to face.

'What the hell is going on Ethan?'

Ethan loosens his tie and places his briefcase on the bonnet of his car as he looks around for any eavesdroppers, but thanks to the bus and helicopter, this side of the garage is out of sight.

'Like I said to Nix, I deem it too much of a risk. We don't know what's going on with Shep, and Davyn isn't well enough to go anywhere. There's no way I'm going to sign off on sending five of you into that kind of situation. It's not happening. Nix understands, so can we just leave it at that?'

'Bullshit,' Bastian spits back. 'You honestly expect me to believe one word of what you just said? How about you try again - without the lies this time. Flann hurt one of our brothers. He's been torturing vampires for decades for sport. You're really going to stand there and tell me we can't go?'

'It's too much of a risk.'

Bastian looks at him with undisguised disgust. 'I thought better of you, Ethan. I thought you were on the level.'

'What exactly do you want me to say?'

'The truth, but I guess that's not going to happen,' he replies as he pushes off his bike and walks away.

'Okay, fine! You want the truth?'

Bastian stops and peers over his shoulder at Ethan.

'I grounded you, because I don't want the male I'm sleeping with, getting hurt like Davyn was.' He pauses and takes a breath as he struggles to get his emotions under control. Bastian turns around and flashes him the smallest whisper of a smile.

'When Nix told me you were planning to go back to take him out, I panicked. The first thing that jumped into my head, was you lying on a gurney with your lips sewn shut. I... fuck it, Bastian. I got scared, okay!'

Bastian slowly approaches him, moving like a predator towards his prey. He stops mere inches in front of him and Ethan is instantly surrounded by the scent of Bastian's cologne, the deep, dark spices doing things to him no scent should.

'When we started seeing each other, you made me agree that if it affected the Blackjacks it would end. You said that to me over and over again. Blackjacks first. You broke your own rule tonight.'

'Do you not think I know that, Bas? I'm a damn hypocrite! I admit it. But the bastard tortured his own son. What would he do to someone he wasn't related to?'

'He did that to Davyn because he is his son. You need to let us go after him.'

'Bastian—'

'No, Ethan. You need to do your job and let us go.'

Bastian's face softens slightly as he scrubs a hand through his dark hair. He looks particularly gorgeous today, which just makes Ethan feel even more pathetic, clingy, and irrational.

'I get why you're cautious about sending us – sending me, but I was a Blackjack long before us. I know what I'm doing.'

'Are you saying that Davyn didn't?'

'He was caught off guard. Now that we know who we're dealing with, we can go in prepared. He isn't getting his hands on any of us again.'

Ethan slumps back on the bonnet of his car and crosses his arms. He knows Bastian is right, but that doesn't mean he's willing to take the risk. He looks up at the Blackjack and knows he doesn't want to give the okay to go to Ireland. He doesn't want to risk Bastian.

When he started working with the Blackjacks, he never expected to find Bastian, but over time, the fighter had captured his attention and refused to let it go.

He didn't notice it at first, but more and more often, Ethan found himself staring over at him while on video calls with Nix. It wasn't until six months ago that things turned physical. He hadn't been aware of it at the time, but Bastian had been looking at him the same way. When Nix had arranged for Bastian to bring some sensitive intel to Ethan, the Blackjack had made his move.

Initially, the attraction to Bastian had been based on looks. The male was absolutely stunning, but there was so much more to him. He's strong and fearless and unquestionably loyal, but there's also a vulnerability deep underneath. He tries to hide it, but occasionally Ethan catches glimpses of it, and it does nothing to stifle the growing feelings he has for him.

They had agreed to keep it casual, and for the first few months it had just been sex. Bastian had brought sex to a whole new level for him - one he doubts any other lover would be able to reach. Unfortunately for Ethan, the more he sees Bastian, the more he wants to be with him - and not just in bed. He knows Bastian doesn't want anything more, so he's kept his feelings to himself.

And it's not like Ethan can ever bring someone like Bastian home to his grandparents. Leaving aside the fact he's a fighter, someone with no lineage – at least none that would please his grandmother, there's also the small detail about Bas being male.

No, all he can do is continue to keep up the many charades. Pretend to be straight. Pretend not to care about Bas. Pretend he's happy with his lot in life, and the never-ending circle of pretending to be something, and someone he's not.

But he may just have blown his deception out the window with his pathetic display tonight. What was he thinking? He knew by grounding the Blackjacks, Bastian would guess why, and confront him about it.

Was that what he wanted? Was it his subconscious breaking the rules, in the hope Bastian would guess his true feelings?

Ethan shakes his head and takes a deep breath before looking back at Bastian again. Bastian's strong jaw is sporting a day's growth of stubble, and his thick hair is tousled. Just how it looks after they've been in bed together. If they weren't having a disagreement, he knows exactly what he'd like to do to him. Ethan shakes his head again.

'What?'

'Nothing. Ignore me.'

'Impossible,' Bastian says with a smile. He joins him on the bonnet. 'I understand your reservations, but Davyn deserves his revenge for what happened. The least we can do is have his back. With the full team of Blackjacks, we will get Flann and put an end to his fighting pits. You've sent us in to dangerous situations before. Why the problem giving the order now?'

Ethan shrugs as he stares at the base of the pillar in front of him. 'First Court gets taken, then Davyn... who's next?' he asks, turning to face Bastian. 'I always knew I was sending you in to potentially life threatening situations, but after seeing Davyn like that... it brought the reality home. I know Nix is the one to actually lead you in to those situations, but I'm the one that gives her the information. She made the order to leave Court and Davyn behind, but I'm the one that sent them in the first place. I don't want to be the one to send you in to something like that.'

'So you ground us indefinitely to keep me safe?'

He shrugs. 'I hadn't thought beyond today.'

Bastian reaches down and takes Ethan's hand in his gloved one. Ethan would prefer skin to skin, but Bas rarely takes off his gloves. Both arms are entirely covered in dark ink, the symbols tattooed on his skin, a detailed and graphic report of his past. A past Ethan knows nothing about.

All he does know is that Bastian worked for a notorious group in Spain before joining the Blackjacks, and that he had been quite efficient completing the tasks he was given. It's a past Bastian has moved on from, content to show the marks on his arms among their group. His hands are another matter. Whatever the tattoos on the back of each hand represent, Bastian is far from happy about them, preferring to keep them covered, unless absolutely necessary. Perhaps in time Bas will open up to Ethan, but he seriously doubts it.

'You have to separate us from the Blackjacks,' Bastian says, still holding his hand. 'Otherwise this won't work. You said the Blackjacks have to come first, and I agree. As much as I enjoy being with you, we made a deal, right?'

Ethan nods feeling defeated. 'I'll call her from the car. I'll give the go ahead.'

'It's the right decision. I'm a good fighter, Ethan. Hell, I've been fighting since I was young. I never take unnecessary risks. Never. Trust in all the training. Trust in what you've created.'

'It's the people I'm sending you up against that I don't trust.'

'That's something none of us can control. You'll drive yourself crazy thinking about it. I need to do this, Ethan. Let me do my job.'

He nods, hating how pathetic he's coming across. 'I know. Ignore me. It's been a stressful few months. I just—'

The Blackjack cuts off the rest of the sentence by pressing his lips to Ethan's. Bastian fists Ethan's hair in his gloved hand as his kiss deepens. Bastian's other hand pushes in between his legs and Ethan groans, growing hard under Bastian's touch. The Blackjack breaks the kiss, and gives him a smile that hits him straight in the groin.

'Bit public,' Ethan mutters as Bastian's eyes begin to glow. Bas pulls off a glove and places his palm against the pillar beside Ethan's car. He closes his eyes then smiles wickedly. 'They're in the bedrooms, kitchen, and training room. No one on this level or anywhere near it.'

Ethan closes his eyes as Bastian pulls down the collar of his shirt and slowly licks along the bite mark he left there a few hours ago, the sensation sending shockwaves straight to his dick.

'It's just us down here,' Bastian whispers as his tongue drags across his neck again, drawing a groan from Ethan. 'Still sensitive after last night?'

'You know I am.'

Another long lick sends a shiver straight to Ethan's balls.

'You thinking about last night?'

'You know I am,' he repeats, hoping Bastian stops talking about it. Thinking about it is one thing, without Bastian painting the picture for him.

'What are you thinking?' This time his fangs scrape the sensitive skin. 'Tell me.'

'I might have liked when you had me pinned down with your teeth and dick. But don't talk about it. I'm on the edge here.'

Bastian sighs contentedly. 'Yeah. I liked that too,' Bastian presses the tips of his fangs against Ethan's skin. 'You taste so damn good, Ethan.'

'Oh God, Bas.'

Bastian purrs deep in his chest. 'I love when you say my name like that. All low and husky.'

Ethan swallows and tilts his head, giving Bastian more room to tease him. Bas knows every single sensitive spot on his body and how to drive him out of his mind. Ethan groans as Bastian's uncovered hand cups the side of his face, holding him in place. 'You keep that up and I'll come.'

'I know,' Bas mutters in his ear. Ethan's breath leaves his lungs in short pants as Bastian's fangs graze along the length of Ethan's neck.

'Bastian...'

The hairs on Ethan's arms stand upright when Bastian growls. 'You say my name again in that voice and I'll be the one in trouble. Fuck this, Ethan. I need to bury my dick and teeth deep inside you, right now.'

He pushes his hips forward and Ethan groans as Bastian's dick presses against him. 'I think you should do that.'

Bastian scrapes his fangs along Ethan's neck, then curses, and pulls out his ringing phone. 'Fuck. It's Nix. I can't ignore it.' He moves away from Ethan and scrubs his hand over his face before he answers the call, as irritated about the interruption as Ethan is.

'Hey Nix.' Bastian closes his eyes and nods. 'Yeah.' He glances over at Ethan. 'No, nothing. Okay. I'll be right there.' He ends the call and curses again, this time in Spanish which usually means he's moved beyond mere irritation.

Ethan knows what's coming and is already losing the high he was just experiencing. 'You have to go.'

'Nix wants me to get the weapons ready, in case you change your mind and let us go. I'm sorry. I... fuck it. I don't have a choice, Ethan. I want to finish this. I want to be with you, but...' He angrily shakes his head as he stares over at his motorbike.

This is how things are between them. Secret meetings and painfully short snatched moments. It's not what he wants. By the look on Bastian's face, it's not what he wants either.

But that's what they agreed to.

'I want to see you as soon as you get back from Ireland. I'll be waiting in my apartment so you can show me exactly what you had planned.'

Bastian looks over at him and smiles, but it's forced. Is he pissed off about being summoned by Nix, being worked up and getting no relief. Or is it because he has to leave Ethan?

Probably a mixture of the first two, Ethan thinks to himself as Bastian leans down and kisses him before moving away again.

'It's a date. I better go.'

'Bastian?' He turns to face Ethan, his dark eyes still glowing from their heated encounter. 'Stay safe, okay?'

'I promise. I'll see you when I get back.' He glances down at Ethan's groin and smiles seductively. 'You better think of me when you deal with that.'

'Always,' Ethan replies as he attempts to adjust his still hard cock in his trousers.

Ethan watches as Bastian walks away, and disappears behind the helicopter. Ethan stares after him with a sinking feeling in his gut. He doesn't want to make the call to Nix, but this is bigger than his feelings for Bastian.

With a sigh he unlocks his car again and slips behind the wheel. He closes his eyes and hits his head against the leather headrest. 'Fuck!' he shouts before opening his eyes and glaring out the windshield. He pulls his phone out of his pocket and waits as it connects with his car. He could easily go back upstairs and speak to Nix, but he can't face anyone right now.

All he wants to do is get into bed with Bastian and stay there. He wants to feel the fighters solid body pressed against his, pinning him to the bed. Wants to feel Bastian's strong hand around his neck, holding him in place as he feeds and fucks. Desperately wants to hear Bastian's animalistic growl as he comes, marking Ethan as his.

'Fuck's sake, Ethan. Like that's helpful,' he reprimands himself. Bastian isn't the sort of male who would ever settle down like that. He's one of the few truly selfless people Ethan has ever known. Bas is devoted to the Blackjacks and nothing else. Of all the fighters in the team, he's the one who doesn't answer back, doesn't argue against his orders, never questions Nix or Ethan – well, until today, but Ethan knew that one was coming.

No matter how much Ethan wishes otherwise, Bas will never put himself, or his needs before the good of the team. If Ethan wants to be in Bastian's life, it will have to be like this. The only person he's hurting is himself, and he can handle that. If it means he gets Bastian, he'll take it.

Ethan glares down at his cock, clearly defined through his slacks. He won't even make it home before he has to take care of himself, and, like Bastian suggested, his thoughts will be on the fighter as he does it.

With one last look after Bastian he clears his throat. 'Call Nix.'

Fallon yawns as she opens the outer door to the cell. She desperately needs a shower, and some sleep before they leave to go back to Ireland. But she needs to see him first. And that irritates her.

She shouldn't have to personally check on Austin before she goes into a battle. It's not where her head should be. Fletch and some of Ethan's support staff were keeping a close eye on him. Technically, she doesn't have to see him at all. But she can't keep away. The unconscious human has somehow managed to get to her, like no one has for a long time. No one since...

She shakes her head. Thinking about her mate certainly won't help.

Fallon unlocks Austin's cell and freezes when she sees a pair of light brown eyes focused on her. She wasn't expecting him to be awake. No one told her he'd woken up. His restrained fists clench as he tries to free himself.

'Hey.'

He continues struggling, his chest rising and falling rapidly as he looks at her.

'You're wasting your time. You won't be getting out of those restraints. I suggest you lie still and save your energy.' Apart from pulling at his restraints, he doesn't reply. 'You got a name?'

That earns a frown which is good news. If he was completely out of it, the question wouldn't have registered with him. 'No? Nothing coming to you, or are you playing hard to get?' He licks his lips then looks back in her direction, the frown still firmly in place. 'Nothing. You're not making this easy. Well, one of my comrades gave you a name. Until you decide to be friendly and open up, we'll be calling you Austin. That okay?'

Nothing.

'I'll take that as a yes. Pretty impressive tattoo you've got. So, are you from the States or are you just a wannabe cowboy?'

Still nothing, not that she was really expecting a response.

Fallon opens the cooler to grab another bag of fluids. Austin turns his head to watch what she's doing, his eyes locking on the bag of blood she takes out of the cooler, to get to the fluids underneath. Like a switch has been flicked, he freaks out, trying to get off the bed. At first Fallon assumes his bizarre Blood Fever is making him crazy for the blood, but she quickly realises he's trying to get away from it. He's terrified.

'Hey, hey! Calm down. It's gone, okay!' She dumps it in the cooler and closes the lid. Fallon stands up and holds out her hands.

'See. Gone.'

He either doesn't hear her, or doesn't understand. She's not sure which one, but if he doesn't calm down he's going to hurt himself. The chains securing the padded restraints to the bed rattle as he desperately attempts to free himself. Fallon leans over him and takes his head in her hands, holding it still on the bed. She's a hell of a lot stronger than him and has no difficulty holding him steady as she forces him to look at her.

'Look at me! Look at me!'

His brown eyes look up at her, and she can clearly see the terror in them. 'It's okay. No one is going to hurt you here. I promise. You have my word. Keep looking at me and just breathe.'

Austin's chest rises and falls dramatically as he stares at her. It takes a few minutes of keeping eye contact with him for Austin to begin relaxing. When he lies still on the bed, Fallon reluctantly releases his head and straightens. 'Fuck, Austin. What the hell was that about? The guys that had you, did they feed you blood?'

He frowns and licks his lips but doesn't stay anything.

'I'll take that as a yes.' No wonder the guy is freaking out. What the hell did they do to him? 'Right, you're dehydrated so I'm going to give you fluids. Not blood. You've got my word.'

While keeping eye contact with him, she crouches down to lift the bag of fluid from the cooler. 'See. No blood.'

Austin keeps his eyes on her as she replaces the bag then lifts the head of the bed and drapes a sheet over his legs.

She steps back from the bed, but can't bring herself to look away from him. 'Listen. I'm going to give you the benefit of the doubt and assume you understand what I'm saying. My name is Fallon. You're safe here. I have to go out for a while, but I'll be back to check on you later.'

His hand lifts from the bed briefly before he settles again and turns his head to look at her.

Fallon checks her watch. She could probably spend a little longer with Austin before she has to go and get changed.

'How about I sit with you for a little longer?'

It could be entirely in her mind, but she could swear his body relaxes a little when she says that. Fallon pulls up the chair and places it facing the head of the bed.

'Try to get some sleep.'

She takes out her phone and absently scrolls through the training schedule for the coming week. Or would do, if she didn't keep stealing glances at Austin. His brown eyes are still locked on her, but his breathing has steadied.

For a human, his strength and courage are hard to ignore. He woke up in a strange place chained to a bed. If Fallon were in that situation she doubts she'd be so calm. Anger would come to the front. He hasn't shown anger at all. No fear either, apart from when he saw the blood. That speaks volumes about the man.

'You're safe. I'll stay with you for a while. You really should sleep.'

Fallon has no idea where this nurturing side is coming from. She's a damn good medic, but Fletch was the one who did the whole comforting side of things. Her brother could instantly calm anyone who was getting agitated. Her, not so much.

Austin's eyes close and he takes a deep breath. Fallon gets to her feet and moves closer to the gurney. He's calm now, his chest rising and falling steadily. She finds herself wondering what he would look like with a few weeks of food in him. He's certainly got the potential to be a great warrior. It's ridiculous to even consider where his future lies, but it wouldn't be a bad thing if he stayed here with them.

She sits back down and crosses her arms. No doubt he has a mate, or girlfriend. Perhaps a wife. Someone is bound to be waiting for him to come home. Someone he'll want to go home to. Why would he want to stay with a group of vampires after what he's been through?

But if he has no memory, there might not be anywhere else for him to go.

Then again, unless they figure out what was done to him, Nix may not be laying out the welcome mat for him.

Fallon slowly reaches out and touches her fingers to his. He closes his hand around hers, but doesn't wake up as far as she can tell. She'll stay another bit, then go and get ready to take down Dav's father. Hopefully she'll survive what's to come and she can return to him in a few hours.

~

Davyn stares out at the fountain in the centre of the garden. He'll never say anything to the rest of the team, but the sound of the running water is freaking him out. He's forcing himself to stay out here. Forcing himself to control the fear of water. It's a fucking fountain. It's not like it's going to get up and attack him. He's not going to be a solid member of the team if a water feature is scaring him.

He lives on a damn island, so coming up against the sea, or a river, or even a fucking stream is bound to happen. If he freezes at the sound of water, he's going to get someone killed.

He closes his eyes and concentrates on his breathing. But it takes less than a minute for the sound of running water to drag him back to his submerged cell. Then the panic sets in, the overwhelming fear as the water rises, stealing the air from his lungs.

Davyn forces his eyes open and pushes back against the railing. 'Fuck!'

'Are you okay?'

He straightens and winces at the look of concern on Nix's face. 'Yeah. I'm fine.'

Nix leans on the railing next to him and nods as she looks out over the garden. 'I've been looking for you. Missed you at training earlier.'

Davyn clenches his hands together as he stares out at the mountains in the distance, trying to ignore the fountain. 'Sorry. I didn't think...' He curses and shakes his head.

'You're questioning your place on the team, aren't you?'

He glances across at her. 'Maybe.'

She nods solemnly, still keeping her focus on the garden. 'I thought as much. Care to tell me what's on your mind?'

He holds out his hand and clenches his fist, trying to stop the trembling. 'For starters, that isn't helping. I'll fall to the Fever at some stage. I don't want to put anyone else at risk.'

'Fletch said you're doing better than he expected. The tremors should ease as your body heals. It's still early days, Davyn. You are without a doubt the best fighter on this team. Even better than Shep, as much as he'd argue otherwise. Nothing can change those instincts, Dav. Just give yourself time to heal.'

'Are you sure you still want me on the team?'

'Why wouldn't I? Did you not listen to what I just said?'

'Yeah, but I'm a Prime, Nix. I'm what we're fighting against.'

She turns around to face him and Davyn forces himself to meet her eyes. 'Do you really believe that?'

'Yeah.'

'Davyn, we're fighting the True Order - not the Primes.'

'I know that, but the True Order are Primes.'

'That doesn't mean we take out just any Prime we see. Never, not for one second, did I condone or promote targeting Primes.' She pauses and takes a deep breath. 'Our purpose is to ensure all vampires - pure bred or mixed - get a fair shot at having a life. To be honest, having a Prime sitting at the table with me is an honour.'

He snorts loudly.

'I'm being serious, Davyn. Just because your father is quite frankly a vile and repulsive male, doesn't mean all Primes are like that. I know Primes who would give their life to help someone in need. Primes who would sacrifice themselves, so another could be freed. Who would put themselves through hell to save someone they love.'

He doesn't want to react to that statement. It's bad enough that it's true, but if he admits it out loud, he'll feel more pathetic than he does right now. He looks down at his clenched hands before focusing on Nix. 'What's that look for?'

'Thea. You care for her, don't you?'

He nods. 'Yes. More than anything. That still doesn't mean I should be with her. She's human. She should be with a human. I'm sure Court agrees.'

'Court wants his daughter to be happy. She is happy with you.'

'But why?'

Nix laughs. 'I think you'll have to ask her that, not me. Davyn, I made a big mistake with Court when we decided to take things further than just team mates. I told him to hide the fact we were together. I know it was only a few weeks, but keeping it to ourselves... when he disappeared, it was like that time never happened. It was a figment of my imagination. I couldn't talk to anyone about it. Couldn't cry on anyone's shoulder. I was mourning the loss of my lover, but as far as everyone else was concerned, he was just my team mate. That nearly killed me.

'It's clear she likes you, a lot. No one spends hour after hour, sitting beside someone's cell reading to them, if they don't have feelings.' She takes a deep breath and looks at him again. 'I'm not trying to interfere. Whatever is, or is not there, it's your business. I just don't want you to let what your father did to you, ruin your future happiness and your legacy.

'I've done some checking. The Oldranson family were well regarded centuries ago. You come from a line of honourable vampires. I don't know what happened with your father, but he put an end to that. However, he's just one cog in that much larger wheel. You should be proud of who you are, Lord Davyn Oldranson.'

She picks up a package from the ground and passes it to him. 'What's this?'

'Open it.'

He tears open the box and stares at the contents. The pauldron is old - the metal dulled with each passing century. The fierce skull is demonic in nature, with large horns on the creature's head and fangs sticking out of its jaw. 'Where did you get this?'

'Ronan. He gave it to me when he met with us. He made me promise to give it to you when I thought the timing was right.'

Davyn hesitantly reaches out to touch it. He remembers Ronan showing him paintings of his grandfather wearing the piece on his armour when he went in to battle. Each Prime family had their own symbol or image associated with their name - much like a family crest. This was Davyn's, although he never thought he would see it in the flesh. His father had destroyed anything of historic value in the castle. In true Ronan style, the man must have somehow managed to save this from destruction.

'Your father tore apart everything his father created. He destroyed the legacy left to him. I think you should follow his tradition. Throw out everything he created. Start fresh. Live the life you want. Live it with Thea, if that's what you really want. Nothing that happened in your past, matters.'

Davyn looks down at the package in his hands, still not sure he wants anything to do with his family, or their legacy. Thea, however, he does want.

Nix squeezes his arm. 'This is a whole new chapter for you Davyn,' she says, then nods to the pauldron still in the box. 'Wear that when you take your father down, and claim his title. Ethan just called. He's given us the green light.'

'He has?' That surprises him. The way Ethan was speaking during the meeting, he was sure it was a definite no. 'What made him change his mind?'

Nix shrugs. 'I honestly have no idea.'

'I don't think I'm ready.' He frowns over at the fountain again.

'Davyn.'

He looks sideways at her.

'Let us help you. We can train you around water. Help you deal with the fear.'

He stops himself from saying he's not scared. Nix has a way of seeing things about her fighters they can't see, or admit about themselves. 'How did you know?'

'I've never seen anyone curse at the fountain before.' She smiles and Dav can't help but smile back.

'We all have weaknesses, Dav. Every single one of us. If we can help you deal with this, we absolutely will.'

'I can't tell the others I'm scared of water.'

'Why not? Seriously Dav, I'd challenge anyone not to feel the same after what you've been through. Even Shep.'

He laughs and takes a moment before looking at her again. 'I want to get back out there.'

Nix nods and gestures towards the house. 'Glad to hear it. Come on. I've got Murt ready to take a call. Let's finish this, so you can put it behind you and focus on looking to your future.

He follows her back to the meeting room and takes his seat opposite Thea. She winks at him and smiles widely. She's ready to get this done with too.

When everyone has taken their seat, Nix turns on the screen and Murtagh Whelan's face appears.

'Didn't think I'd be hearing from you so soon, Nix.'

'I didn't think we'd need your help again so soon. We appreciate you taking the time to speak with us again. I know it puts you and your brothers in a difficult position.'

'That's a normal day for us. Don't go worrying about us. We can handle the heat. Besides, you mention potentially getting another crack at our enemy and you're bound to get our attention,' Murt says with a smile.

'We appreciate that,' she says and Davyn is grateful she's taking the lead on this one. He's not keen on talking about his father - even if it is about killing him.

'Davyn was jumped a few days ago by some of his father's men.'

Murt leans forward, clasping his hands together on the table. 'I wasn't aware Flann had left Ireland.'

'He didn't. He sent some thugs to do his dirty work. There's a hefty bounty on his head, so it's not going to end until Davyn is taken back to Flann. Obviously we won't let that happen. So we decided to go back to Ireland, and take care of the problem once and for all.'

Murt leans back in his chair, rubbing his jaw as he considers what Nix said. 'We're in. We can meet you in the same location as the last time.'

Davyn has been told time and time again that he's part of the team, but it still hits him every time they step up to defend him. It should have sunk in by now, but clearly it hasn't. Everyone at this table - vampire and werewolf alike, is willing to fight for him. And that floors him.

'Okay,' Nix says, getting the attention back on her. 'We'll leave in the next few hours. I'll send you our ETA once we're underway.'

The wolf nods and cuts the connection.

'Dav and Shep, I want you both to get checked and cleared by Fletch before you leave. If he has any issues with either of you, I won't hesitate to ground you.'

'Yes, boss,' Shep mutters.

'Dismissed.'

Nix stops Davyn just as he's about to escape to his room. 'Are you sure you want to do this? No one would blame you for wanting to sit this one out. Or even call it off. He is your father after all.'

'I'm sure. Flann means nothing to me. I have to do this, Nix.'

She nods and smiles at him. 'Make sure you feed before we go.'

She steps aside and Davyn finally escapes. His father needs to die. He has no problem with that. It's the castle he doesn't want to see again. It's just a building, but there are so many hellish memories for him in that place, that he doesn't want to go anywhere near it.

It was never really a home. Even when his mother was alive he didn't like it. Her quarters were inviting and homely, but the rest of the building was a prison. That's all it ever was. A monstrous prison himself, his mother, and Ronan were kept in.

Until he met Thea, he didn't think he'd ever have a life that resembles anything remotely normal. He survived from day to day.

Fighting and hiding in his room. There was nothing else. He'd planned on doing that for the rest of his life - however long he had left. But now he has Thea, things have changed.

Which just makes going back to the castle so much more difficult.

He gets to his room and closes the door behind him. There's no way he can even contemplate a future with Thea while his father breathes. It's just not possible. If he's to have any control over the rest of his life, he needs to kill his father and claim his title.

He smiles as he faces the door, turning the key in the lock. 'You're supposed to be getting rest before we leave.'

'Can I not rest here with you?' Davyn turns around, and any thought of resting disappears from his mind when he sees his beautiful woman stretched out on his bed, naked, and no more interested in resting than he is.

49

Thea smiles as his eye begins to glow in the dim room. Clearly coming here to spend some time with him was a good idea.'

'What if I don't want to rest?'

She shuffles over and pats the bed. 'I'd say that's absolutely fine with me.' Davyn lowers beside her and she can feel the weight of his gaze as it travels up her naked body. The way he looks at her, full of wonder and want, is heart-warming.

She wraps her hand around the back of his head, but he resists her attempt to draw him closer.

'What's wrong?'

'Are you sure you don't want the chains?'

Cupping the side of his stubbly cheek she meets his eyes. 'I'm sure. I'm being honest with you. You can probably tell that, right?'

He nods. 'Yeah. I can tell.'

'Good.' She lifts her head, kissing his lips when he still resists. 'I want to be with you. Please.'

It could go either way. She can tell that without any of the vampire senses he has. His entire body is rigid.

She leaves him to his thoughts, but he doesn't need long. Less than half a minute later, he stands up and, after tearing off his clothes in record speed, covers her with his warm body. With a moan, Thea wraps her arms around his neck, dragging her fingers through his hair as she kisses him.

Davyn pushes back and peers down at her. 'I don't know what to do.'

'Yes you do. Just touch me. Feel me.' She arches her back, loving the way his attention immediately goes to her breasts. 'Why not start there and work your way down?'

His touch is barely there at first, gentle and unsure as his tongue traces over her nipple. His hand moves down her body, caressing and stroking her skin as he licks. Then he sucks her nipple into his mouth, teasing it with his tongue.

She buries her hands in his hair drawing him closer. 'Oh God... Davyn...'

'You taste so good.'

'Mmm, and you're not even at the good part yet.'

She moves under him and spreads her legs. Instinctively, his hand runs down her body, skimming over her hip.

After sucking on her nipple once more, he turns his attention to further down her body. He moves down the bed, spreading her legs so he can settle between her thighs.

Tentatively, he strokes her, his fingers sending a shockwave of pleasure through her with the briefest of touches. 'That's it, Davyn. Don't stop...'

'I don't want to hurt you.'

'You won't. I trust you.' She reaches down and takes his hand, placing it back where it was. 'Please. I don't want you to stop.'

He licks his lips and caresses her again, but this time his finger presses against her, sliding inside ever so slightly. Thea gasps and writhes against his hand. 'So good,' And she means it. For someone who's never done this before, he's a quick study.

'Can I taste you?'

'I'd like that.'

His breath sends a tremor up her body, then his tongue brushes against her. The deep animalistic growl that follows, hits her straight at her core. 'More, Davyn.'

He licks her again, harder this time. 'You taste incredible.'

She gasps, arching her back off the bed as he slowly explores her, lapping, sucking, and licking her into a frenzy.

'It that okay?'

She grabs his hair, pulling him against her. Taking that as a yes, he reaches under her ass, lifting her hips off the bed. Then his tongue slides in, the new position only adding to the pleasure.

'You okay,' he asks as he peers up at her.

She nods quickly. 'Oh yeah. Just keep doing that. I'm close.'

His eye glows brightly as he lowers to finish what he started, his tongue and mouth hitting all the right spots with increasing urgency.

When her back arches again, he places a heavy hand on her stomach, holding her exactly where he wants her. The growl builds in his chest, helping to steamroll Thea towards the edge, and push her over.

But he's not finished.

Davyn keeps her spinning, his tongue in no hurry to let her come down.

When Thea finally comes back to her body, she meets his glowing eyes, full of wonder.

'Was that okay?'

She nods as she waits for her voice to come back to her. 'Yes. That was... wow. My brain is fucked at the moment, so that's the most descriptive word I can come up with. Are you okay?'

He grins, looking especially sexy all flushed and turned on. 'I liked that.'

'I can tell.' She looks at his dick and smirks. 'I think you're ready for more.'

He frowns, then glances down at his groin, which makes her want to laugh.

'Yes, Davyn. I'd like to finish what you've expertly started. Please.'

~

Davyn wants to. As much as he needs to protect Thea, to keep her safe, he wants her like this. He wants to feel her body under his hands, wants to be with her again, with no chains this time

Her seductive smile comes back and his dick throbs in anticipation. Thea moves her hips, rubbing her groin against his thigh, bringing out the growl she seems to like so much.

'Come on, Davyn. You won't break me, I promise.'

He licks his lips and positions himself at her entrance. He's a fucking idiot. It shouldn't be like this for her. He should be able to sweep her off her feet, or whatever people in movies do. He should know how to be with her, without freaking out.

Her hand runs up his arm and she grips his bicep. 'Stay with me. It's just you and me.'

Her words ground him and he shuts off the second guessing. She trusts him, justified or not, and he's not going to let her down.

He brings his hips forward, sliding inside her tight body as slowly as he can. Thea gasps and pushes her head back into the pillow. 'That's it. Keep going. Just keep it slow for a minute.'

He holds himself back, even though his body wants to claim her in every way possible. Watching his dick slowly disappearing into her body is the best thing he's ever seen. They fit perfectly. Like two pieces of a puzzle.

That fucking growl rises in his chest as he fills her, her delicate body accepting every inch of him. Thea peers down at him, her eyes hooded. He stretches out over her and kisses her, remembering she did the same to him, while she was getting used to him inside her. Thea moans against his mouth, hungrily devouring his tongue.

She tastes like nothing he's tasted before. Warm and sweet and completely addictive. His hips begin moving before he even knows what he's doing. She wraps her legs around his waist, holding him close so he moves a little faster, desperately trying to hold himself back. But she feels too good. Her mouth, her smooth body under his, the way she grips his dick. It's all too much for him.

'More, Davyn.'

Her fingers rake over his shoulders, her blunt nails brushing against the ridges running down his back. The contact sends a vice of pressure down his body to his balls. He's never let anyone touch him there.

'Did I hurt you,' she asks, her breath ragged.

He growls again and fights to keep his fangs pulled up. 'Do that again.'

His hips pump harder, before she even touches his ridges again. This time she drags her fingers up them, and his fangs lengthen. Usually there's no feeling on the ridges, but the way she's touching him, is like she has a hand wrapped around his balls.

Thea moans as she looks at him. 'There he is. God you're stunning.'

When she touches his back again, he has to stop himself from digging his teeth in to her neck.

He has to keep control. He's so close, but he needs her to finish first. Pushing upright, he grips her thighs, spreading her wide. Transfixed by the sight of their bodies moving together, he can't look away.

'I want to see you when I come.'

He lifts his eyes and she groans aloud. She's close. Her stomach is tightening, her breathing speeding up. He's doing this to her.

Her body clenches around him as she arches her back. 'Davyn!'

Hearing her scream his name as she comes undone, helps unravel whatever small semblance of control he had left. With a roar, he comes, her body still pulsating around him, drawing out his own release.

~

Thea runs her hand over the tattoos on Davyn chest as she listens to the steady beat of his heart. She has no idea how much time has passed since they both came loud enough to be heard throughout the house. And she honestly couldn't care less. She can't move, not that she wants to. She's quite happy to stay huddled against Davyn's chest.

He pushes up onto his elbow to look down at her. His eyes are back to their normal colour and his fangs have withdrawn again. Seeing him let go like he had was, not only a turn on, but a big step for him.

'Did I hurt you?'

She runs her hand down the stubble on his jaw. 'Of course not. Every single thing you did felt perfect.' Thea could cry every time he asks her that. He's so careful with her, she doubts he even dislodged a hair while they had sex. The fear of hurting her is crippling him, and she hates it. She pushes up the bed and rests her head on the pillow beside his. 'I love being with you like this, Davyn.'

'Really?'

'Of course.' She reaches across and kisses him. 'I wish you'd enjoy yourself too.'

'I do.'

'You're still holding back. But it was amazing to see you let yourself go a little more. I really like seeing you like that.'

He flashes her a quick smiles. 'I think I picked up on that.'

'Now you just need to release those wings of yours.'

'And cut you to pieces. No.' He checks the time on his phone. 'Fuck. We have to get ready to go soon.'

'Are you sure you want to go back there?'

He wraps his arm around her, pulling her into a tight hug. 'I'd give anything not to go. I'd much prefer to stay here with you like this. But I have to. I need to be the one who ends this, once and for all. If I don't, I'll be looking over my shoulder for the rest of my life. I'm not living like that. I won't have you live like that either.'

'Do you really think he'll keep coming for you?'

'It sounds like he's put an impressive bounty on my head. He doesn't even have to leave his miserable castle. There are enough people who would do it for him. For some reason, he's got a never ending supply of followers who are willing to die for him.'

Thea knows he has to go, but hates the thought of him going anywhere near that place again. She doesn't want any of them going near it. If this goes wrong, she risks losing her father, and the man she loves in one night.

He tilts her chin up so she's looking at him again. 'We'll all come back again.'

'That's so unnerving the way you do that.'

'I'm getting to know you.'

'I like that. I really do, but you can't promise nothing is going to happen.'

'We're damn good fighters, Thea. Your father trained most of us and, thanks to your blood, I'm stronger than I've been for a long time. I promise, he won't take any of us down.'

'Is Shep going?'

Davyn rolls onto his back and laughs. 'After a lot of fighting, Nix gave in. Physically, he's been cleared, and whatever is going on with his body hasn't progressed at all. Nix either lets him go, or he's going to destroy the place in protest. He needs to vent. My father is responsible for whatever's going on with him too.'

'Seems Flann's cards are marked.'

'Yeah. They were marked centuries ago. I need to kill him, Thea. I hate saying something like that to you, but it's the way it is. I'd prefer you weren't coming too though. I'm not happy about that decision. Can I convince you to stay here?'

'Not a chance. I'll stay in the Whelan's cottage with Fletch. I promised I would, and I'll stick to that. But I want to see this through with you. I want to be nearby if you need me.'

'Come to my rescue again?'

She smiles at the grin on his face. 'Hopefully not. I think you can take care of yourself.'

He nods, realising he's not going to get anywhere with her. Nix had, after a lot of persuasion, agreed to let her tag along. Being confined to the helicopter, or the cottage wasn't exactly what she had planned, but it's a start. And she's going to follow the rules. She needs to prove to the whole team that she's not a liability. That she can obey orders and carry her own weight.

She laces her fingers with his. 'Just be careful. Please. I don't want to lose you, Davyn.'

He kisses her, something he's becoming increasingly proficient at. 'I've got a beautiful, strong, incredible, stubborn woman to come back to. Of course I'll be careful.'

Thea climbs onto him and kisses him deeply. Hearing something like that from him, makes her feel like she can take on the world. This century and a half year old vampire thinks she's strong, so that's what she will be. For him and for her father. If she's to be part of Davyn's world, she'll have to get used to him leaving, and potentially not coming back to her. If she gets upset every time he does his job, it'll make her miserable.

'I love you, Davyn.'

'I love you, Thea. Can I show you how much?'

'Again? Do we have time?'

She squeals when he rolls her over, trapping her under his immense body. 'Yes. You're ready for me.'

The way his vampire senses can tell what her body is doing, takes having sex with him to a new level. 'How can you be so sure?'

He nuzzles the side of her neck and growls softly. Thea moans and, if she wasn't ready before, she is after hearing that. He presses his cock against her and rubs it along her entrance. 'I can smell you. It's intoxicating.' His fangs scrap against her neck and, not for the first time, she wishes he'd bite her while they have sex. She's desperate to be with full Prime vampire Davyn. Desperate for him to stop holding back. Desperate for him to claim her in every possible way.

But then he slides inside her and all thoughts disappear.

Thea follows her father to the hangar, hurrying to keep up with his long strides. A heavy weight is pressing on her heart, increasing with each step towards their destination. Finding the Blackjacks had been exactly what Court needed, but she had never thought of the effect him being part of the team would have on her.

Their relationship may be altered forever, she may still be angry at him for telling her he was her brother, instead of her father - as irrational as it sounds, but she's not ready for him to go on missions.

She's not ready to stand back and watch her father and Davyn walk away from her. She doesn't know much about what the Blackjacks do, but she does know every time they leave the compound like this, they are going on potentially dangerous missions, against the people who may have been responsible for Court's blasted amnesia in the first place.

He reaches down and takes her hand in his as they walk through the steel doors in to the hangar. Thea squeezes her father's hand, needing the silent reassurance. Nix, Willow, Shep, and Fallon stop talking and turn to look at them as they approach.

'Hey big guy, you ready to try out that new move I showed you yesterday? Use it on some of Pastry King's goons?' Shep asks, a wide grin on his face. Shep nudges his sister in the side. 'It's a classic, sis. I'll show it to you when we get back.'

'Oh yay,' Willow replies, rolling her eyes. 'I get to listen to you going on about how great a teacher you are, over and over again. Any chance you could show me the move while not talking?'

Shep feigns hurt as he places a hand on his chest. 'That hurt me bad, Wills. I do not go on and on. It's called bragging and I only do that because I've got every reason to. I'm the best.'

'How are you still single?' Fallon asks sarcastically.

'About time. Having a bad hair day?' Shep calls as Bastian joins the group, with Ethan walking beside him.

Bastian throws a black bag at Shep's chest. 'You forgot your kit, smart-arse.'

Thea instantly notices Ethan is far from happy. His shirt is creased and he's not wearing a tie. It's probably the first time Thea's seen him without a tie since she first met him. Ethan usually took impeccably dressed to a new level.

'Fuck me, Ethan,' Shep says. 'You look like you haven't slept for days. You good?'

'Thank you for that, Shep. We're just working around the clock at the moment. I'm fine.' Thea catches Ethan glancing at Bastian before he walks away to speak to Nix. Bastian keeps looking over his shoulder at Ethan. He's trying to be discrete about it, but Thea notices.

Whatever is going on between Bas and Ethan fades into the background as Davyn stalks into the room. He's dressed like everyone else in his black fighting clothes, with the addition of a black leather jacket, with flashes of red to match his wing colour. On his left shoulder is a large metal horned skull attached by leather straps to his jacket. She stays at the edge of the group as his team mates welcome him with slaps on the back, and various smart comments. All the while, Thea can't convince her eyes to move from him for even a second.

A few weeks ago, she would have struggled to see how the badly beaten, starved man the Blackjacks rescued would survive, let alone be cleared for action again. Apart from the black eye patch hiding his ruined eye, you'd be hard pressed to believe anything happened to him.

Eventually, the team breaks up to go through last minute weapon and vehicle checks. Left alone, Thea wanders through the hanger, weaving past the assortment of bikes and cars, and stops beside Davyn's new car. He'd taken delivery of the Range Rover a few days ago, to replace the one destroyed by his father's men. Hopefully this one will have a longer life than the old one.

She leans against the bonnet and watches the group as they prepare to leave.

Court and Nix are deep in conversation with Davyn while Shep, Willow, and Fallon squabble over weapons. Bastian is in the cockpit checking the craft before they take off. It's who's hanging around him that surprises Thea. Ethan is sitting in the co-pilot seat speaking to him as he works. If she's reading the situation right, it's one hell of a serious chat.

And whatever Bastian is saying isn't easing the situation. Maybe Ethan is as apprehensive about Bastian going on this mission as she is about Davyn.

Thea smiles as she watches them. The more she sees of them together, the more sure she is that there's something going on. She knows Ethan is gay, but she didn't know Bastian is. Not that he'd come up and tell her if he was. Bastian's sexuality is his business.

But what does surprise her, is that no one has mentioned anything about them being a couple. Does that mean it's a secret? She knows Nix was unsure about being in a relationship with one of her fighters. Maybe Ethan is thinking along the same lines.

Ethan leaves the helicopter, appearing more flustered than he did when he went in. He quickly makes his way around the front of the craft, and goes over to speak to Nix again.

Her thoughts drift back to Davyn. She's actually surprised she made it to the hangar on time. Davyn had refused to let her out of his arms until ten minutes before they were meant to meet the rest of the team. The more they are together, the more his confidence is growing, and she can't get enough of him like that. Can't get enough of his immense body towering over her, his fangs out and eyes glowing as he pounds into her. That intoxicating growl building in his chest as he—'

'You better not scratch my new car.'

She spins around and smiles at Davyn. Her cheeks flush warmly as she licks her dry lips. 'Hey. Of course I'm not scratching it. So, you all set?'

Davyn nods. 'I'll find out soon enough.' He taps a finger on his leather eye patch. 'As long as no one comes up on my right side I'll be grand.' He pins her against his car, caging her with an arm to either side.

'Don't scratch your new car.'

'Fuck the car,' he replies before kissing her, grasping her hair in his hand as he places the other hand on her hip and pulls her close against his body. She runs her hands over his backside, groaning at the feel of the leather under her palms. Her tongue scrapes off his newly repaired fangs as they extend. Too soon, Davyn breaks contact and rests his forehead against hers as he continues to grip her hair. 'You'll be the death of me, Thea.'

She laughs, trying to stop herself from taking this much further. Whatever about her being the death of him, the way he looks right now is making him almost impossible to resist. His fangs, glowing green eye, and all the leather, isn't helping to quench the need building in her. The need for him to take her wherever they can find some privacy. 'I want you when we get back.'

'Oh you can have me. No arguments there. You can have me as many times as you want, Thea. We better go. The sooner we end this, the sooner I can bring you home.'

'Hey, can I ask you something?'

'Of course.'

'Is there something going on between Bas and Ethan?'

Davyn frowns and steps closer to her. 'I don't know. Why?'

'I might be seeing things that aren't there, but Ethan acts differently around Bas. He's more flustered, more emotional I guess.'

Davyn thinks about that for a moment. 'It's not impossible. Ethan prefers males, but I have no idea about Bas. I don't know much about him at all. If they are together it would have to be in secret.'

'Why?'

'Ethan is old blood, Thea. His grandparents wouldn't accept him unless he fits with the ideal image of a straight, well-bred male. If they find out he's with a male fighter, they would probably disown him.'

'Poor Ethan. That's horrible.'

Davyn shrugs. 'Vampires live for centuries, Thea. That means our somewhat archaic rules also live for centuries. We appear backward in some of our views. That won't change overnight, as much as we want it to. Nix won't have a problem with Ethan and Bas, but others would. Leave them to it. They're both decent males. They deserve a semblance of happiness.'

He cups the side of her face and draws her close, kissing her passionately.

'So, you ready to load up?'

'Absolutely,' she lies, hoping she convinces him otherwise. She doesn't want any members of her new, and slightly messed up, family anywhere near that castle.

He smiles at her, his fangs retracting as he gets control of himself again. 'Let's get this over with. I promise by the end of the night, only one of my line will be alive. I'm going to make sure it's me. I've got this,' he adds with a smirk as he steps aside and gestures to the helicopter. 'After you.'

Davyn grips the edge of the bench, squeezing until his fingers ache. Bastian is bringing the craft down, which means they're near the cottage where they'll be meeting the Whelans.

Then it's on to the castle. He stopped thinking of it as his home over a century ago. Right now, he wants to see it razed to the ground in a ball of flames. Thea meets his eye and smiles. He smiles back, trying to put her at ease, but he knows it came across as more of a grimace. He wants to be far away from this place. Ideally in bed with her.

He glances at Court and instantly feels shame washing over him. What right does he have to think of his team mates daughter like that? Court deserves more from him. Fuck, Thea deserves more than him. He can't for the life of him figure out why she wants anything to do with him. He keeps waiting for her to see sense and run for the hills, but it hasn't happened. He knows he can easily slip into needing a life with her. A life he doesn't deserve.

The helicopter touches down, and Bastian gives the all clear from the cockpit. He joins the others in the hold, leaving Fletch to take control of their transport.

The door opens, and they step out to their welcoming committee. Murt Whelan steps forward and smiles at the group. 'Thought we got rid of you lot?'

'Shep enjoyed your company so much we had to come back,' Nix says.

Murt winks at Shep, who is grinning back at him. 'I'm sure he did. Let's get inside.'

Davyn follows everyone inside the cottage and takes the nearest seat.

'You look well, Davyn,' Murt says as he sits by the fire. 'That's good to see.'

'Thanks. I appreciate what you did to get me out.'

'You're welcome. To be honest, we weren't convinced initially, but Thea changed our minds. You've got her to thank for our involvement.'

Davyn looks over at her. He didn't know that. 'You did?'

'They took a little persuasion.'

'More than a little,' Murt says. 'Damn near dragged us back into the house. So, are you sure you want to kill your father? I know he's not going to win any father of the year contests, but killing him... you sure?'

'Never more sure of anything in my life.'

'Convinced me,' Garret says. 'How about we get to talking about how the fucker is going to die.'

'I'm liking him more and more,' Shep says, as he nods at Garret.

'Wow, if that's not a compliment and a half. A blood sucker approves of me.'

'Bite me.'

'You first.'

'Oh would you both knock it off?' Murt says, stopping the two men from their back and forth. 'You're like a bunch of fucking kids.'

'Has there been any activity around the castle?' Davyn asks, desperate to get this over and done with, so he can get Thea away from here again.

Murt nods as he sits back in the chair. 'We haven't been able to get too close, but from what we can tell, Flann hasn't left since you escaped. There have been other vampires coming and going regularly. Not part of your father's court.'

'Any idea who they are?' Nix asks.

'I'd imagine they're True Order. He's linked to them somehow. It's not a concern right now. We can take whoever we come up against. The problem is getting in. We've tried to breach the castle countless times. It's impenetrable.'

'No it's not,' Davyn says. 'There are tunnels under the castle. Dozens of them. My father knows of a few, but I know of one that will be clear.'

'How can you be sure it's still there?' Murt asks.

'It's submerged most of the time. The only way to go through it, is at low tide, and even then the water will be up to our chests.'

He can feel Nix glancing over at him, no doubt already worrying about his fear of water. 'It leads up to the old food store. From there we have access to the entire castle.'

'So we're heading in for a swim,' Murt says, 'Can't say I'm thrilled about that, but so be it. Where will he be?'

Davyn licks his lips and pauses as a cramp twists his gut, momentarily silencing him.

'You good?' Court asks, and he nods.

'He'll either be in the great hall, or his office. It's on the floor above the hall. You can get to it up a stairs at the back of the room. His personal quarters are connected to it. He doesn't usually stray too far from there. Well, unless he has a prisoner he wants to taunt.'

'So when's low tide?'

Shep check his phone. 'About two hours. So I presume we'll need a boat of some sort to get us there.'

'Unless Nix, Fallon, and Willow fancy carrying the rest of us,' Davyn replies. 'Which I wouldn't suggest. He's prepared for an aerial attack. We'll have to go by boat. And I don't mean a boat with an engine either.'

Murt looks over at Garret as his brother nods. 'I'll sort that out.' He gets up and leaves the room to make a call.

'I have one favour to ask,' Davyn says. 'I want the kill shot. I don't want him to escape, but if possible I want to take him down.'

Nix nods and everyone else joins her. 'Whoever finds this bastard, call it in, and make sure he can't go anywhere until Davyn gets there. We hunt in pairs on this one - no excuses. This guy is not to be underestimated or trusted. He'll want to get out with his head attached, and will do everything he can to make sure that happens. We're here to make sure that doesn't. We'll leave in an hour. Make sure we're in place to hit, as soon as the tide drops.'

The team heads off in different directions to make preparations. Davyn looks into the fire, trying to breathe through the cramp that's gradually getting worse. Adrenaline isn't helping in any way. He's gearing up for the fight, getting set for meeting his father again and killing him. It's something he badly wants, but he's not embarrassed to admit the man scares him. Always has.

'How are you doing?'

Court sits on the stool beside him bringing him out of his thoughts. 'I'm fine.'

'How bad is the pain?'

Trust Court to notice. Very little gets by him. 'It's bad. Easing though.'

'You look on edge with me now. You don't have to be.'

Davyn smiles briefly. 'You burst into my memories, Court. I know you didn't mean to, but you released some stuff I'd tried hard to forget. I'm not keen on a replay.'

Court nods and looks down at his hands. 'I'm sorry, Davyn. I think I can push the memories back for you, if you want.'

Davyn frowns at him. He knew Court's powers had strengthened while Rhain had him, but he had no idea what he can do now. 'You can do that?'

'Yes, I'm sure I can. I've got a better handle on my powers. I know how to draw the memories out. I'm sure I can do it in reverse. It wouldn't be a good idea to give it a go now, but when we get through this, I can try to lock then up for you again. I had no right going near you like I did. The very least I can do is make it better. The offer is there if you want it.'

'Thanks. I'll think about it.'

Court stands up and stretches. 'I'm going to check on the boat.' He takes a few steps away, then stops and turns back to him. 'By the way. I approve. It means fuck all, I know, but I just thought I'd tell you.'

'Approve of what?'

'You and Thea. I learned a long time ago that she's very much her own person. Even when I thought we were siblings she was the same. And I have to admit you're a good match.'

Davyn stares after Court in shock as he walks across the room and joins Garret and Murt. What the hell just happened? He wraps his arms around his stomach and looks back at the fire. Court giving his approval is a monumental thing for him. He knows Thea wasn't bothered either way. Of course she would have preferred that he didn't hate the idea, but to Davyn it's important.

He has to work with Court. Has to trust him with his life and vice versa. If there were any doubts, or bad blood between them, it would have made things awkward. Hearing what he just did, takes a huge weight off his shoulders.

Garret slams his hands against the counter and everyone looks at him. 'Boat is organised. Looks like we're on.'

~

Davyn stares at the cliff facing them instead of the water surrounding them. The trip on the fishing boat had taken less than thirty minutes, but he felt like he was going to puke for each of those minutes.

And this is the easy part.

Once they get to the cave they'll be wading through a low tunnel with barely enough head room. One problem at a time. First they need to get there without being shot down.

Shep is sitting beside him, his eyes closed as his head moves from side to side. He'll be picking up on the vampires in the castle but, as long as they're far enough away from the castle, they shouldn't be a problem.

Murt and his brothers lie on the floor at their feet. They'd shifted into wolf form just before they got on the boat. Their rule about not letting any other species see them transform, meant they had to make this journey on four legs.

Shep hadn't even made a joke about wet dog hair. The time to joke will be later. After the last time, they know what forces they'll be up against. No one is taking this lightly.

Davyn looks down at the scars around his wrist and his resolve strengthens. More than a century of being hurt. Of being cold, alone, and terrified. It's about to come to an end. He'll make damn sure it does. He closes his fist and looks up as they round the corner.

On the top of the cliff, towering above everything around it, stands the castle. 'Fuck me, Dav,' Fallon says when she spots the hulking form. 'That's where you grew up?'

'Yeah. Home sweet home.'

Nix taps Shep on the knee, startling him out of his daze. 'Sorry, are you getting anything?'

'Yeah. A fucking heart attack. Don't do that again. As for us sailing into an ambush, we're clear for now. Lots of bodies in the castle and surrounding it, but no one out this far. We're good.'

'Whereabouts is the cave?' Bas asks, as he steers the boat nearer to the cliff.

'Just in the next bay. Keep out from the cliffs though. There are hidden rocks.'

They stop near the cave and sit, waiting for the tide to drop enough to let them in. Davyn used this way to get in and out of the castle when he was a child. His father never knew of it, so he could come and go without being noticed. But that was before he had been locked in the water for decades.

'It's time.'

'I'll let you lead the way,' Nix says, moving aside to give him access to the steps leading from the back of the fishing boat.

He has to go first. He knows that. He's the only one who knows the way.

Tell that to his fucked up mind which is in full control of his body.

Nothing happens except for a lot of staring at the moonlit water swelling around the boat surrounding him, suffocating him. Then Court is in his face, his pale eyes glowing slightly in the gloom. 'Let me help you.'

'I can't.' Davyn hates how pathetic he sounds, but he's about to freak out.

'I know. I can block the fear for you.'

'It's just the water.' He keeps his voice low but it's not a cruise ship they're on. Everyone will be listening to his breakdown.

'Let me help,' Court says again. When Davyn looks up he sees nothing but sincerity in Court's face. He genuinely wants to help.

'Okay.'

'Keep looking in my eyes. Don't look away.'

Courts eyes burn, locking on to him, but unlike the last time, he doesn't resist. When Court blinks, releasing him, Davyn feels no different.

'You okay?'

'Yeah. Did it work?'

'Look at the sea.'

Davyn does, but instead of the suffocating fear, there's nothing. He smiles and looks back at Court. 'It worked.'

'Good. Can we get in there now? I'm fucking freezing sitting on this boat.' Court slaps him on the shoulder, then moves out of the way to let him off the boat first.

Davyn slips into the sea, feeling nothing but a clear headed determination to get to his father. Concentrating on the cave ahead of him, he wades towards it and lowers his head as he goes inside. The others follow after him, with Shep taking up the rear. Davyn keeps putting one foot in front of the other, counting the steps in his head. He's taller so his strides are longer, but counting gives him something to do.

Eventually, the narrow cave opens out into a large cavern. Davyn quickly pulls himself out of the water. He climbs up the rough rock path and stands aside to let Bastian move to the door at the top. Bas takes off his gloves and places his hands on the door. Now he's touching the actual building he'll be able to tell them exactly where everyone is.

'No one on the other side. Most are in the great hall.' He frowns and looks at Davyn. 'Your father is in his study. Room above the Hall right?'

Davyn nods. 'He alone?'

'Yes. Will I open the door?'

Nix signals yes, so Bastian places his hands over the lock and closes his eyes. A minute later he stands aside, pulling the door open.

Davyn and one of the wolves lead the rest of the team through the underground rooms, up to the main residence. Bastian keeps one hand on the wall as he walks, tracking everyone in the castle.

The wolf beside him growls at the same time Bastian speaks. 'Two ahead. Armed.'

Davyn creeps ahead and shoots them both before they even see him.

'Clear again,' Bas says. 'But not for long. We've got company moving our way.'

'He knows I'm here.' Davyn curses himself. 'They fed from me. If even one of them can pick up on me, he'll know.'

'Time we stop sneaking about in the basement then.' Nix moves to the front of the group with Murt beside her. He's the only one Davyn can tell apart due to his size. 'Are you wolves ready to play?'

Murt growls and nudges Nix's hand.

'I'm going to take that as a definite yes. Murt, you stick to Davyn. Everyone else, you know the drill. If you find the King before Davyn does, call it in. Davyn gets the kill.'

Davyn climbs the stairs to the upper level. He knows his father will be hiding in his room, waiting to make a run for it when the time is right.

'Can you smell Ronan?'

Murt nods and lifts his head towards the top of the stairs.

'Is my father there too?'

Murt does what he can only describe as a shrug. 'You don't know his scent?'

He shakes his head.

They get to the top and Davyn composes himself before looking down at Murt. The wolf's green gaze is confident and gives him a little strength. He can do this.

Davyn slowly opens the door, pressing himself back against the stone wall as it swings open with an ominous creak.

Gun raised, he steps in to the room and hears the heavy shifting of gears. Next thing he knows, Murt's immense weight is on his back, sending him forward onto the rough wooden floor. Air driven from him, Davyn coughs, trying to get his lungs working again. It would help if there wasn't a two hundred and fifty pound wolf on his back.

'Murt?'

The smell of fresh blood hits him. 'Shit. Murt?'

The whimper is both a relief, and the last thing he wants to hear. He gently pushes the wolf off his back and rolls over. Murt is bleeding heavily, a thick wooden stake, about the thickness of his arm, embedded in his hip.

'Damn it, Murt. Why the hell did you do that? You should have let it hit me.'

The wolf whimpers again, but pushes Davyn away with his paw.

'Stop. I have to help you. Fuck. My father must have boobytrapped the place. I didn't know.'

Murt fixes him with a 'don't mess with me' wolf stare and shoves him in the leg with a massive paw.

'I can't leave you like this.'

When he growls Davyn gets the message. 'You're a stubborn fucker, you know that.'

Murt snorts.

'Okay, I'm just going to move you out of the way of the door, okay?'

He grips Murt's two front legs and hauls him over to the side of the room, out of immediate sight of the door. Murt breathes heavily and pushes Davyn in the leg.

'Just a second.' Davyn pulls a roll of bandage from his field kit and wraps it around the piece of wood, holding it in place until Fletch can take it out without ripping Murt's leg apart. 'That'll hold it for now.'

Murt nods then growls, lifting his lip to give Davyn an eyeful of some of the most vicious teeth he's ever seen. 'I know. I'm going.' He stands up and hits his earpiece as he walks over to his father's desk. 'Murt is down. He's alive but out of commission.'

'Got that,' Nix says, her breathless reply cut off when she fires. 'We've hit heavy resistance. We're keeping them from you, but you better get a move on. I'll send back up for you.'

He checks his father's desk and places his hand on the seat. It's warm. 'The bastard was just here. I'll find him.'

'Wait for support. Do not go after him alone.'

But Davyn isn't listening. Where would the fucker go?

Davyn thought he knew the castle, but it seems his father had planned for something like this. He slowly peers into the tall fireplace at the device that caught them out. There was only one stake loaded in the contraption. 'Don't suppose you can smell any more of these hidden away?'

Murt slowly shakes his head.

Davyn checks the stone walls, testing each brick. He curses and leans back against the fireplace, stumbling back a step when the whole thing shifts.

'Crafty bastard.' Davyn shoves the mantle and uncovers a spiral staircase. 'There's a secret staircase in his room,' he says over his radio. 'I'm going after him.'

Murt growls deep in his chest.

'Someone down there?'

He growls again and whimpers.

'I'll take that as a yes.'

Ignoring the burst of arguments over the radio, he hurries down the stairs, keeping the gun in his hand. By the time he reaches the bottom, the radio has been silenced. Nix will have his neck for this, but he doesn't care. He's too close to risk losing his father while he waits.

Davyn steps into the cave and looks around him. He doesn't recognise this area at all. He explored most of the underground caves when he was a child, but this place is somewhere he never ventured. He grunts as something impacts the side of his face, knocking his teeth together.

Davyn wipes the blood off his mouth and looks over at his father.

And Ronan.

Flann has his arm around the old man's neck as he steps backwards, crossing the wooden walkway over the water splitting the cave in two.

He silently watches the man who has haunted his dreams and ruined his life since the day he was born. Today that ends, and he can't fucking wait. 'There's nowhere to go.'

Flann laughs as he paces the walkway at the far side of the water. 'Is that so? Do you expect me to quiver and kneel before you?'

'No. I expect you to die.'

Flann laughs but it fades away, his eyes turning cold as he spots the pauldron on Davyn's shoulder. 'Where did you get that?'

'I gave it to him,' Ronan mutters around Flann's grip on his throat.

'It seems being lenient with you was a mistake.'

Ronan winces as Flann tightens his grip.

'His... grandfather would... have wanted him... to have it.'

Flann dismisses Ronan's words, sneering over at Davyn again. 'You're not worthy, Davyn. Never were, and never will be. But if you want to pretend, who am I to stop you? I'll be tearing it from your dying corpse in a few minutes. Then, Son, you will be thrown back in your cell and I will walk away. Forever. Let you rot in the sea where you belong.'

'I'm taking back what's mine, Father. By force.'

'I see. I must say I'm damn impressed, Son. Many a strong male has succumbed to the Binding. In fact, I don't think I've heard of anyone surviving it. Even if they somehow get out of here, they're never the same again. Is that the case with you?

'Do you think of it often? Think about each and every precious breath. Think about the weight on your chest as you fall prey to the panic, and slowly suffocate. I must admit, I never thought I'd see you standing in front of me again. Yet, here you are. Not only still alive, but daring to threaten me? To try and take what's mine? Ungrateful bastard to the end.'

Flann draws his sword, slicing it across Ronan's throat before Davyn can react.

'No!'

Flann shoves Ronan into the water and makes a run for it. Davyn leaps into the water and wades over to him. He turns him onto his back and holds him to his chest. 'Ronan?'

Ronan opens his eyes and smiles at him. Familiar eyes stare up at him and a shaky hand raises to rest on the side of his face.

'Go finish this, Davyn,' he whispers. 'Kill him. Be free.'

He doesn't know if he's seeing things, but he could swear the old man is smiling as the light fades in his eyes and his hand drops.

Davyn stares down at Ronan, but his friend is dead. He knows it. He can feel it. He can hear his heart take its last beat. He carefully lifts him out of the water and lays him down on the walkway. Tears stream down his face as he closes Ronan's eyes.

Ronan did more for him than anyone else he's known. Davyn always considered Ronan his father. He risked his life every day to make sure Davyn was as safe as he could be. Davyn lifts his head and growls. Ronan didn't deserve to die. Not like this, and not by that bastard's hand.

'I will end this, Ronan. For you and for me. I promise. We'll both be free.'

With one last look at his friend, Davyn takes off after his father. The Prime blood in him roars as he follows. The hunter in him charges to the surface, brought out by the thrill of the chase. His boots hit the stones without a change in momentum. The moon is high in the night sky, casting an eerie glow on the beach and Flann. He can sense Fallon and Willow in the sky somewhere above him, but instead of landing to help him, they move away. Davyn smiles. This is between the two of them.

Once clear of the cliffs, Flann releases his wings. Davyn pulls the twin blades from his waistcoat and flings them at his fleeing father.

Each blade hits home, driving deep into Flann's back where his wings protrude. He shouts and falls in to the sea. Davyn doesn't halt his pursuit, crashing into the surf after his flailing father. Whatever fear he had has been masked by Court, and he can't be more thankful.

Davyn grabs him by the back of his shirt and pulls him to his feet. Flann coughs and splutters as he tries to clear his lungs of sea water. Flann swipes at Davyn with his wing, but the weight of the water against the limb, slows his attack down enough to give Davyn time to back away. His father rams his head back, forcing Davyn to let go to avoid a broken nose.

Flann launches himself at Davyn, driving him underwater as they collide. He wraps his hands around Davyn's neck, holding him down as he squeezes. Davyn claws at his father's hands, but the male has an iron grip. Instead, he drives his feet into the seabed and pushes upright. His head breaks the surface and he takes a deep breath.

'You're an ungrateful bastard, Davyn.'

He wraps his hand around his father's wrist and twists, snapping the bones. Flann shouts in pain and releases him, clutching his shattered arm to his chest.

'How the fuck did you do that?' he grinds out through clenched teeth. 'You find yourself a new donor, boy? That must have been a real sell to convince someone to get that close to you.'

Davyn braces himself as a wave breaks over his back. He knows what his father is doing. Trying to get under his skin. Trying to make him doubt himself.

Flann glares over at him. 'Your lips still sewn shut, Son? Nothing to say?'

Davyn keeps his response to a simple shake of his head.

Flann growls as he draws his sword, slashing it at Davyn. He ducks out of the way and kicks his father's leg, knocking the older vampire off balance. 'Damn you! Why won't you die!'

Davyn punches his father in the face before he can recover, and pull his sword up. Flann rears back, using his wings to keep himself upright.

'Just thinking the same thing.'

Father and son face each other as the waves crash around them. Davyn releases his wings and his father scowls at him. 'How the fuck did you fix them?'

Instead of answering, Davyn rams his talon towards his father's head, but Flann blocks the move with his own wing.

'Should have killed you when I took care of your mother.'

Davyn pauses, and Flann takes advantage. He drives his talons towards Davyn. He gets his hands down, catching the thick bone just above his father's razor sharp talons. His father growls, pushing against Davyn, but he fights back, keeping the talons from spearing his flesh.

Davyn digs his fingers into Flann's wings, trying to stop them from tearing him in two. His father is strong. Always has been. But with Thea's blood powering him, he's got the upper hand. And his father knows it. For the first time in his life he's not scared of him.

'What are you smiling about?'

'Just thinking about killing you.'

'We'll see about that.' Flann growls as he lifts up his wings, bringing Davyn with him.

'You're just like her. Delusions of grandeur. Thinking you're better than everyone else. She was damn lucky I agreed to marry her. Damn lucky I didn't kill her the second you were born. As soon as I saw you, I knew you'd bring shame on my name. Shame on my house.'

'What did you do?' Davyn forces the words out through clenched teeth.

'Thought a big-shot Blackjack such as yourself would have figured that out by now. I killed her.'

Davyn digs his fingers into Flann's wings but his father doesn't react. He roars at his father and tries to ram his boots into Flann's face, but his father's wings are too long.

'Why?'

'Bitch tried to run off with you. I caught her about a mile from the castle. Put her out of her misery and brought you home.'

'Never wanted me. Why not... just let her... leave?' His father is going to slice him in half if he doesn't find a way out of this in the next minute. Holding his own weight, while pushing against his father, is draining his energy levels.

'You may have been a disappointment from the start, but you were my property. She had no right taking you. Now, I'm going to kill you, like I should have done that night I killed her.' Davyn feels his father's talons push against his side.

Bastard is going to tear him apart. After nearly a century of fighting, his father is going to be the one to take him down. Just like he took down Ronan and his mother.

He was just a kid when he lost her, but he remembers her like he saw her a few hours ago. Apart from Ronan, she had been the only good thing in his life. He lifts his head to look at Flann. The man who took her from him. The man who took Ronan from him. Something burns inside, something that blocks out the pain of his father's talons slowly tearing into his skin. He grits his teeth and begs his wings to do what he needs them to, for the first time in his life.

He beats his wings and he rises into the air, dragging a very surprised Flann with him. Flann releases his hold on Davyn, pulling his talons away from Davyn's sides and dropping back into the sea. Davyn lifts his wings above his head and lands on his father, driving him under the water.

Before Flann can resurface, Davyn twists both wings around, bringing the razor talons down. His thick black talons tear into his father's neck, cutting through flesh, muscle, and bone. Davyn stares at the wound spilling blood into the sea as the life drains from the bastard.

But the King has one last trick up his sleeve. He rams his talon into Davyn's leg, locking them together. Davyn pulls against him but he can't get his leg free. He thrusts his wings upward, trying to push against the water to get some leverage, but his damn father won't release him, even in death. He takes a deep breath, as his father's lifeless body pulls him downward under the icy waves.

53

Shep races down the beach and stops a few feet from the shore. 'Dav! Fuck! You getting him?'

The wolf beside him takes a step towards the sea and Shep groans. 'Oh perfect.' He walks to the water's edge with the wolf beside him. He doesn't know which one it is. They all look the same as far as he's concerned.

Shep closes his eyes and takes a deep breath. He curses as too many scents hit him at once - his teammates, the vamps in the castle, the dog beside him, the sea... blood. Dav's blood.

'He's out there all right.'

With no time to wait for the winged backup, Shep points a finger at the wolf. 'You stay. Watch my back, okay?'

He gets a small nod from whichever wolf it is, then takes off his jacket before charging into the surf, diving over a wave before it knocks him off his feet. He swims past the breaking waves and tries to keep above the water while he searches for Davyn's scent. He turns to his left and swims. There's nothing floating on the surface which means he's under it.

Shep swallows a mouthful of water as one of Davyn's wings suddenly bursts from beneath the water to his right, then disappears again.

'Fuck.'

He dives under and sees Davyn struggling to free himself from his dead father. Fucker's head is barely attached. Good for Dav. Shep pulls at Davyn but he won't budge. Shep surfaces, takes a deep breath and dives back down.

One of Flann's talons is embedded in Dav's leg, locking the males together. He knows it's going to fuck Dav up, but he has no choice. He pulls the claw out of his leg, and grabs his teammate by the arm as he heads for the surface again.

He splutters to clear his lungs. 'Hey. You with me?'

Davyn nods. 'Yeah, thanks.'

'Can you swim?'

Before he can answer, he drops below the surface again. Shep grabs him by the arm and holds him up. 'Wings are too heavy,' Dav says as he struggles to keep himself afloat. 'Shep. I need to get his sword.'

'I know. How about we save our own asses first. Hang on buddy. I've got you. Hey, you guys hear me? Dav and I need a lift. Anyone free?' Shep is fit and pure muscle, but Dav's wings are royally screwing with him. The current is winning over his strength, threatening to drag the two of them under. Davyn slowly spreads his wings, laying them on the surface to keep some weight from Shep.

'On my way, Shep,' Willow responds. 'Where are you?'

Shep coughs and splutters. 'In the fucking sea. I'm the one holding the fucker with the wings. Can't miss us.'

'Thanks, Shep,' Davyn says as they try to keep above the surface.

'How about you treat me to a beer if we get out of this?'

'Sounds good.'

Willow flies over the cliff and dives, extending her wings as she reaches the sea. She hovers above them and grabs Davyn's arm. 'Are you strong enough to pull your wings back?'

Davyn shakes his head. 'Tried. I can't. Need to get his sword.'

'I'll get the fucking sword, Dav. You go with Wills.'

Shep ducks under, moving the wings to stop the resistance as his sister rises into the air, hauling Davyn's body from the sea. 'You good?' Shep shouts up at her.

'I'm fine. Get the sword.'

He waits to make sure she doesn't drop Dav's ass back in the sea before he takes a breath, and goes to get up close and personal with Dav's dickhead father again. Even in death, the asshole isn't giving up the sword without a fight, but Shep eventually pulls it free from the dickhead's hand. After kicking Dav's father in the nuts, he pushes himself up, breaking the surface just as Willow arrives back to give him a lift.

He grabs onto her hand and grins up at her. 'Thanks, Sis.'

'You can thank me by losing some weight.'

'Hey, watch it. I'm pure muscle thank you very much.'

She reaches the beach, dropping him on his ass. He holds up his middle finger to her before going over to Davyn. 'You good?'

'Yeah.' He leans on the back of the wolf and pushes himself to his feet, then takes the sword from Shep.

'Any word on Murt?'

'Still breathing,' Shep says as he slips his jacket on over his wet t-shirt. 'Oh fuck that feel horrible. I hate being wet.'

Davyn takes an unsteady step towards the cave leading to the castle, leaning heavily on the sword for support.

'Hey! Dav, where the fuck are you going?'

'Castle.'

Shep gestures to the wolf and Willow, and the three of them join Davyn as he slowly makes his way up the beach. 'Would you stop being a stubborn ass and at least lean on me.'

He begrudgingly accepts Shep's help which makes the going a little faster. 'Wills and Wolfie, you two are going to have to take the lead. I've got my hands full.'

'It's Fionn.'

'What is?' Shep, throwing his sister a confused look over his shoulder.

She nods to the pissed off looking wolf glaring up at him. 'It's Fionn.'

'How the fuck do you know that?'

She shakes her head as she overtakes him with the wolf by her side. 'Because they look different, dumbass. Even as wolves.'

Shep glances at Davyn, but the guy is concentrating on putting one foot in front of the other. 'Whatever, just don't let me or Dav get shot.'

~

Davyn leans heavily on Shep as they make their way back through the cave. He looks down at Ronan as they pass his body.

'Don't worry, buddy. We won't leave him behind.'

'You're assuming we'll be alive to get him.'

Shep laughs and adjusts his grip on Davyn's arm. 'Oh we will be. I'm far too amazing to die here.'

Davyn laughs in spite of the situation.

Thea's blood in his system is already healing his leg, but he's far from ready to take on any of his father's men. All he can do is hope when they see he has the sword, they'll realise what it means and back off. If not, they'll have to be taken out. He's not going to spare a thought for any of his father's men. Not after what they did to him the last few months.

'How much further?' Shep asks as they reach the far side of the cave.

'Not far. There's a staircase hidden around the corner.

Shep readjusts his grip on Davyn's arm again. 'Stairs. Yay. That'll be fun.'

With Willow and Fionn in the lead, they climb the stairs back to the great hall. By the time they get to the floor below it, Davyn is able to support himself, just highlighting the power Thea's blood has on him.

Willow holds up her hand, stopping them before they reach the next landing a few feet from the hall. Three of Flann's men hurry up the stairs to their right and join the others in the great hall.

'What's down there?'

'Kitchen,' Davyn says. 'Some sleeping quarters too. It leads out into the stables.'

'Fionn, you make sure he gets where he needs to be without falling on his face.' Davyn glares at Shep. 'Sorry. Escort him to the great hall please. That better?'

Dav shakes his head. 'Where are you going?'

'Wills and I will make sure you don't have any interruptions. Good luck.'

'You too.'

Shep and Willow wait until Fionn and Davyn have cleared the next flight before they take the door to the left, and hurry along the corridor into the vast kitchen. The aroma of stew makes Shep's stomach growl loudly.

'Are you seriously thinking about food at a time like this?'

He shrugs. 'Nothing wrong with having a healthy appetite.'

She grabs him by the jacket, dragging him to the ground behind a counter as a group of Flann's men step into the room and fire at them. 'Still hungry?' she asks as she returns fire.

Shep peeks over the counter, ducking quickly when a bullet embeds itself in the wooden surface. 'You know me, Sis. Not much will turn me off my grub.' He springs up and fires, hitting one guy in the arm. 'Ha. That'll slow him down.'

'What about his friends?' Willow asks as she risks a quick look.

'I'm sure we can handle that.'

'Yeah? So what's your big plan then?'

Shep looks over at her. 'Me? Why am I coming up with the plan?'

'Because you were second in command while Court was gone.'

Shep glares at her. 'Yeah and you did fuck all I told you to do, so you can't pull that one out now.'

She fires over the counter before responding. 'That's because you were ordering me to make you macaroni and cheese.'

He fires then ducks down again. 'All part of the team building, Sis.'

'Piss off, Shep.'

Shep grins as he spots a basket by his feet. 'Gladly. Okay, so how's this for a plan? I'll cover you. Head left and take them down while I distract them.'

'How exactly are you going to do that?'

He winks and grins at her. 'All will be revealed. Trust your big brother. Now go.'

She waits until he fires then crawls out from behind the counter to the large armchair by the open fire. It's brought her alongside the goons so she'll easily take them down.

'Hold your fire!' Shep shouts. 'I've got grenades and I'm not afraid to use them!'

The goon at the front takes a step forward. 'Stand up slowly.'

'No problem.' He gets up and smiles at the group of men. 'I hope none of you have itchy trigger fingers, or else this whole place will go boom.'

'Show us your hands. Slowly.'

Shep raises his hands but keeps them closed. 'Can't really open them or else... well they'll be picking the lot of us off the walls. Don't fancy being in a vampire soup with you twits. No offence.'

Then Shep throws the grenades and the men duck. He bends down and collects another one, launching it into the group.

'Wills!'

As he pelts them with grenades, Willow takes them down, using the confusion to kill them all within seconds. When the bad guys are bleeding out on the ground, Shep steps out from behind the counter and nods. 'Not too bad if I do say so myself.'

Willow bends down and picks up what Shep was throwing at them. 'Are you serious? You've finally lost your mind.'

He grins widely. 'Vampire grenades. There's a whole basket of them behind the counter.'

'It's garlic, Shep.'

He grins widely. 'Yep. We just took down a bunch of vampires with garlic. How hilarious is that!'

She throws a bulb at him, hitting him on the side of the head.

'Ouch.'

'How the hell am I related to you? You're... I have no words, Shep. You're unbelievable, you know that?'

'Shucks, thanks Wills. But yeah, I know. Hey, maybe next time we can launch bottles of holy water at them. Kind of like putting our own twist on the pop culture myths.'

'How about next time I come up with the plan?'

'Hey, don't knock it. Worked didn't it? Anyway, you can thank me later. We better head up and make sure the others are okay.'

He bends down and fills the pockets of his jacket with more garlic.

'I'm almost afraid to ask.'

'I'm adding these babies to my arsenal. Powerful stuff.'

'I seriously worry about you sometimes, you know that? You're unstable.'

Shep grins and follows her up the stairs to the great hall. 'All the best vampires are.'

54

Davyn straightens his shoulders as he nears the great hall. He's tired and sore but, if this is to work, he needs to at least pretend he's a credible threat. He tightens his grip on the hilt of his father's sword. His sword. His grandfather's pauldron weighs heavily on his shoulder as he takes a few calming breaths. A lot is riding on this. He'll have to prove himself and, if that means killing more vampires, he'll do it. Thea's safety depends on this madness ending. To keep her safe, he'll do whatever he has to.

Fionn waits with him while he catches his breath, the wolf's thick coat bristling as he growls. He's eager to join the fight. 'You go. I need to do this part alone.'

Fionn dips his head then leaps up the last few steps, growling loudly as he launches into the battle.

Davyn steps out of the staircase and walks into the room. His team mates are embroiled in a fight with his father's men, blood, and bullets flying through the ancient building, tearing holes in flesh and stone.

He's not surprised the Blackjacks are holding back the greater number of attackers. It's what they do. But they can't hold them back for long. His father has an endless supply of mindless drones willing to die for the cause.

Nix leaps off the balcony running around the hall, landing on the back of one of his father's men, putting a bullet in his head before they both crash to the ground. Monstrous winged males slash through the room, causing carnage as they push forward.

Time to end this.

He climbs onto the throne and releases his wings. The pain is intense thanks to his various injuries, but he needs them out. It's all part of the show he needs to put on. He lets his fangs drop, calling his Prime side out to play. Then he draws the sword and holds it to his side.

'Enough!'

His booming roar has the desired effect, which surprises him. He didn't think it would be heard over the fighting.

The room falls silent, and he catches Nix smiling at him as she wipes blood from her face. There must be a few dozen of Flann's men still alive. Enough to cause a problem if this goes wrong.

He stretches his wings out to either side, showing two near on perfectly formed wings, complete with years of scars and tears from his father and brother.

'The Raven King is dead.'

A few murmurs break the uneasy silence.

'I killed him. I drove my talons into his neck and watched as he sank to the bottom of the ocean. I hold his sword. I claim his seat as my own. Kneel before me. Now!'

He pauses and tries to keep breathing. Everything rides on the next few seconds. If they kneel, it's done. If not... well, they're back to fighting. He looks to his left as his father's aide, Fergus, steps forward. If anyone will object it'll be that dick.

He looks at Davyn, taking in his wings, then settling his gaze on the sword in his hand. When he rests his palm over his heart and drops to his knee, Davyn can't believe what he's seeing. Then one by one, the rest of the room fall to their knees.

He looks over at Nix who is smiling and nodding in approval. She slowly takes a knee in front of him, followed by the rest of the Blackjacks, each one beaten and bleeding from the fight.

Davyn lowers his sword. As he takes in the sight in front of him, more men and some of his father's servants file into the room, dropping down in front of him, showing their allegiance.

It shouldn't have been that easy. These vampires have followed his father for centuries. They loyally obeyed his command. He can't believe they knelt so quickly for him.

Then he notices something.

Fergus has a scars on his face. The man next to him has scars on his arms. In fact, most of the men and women in front of him are scarred in some way. He remembers Ronan's injuries caused by his father. The bastard hurt all these people. Just like he hurt Davyn and his mother. He ruled through fear and pain. These people were never loyal to his father. They were terrified of him.

No wonder they were so quick to kneel.

'I'm not like my father.' He wasn't planning on saying anything else, but the words just come out. 'I don't demand loyalty. I won't threaten or hurt you if you disobey. I've lived like that for too long and I'm done with it. The fighting stops now. The pain stops now. The fear stops now. You're all free to go. I'm not going to rule this house.'

~

Thea follows her father into the castle, a cold shiver running through her body the further in to the building she goes. The castle is damp, dark, and miserable. And Davyn is now the heir to all of it.

Court glances over his shoulder at her. His left eye is swollen shut, he's got an impressive gash on his forehead, and he's cradling his arm to his chest. He's alive though, and that is all that matters to her. He will heal in time.

They all will, although some will take longer than others.

Fletch has been given two rooms next to the great hall for treating the injured. He was stitching Bastian's stomach, while next door Fallon was working on Murt's leg. Thankfully the stake hadn't caused any long term damage, but it would be a few hours before he could shift back.

As soon as he's cleared for visitors, she will be the first one there. Murt had saved Davyn's life by doing what he did. Yet again, she owes the clan leader a debt she doesn't think she'll ever be able to repay.

Ethan had been all for jumping on a helicopter and joining them for the clear up, but Nix had told him to stay put. After seeing his reaction before they left, Thea knows exactly why he was so desperate to join them.

She was there when Nix had made the call. Ethan was concerned for the whole team, but when she told him that one of Flann's men had tried to gut Bas, his demeanour shifted. Bastian will recover in time, but the injury was serious enough to knock him out for a while.

Ethan cares about Bastian. She has no doubts about that. She only hopes the fighter feels the same for Ethan. Knowing the team can find happiness with all this madness unfolding around them is uplifting.

'Where are the cells?' she asks as she follows him through the castle.

'In the foundations. They've been emptied.' He takes her hand and guides her through the maze of corridors until he stops outside a heavy double wooden door. 'He's in there.'

'Thanks, Dad.'

He looks around the gloomy corridor. 'We've got the castle covered, but Davyn doesn't want to hang around for long. Stay with him while you're here.'

'I promise.'

As Court walks away, Thea faces the enormous door and pulls the left one, opening it with an ominous creak.

Thea stops a few steps into the room and looks around the vast space. The entire room is decorated with wolf heads, just as Murt has said. Heavy chains hang from the ceiling around the metal chandeliers leading to a stone platform at the front of the room. Thea swallows thickly. That must be where Davyn was displayed after his fights.

Her eyes move from the platform to the impressive throne at the head of the room. Davyn is slouched back in the chair, his legs stretched out in front of him. As much as she hates to admit it, he looks at home.

He's frowning - nothing new there. Davyn's 'go to' expression is a frown, but he's repeatedly running his hand over his tight beard - something he only does when he's got something on his mind. The other big clue he's not in a good place, are the massive black and red wings hanging to either side of the throne. The impressive limbs are twitching, the talons scraping along the floor, tearing grooves in the stonework.

Even though he's not in a good place, Thea can't help but take a minute to marvel at the man she's fallen in love with. The attraction to Davyn had been instant, but she never hoped for anything between them. Looking at his tall, solid body with the Celtic tattoos, the piercings, and his incredible wings... she has to pinch herself. He's hers and she's all his.

He pulls his hand away from his face and clenches his fist, trying to ease the tremor she can see from the doorway. Blood Fever is still after him. It's a race she knows he can't win, but at least her blood can keep it from taking a hold of him. For now.

'Stop staring at me and get your sexy ass over here.'

She smiles and approaches him. 'Of course, my lord.'

He shakes his head. 'What have I said about that fucking title?'

Thea straddles him and runs her hand through his thick hair. 'Hiding from your title won't help anyone. Besides, I kind of like the way it sounds.'

He kisses her, then pulls away, resting his forehead against hers. 'Are you okay?'

'I'm fine, Davyn. How are you?'

He shakes his head as he looks around the vast room. 'Still can't believe it's done. He's dead, Thea. He's finally dead.'

'It's over then.'

'Yeah. I don't think I realised how many people he'd hurt while he ruled. I hadn't planned on everyone taking a knee in front of me. Not until I saw their scars. They were terrified of him. Just like I was.'

'At least now they're free. You've done a great thing for them.'

'Yeah. I hope so.' They both look over at the door as Fallon steps inside the room. 'Got Fergus for you, Dav. Won't take no for an answer.'

Thea gets off him, but he grabs her wrist, stopping her from leaving. 'Send him in.' Davyn looks at her as he gets to his feet. 'You stay with me.'

Fergus walks into the room, carefully making his way over to Davyn. 'Thank you for seeing me, sire.'

'What is it?'

Fergus casts a curious look in her direction, but the growl that emanates from Davyn directs his attention back to his ruler. 'We have spoken, sire. The servants and I. Can I inquire what you plan to do with your title? Are you remaining here to take his place?'

'No one is taking that fucker's place. But no, I'm not planning on staying. There's no need.'

Fergus stares at him for a moment then clears his throat. 'What if there was something here to rule?'

'What?'

'Sire, many of the servants have been under this roof all their lives.

They served your grandfather, served your mother and you. When your father took over, we did not remain through choice. Like you, we were trapped, although not in the same way.'

Fergus drops his gaze to the floor and shuffles uncomfortably.

'We were unable to assist…'

He's feeling guilty about not stepping in to help Davyn. She can't imagine what it was like to live in this castle, witnessing what all of them had, but being unable to help themselves, or anyone else.

Davyn knows it too. His broad shoulders drop and his confrontational glare weakens. 'What are you trying to say?'

'We wish to stay here, sire. We wish you to take your place as head of this house and rule, following in your grandfather's footsteps.'

'I'm a Blackjack, Fergus. Not a king.'

'Why not both, sire? We understand there is little to keep you here, but if you could please consider what I've said, we would be grateful.'

Davyn nods and gestures to the door, so Fergus bows deeply and leaves them alone.

'Fuck,' Davyn mutters as he drops back into the throne.

'Wow. That was unexpected,' she says as she sits on his knee.

'Yeah. I thought they'd run as soon as I opened the door. Why do they want to stay here? This place is fucking miserable.'

'True, but that was while your father was in charge. Like he said, your grandfather was a good man. Is it so difficult to believe that can't be the way again? That this castle, and your name, can't rise above all that to become something to be proud of.'

'I don't want to stay here.'

'You don't have to. Listen, so much has happened the last few months. You need time to think. Time to get your head around everything. You don't need to make any decisions at this moment. There's nothing wrong with going home, taking a few weeks to recover, then make a decision when your head is clear.'

He nods thoughtfully. 'Yeah. You might be right.' He kisses her forehead, then gently lifts her off his knee. She watches as he pulls his wings back into his body, then walks around the room, lost in his thoughts.

Thea feels the bile rise when she focuses on the dozens of wolf heads hanging high up the stone walls. Murt's family.

Davyn suddenly comes to a stop. 'You might be right. But, if I'm leaving this place standing I need to deal with some things first.'

'What things?'

'You were just thinking the same thing,' he says, nodding to the wall over her head. 'I need to talk to Murt. It's time the Whelans put their family to rest.'

Davyn pulls Thea closer to his side, trying to shelter her from the wind howling around the castle walls. The sparse, desolate landscape surrounding the structure offered no shelter from the elements. It also helped to add to the ominous feeling enveloping it.

It's a very different place in the summer months. Before he was locked in that cell, he spent a lot of time outside with his mother, walking through the fields. He'll bring Thea back here in a few months when the grass has grown and the weather warmer. Maybe.

He's still not entirely convinced he ever wants to set foot here again.

In the courtyard in front of him, the wolves are loading the heads from the great hall into the back of a vehicle. The vampires had offered to help, but it was something the Whelans wanted to do alone. Murt and his brothers will take them away from here so they can bury them with the rest of their clan.

The clan leader is back on two legs, but one of those legs doesn't seem to be able to carry his weight. He doubts Fletch was able to get him to stay off his feet while this task needed to be completed. There's time for everyone to recuperate later.

Behind him, the servants are emptying Flann's living quarters, under the watchful eye of his team mates. They pile the furniture and clothes on top of a large fire they built to the left side of the courtyard.

Thea squeezes his hand as the Binding rack is brought out and thrown on the fire. Davyn's throat constricts, the suffocating terror of being secured to it coming back to him as the gruesome contraption smoulders then ignites.

The huge throne follows, crushing the rack as it lands on top of it, quickly catching fire.

Murt climbs into the car with his brothers and pulls out of the courtyard. 'Will they be back?' Thea asks.

'Yes. They'll meet us back here in a few hours.'

'So what now?' Thea asks as the fire blazes.

'Great hall. I have to talk to everyone.' He walks away, then stops and turns back, holding his hand out to her. 'I need you by my side, where you belong.'

'Are you sure?'

'Thea, I love you. You are my life. Any decisions I make in the coming weeks will be with you. I want you by my side always.'

Thea grips his hand, squeezing it as she walks back inside the castle with him.

The crowd parts as Davyn enters the room, giving him a clear path to the empty space at the front where the throne used to sit.

As well as Fergus and the servants, his teammates... his family, are there, supporting him.

He hates speaking in front of such a crowd. Even voicing his opinions in team meetings was uncomfortable, but with Thea's hand in his, he feels a confidence he didn't know he had.

'Fergus spoke to me about what you want for the future. I haven't made any decisions yet and won't for a few weeks. I'm a Blackjack,' he says, glancing over at Nix, who smiles encouragingly at him. 'That's what I am. I never wanted any of this, but that doesn't mean I'm going to walk away from it. What I'm asking for is some time to think. To decide on the best way forward. While I'm gone, Fergus will be my eyes and ears.'

The man visibly whitens at the words. He wasn't expecting that.

'Do you agree?'

'Me?' he stutters. 'Of course, sire. But are you sure?'

'You know this place better than anyone. I'm sure.'

Fergus bows and smiles which throws Davyn off track for a second. He's never seen the man smile. 'Thank you, sire.'

'We'll set up some ground rules but, needless to say, there will be no one in the dungeons. There will be no extortion. No beatings. No pain. You will all work to keep this monstrosity well maintained and, in return, you will get food and board. A hell of a lot better than you have so far. Once it pays for itself, there will be wages. That's the best I can do for the moment. Take it or leave it. I'm not going to force any of you to stay.'

He scans the room but no one leaves. Thea silently squeezes his hand in support, and he couldn't be more grateful. Everything that's happening is so out of his comfort zone, he's making it up as he goes along. But Thea is right. He needs to take time before he makes any decision about his fucked up legacy.

With nothing else to say, he clears his throat again. 'Dismissed.'

As they file out of the room Nix approaches him, a wide smile on her face. 'I'm impressed. It looks like the unwilling King has an eager following.'

'I have no idea why,' he says, leaning against the wall. 'I haven't got a clue what I'm doing.'

'There's time to figure it out, Davyn. I just got a call from Murt.

They're on their way back. Do you want to stay longer or—'

'No,' he interrupts, 'I'm done here.'

'No problem. We'll be outside. Take your time.' She leads the rest of the team out, leaving him alone with Thea in the vast, bare room. Stripped of the throne, the chains, the heads, he realises the room isn't as intimidating as it had been. It was his father's personal touches that added the fear and intimidation. Without that, it's just an empty castle.

Thea leans against his chest, and he wraps his arms around her. 'Is there anything left here you want to take?'

He shakes his head then stops. 'Yeah. Actually there is something. I don't know if it's still there. I completely forgot about it until just now.'

'Still where?'

'I hid it in my cell.'

Thea goes still in his arms. 'You need to go back down there?'

'Easier than explaining where it's hidden.'

Thea gets up and holds out her hand. 'Let's go and get it, then we can go home.'

'You don't have to come with me.'

Thea squeezes his hand, giving him support through her touch. He never thought he'd tolerate contact like this, but after being with her, even for a relatively short length of time, he knows he not only tolerates it, he needs it.

'I'm coming with you, so stop arguing.'

'You sure you want to see it?'

She squeezes his hand again as he leads her along the corridor. 'I don't want to see where you were kept, but I think I need to. Does that makes sense?'

He rubs his thumb over her hand and smiles. 'Yeah. It does. Thank you, Thea.'

He brings her down the wide staircase, following it to the bottom of the structure. The deeper they descend, the colder the air surrounding them. Thea shivers beside him, so he stops and shrugs off his jacket. 'It's only going to get colder. Put this on.'

She takes it with a small smile, and he pushes open a well rusted metal gate at the bottom. He holds it open for her, and takes her hand again. In the distance, he can hear the sea hitting against rocks.

'I always thought the sound of the sea had a calming effect. Something about this place makes it sinister.'

'That's what this place does. It destroys everything good.' Davyn stops at the end of the corridor. 'You sure you want to see in there?'

'No, but I need to.'

He leads her into the cells, and Thea's grip on his hand increases. He brings her along the wooden walkway suspended from chains above the cavern floor. Water churns under their feet as they make their way over to the cell he called home for most of his life.

'Watch your step. The walkway can be slippery.'

'How many cells are down here?' she asks, her voice quiet.

'Twenty-four down here. Another ten on the level above.'

'Were they ever all full?

'Unfortunately. He enjoyed the power that came with keeping other people prisoner. He got off on it.' Davyn points to the door at the end of the walkway. 'That's the one.'

Thea bends down as they get closer to peer into the cell. Apart from about two foot of headroom, the entire cell is under water. 'This is your cell?'

'Yeah. Best room in the prison. You stay here.'

Davyn pushes open the door and slides into the icy water up to his armpits. He pushes through the water to the far wall and reaches up, running his hand along the wall of the cell, until he smiles as his fingers brush against the loose stone. He takes a package from under it, and makes his way back over to Thea, handing her the leather wrapped package, before hauling himself out of the sea.

Once he's out of the water, she gives the package back to him. 'Is that everything?' she asks, looking around the cells, taking in everything about the miserable place.

'Yeah. Time to go.'

'I couldn't agree more.' Thea takes his hand, then follows him out of the cells and back into the castle.

They walk outside in silence, joining the others just beyond the main gates. 'You ready?' Nix asks.

Davyn looks back at the helicopter. Ronan's body is strapped to a gurney inside the craft. They'll take him away from this place. Put him to rest somewhere he'll be safe. Somewhere Davyn can make sure nothing happens to him.

He wasn't able to save his friend's life, and that will be a regret he'll carry with him for the rest of his life. All he can do now is protect him in death. He only wishes he could do the same for his mother, but his father destroyed her body long ago.

His arsehole of a brother is buried in the family crypt. Seems his mother wasn't worthy of the same curtesy.

He pulls the small package from his pocket and turns is over in his hand. This is the only thing of hers he has left. Nearly a millennium of lineage reduced to a pauldron and this package. Fucking pathetic.

'Yeah. I'm ready.'

He can feel his teammates behind him. His friends. His family. With their help he can put this hell behind him, and make sure his legacy is something to be proud of.

Davyn frowns as the courtyard in front of him fills with the fellow victims of his father's abuse. Fergus moves to the front and, without a word, they all drop to their knees in front of him.

But when the four wolves move from behind to stand in front of him, his confusion grows. Murt looks him dead in the eye, then does something that makes Davyn fear his hallucinations have come back. With help from Con and Garret, Murt lowers to one knee. The other three brothers follow their leader, silently pledging allegiance to Davyn.

Behind him he can hear the mutters and gasps of surprise from the rest of the team. Wolves don't kneel to anyone, especially not a vampire. It's unheard of.

Davyn walks over to him and lowers his voice. 'Murt? What the hell?'

He grunts as he adjusts his position. 'Thanks to you, our clan members are resting as they should be. I can't speak for the rest of the wolves, but you've earned our respect, Davyn. You and the Blackjacks as a whole.' Murt grins at him and points to his hip. 'Can I get up now? My leg is fucking killing me.'

Davyn smiles and helps him to his feet. 'Thank you, Murt.'

The wolf's grin widens. 'Just don't make me regret this.'

'Never.'

Murt nods and hobbles after his brothers over to the helicopter. By having Murtagh Whelan and his brothers kneel before him, they weren't just swearing their allegiance to Davyn. They were making a statement to the other wolf clans, and the vampires. New beginnings for everyone. Beginnings that involve wolves and vampires working together.

Davyn smiles in spite of himself. 'Time to go.'

He turns his back on his childhood prison, as he takes Thea's hand and walks away.

56

Murt watches as the helicopter takes off from outside the cottage, ferrying the vampires home. He takes a deep breath, sorting through the various scents surrounding them, but they're alone.

The pick-up they left hidden in the garage off the small cottage, is still there. Nothing seems to have been tampered with either. Without a word, he leads his brothers into the cottage where they met the vampires for the first time. After checking again just to be sure, he finally relaxes, and drops into the chair by the fireplace. He's sore and tired, but there's no time to recover.

He leans back against the worn chair, and lifts his leg onto one of the stools, pulling on the still healing wound. According to the human doctor, he'll be lucky to walk without a limp from now on. Fletch had mentioned nerve damage but, after swearing him to secrecy, Murt had left his care, and seen to his clan members. That was more important than his leg.

He's still young... well, young enough for a wolf. There's a chance he will heal fully. If not, he'll have to live with the limp, and so will his wolf.

He scrubs his hand over his face, trying unsuccessfully to wake himself up. What he wouldn't give just to crawl into bed and sleep for a week. Even his wolf is weary and that very rarely happens. The beast is usually itching to break out as often as possible.

Con still isn't back and that worries him. While they were putting their dead to rest, Murt had received a message from the other clan elders. Con had offered to go in his place. It's never a good idea to meet the elders when you're not fighting fit.

Garret passes him a drink, which he accepts with a tired smile. 'Do you think she's still alive, Murt?'

'I don't know.' He's been mulling over that very question non-stop since they examined each of the heads the King had on display. Murt absently rubs his thumb over the clan tattoo on the back of his hand. The Celtic knot surrounding the wolf has five points to it – one for each sibling. Four brothers and one sister.

They assumed the Raven King had captured and killed Sorcha years ago. She had disappeared while out for a run with her boyfriend, and no one had heard from her since. Usually, the King would be the one blamed for any mysterious disappearances.

The four of them had come to terms with the fact Sorcha's head was probably on the wall with other clan members.

But it wasn't.

Her boyfriend's head was, and that sickens him. Cian was a good wolf and he had loved Sorcha deeply. He didn't deserve to die like that. None of the wolves in the great hall deserved the death they received.

They'd searched the cells but Sorcha wasn't there either. So, instead of being able to put her disappearance to rest, they're back to wondering what happened to her.

Murt is startled out of his thoughts when Con bursts through the door.

'So, Con. Out with it. How much trouble are we in?' he asks as Con helps himself to a drink, then drops onto the nearest vacant chair.

His brother looks just as worn out as he does. They all do. Beaten and worn down. But alive and, for the most part, not seriously injured. But if Con's face is anything to go by, that's the only good news Murt is going to be getting.

'Shit loads, Murt. It's pretty much as bad as it gets.'

'We in the bad books again?' Garret asks, smiling widely at the thought, then wincing when the cut on his lip splits again. Murt shakes his head as he glares at him. His brother is notorious for enjoying trouble a little too much for his liking.

'You can wipe that smile off your face, Garret,' Con says. 'The Elders met while we were with the Blackjacks. They've made their decision.'

That gets their attention. Fionn's eyes dart to Murt's, the fear in his gaze unsettling Murt. His youngest brother wasn't a fan of confrontation like Garret. 'That's impossible. They didn't talk to you, Murt. Can they do that?'

Murt shrugs, trying to come across as nonchalant, even though inside he's not liking where this is going. 'It's not unheard of. We must have really pissed them off.'

Con nods. 'Understatement of the century brother. Decision was unanimous. We've been exiled. Our land and property has already been divided between the other clans. We've got the clothes on our backs, the truck, and fuck all else. Well, as far as they know. They don't know about this place or the cash we've hidden.'

Murt nods slowly, dropping his head back onto the chair. This has spiralled into a fucking nightmare. He knew as soon as they agreed to help the Blackjacks, they'd be rubbing quite a few of the other clans up the wrong way, but he wasn't expecting exile. Usually, when laws are broken, the Elders call a council meeting and hear out both sides.

Leaving aside the fact that associating with vampires shouldn't be a fucking crime, as the oldest living member of their clan, he should have been called to speak for his brothers. By making the decision without hearing from him, the Elders had set a new precedent. With no way to plead their case, Murt and his brothers are out of options. Punishment stands and they're out in the cold.

'I presume they don't know we took a knee in front of a vampire?'

Con laughs loudly. 'Are you fucking serious? We're still alive, aren't we?'

'For now. We knew the risks when we agreed to help. Must admit I wasn't expecting them to react so dramatically.'

'It was worth it,' Con says from opposite him. 'I've no regrets. We needed to do this for them.'

'Second what he just said,' Fionn says. 'That bastard had to die. Glad I was there to witness it.'

'You know I never regret anything,' Garret says. 'No point.'

Murt laughs at Garret. 'Yeah. I think we all know that.'

'You tell the vamps what was at stake for us by agreeing to help them?' Garret asks.

Murt shakes his head as he stares at the ash in the fire grate. 'Like I said, we knew the risks. It's our burden. They've got enough to deal with at the moment.'

Fionn leans forward and wrings his hands together. 'So what are we going to do, Murt?'

Con blows out a long breath and Murt groans. 'You haven't told us everything, have you. What else?' Murt asks, the feeling of dread weighing heavy on him.

'They're sending us to Mount Leinster. If we're seen anywhere outside the area, we'll be taken down.'

Murt, Fionn, and Garret stare at Con for a long few minutes before Murt says what they're all thinking. 'They're sending us to the place where the last non-shifter wolf in Ireland was killed. They've never done that before.'

'Fuckers are making a statement all right,' Con mutters. 'Talk about a kick to the gut. Wolves don't come back from there. The Elders have just signed our death warrant.'

Murt closes his eyes, the uncertainty of their situation threatening to break him. He's the leader of his clan. It's his job to look out for his family. To keep them safe. He's already failed Sorcha. He couldn't protect her from whatever happened, and he'll never forgive himself for that. Now he's failed his brothers by getting them exiled or hunted by other clan members.

If the punishment was handed down to him and him alone, he could accept that. But to drag his brothers down with him is unacceptable, and is seriously pissing him off.

'We rest here tonight. Take it in turns to keep watch. Tomorrow we get some cash, and take our punishment.'

Garret launches to his feet. 'No fucking way, Murt. You're just going to accept it and go with your tail between your legs?'

'I'm not accepting anything. We're all injured and tired. Going on the run in this condition will get us all killed.'

'I don't want to go there.'

'You think I do?' He pushes to his feet, ignoring the pull of the wound in his leg. 'I lead this clan, and I will not accept this exile. I will fight until my last breath to get this overturned. I swear. But fighting while we're not fit will end with us dead.

'We rest, then we go, and let them think we're playing by their rules. We bide our time, train hard. Then we take back what was ours.'

'What about Sorcha? How the fuck are we going to look for her from that place?' Garret asks.

'We didn't take a knee in front of a vampire for nothing. We did it so we'd have a link to the most powerful vampire in Ireland. Do you not think he'd tell us if he discovers that his father had, or still has, a wolf hidden away somewhere?'

'You really trust him.'

Murt nods at Con. 'He hasn't given us a reason not to. If our sister is still alive, we will find her. Don't doubt that. And when we do find her, I won't hesitate to call in the favour Davyn owes us. I need you all to trust me.'

One by one his brothers nod, holding out their hands in front of them. Murt places his on top, and looks at each of his brothers in turn. 'Our day will come again. I swear. Now get some rest. I'll take first watch.'

They leave him alone in the living room, and Murt settles back in the chair by the unlit fire. He and his brothers had never been top of the popular list among the other clans, but being exiled to that place is going to make things incredibly difficult for them. No home. No livelihood. No friends. No hope of clawing their way back from their fate. Once they go there, their clan will be blacklisted.

Sounds like life is going to be a bit rough for a while.

But he has no regrets. If they hadn't helped the Blackjacks, they would never have found out that Sorcha could still be alive. There's still a chance the brothers can reunite with their sister.

He smiles to himself. Then the Whelans will rise again and show the other clans the error of their ways.

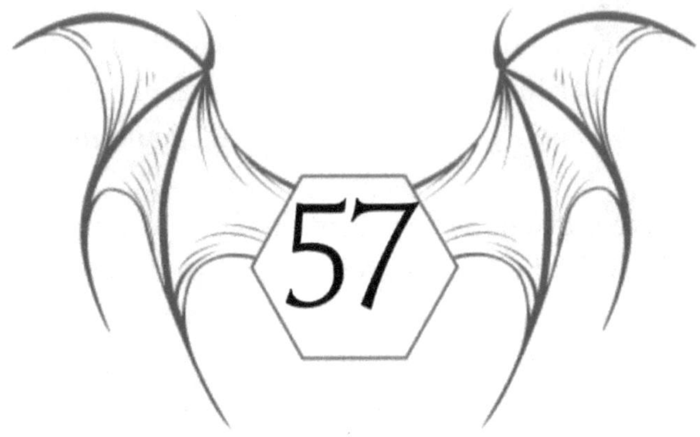

57

Rhain clenches his hands together on his knees in a vain attempt to control the tremors. He woke up with them and fears they will keep him company for the next few hours. Training had done little in the way of relief, as it had in the past. Nothing offers relief the last few weeks and that is the problem.

He peers up at the full moon, taking a few minutes to push all thoughts from his mind and just be in the moment.

Then the wind carries a familiar scent, calling an end to his peace. Ethan walks around the corner, his formidable bodyguard right beside him. Ethan sits beside him and straightens his coat as the Spaniard stands watch a few feet away.

'I hear the Raven King is no longer breathing.'

Ethan nods slowly. 'You heard correctly.'

'And your man is safe?'

'He is.' Ethan glances sideways at him. 'Thanks to your assistance.'

Rhain hides his sigh of relief. He has heard rumours and supposition from members of the Order about the fate of the King and the Blackjack, but nothing he could confirm with absolute certainty.

'I, for one, will not be mourning the King's death or that of his house.'

'His house is still very much intact,' Ethan says with a coy smile.

'How? He has no heirs?'

Ethan raises an eyebrow but does not offer an explanation, allowing Rhain to slowly reach it without his help.

'Davyn. Of course. He's the disgraced son. Well, that certainly explains the King's obsessive need to reclaim him.'

Hearing that he'd saved the King's son gives him great relief. Not only will he now have earned a brief respite from the Blackjacks, he could have the favour of the new King.

'Don't get excited,' Ethan says, his look telling Rhain he suspects what was going through his mind. 'It's early days.'

'I understand. So does this mean your protector is less keen on tearing my head from my body?'

Ethan laughs as the Spaniard growls and bares his teeth. 'How about we say he's less keen on tearing your head from your body, today. We will have to wait and see what tomorrow brings. I don't trust you, Rhain. I have no idea what your end game is, not that I'd necessarily believe you, even if you told me, but I am more open to seeing where this goes.'

'That's all I can ask for at this stage.'

He glances over at the Blackjack who levels his cold gaze on him. He disagrees with Ethan's decision. No surprise there.

'I am no doubt going to rub your friend here up the wrong way by asking, but I hear another member of the team was exposed to the enhancer.'

Right on cue, the Spaniard growls deep in his chest. Ethan holds up his hand, silencing the Blackjack. 'Yes. You heard correctly.'

'How is he?' The Spaniard takes a step closer to the bench, baring his teeth.

'Bastian! Stand down. Now!'

The Blackjack flashes his teeth at Ethan, but does as he's told. Ethan holds his glare for a long time, and Rhain is in no hurry to interrupt. Ethan eventually turns back to Rhain and smiles. 'He is alive. I don't suppose there's anything you can do to help?'

Rhain looks back at the bodyguard. 'I'm going to get a file from my pocket.'

Bastian narrows his gaze, but doesn't make a move to kill him, so Rhain takes out the thumb drive and hands it to Ethan. 'I'm not going to ask how the enhancer is affecting him. The less I know about it the better. What I will say, is that there's a formula to a drug on that you'll need. If his body... evolves in any way, you will need to give him that to stabilise him.'

Ethan turns the thumb drive over in his hand. 'Stabilise?'

'Most Hybrids given such a pure form of the enhancer have died within a few weeks. If their body accepts the drug, it will alter them, enhancing the vampire side. But the alterations can also kill them.'

Bastian snarls. 'You're not helping yourself.'

'I know,' Rhain answers. 'I am attempting to help your team mate. He will need to be given that drug two months after he was first injected. It's imperative. Do you understand?'

Ethan meets Rhain's eyes, searching for the deceit. He can't blame him. If his enemy told him to inject someone in his team with an unknown drug, he wouldn't be too keen on instantly agreeing.

'I am not going to help you save the life of one of your team, and then take the life of another. How would that benefit me?'

Ethan shrugs. 'That's what I'm trying to figure out.' Ethan tucks the drive into his pocket. 'We'll examine the data.'

'Very well. Eight weeks, Ethan. The timing is crucial.'

'I understand.' Ethan brushes some lint from his expensive trousers. 'I may be about to overstep my mark here, but have you put things in place to protect yourself?'

Rhain is completely derailed by the question, taking a moment to regain his composure before he speaks. 'Thank you, but yes. I have lived with a target on my back for centuries. If the Order make a move against me I will fight back.'

The Blackjack laughs harshly.

'I may appear a mere businessman to you but I assure you, I can defend myself.'

The Spaniard flashes him a predatory smile. 'Don't care either way. You die I won't be welling up.'

'Bas... please.'

Rhain supresses a grin when the Blackjack clenches his jaw, but backs off. That's quite an impressive hold Ethan has on the fighter.

'We'll let you enjoy the rest of your evening,' Ethan says as he gets to his feet.

Rhain nods, unable to get to his feet thanks to a badly timed cramp. Showing weakness in front of these two vampires is not ideal, but there's little he can do about it.

Unfortunately, Ethan picks up on his discomfort and sits back beside him again. 'Is there anything I can do to help?'

Rhain shakes his head. 'No. It will pass.'

Instead of leaving him alone, Ethan signals to his bodyguard who sighs loudly, then sits down beside Rhain, the bench groaning under his impressive weight.

'What's he doing?'

'We'll stay until it passes. He'll watch out for both of us.'

Without saying another word, Ethan takes out his phone and scrolls through some emails as Rhain rides out the cramps under the strangely comforting protection of Ethan and his bodyguard.

~

Davyn stands at the fountain in the courtyard of the compound and peers into the water. Thanks to whatever Court did in the boat, his fear of water is gone. He thought Court's powers were dangerous. Being able to meddle with someone's mind is something that can be easily abused. But Court had helped him. Genuinely helped take the fear away. And he's grateful for that.

Maybe he would be okay. Maybe his father hadn't completely destroyed him.

Maybe he could be a valued member of the team again.

He had toyed with the idea of asking Court to hide or remove other memories, but decided against it. If he forgets what his father did, he forgets what happened to his mother and to Ronan. They're a part of what happened to him. Instead of hiding from the memories of his life in that castle and the pit, he'll deal with it. He'll face it. He'll make sure it never happened again to anyone else.

He trails his hand through the water and smiles at his distorted reflection in the surface, before heading back into the compound and back to his room.

When he opens the door, the smile comes back in force. Thea is lying on his bed, fast asleep under the covers where he left her.

He'd never expected or believed such a life would be his. Dying alone in the cell had been the end he'd accepted he'd meet. Then he joined the Blackjacks and dying in battle had been the end he wanted.

But now, growing old with Thea is all he can think about. It's all he wants.

He sits on the covers beside her and gently runs his hand over her hair. She stirs and smiles lazily up at him. 'Hey. You good?'

'Just went to clear my head. You sleep okay?'

'Eventually,' she says with a grin. 'Someone kept me up for hours.'

'Yeah. Sorry about that.'

'I'm not. Are you getting back into bed?'

'I think I just might do that.' He takes off his clothes and climbs back under the covers with Thea. He pulls her into his arms and looks over at the package he took from the cell, still wrapped up on his bedside table.

'What is it?'

Davyn reaches out and takes the small parcel from the table. Davyn unwraps it from its protective case and his breath catches in his throat when he sees the cover. 'My mother was a fantastic artist. She loved drawing flowers. It's probably my most vivid memory of her. She'd spend hours walking the grounds of the castle with me, stopping to draw any new flowers she saw.'

Until his father killed her.

'Can I see some of the drawings?'

Davyn hands her the small notebook and Thea flicks through the pages. 'These are beautiful, Davyn. How did you get this?'

'Ronan. He took it from her room before my father destroyed all her belongings. We hid it in my cell, cause we knew it would be the only place it wouldn't be found. When I was a child, looking it at gave me a little comfort. But I stopped after a while. It just made being in there so much more difficult.'

'It sounds like Ronan was a good father to you.'

'He was more of a father to me every single day than Flann ever was. I just wish I'd been able to take him with me when I escaped the first time.'

'I'm sure he understood. You needed to get out of there, Davyn. You had no choice.'

'I know. Doesn't make leaving him behind any easier. I'm just glad we were able to bring his body back.'

'He's safe now. And he'll be with you, resting in the courtyard whenever you need to talk to him. Why don't you get some more sleep.'

Davyn holds Thea against his chest and closes his eyes. Ronan got his wish in the end. He just wanted Davyn to be safe and now he is. They both are.

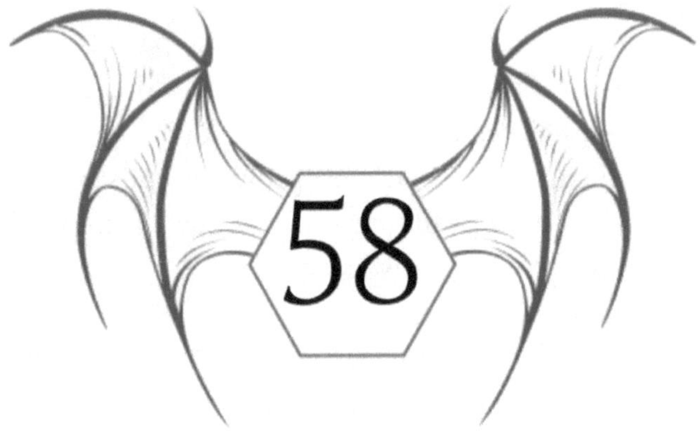

58

Thea stares over at the magnificent vampire fast asleep beside her and, not for the first time, wonders how she managed to attract his attention the way she has. She's in love with a century and a half year old, spectacular, vampire lord. Not quite the way she had planned out her life, but she couldn't be happier. There is one thing missing however, and she's been struggling with how to broach the subject with him, without sounding ridiculous.

Since their first moment together, he's been holding back. Fear of hurting her, fear of losing control, had kept him guarded while they were together. He does everything to make sure she enjoys herself - and she absolutely does, but she wants him to be able to be as free as she is in the moment. She wants him to be able to let go with her. Wings, fangs, the full works. Instead he offers her a little of himself, terrified of going too far.

He frowns in his sleep, and moans in pain, so she gently strokes his arm, working her fingers in steady circles until he relaxes again. No doubt he was dreaming about his life in that castle. About a life scared, alone, and in the dark.

He'll never feel like that again. She'll make sure of it. She'll tell him every single day how much she loves him, and how important he is to her.

Davyn opens his eyes and smiles at her. The scars around his right eye have faded to faint pink lines which stretch down his cheek. He's not wearing his eye patch around her all the time, which makes her incredibly happy. He's not embarrassed about it or trying to hide it from her. Each and every scar is a testament to his strength. To the fact he survived what most would not.

'Good morning. You've been asleep for nearly ten hours.'

He groans and stretches. 'I don't think I've ever slept that long. Guess that's thanks to you. I've never felt this relaxed before.' When his eyebrow lifts slightly and his lips curl into a smile, she knows what's coming.

'You're becoming less relaxed, aren't you?'

Davyn wraps his arm around her waist, pulling her firmly against his hard chest. Thea groans as his arousal presses against her stomach. 'I think I might be.'

She rubs against him. 'I agree.'

Davyn rolls over, covering her body with his, as he kisses her.

'Tell me what you want.'

Thea freezes at his words, both turned on, and yet slightly confused where they came from.

'Sorry?'

'You're not with me. You want something, and it's occupying your mind.'

She smiles up at him as she rubs his arm. 'How do you do that? How do you know when I'm thinking about something?'

'We're linked by your blood. I can tell when you're distracted.'

She continues to rub her hand over his arm as she collects her thoughts. 'Okay, so please don't laugh at me.'

'I don't laugh.'

'That's true and something else we need to work on.'

Davyn nuzzles against her neck, slowly tracing his nose along her skin. 'And now you're stalling. Tell me what you want.'

His growing confidence is noticeable, and she can't get enough of it. He's finally free from the burdens weighing on him for most of his life. She sighs as he moves around to the other side. 'That's seriously distracting.'

'Sorry,' he mutters as he continues to breathe in her scent. It's something she doesn't understand, but it seems to drive him crazy, which in turn drives her crazy. 'I was wondering if it would be possible for you to maybe be with me with your...'

He peers down at her, his green eye glowing brightly. 'With my what?'

'Can you release your wings? Please don't make this the first time you laugh.'

Instead of laughing, Davyn sits up and frowns at her. 'You want them out?'

'Absolutely. But only if you're comfortable like that.'

'But why?'

'I want you to be yourself with me Davyn. I want to see it all. Feel it all. You told me that feeding can be intense. But you won't feed from me when we're like this.'

'I don't need to feed again for another week or so. If I take too much of your blood I could kill you.'

'Not exactly great pillow talk.'

'It's the truth.'

Thea smiles and shakes her head. 'Okay. I get that. How about you humour me. Don't feed then. Just bite me.'

He rolls off her, and rubs his hand over his face as he looks at her. 'You really want me to bite you? You like that?'

'Were you not there when you fed from me months ago? I know you can sense when I'm turned on. Was I turned on then?'

A small smile pulls at the corner of his mouth.

'Exactly. You should be able to let go and be yourself with me, Davyn. I don't want you to hold back because you're afraid I'll break.'

Davyn keeps the frown going for another few seconds, then climbs off the bed and hunches his shoulders. Then he straightens and the wings come out. Thea watches in amazement as they reform, the bones sliding into place to create two monstrous wings that, paired with a naked Davyn, create one hell of a gorgeous sight.

He stretches them out to each side and flaps them gently. 'Do not touch my talons. They're like razors.'

'Got it.'

She gets up and walks around him, taking care not to go near any of his talons. Thea runs her hand over the scars on his back to either side of his wing ridges. Most were caused by releasing his damaged wing over the years, but some she knows are from his father and brother. The thick muscles in his shoulders and arms tense as she traces her fingers over them. He's still not fully comfortable with being touched and that upsets her. Over a hundred years of pain is going to take time to get past that feeling for him.

She smiles as she draws her hand over the thick skin on his damaged wing. It's taking time to regenerate, but not being torn apart every time he releases it is helping. He closes his wing and his shoulders drop.

'Are you okay?'

'It's just strange having someone touch my wings. I'm not used to it.'

'Your wings are beautiful, Davyn.'

He smiles a little, but he's far from convinced. She reaches up and runs her fingers along the scarred skin on his face and Davyn finally looks at her.

Each and every scar on his body is from a battle he fought and won. He survived and that is something he should be proud of.

'You know what I see when I look at you, especially like this?'

'What?'

'I see a gorgeous, strong, fearless warrior. I see the vampire I've fallen in love with. The person I want to claim me as his and his alone.'

Thea knows it's even odds he'll respond to what she just said. It doesn't mean she made any of it up. Every single word she said is the truth. She absolutely loves him and wants him to claim her or mark her - whatever vampires do when they find a mate. She honestly doesn't care what it's called. All she knows is that she doesn't want anyone except Davyn. Ever.

He tilts his head a little and looks at her. In that moment she knows he's on board with what she just said. His eyes are glowing - both of them. Then she hears the rumble in his chest and her heart races.

'You mean that? Don't say it unless you mean it.'

'I mean it. I don't want to leave you alone again. Not ever.'

When he smiles at her, it's the single most stunning smile she's ever seen. *Mine forever?*

Thea hears the words but his mouth doesn't move. 'What was that?'

'Sorry. I didn't mean to do that.'

'You spoke in my head when you were in the pit. I thought it was a one off. You can do that?'

'Not all the time. Usually only when my wings are out. It's a Prime thing.'

'Ask me again. In my head.'

She reaches up and kisses him. Then the words echo in her head again. *Are you mine forever?*

She breaks the kiss. 'Wow. That's different. And yes, I am absolutely yours forever.'

Having sex with Davyn is intense, but this is going to be so much more than that. This is going to be the full blooded, male vampire, and the way he's staring at her is such a turn on.

He takes a step closer and she has to tilt her head back to look up at him. 'You absolutely sure you want this?'

His voice is deeper and huskier than usual. 'Yes, Davyn. I want this.'

He leans closer and his hair tickles the side of her neck as he brushes against her. *'You sure?'* Hearing him in her head as his mouth is driving her crazy, is more than just intense.

'Yes, Davyn.'

He growls again and his fangs scrape along her skin.

'Please, Davyn,'

'Please what?'

She could absolutely get used to hearing him in her head like this. She loses track of what she was going to say. All she can think about is the gentle growl coming from Davyn, almost like he's purring, and she absolutely loves it. 'Is everything heightened for you with your wings out.'

'Yes.'

'So this is going to be intense then?'

He growls again and picks her up. 'Yes.' Davyn lowers her onto the bed, keeping his wings outstretched so he doesn't tear the bed to shreds. Not that she'd care.

Davyn's hands spread her legs, his wings twitching as he hunches over her. His tongue caresses her, lightly at first, then with a growl, he replaces his tongue with his whole mouth, kissing, licking, and sucking her core.

This is so different to the last time. He's not holding back anymore. This is the unleashed Davyn and the sight alone is nearly enough to have her screaming out his name.

Behind him, his striking wings move, the twitching and tremors working through them in perfect timing with his mouth. He's keeping them far from her, but watching the mesmerising movements while he's devouring, her leaves her gasping for breath.

'Davyn... I'm close.'

'I know,' he growls against her pussy, pausing to give her clit a flick of his tongue. She rears up in the bed, but he pushes her back down, leaving one hand on her stomach to hold her in place.

'You're mine.'

His voice sounds so much louder in her head. She nods as he gets back to work. 'All yours.'

The growl turns to a deep purr and she could swear he smiles before his tongue is back, sliding in and out at a mind-blowing pace. Her fingers dig into his biceps as she tries to keep herself in place as the tingle builds in her chest.

She comes undone the second he flicks his tongue against her clit again. 'Davyn!'

But he doesn't stop. If anything, his licking becomes more frenzied as she comes, the waves rolling through her body over and over again, until she finally stops trembling and looks down at him.

'All mine.'

She laughs and smiles at him. 'Oh yeah.'

He crawls up the bed, covering her with his body and kisses her. His arousal presses against her entrance, teasing her with what's to come.

Davyn brushes her hair back from her face and, when he looks in to her eyes, she can't quite believe how powerful her feelings are for this man. This vampire. 'I love you, Davyn.'

His eyes glow and the smile he gives her is one of the most beautiful things she's ever seen. He doesn't smile enough. Something she will work on. He needs to have more to smile about.

'I love you, Thea.' He brings his wings forward, resting them to either side of the bed. 'You don't know how much you've changed my life. I'll never be able to thank you.'

'You never have to. Just being with you like this, is more than I could ever want. I don't want you to ever hide who you really are,

Davyn. Never again. You're spectacular. Every part of you.' She runs her fingers up his chest, tracing the tattoo along his skin. 'And if I can say, you're also incredibly sexy, my lord.'

He flashes her a quick smile. 'How do you do that?'

'What?'

'Every time you say my title or call me 'sire', even in a joking way, you do this to me.'

He takes her hand from his chest, kissing it before placing it on his arousal. He closes her hand around his dick, leaving his own hand over hers.

She strokes him, loving the way his ab muscles clench. 'Interesting. So I should keep calling you sire while I do this?'

He groans as she runs her thumb over the head, circling over and over.

'I think it's the way you say it.'

She positions him at her entrance and rotates her hips, pressing him against her. 'Please, sire, make love to me,' she says, moaning as she says his title.

~

Davyn grew up hating his title, but the way this stunning woman says it, while she's looking at him with her eyes half closed and her lips parted, has a very different effect on his body.

She makes him proud, unashamed of who he is.

He's not scared anymore. Not worried about hurting her. Every part of him loves her so deeply. He can make love to her like this. He can show her how much she means to him.

Thea smiles as he looks down at her. She's not rushing him, just slowly moving, their bodies brushing against each other. He stretches his wings out and Thea moans quietly, but he hears it as if it was at full volume. He loves the way she reacts to his wings.

Davyn holds her thighs to each side and next time she moves, he pushes forward, sliding in a little further. She feels even better than she did the first time.

'You okay?'

She nods. 'Never better.' Thea wraps her hands around his wrists, bracing herself as he thrusts into her, their bodies fitting together and moving in perfect unison.

His wings extend to either side and the large talons scrape across the carpet. Time to give her everything she asked for. He pauses for a second then growls as he releases his canines.

'Oh God. Wow.'

Davyn runs his fingers over her smooth skin, tracing the faint scars left by training. By fighting to take care of herself in his world. *'Beautiful.'*

She blushes as the compliment echoes in her head. Thea crooks her finger at him, calling him closer. Her smile is wicked as she kisses him, her tongue taking over his mouth, tasting him, running her tongue over his fangs as her movement against his hips grows more desperate.

He's trying not to go too fast. He's so close. If she keeps this up he won't last long.

Then he hears the sound of her blood rushing through her veins, the pull so intense thanks to his wings being out. Her small, dainty hands trace along his shoulders to the base of his wings. Davyn's hips buck, driving himself deeper when she grips each of the bones in her hands. Everything is so fucking sensitive.

He drops his head to her neck, breathing her in. 'I want you, Thea.'

She turns her head to the side, a silent invitation he is eager to accept.

'Are you sure?'

'Don't make me beg,' she responds, gripping his wings tighter in her hands.

Unable to hold back any longer, he licks the side of her neck, the taste of her skin better than the sweetest desert he's ever sampled. He won't drink from her, but he needs to taste her. Desperately.

Davyn's teeth sink in to her flesh, her blood hitting his tongue like pure heaven. He sucks once and she moans loudly, pulling against his wings as her body rolls under his.

Instead of drinking, he laps his tongue over her skin as he keeps a hold on her neck. The sounds coming from her are exquisite, deep and full of pleasure. Pleasure she's getting from him.

He pulls his wings forwards, cocooning them and giving her more to touch. Her hands massage the base of each wing, harder and faster in time with his thrusts. Her blood on this tongue, her hands on his wings, her flesh between his teeth. He knows now why she wanted this for him. For them.

The freedom, the loss of his restraints – both physical and self-inflicted, it's elevating this moment. The pressure builds in his body, tightening his balls and sending quivers through his dick and wings.

Thea first. Always her first.

He sucks her neck again, the possessive growl rumbling deep in his chest. Thea goes rigid under him, her short nails digging into his wings as she tightens around his dick. He pulls his wings up a few inches, then rams them down, driving his talons into the ground as his own orgasm rides through him. He pulls out of her neck and shouts loudly as he pumps into her. He feels like he's falling, over and over again. There's no end to it.

When his finally reunites with his body, he's being kept upright thanks to his wings support. He shudders one last time then peers down at Thea. Her eyes are closed, her skin damp and flushed as she breathes heavily.

'Are you okay?'

She gives him a thumbs up, cracking a small smile before she drops her hand again. He laughs and slowly draws his tongue along her neck over his bite mark. 'Dear God would you let me recover first,' she jokes, 'I can't move.'

'I'm just making sure I don't waste any of this.' He restricts himself to one more lick before he grabs a tissue from the bedside table and presses it to the wound. 'I didn't take much. Just a mouthful at most.'

'Mmm, well it felt... '

'Wow?'

She laughs and opens her eyes. 'Yeah. Wow will do just fine.' Her attention moves from his eyes to his mouth, her lids dropping a little when she sees his fangs.

'It'll take a minute for them to withdraw.'

'No rush whatsoever. I like them.' She turns her head, her eyes moving over his wings, still buried in the ground to either side of the bed. 'You didn't destroy the bed.'

'No, don't think the floor survived though.'

Thea reaches out and touches the tip of his wing, her fingers sending shivers through him. 'They are sensitive, aren't they?'

'Didn't know how much until you touched them.'

'So can I expect them to make an appearance again?'

'Oh yeah.'

She shuffles over and, after pulling his talons from the floor, he lies down beside her, leaving his wings resting on the floor behind him.

He takes her in his arms, loving how she fits so perfectly against his body. She's his. He looks down at the scars on his wrists. The marks from the shackles will never fade. No more than his eyesight will return in his right eye, but he doesn't regret any of it. Everything that happened brought him to Thea, and she's given him more than he ever thought he'd have.

He kisses her forehead and combs his fingers through her long hair as she holds on to him. He wants to spend the rest of his life with her. He knows that without a doubt.

There's still the whole mess in Ireland to deal with. A castle full of people eager for him to lead them. A legacy to tear apart and rebuild the right way. The future is still so unclear, but with Thea by his side, he is confident he'll be strong enough to face it.

His hand trembles slightly as he runs his fingers through her hair. The Fever problem hasn't gone away either. It's still there, lurking in the background, waiting for him to drop his guard. At least with her blood sustaining him, the pull should be controlled. Hopefully.

It's all so new. Who knows how things are going to play out – with Thea, the Fever, and his legacy.

For now, he's going to enjoy his beautiful mate, enjoy just being with her like this, without any of the complications of life, title, or illness.

There's time to think about that later. He's got his life back thanks to her. There's no rush to make any decisions. That time will come later.

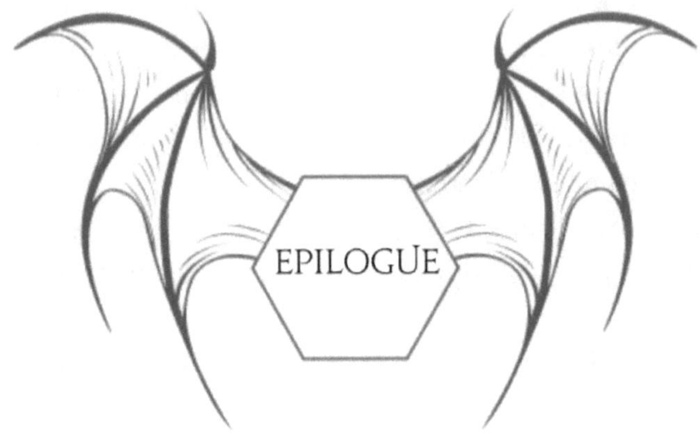

Shep tries to get out of bed, but he can't. He opens his eyes, but he's surrounded by pitch black, which doesn't make sense. He can see in the dark. He turns his head, feeling the pull of something over his eyes. He's blindfolded.

Panic immediately takes over. He pulls at his arms and legs, but he still can't move. He's restrained to the bed.

This isn't right. He can't be back there. Not again. Trying desperately to calm down, he breathes slowly, but his heart is racing in his chest. He went to sleep in his room in the compound. He's sure he did.

It's just a dream. It has to be. He moves his hand, but instead of finding his pillow, his fingers brush against chain.

He whips his head to the side when he hears the door open and someone lock it behind them. Then the bed moves as someone sits on it, sickly sweet perfume filling his nostrils and making him gag.

Shep wakes seconds before he vomits, just managing to aim for the floor instead of his bed. His head spins, throwing the room on its side and him on to the floor. He crawls away from the vomit and rolls onto his back, but that doesn't work. Two spears dig into his shoulders forcing him onto his front again.

What the fuck is wrong with him? The nightmare he understands. The damn things hit when he's overdone things, and missed sleep or a feed.

He takes a deep breath, gagging when the smell of perfume threatens to empty his stomach again. It's not really here. He knows that. It's his head playing tricks on him.

A head that's not happy right now. He grips it in his hands and moans. He'd swear it's about to crack open. Using the bed to pull himself up, he takes a ridiculous amount of time to get to his feet, wobbling when the whole room spins again. He bumps into the wall, hitting his back. This time he shouts in pain. There's something seriously wrong back there.

Supporting himself against the wall, he reaches over his shoulder, but even the smallest touch of his fingers against his skin sends the knives into his back again.

Moving slowly, he circles the perimeter of his bedroom and finally makes it to the bathroom. After throwing up again he faces his reflection. Fuck. He looks half dead. His eyes are glowing, there's blood coming from his nose, his fangs are down, and his gums throbbing. It's like he hasn't fed for days, which makes no sense. They'd all fed after the fight. Shep runs a hand over his skin. Sweat beads on his naked chest even though he's cold. What the fuck is wrong with him?

He laughs harshly to himself. Who exactly is he trying to kid? It's the drug he was lucky enough to get jabbed with. Fucking stuff is still changing his body. His skin itches like crazy across his back. Either his skin is shrinking or his body is getting bigger. He can feel the fuckers growing inside him. Both of them. Turning him into something he shouldn't be. Turning him into an abomination. A freak.

He doesn't want to turn around. Deep down he has a horrible feeling he knows what's going on, but he's too chicken to deal with the visual confirmation. He's already been through so much, he can't handle having that thrown at him too. If he doesn't look, then he can pretend it's not happening.

Perfect mentality for a highly trained fighter. He can face anything head on. Never shied away from a fight. Never hid like a fucking coward. That's not how he does things.

Shep squares up to his reflection. He's no coward. Not after everything he's conquered in his life.

As if to prove him a liar, the scars on his sides and legs sting like crazy, but he knows it's not real. He's had them for decades. They've healed to faint pink marks, but what each of those marks stands for, won't fade. It'll never fade. The fear will never fade.

'Knock it off, Shep. Stop acting like a pussy.'

It's either dwell on that fucked up time in his life, or face what's going on right now. He turns around, then slowly looks over his shoulder at the reflection of his back.

The nightmare. The scars. It all fades to insignificance when he sees a raised ridge to either side of his spine. As he stares in disbelief at his new wing ridges something moves inside his back, sending him bolting for the toilet again. The stretching and sickening movements deep in his body ramp up, and he retches until there's nothing left to come up. He grips the edge of the sink and pulls himself to his feet again.

The new ridges burn as something sharp pushes against them, trying to tear out of his body. The confusion turns to horror as a thick black talon slides through one of the ridges before disappearing inside him again.

'Oh fuck.'

Thank you for reading *Reviving Davyn*.

I hope you enjoyed meeting Davyn and the rest of the Blackjacks. There's plenty more to come!

The sequel, *Defying Shep*, is coming in 2023.

Do you fancy staying updated with news about my books?

• Join my mailing list at: www.kafinn.com/

• Like me on Facebook: www.facebook.com/kafinnauthor

• Follow me on Instagram: www.instagram.com/kafinnauthor/

• Keep up to date with new releases:
https://books2read.com/ap/nE2Kdj/KA-Finn

Also, if you have a moment, I'd appreciate if you could review *Reviving Davyn* at the store where you purchased it. The Blackjacks and I would love to know what you thought of the book.

Thanks for your support!

K.A. Finn

Coming soon...

BLACKJACKS BOOK 3

DEFYING SHEP

K.A. FINN

www.ingramcontent.com/pod-product-compliance
Lightning Source LLC
Chambersburg PA
CBHW060725190726

48285CB00001B/78